JONAH

A NOVEL

OF MEN

AND THE

SEA

HOWARD BUTCHER

LIBERTY ISLAND
LET YOUR RIGHT BRAIN RUN FREE

A Liberty Island Book

ISBN: 978-1-947942-18-9

Jonah: A Novel of Men and the Sea

Cover design by Erik Hollander

Liberty Island

Libertyislandmag.com

Published in the United States of America

For
Sue, Avery, Nolan, Evan,
and
Theron Raines, 1925-2012

ACKNOWLEDGMENTS

I would like to thank the following:

— For his expert advice and camaraderie: Dr. John F. Morrissey. Our months in the Bimini Sea remain, in many ways, beyond the power of words;

— Eric Pearson, an all-around mensch;

— Robert Butcher for his encouragement;

— Andy Gumpper, Troy Tafel, and the whole Buffalo gang: We have heard the chimes at midnight!

— Coach Gordie McAlpin and Max Pearson for turning me into a wrestler and showing me the value of hard work, discipline, and tenacity.

Huge thanks to writer Keith Korman, my agent and editor, for driving the project home.

Blessings and love to my original agent, Theron Raines, for his friendship, wisdom, and belief. He left a real mark.

Most of all, my gratitude and love to Sue for her faith and support over the many years of rejections and countless rewrites. Also, for her grit, grace, and gorgeous piano playing—and to our beloved Avery, Nolan, and Evan for lighting up our lives.

Speak, mighty head, and tell us the secret thing that is in thee. Of all divers, though hast dived the deepest.

—HERMAN MELVILLE, *MOBY-DICK*

God of greatness, god of glory! Grant that Achilles will receive me with kindness, mercy. Send me a bird of omen, your own wind-swift messenger.

—HOMER, *THE ILIAD*

The only other place comparable to these marvelous regions, must surely be naked space itself, out far beyond the atmosphere, between the stars, where sunlight has no grip upon the dust and rubbish of planetary air, where the blackness of space, the shining planets, comets, suns, and stars must really be closely akin to the world of life as it appears to the eyes of an awed human being, in the open ocean, one half mile down.

—WILLIAM BEEBE, *HALF A MILE DOWN*

JONAH

A NOVEL

OF MEN

AND THE

SEA

CHAPTER ONE

THE WHALE'S SKULL

We were sitting on the terrace of the King Fisher Club, sipping iced tea and not talking much, idly watching an old seventy-foot crew boat heading out of the harbor. The boat suddenly hesitated in the water, then shuddered, and in slow motion it raised up with the low grinding sound of a hull hitting bottom.

Sandbar.

You could hear it where we were, overlooking the harbor, and the boat came to rest tilted at a crazy angle. Faint jeers rose up from the men on board, and some of them leaned over the gunwale to see how badly they were grounded. They were oil field workers being ferried out to a pipe-lay barge eighty miles offshore.

We were watching the *Jean-Baptiste*, a crew boat I'd been out on many times before retiring from the oil rigs. She was a steel-hulled vessel, and we could tell by the calm way the deckhand went up the stairs to the wheelhouse that there were no leaks. When there are leaks deckhands run like mad. When there aren't, they take their time.

The captain tried to reverse off the bank, and his screws churned the water brown and ugly. He kept trying, but the boat didn't move, and he gave up. With the tide coming in, he must have decided to wait for it to lift him off the sandbar.

It was late afternoon, and the summer sun glared off the water, silhouetting the nearest oil rigs against silver waves. From the terrace we could see nearly thirty miles, all the way out to the hazy point where the curvature of the earth took the sea around the side of the globe, leaving only empty sky beyond. A flock of snow white egrets waded in the brackish water where the low swamps and bayous fed into the Atchafalaya Bay and then the Gulf of Mexico.

My friend Porter sat on the terrace opposite me watching the crew boat, waiting for the tide to set it free. A pitcher of iced tea sat on the table. Most oil field workers drink hard, but I had quit liquor years ago, and so had Porter. The clear glass pitcher was fogged with condensation and drops of water ran down its side. Two honeybees kept buzzing the table, drawn to the sweetness of the tea. One bee landed on the rim of the pitcher, the sun glinting off its tiny glassine wings. Then it fell into the drink. It buzzed frantically, sending pollen floating off on the surface of the tea, and somehow managed to climb onto an ice cube. It balanced there uncertainly, seeming stunned. Sure, falling into a frozen ocean of Lipton's would have been enough to stun anyone.

Porter was an old hand in the offshore industry like me, and looked it, but he had been a commercial diver. Now he had severe arthritis in his shoulders and hips, and sometimes his vision went blurry. The last time he got the bends he was working at 435 feet and nearly died. The company forced him to retire. So now a few old hands got together several times a month and played poker. Today, the others had canceled so it was just me and Porter on the terrace, with no game. The egrets suddenly rose into the air and flew east, like bits of bright white confetti against the green swamp, and followed the north curving shoreline of the Gulf of Mexico.

"Last week, after the storm, the skull of a whale washed up near my house," Porter said. He had an arthritic way of moving, but he was a friendly, straightforward man. "It was just sitting there on the sand, like a boulder coughed up by the ocean. A whale's skull. Huge. Gleaming white."

"Maybe it was Jonah's whale," I said. A drop of condensation ran down my glass of iced tea and tickled wet across my hand.

"Yeah, possible," Porter said, looking at the crew boat stuck below us. He frowned. "Look at that idiot, running his crew boat onto the sandbar in broad daylight. I'd like to see him navigate at night in a tropical storm, when the ocean really lets loose."

Porter was right. You have to respect the ocean, and I'd seen the strangeness, the quicksilver changes in weather, the sudden eruption of magnificent sea life after weeks of apparent lifelessness.

The indifferent cruelty.

A half dozen oil rigs were scattered across the Atchafalaya Bay in front of us. The pleasant breeze that had come up brought the salty wet-earth smell of the swamp. Daylight was fading and a haze had formed over the water; the sky had turned watercolor pink. The tide had come in enough so that the *Jean-Baptiste* was beginning to shift and right itself. The captain reversed engines and the crew boat pulled free, to mocking applause from the men standing on deck.

At last the trim steel boat cut a gleaming wake out to sea, and Porter stood up. Something had come to him. There was a small change in the man's face, and if you knew Porter, you knew he had retreated back in his memory, to a place where he was still diving. He seemed to be turning something over in his mind, looking for a good place to take hold.

"Jonah," Porter said to himself thoughtfully. "You know, I talked to him after it happened. He knew Aleck Brockman. Worked that job."

Brockman. The name took me back twenty years. Brockman was infamous, hated and feared, the source of many rumors. Thinking about the man, I looked at the biggest platform, far off at the horizon. The sky had darkened to purple, and the rig's flare-off fire seemed to be glowing brighter and brighter.

"I remember hearing about Brockman," I said, "the North Sea diver. Never met him, though. What do *you* think happened out there?" What did Porter think? What could you think? The *Nez Perce* deepwater pipelay job ranked among the deadliest in the history of the Gulf offshore oil and gas industry. Nineteen fatalities. The news reported one death as a suicide and the rest as accidental. They blamed the collision on the whale—but the bodies were never recovered. And no whale carcass. No evidence of anything. There were conflicting stories about what really happened and accusations of a cover-up. Whatever the truth was, people certainly tended to die around Aleck Brockman.

Some believed Brockman killed them all.

"Don't know for sure. I only knew Brockman when we were both teenagers. He seemed like a good guy. But I don't think it's possible to really know what's in a man's heart—any more than it's possible to know what's hidden in the ocean," Porter said, turning to face me. "But I'll never forget what Jonah told me about the whale and the crew boat that sank."

There was a distressed buzz from the pitcher: the bee had slipped off the ice cube into the cold tea. Weaker now, it barely moved its legs trying to climb back onto the ice.

"Jonah was the blond diver, good looking, like an athlete?" I'd only seen his face in the newspaper. About a year ago.

"Yeah, that was him," Porter said. "Jonah was a wrestler. Real wiry, broad shoulders, kind of rough-faced, his ears chewed up. But he had interesting eyes, like he understood things about you, without having to be told. He was an easy guy to like. And somehow he got stuck at the center of the whole thing." He took a sip of tea. "And Brockman was the Dive Supervisor."

The honeybee tried to climb onto the melting ice cube again but fell back and sank.

Porter held up the pitcher and nodded at the waitress. After she brought fresh tea, he said, "The first time I met Jonah he was just another new Tender," Porter began. "Just trying to earn a living in the sea . . ."

CHAPTER TWO

A LIVING IN THE SEA

Jonah had fair hair, cut short and now almost white from the sun, and the build of an athlete turned laborer—more wiry than muscular. Large, strong-fingered hands, calloused, raw-knuckled. His right forearm was covered in a red rash like poison ivy, where a stinging jellyfish had brushed against him in the sea the day before. He looked like a typical oilfield grunt, but he had intelligence and an adventurer's enthusiasm in his large blue eyes, an openness and lightness in his face that women liked. They told him so, but he was usually shy about women. He worked in a mind-numbing industry full of blunted, brutal, and cauterized men. Men, it seemed, less able than he to see, feel, and think. He was one of them, but was not like them.

Jonah had two interviews with Mr. Lancaster, the Head of Human Resources, before being hired. This was the only dive company Jonah applied to for a job. For the first interview Lancaster had sat behind his desk, arms clasped behind his head. At first he talked cheerfully about a lot of little things. Lancaster wore a short-sleeved white-collar shirt. Jonah immediately noticed the old dive watch with a heavy-duty casing on his left wrist. Lancaster had short white hair, bald on top, but thick black eyebrows. His facial skin was rough with large pores from drinking, and his once hard body had softened from age and desk work.

He talked about bass fishing and how it took him a while to get used to the Deep South. He acted friendly and said it was like being in a different country to him; especially at first, when it had all been new and he'd just retired from the Navy and moved down from Groton, Connecticut. He said that being in southern Louisiana and its swamps was like being in a tropical rain forest or maybe Vietnam—the flooded rice fields; intense, humid heat; everything wet and packed with green.

The real questions started when he pointed to Jonah's cauliflower ear and asked how he got it. Lancaster liked that Jonah had been a wrestler, that he had worked as a roofer and a mason, and that he had a high school diploma. After studying Jonah's dive log from trade school and seeing that he'd done more than fifty training dives, Lancaster asked some medical questions.

Most of the questions Jonah had already answered in writing in the doctor's office before taking the physical.

Did he or anyone in his family have a history of emotional instability?

Asthma? Cardiac abnormalities?

Was he subject to fainting or blacking out? Was he claustrophobic?

Did he scare or panic easily?

He figured Lancaster was asking him again because he wanted to watch his face as he answered; maybe spot a weakness.

Then Lancaster asked questions not in the paperwork. Did Jonah have a criminal record? Had he been arrested or jailed anywhere? Had Jonah ever seen somebody killed or badly hurt in an accident? Had he been in any serious fights or other high-stress crisis situations? Jonah had never seen anyone killed and said he'd won all his fights. Lancaster said coldly, "Good divers know how to keep their cool in a crisis."

At the close of the first interview Jonah felt pretty sure they were going to hire him.

By the time of the follow-up interview, the paperwork from the doctor had arrived. He was healthy and drug free. Then Lancaster asked again whether he ever got claustrophobic and whether he spooked easily. Jonah answered as he had before.

"That's it, pal," Lancaster said cheerfully. "You're hired. Welcome to Abbott Divers. You can start work today."

"Good, I'm ready." Jonah started to get up, wondering where to report.

"Hold on," Lancaster said. He paused for a long moment and seemed to carefully consider what he wanted to say. He leaned forward over his desk, suddenly serious. "I want to give you a little advice before you leave this office. You know by now this is extremely dangerous work. At this company it's sink or swim. There's a lot of pressure, especially at first. Keep in mind that more accidents occur on deck than underwater. Use common sense and ask questions. You'll find that you don't know shit about oil field diving coming fresh out of trade school. You have to learn on the job. I'm telling you this cause you seem bright. So understand this and remember it; it's going to be hard at first, but it'll get easier after a few jobs, when you have a handle on it. You'll be in the water before you know it and then you'll know—then *we'll* know—if you can cut it. We don't coddle our recruits here. Good luck."

Then Lancaster gave Jonah an OSHA compliance safety manual, a life jacket, and a hard hat. He said the company would deduct the cost of the life jacket and the hard hat from his first paycheck. Jonah punched in on the time clock and went to work down in the shop five minutes later. And two months passed before Jonah could count the weeks.

CHAPTER THREE

THE FALSTAFF

A northwest wind pressed steadily on them, driving a mild chop of waves that struck the workboat sideways. Five men were on board: a three-man dive team plus the captain and his deckhand. Captain Ira guided his workboat, the *Falstaff*, out of the Houma port into a shallow, olive-dark sea. They were going to perform routine inspections of nine pipeline crossovers—places on the sea floor where different oil and gas pipelines crossed—and make sure that there was a minimum of a three-foot buffer between the overlapping pipelines. There was more than twenty thousand miles of offshore pipeline infrastructure crisscrossing all over the sea floor in the Gulf of Mexico, ranging in size from three and a half inches in diameter to 42 inches. All of it needed divers for regular maintenance and repair, and grew with the continuous exploration for oil and gas.

Captain Ira was a sturdy Creole with a thick lantern jaw that hardly moved when he talked. Sunny days on deck he wore a broad-brimmed palmetto hat and a bandana knotted around his neck. He had worked with the senior diver on board before, but not the Tenders—apprentice divers. It mattered to Captain Ira who set foot on his boat not because he couldn't tolerate assholes, but because he was a superstitious man. He believed the men on board affected the sea. He'd made mistakes before in that regard, then encountered dangerous squalls and water spouts so close he saw the fish in the funnel whirling into the sky.

Also, this was a live-boat job. Unlike more typical jobs, the *Falstaff* wouldn't be tied alongside an oil rig, barge, or pier. It would be *alive*, rocking in the waves, propeller spinning, with the divers in constant danger of being ripped toward the surface by an unexpected swell lifting the boat. Such an abrupt and uncontrolled ascent could kill a diver, because the pressured air in his lungs would suddenly expand and might cause an arterial gas embolism or pneumothorax. A diver might also have his umbilical hose severed by the propeller blades if a Tender let out too much slack, or if the captain overran the diver. Without a good dive crew, a good captain and good weather, a live-boat job was suicide for a diver.

Jonah stood on the aft deck of the *Falstaff,* leaning on a gunwale. His stomach felt sour from bad coffee and he worried about tending the divers. Seed, the new Diver-Tender he was supposed to trust and work with had a hangover. Jonah had met Seed that morning right before the job. Supposedly, Seed had more than a year of experience at a different dive company and held the rank of Diver-Tender. He was therefore slightly senior to Jonah who was ranked and paid as an entry-level Tender.

As apprentice divers, Tenders set up the dive stations, helped dress the divers, operated the decompression chambers, tended the divers umbilicals, and performed dive work in shallow water. Even though they literally held men's lives in their hands, they were paid less, abused more, and worked longer, harder, topside hours than full divers. Divers had to reserve their strength for underwater labor because exhaustion increased the chance of getting the bends. As Tenders gained experience or as the company chose or needed qualified divers, they were graduated or "broke-out" to a higher rank and salary.

⚓ ⚓ ⚓

Seed had shiny black hair and a deep tan like a model or a TV gameshow host, and a handsome, square-jawed face. But he had bad skin. His arms and neck were covered with small round scars like he'd had the worst case of chicken pox in the world. Aside from that he had a rough, kicked-around appearance with jagged scars in his eyebrows and on his knuckles. Like he knew how to fight.

When Jonah first saw him, Seed sat in the office tired and drunk-looking and ate pistachios. The only sound in the room was the clipped *crack* as he opened the nuts between his teeth. He then spit the shells into a paper lunch bag balanced carefully on his knees.

"Are you the new guy?" Jonah said.

"Yep." Seed stood up, suddenly friendly, and shook Jonah's hand. "You mind driving my truck?"

"I'll drive," Jonah said, thinking it would be better if Seed didn't. He could smell alcohol on the man's breath.

"I had a late night," Seed said. He crunched up the lunch bag and dropped it in the trash can next to the secretary's desk. He followed Jonah out of the office.

As they walked out to the parking lot Seed said, "I know we just met, but I need to tell you something about me." Seed stopped walking to say what he needed to say.

"What?" Jonah said impatiently, and stopped walking too. So what kind of flake was he being made to work with? They needed to get driving. They could talk on the way to the job if necessary.

"I'm on parole from Angola," Seed said.

"Is that it?" Ex-cons were pretty common offshore.

"You should see the look on your face," Seed said, smiling. "What did you think I was going to say?"

"I had no idea. Maybe you were in a twelve-step program, or were gay, or wanted to convert me to your religion," Jonah said. He didn't like total strangers spilling their guts. You ought to at least be friends before doing such a thing.

Seed smiled wider. "You're funny. Nothing like that. I'm trying to fly straight now. And being upfront with people about my history is part of flying straight."

Behind Seed's smile and friendly demeanor there was something aggressive and measuring looking at Jonah. Yet, he also seemed genuine about trying to reform himself.

"Where's your truck?"

"Over there." Seed pointed to a Ford Bronco with oversized wheels, a jacked-up chassis, and a license plate reading 2BIG4U. They started walking to the truck.

"That's quite a rig," Jonah said looking at the truck, thinking, *What a waste of money.* Seed took the remark as a compliment.

"Girls like it, especially the backseat. I could tell you stories."

"What'd you do to get sent to Angola?" Jonah said, already wishing he'd never laid eyes on this guy.

Seed said, "Came home from a job offshore and my girl was fucking another guy. The counselor in prison told me I have anger management issues."

"Did you kill her?" Jonah didn't believe for a second Seed was putting everything on the table.

"Hell no. She's okay now. If I'd a killed her, I'd still be in Angola."

CHAPTER FOUR

HELMETS, UMBILICALS, AND THE SHADOW

J onah looked down at the water churning past, then up at the soft violet sky. A hot yellow sun beat down but its heat was tempered by the wind. They were still hugging the marshy coast with its run-down oil and fishing wharfs built up from sun-bleached clam shells. Along the shoreline, palmetto fronds waved in the breeze; Spanish moss clung to giant live oaks that lined ancient beach promontories called cheniers.

The *Falstaff* turned south toward the waters of the open Gulf, and the wind shifted. Crossing the shallows of Terrebonne Bay, the boat sped past several small non-production satellite rigs. Seagulls strutted and cawed on the scaffoldings and decks. Jonah knew that concealed below the waterline, fish schooled near the rig legs and sought shelter there. The platform legs undersea would be weed-wigged and alive with sponges, polyps, and the beginnings of corals.

Further out, when the coast had receded to a wispy green smudge, the Gulf waters cleared to a dirty blue. The silhouette of a hunting frigatebird glided over the bright surface on narrow wings, angling almost imperceptibly. A bit of silver winked in the sun as the fork-tailed bird scooped up a small fish and soared away with it.

In the pale distance two oil rigs rose up from the ocean, seeming to float above its bright haze and looking like bleak castles made of scrap iron. They bristled and glinted with steel fixtures, flare-off fires, cranes, and derricks reaching skyward.

Secured and tied down on the boat deck near Jonah were the two compressors he had prepared, umbilicals, buoys, probes, and pallets stacked with sandbags. On this shallow job the divers would breathe compressed surface-supplied air delivered to them through their umbilical dive hoses. Only at depths greater than 180 feet would it become necessary for them to breathe a mix of helium and oxygen to avoid oxygen toxicity and the opiating effect of nitrogen narcosis or as the French call it, *l'ivresse des profondeurs*—rapture of the depths. Jonah had learned the phrase in dive school. It was the only French he knew.

On a live-boat job a Tender had to give out enough slack for a diver to move, but without feeding the umbilical hose to the propeller. The sea was calm and the wind weak, so at least conditions were good. Still, Jonah wanted to talk to Seed, make sure they were on the same page, before the work started. But Seed was still out of it. He lay on deck in the shade next to the deckhouse with a life jacket for a pillow. Jonah knew the man was waiting irritably for the five aspirins he'd swallowed to ease the pounding at his temples.

"Seed, you need some coffee?" Jonah said.

"What?" Seed said, cracking his eyelids.

"Coffee. You want a cup?"

"No." Seed closed his eyes.

"You better get it together," Jonah said. He wasn't going to let Seed screw up. Mistakes in this line of work got you maimed or killed.

"Don't sweat it. I've worked live-boat jobs before."

The coffee pot had half a cup in it, bitter dregs. The deckhand had guzzled the rest. Jonah stood in the galley and drank it anyway. Pike, the lead diver and supervisor on the job, sat in the galley watching a video on the small-screen TV. He was a large muscular diver with thick black hair and sideburns. His eyebrows, joined in the middle, gave his face a wild and deceptively simple expression. Pike nodded at Jonah.

In the afternoon, twenty miles from land, they were watching for a red marker buoy in the sea. The Loran, a radar navigation system in the wheelhouse, indicated they'd arrived at the coordinates of the first pipeline crossover they were looking for and the buoy should come into view anytime now. Jonah climbed up the ladder on the side of the wheelhouse and looked around. The mild wind let down even more, and the resting sea swayed gently. Here and there on the horizon Jonah saw other platforms and traveling vessels. The sea blurred in rippling eddies off the stern and glowed with an inviting luminous light.

No buoy anywhere.

"The buoy's missing," Jonah called up to the bridge.

"It's always missing on these fucking live-boat jobs," Pike yelled down. His voice was angry.

Pike and Captain Ira stood in the wheelhouse trying to figure out how to find the crossover without a marker buoy. The bosses were pissed off.

"Jonah, come up here!" Pike shouted from the doorway.

Inside the wheelhouse Pike said, "While we figure out what to do, I want you watching for the buoy."

"Yeah." Jonah looked out the windows. If he found the buoy it would save them all a lot of time.

With brown leathery hands Captain Ira unrolled a chart which he and Pike studied intently. Then, with equal gravity, they consulted the engineering blueprints provided for the job.

"You see that buoy yet?" Pike asked.

"No," Jonah said.

"Probably some trawler ripped it off," Pike said gruffly. After a short deliberation he and Captain Ira agreed to backtrack to the small platform nearest the pipeline crossover. According to the blueprint, the crossover could be found by diving down the small platform's riser pipe to the sea floor and then following the pipeline on bottom six hundred yards west where the second pipeline crossed over it. "That's the plan," Pike said.

As Jonah came back down on deck, Seed finally stirred and got up. He didn't look any better.

Jonah asked in a low voice, "Can you do the job?" Having to partner with Seed was like unclogging a toilet with bare hands.

"I'll be fine, Mom. What's going on in the wheelhouse?" Seed asked.

"Searching for the crossing. Time to set up."

Jonah and Seed set up the dive station at the bow. Jonah dumped the 375-foot umbilicals coiled in separate figure eights on the foredeck, one for the diver in the water and the second for the standby diver. He braced the telephone communication box and pneumofathometer gauge, an air-pressure gauge that measured the diver's depth, behind the dive hoses on a rack against the deckhouse. Using the twelve-inch crescent wrenches that all Tenders carry like a best friend, he hustled around the workboat tightening fittings and mating different-size hoses with adapters. Jonah worked fast. They'd already lost time because of the missing buoy, and they had to find the crossing and do the job before dark. Ultimately they rigged the system so that the diver in the water could draw air through his umbilical hose from the pressure air-supply tank of the primary compressor on the stern deck. Jonah cranked both compressors to a start and moved away from them. The engines were loud as hell.

While Jonah finished preparing the dive station, Pike and Seed pulled on their neoprene wetsuits. After sucking on the non-return valve of Pike's helmet to be sure it was seated properly, Jonah screwed the umbilical air-supply hose to the nipple on the dive hat. When he was done setting up the helmets, the two-way telephone system in each helmet was on and air from the compressors pumped through the two umbilicals and directly into the dive helmets. This way, divers could breathe unlimited air from the surface and talk to their topside support at all times, regardless of depth. The dive station was ready, the compressors on, the volume tanks full, and two dive helmets were online. Jonah leaned against the bulwark and waited for Pike.

He looked at Pike's helmet sitting on its bag. Pike's hat had a lead anode affixed to its handle grip to slow the corrosion caused by the electrolysis of the seawater. It was a yellow Kirby Morgan SuperLite, the very brand Jonah planned to own. Made of fiberglass and weighted with brass, it resembled a space helmet sealed in front with a faceplate and a regulator. When Jonah put one on, the SuperLite completely enclosed his head, provided a small volume of air, an oral nasal demand regulator, and a single viewing port defogged by turning the free-flow valve on the side. A diver's helmet was the most prized and expensive piece of equipment he could own. Some divers even gave their helmets names. One diver Jonah had worked with was nicknamed the "Kansas Cowboy," and he called his helmet Sea Horse because it was aquamarine.

Once Pike was dressed for work, he walked to the foredeck. Jonah watched him plod in his cumbersome underwater gear, taking careful measured steps on the slightly swaying deck.

For the final preparation Pike pulled his neck dam over his head. The neck dam made it possible for his helmet to lock over his head and keep water out. Jonah gave him his weight belt then helped him put on his bailout bottle. The bailout bottle was a small scuba tank that served as a backup air supply in case of an emergency. After sealing his helmet to the neck dam around his throat, snapping the umbilical to the quick release on his harness, and checking with Jonah that his bailout bottle was turned on, Pike stood ready to dive.

In full gear he looked like a jet fighter pilot, his body completely sheathed in faded and patched tight neoprene. His hands were gloved, his feet booted, and his head shielded to the neck by his domelike helmet. The dive hose fed air to him and snapped on to his harness quite literally as an umbilical to the surface. Pike's dark eyes became wider and more alert as his departure from the upper world became more imminent. He spoke in a distant wire-transmitted voice to Jonah over the diver's telephone. Jonah gave him the go-ahead.

Captain Ira nosed the *Falstaff* up to the small platform whose location would help them find the pipeline crossover. Seed led Pike to the tip of the bow. The diver's amplified breathing sounded tinny and exaggerated over the communication box. Jonah could now tell when a diver was afraid, just by his breathing. Usually it was the older divers who sucked nervously at their regulators just before entering the sea. They were the ones who'd had many close calls and knew that if luck came in hundred-dollar bills, they had only pennies left to spend. But Pike was not afraid, and Jonah heard his breathing slow and measured.

Holding the end of a spool of yellow nylon rope, Pike climbed up onto the prow of the boat. The yellow rope was going underwater with him. He would tie the end to the pipeline crossing as a downline marking their work site. Seed fed out the umbilical halfway to the water and Pike jumped, going in with a modest splash. The spool of the downline spun on its axis. In a flurry of arm movements, Jonah swiftly fed out the umbilical to Seed, and Seed fed it out to Pike descending.

"Going down," Pike said over the telephone speaker.

Right beneath the surface of the sea, like some strange marine creature separated from its viewer by a mere pane of glass, Pike glowed blue among silver bubbles down in the water. His form distorted and rolled with the motion of the sea; the forces of the water were at play on him now. Pike's body had to operate and gain some kind of traction in a world where the physics was vastly different from that on land: gravity was almost nullified; unpredictable currents like undersea rivers could bedevil him and sweep him off course; thermoclines could make him suddenly warm or cold; every 33 feet deeper another atmosphere of liquid weight (14.7 psi) buried him and heaped on him greater pressure; the light faded and dimmed the deeper he went. Optically, everything appeared closer and larger, if he could see much at all.

Pike's breathing was deep and fast over the communication box. Entering was always a shock to a diver's system; he had no gradual transition, no time to ease in. Jonah watched Pike grow smaller and purplish as he swam deeper down the platform's riser pipe toward the sea floor. His breathing was already becoming regular, slower. Pike was a good diver. He knew how to settle in, how to find his groove quickly. His body form became even smaller—and then he was gone. Jonah watched him disappear, a little envious.

"On bottom," Pike said over the speaker moments later. His voice sounded as if he were calling from very far away.

"Roger, on bottom," Jonah replied. He made a time entry on the dive sheet.

Where Pike had gone in, the sea gently swelled, cool and dark blue, with light playing down inside. Suddenly a large shadow crossed under the water going away from where Pike was diving.

Jonah stepped closer to the gunwale.

The shadow seemed to race toward the surface, growing larger, then eased downward. It happened in three seconds. Jonah didn't see a fin or a tail or anything distinct. It never fully emerged from the moving shades of blue and refracting sunlight. He couldn't tell what it was, but it was big and fast and he was suddenly afraid of the water, even though Pike confirmed a depth of only 62 feet.

As Jonah worked he watched the waves for another sight of the shadow. What was it, and was it still around? Maybe he should warn Pike. But what would he say? *I saw a shadow in the sea?* They'd laugh at him. Best to say nothing.

Captain Ira, mindful of the drift of the sea and the direction of the wind, carefully began maneuvering the vessel, his eyes fixed on the diver's bubbles and the pointing arm of Seed tending at the prow.

Easing the throttle, Captain Ira cautiously and slowly followed the diver's bubbles like a blind man being guided by a leashed seeing-eye dog. Pike, on the sea bottom, scampered and strained at his harness. He moved along a pipeline resting on the sand and looked for where it crossed over a second pipeline. His job was to inspect the point where the two pipelines crossed for any damage and to make sure there was atleast a three-foot gap between the two pipelines.

The CB radio in the wheelhouse crackled and squealed on and off as vessels out on the water talked to each other. Two mackerel boats discussed the marine forecast and where the king mackerel were running today. Someone claimed to have seen a very large whale and was told by someone else that was unlikely, because all the whales left the Gulf during the summer. Captain Ira turned the volume down. He wasn't interested; he had to watch the diver's bubbles.

⚓ ⚓ ⚓

Jonah stood on the slowly rocking deck set to take in or pay out the umbilical to Seed. He caught a glimpse of Seed's face: better, but still looking sick. Elevated at the apex of the bow, outlined against a calm sea, Seed tightly held the umbilical hose with an absolute minimum of slack. He was sweating profusely and had taken off his work shirt. His entire torso was covered with the same small scars that were on his arms and neck. There were dozens of them. Also, prison tattoos on his chest and back. One big one on his chest was a portrait of a man with snakes wriggling from his scalp instead of hair. Like a portrait of Medusa if she were a man.

"Found the crossing." Pike's voice crackled with static over the communication box. He tied off the yellow downline to the spot where the two pipelines crossed on the sea floor. "Downline's tied off. Bring on the sandbags."

"Roger that," Jonah said.

Jonah went back to the stern and began hauling forward the forty-pound sandbags, one at a time, slung over his shoulder. He brought them to the bow. The sandbags were three parts sand and one part cement. When submerged in water, they quickly turned rock hard. They used them to make a buffer between the pipelines.

Once Pike had moved safely out of the way on the sea floor, Jonah dropped several sandbags into the sea next to the downline. On bottom, Pike would return to the crossing and insert the sandbags between the two overlapping pipelines so they couldn't touch. When Pike was done, he tied a red buoy to the spot, and surfaced. There wasn't enough daylight left to get to the next crossing before dark, so Pike and Captain Ira agreed to tie off for the night to the small platform where they had started that afternoon. Jonah switched off the compressors and began breaking down the dive station.

CHAPTER FIVE

THE WHEEL JOB

A little while later Jonah kneeled on the deck bleeding out the condensation from the volume tank of a compressor. Pike suddenly opened a slide window on the wheelhouse above. He stuck his large sideburned face out the window and called down heartily.

"Hey! You Tenders! Either of you want to do a wheel job? There's a shrimp dinner in it for us. No money."

A wheeljob: where a diver untangled a fouled propeller.

Seed shrugged indifferently. "No thanks."

After being in the sun all afternoon Jonah wanted to cool off in the sea, but he still thought about the shadow. It nagged at him. He told himself he had to dive, he knew he would be fine, he had been trained for this. Besides, on a wheel job, a stupid shadow was the least of his worries. If for some reason the propeller came on while he was working, he'd be chopped to pieces.

"I'll do it," he said.

"Where is it?" Seed asked.

"Over there. That shrimp boat heading this way," Pike said pointing.

The shrimper had run over something in the water that jammed up in her propellers and prevented them from turning correctly—i.e., jammed the wheel. The captain of the shrimp boat had noticed the divers working nearby and asked over the CB if they'd be willing to do the job. He offered them a sack of fresh shrimp for the work. Pike agreed to the deal.

The shrimp boat moved slowly toward them. Black tire fenders stood out as perfect Os against her white paint. A flock of noisy gulls and terns wheeled and turned in the sky about her mast and swooped in low over her drawn nets. Scavengers looking for scraps. As the shrimp boat pulled up alongside, Jonah wrinkled his nose and said, "Catch that smell!"

"Old shrimpers never die, they just smell that way," Seed said. The aspirin hadn't worked, but his hangover was finally letting go of him.

One of the seagulls, cawing in piercing repetition, flew several times close over the *Falstaff* searching with hungry beady eyes for bits of offal. Jonah and Seed worked one of the umbilicals back to the stern. Jonah put the helmet online.

Captain Ira moored the *Falstaff* alongside the fenders on the small oil platform with hawser lines at the bow and stern. Pike manned the communication box and Seed tended Jonah. The shrimp boat tied up next to the *Falstaff*. Seed positioned himself in such a way that he could keep Jonah's umbilical from being pinched between the two vessels.

Jonah wore the old quarter-inch wetsuit top he'd bought secondhand. He put on swim fins, a lightened weight belt, and harness. Seed helped Jonah put the helmet on and clamp the neck dam tight. Jonah stepped up to the edge of the *Falstaff's* open fantail. The surface of the sea now seemed tinged with pewter and stretched away nearly flat all the way to the sky. Three oil rigs glinted in the distance, catching the late-afternoon sunlight.

Once the skipper switched off the shrimp boat's main engines, Pike gave Jonah clearance to jump and Jonah hopped overboard feet first. He had two sharp knives and a stainless steel hacksaw tied to his harness. Seed fed Jonah's umbilical hose into the sea.

Even before Jonah had adjusted to the seeping coolness or the bubbles had cleared, he started breaststroking underwater toward the sun-sheltered recess beneath the shrimp boat's stern. Half gold and half silver, the bubbles quavered and shimmied up in front of him. When they were gone, Jonah concentrated his eyes through the liquid blue prism toward the dark bulk where he was going.

He saw the propeller blades underneath, large steel petals, taller than he was. He grabbed hold of one edge, tentatively at first, then hard, to pull himself across their cutting plane. He put his shoulder and head between the giant blades first, and for a second imagined the blades spinning. The image was too much, and he nearly panicked. All it would take was some idiot on deck ignorantly throwing a switch and turning on the engine.

By the time he worked himself through and forward of the blades, along the propshaft, he was feeling better and a little safer. At least, the water was familiar. He turned and locked his legs around the skeg, a ringed stanchion where the keel of the ship attached to the propeller. He found several heavy fishing lines, lead weights and all, wound up around the propeller shaft. Luckily, he saw no tangled steel cable or anything else that couldn't be cut with a strong arm and sharp blade.

"We can do it," Jonah reported into the microphone in the helmet. "Nothing but a mess of fishing rope. No cables."

"Roger. Go to it," Pike said. "I'll tell the deckhand to put on the pot for boiling shrimp!" His voice came through the speakers in Jonah's helmet.

The lines were tightly coiled between the propeller hub and the stern bearing. Jonah cut easily through the thin lines with the knife then went to work on the heavy rope with the hacksaw. As he sawed through hemp and nylon he began to heat up inside his wetsuit. He thought only of the job and ignored the open water all around and the silver puddle of air forming above him as his exhaust air became briefly trapped against the under stern.

Suddenly an engine started on the shrimp boat; the vibrations ran throughout the boat, down the propeller shaft, and into Jonah's hands. Jonah squirmed and yanked his legs away from the giant propeller blades. He suddenly saw himself shredded into raw meat.

"Pike, they've turned on an engine. I'm getting out!" Jonah checked his umbilical hose to make sure it was free. He was about to dive away from the propeller to safety.

"Wait Jonah. It's only their refrigerator generator; *not* their main engines. Repeat *not* their main engines. Okay. Stay put and finish the job."

"You sure? The engines sound the same to me."

"I'm dead sure," Pike said.

"I'm dead if you're wrong."

"I'm sure; their captain is standing right next to me. You're fine," Pike said firmly.

"Okay."

"Way to stay alert, Jonah. Just their refrigerator engine. They gotta keep those shrimp cold, you know."

Jonah went back to work but the engine reverberations continued and the noise rattled him. Every second Jonah thought the blades would start rotating. He couldn't believe it would happen but he feared it. He put his nerves to work and sawed as fast as he could to finish the job and get the hell out. He gave his exhausted arm a rest, letting the hacksaw dangle off its lanyard from his harness. He worked his hand open and closed to relieve a cramp.

"Jonah, what the hell are you doing? You're sucking wind," Pike said over the diver telephone.

"Are you sure about the engine?" Jonah looked out from the shadow of the shrimp boat, breathing hard. Just beyond his reach the azure depths shifted with the slanting sunlight of late afternoon. Particles and spicules clouded the water and visibility was poor. Below, like a deep well, a chasmal blue mouth seemed waiting to gulp him down.

"Yes," Pike said. The engine sound suddenly changed like somebody was putting the boat into gear. A deeper sound than before.

The propellor blades started slowly spinning like an enormous fan.

For a fraction of a second Jonah couldn't believe it.

This is how I'm going to die. Shredded into raw meat.

Blindly, he dived headfirst away from the propeller shaft.

"Jonah, get out of there!" Pike shouted. "Jonah get out of there! Shit!"

Jonah breaststroked hard and frantically kicked his fins; he was barely in the clear.

Rushing water hit him. Bubbles and blue blurred across his lens.

He knew his feet would be cut off first and heard himself screaming. The ocean churned white, an incredible force of water, spinning steel, a slash across his chest.

Suddenly, he was on the safe side of the propeller.

A second of stillness.

Was he dying?

He couldn't think.

The water was clouding with blood.

Suddenly he couldn't breathe, couldn't draw air from his regulator.

His umbilical was severed by the propeller blades; he had to bail out of the helmet.

The engine was still going. Holding his breath, he unclamped the neck dam and pulled his quick release.

He lifted his helmet off his head and the sea rushed in.

The ocean was cold on his face and head and looked fuzzy blue against his naked eyes.

Did he still have legs? He had heard that amputees feel their limbs even after they are cut off.

Something was making him feel numb all over.

His eyes were open and for a few seconds he let himself drift to safety, away from the propeller, almost like he was dead. He didn't want to swim upwards until he was clear of the shrimp boat's stern. He could see the surface above and the dark silhouette of the shrimp boat.

As he held his breath and drifted, the small iridescent form of a comb jelly floated toward him. Its gelatinous body sparkled in the sunlit water like a snowflake melting and delicate beyond possibility. Crossing within a foot of Jonah's face, the comb jelly gently rolled over and away, fading like a crystal ornament in the current. Jonah only saw a blurry dot against blue and a thin swirl of blood coming from his chest. He had the weird notion that the blurry dot was a small piece of himself that had been sliced away. He tried to grab at it but it was beyond his reach.

The engine above suddenly switched off. Jonah closed his eyes, kicked his legs, and started for the surface.

CHAPTER SIX

ONE OF US

S till underwater, he grabbed a rung of the side ladder and was astonished that he had all his arms and legs, and that they all still worked. He pushed his head out of the water and gasped for air. Immediately he heard shouting. A voice yelled, "I'm sorry!" The captain of the shrimp boat was punching the hell out of the man apologizing.

Jonah looked up and saw Pike wearing a dive helmet and about to jump into the sea, to see what was left of him. Pike and Seed helped him onto the deck. "You made it man! We were *sure* you got smoked!" Seed said.

Pike swatted Jonah on the back.

"I got cut. I'm bleeding," Jonah said pointing to a big slit across the chest of his wetsuit. "Who turned on the propeller?" He was suddenly furious; he wanted to kill somebody.

"That dumb-ass over there," Seed said. The shrimp boat captain had knocked a man to the deck and now stood over him. "You're damn lucky you didn't kill him! Don't you ever do shit like that again! I'll kill you myself!"

Pike took off his helmet and Captain Ira was suddenly there with a first-aid kit.

"Man," said Pike, "I thought I was gonna do a body snatch, then there you were coming up the ladder!"

Jonah shook his head and said nothing. They made him take off his wetsuit top and lie down on the deck. As he took off his wetsuit, blood trickled down his chest and over his stomach.

The propeller gash was nine inches long across the left side of his rib cage. The wound looked clean and the middle was deep enough to need stitches.

"You had a tetanus shot recently?" Pike asked.

"Yes, six months ago."

"Good." Pike parted the edges of Jonah's flesh and poured rubbing alcohol into the open wound. Jonah gasped and convulsed in agony. It felt like a blowtorch, searing.

"It's clean," Pike said. "You can still work and dive."

"Jonah, do you want stitches? I've done it before, but I ain't no doctor," Captain Ira asked.

"No, just bandage it," Jonah said with his eyes closed.

"What'd you do? How did you get around that propeller?" Seed asked. His face looked amazed, like he was proud Jonah was still alive.

Pike knelt down and put Neosporin and cotton pads over the wound.

"I don't know," Jonah said. "I swam like hell and got away from the blades just in time. Before they were really spinning."

Pike taped the cotton pads over the wound and Jonah got shakily to his feet. The captain of the shrimp boat came aboard the *Falstaff* and brought with him the young crew member who had turned on the propeller. He was a pimply, narrow-shouldered man with short black hair. His eyes were watery and he seemed frightened to be near the divers. In his right hand he carried a six-pack of Dixie beer. He looked so beaten and pathetic Jonah couldn't stay angry.

"Hey man, what can I say," he mumbled. "I'm real sorry. I fucked up, not the captain. I thought the captain signaled me to try the screw. I thought you was clear. I'm sorry, bud." His cheek was swelling and angry red where he'd been punched.

Jonah looked at the man's lumpy face then at the six-pack in his hand. This was how you died in the oil patch. Somebody like this screwed up and killed you.

"This is for you, man," said the shrimper. "I know you divers ain't supposed to drink offshore, but this is all I got. I'm sorry for whut I done."

"Take the beer, you earned it," Pike said.

Jonah took the beer and the man ducked his head and hurried back onto the shrimp boat and went below.

Pike put his arm around Jonah. "Jonah, you're gonna be a great diver when you break-out. You're one of us."

"How's that?" Jonah asked. It felt good to get praise from Pike, but what did he mean?

"Nothing," Pike said. "You're just hard to kill."

CHAPTER SEVEN

A SMALL KINDNESS

That evening Captain Ira's deckhand surprised everyone with his cooking skills. Pungent smells of squeezed lemon and curry powder filled the galley. Everyone lined up at least twice for boiled shrimp, white rice, and green beans. The shrimp was extra sweet because it was so fresh. Pike and Captain Ira sat together on one side of the table and Jonah and Seed opposite them. In a golden silence they deheaded and peeled mounds of fresh pink shrimp. Pike kept making soft grunting sounds of satisfaction. Captain Ira put down his fork every now and then to rub his stomach. Jonah ate the shrimp like he'd never had them before, and savored an ice-cold beer. He gave beers to everyone, including the deckhand. He tried to give away the last beer but they insisted he have it. His face throbbed hot from the afterglow of the sun, and the gash on his chest felt raw and open.

Before long, the platform's warning horn sounded, set off by the darkness. At the same time, the nightlight began to blink; the horn and light would go all night to alert vessels traveling in the dark that a platform was there. The shrill nasal screech of the horn penetrated the timbers of the *Falstaff*. Every time it sounded Jonah felt it in his wounded chest.

⚓ ⚓ ⚓

Jonah opened a porthole to let the cool sea air drift in. He was fuzzy-headed from working in full sunlight all day and diving undersea, but also from the accident and the beer. The boat moved gently with the ocean and knocked against the fender of the oil platform. The rolling sensation made him sleepy but he couldn't fall asleep with a wound that felt irritated and itchy. He thought of borrowing the deckhand's fishing rod and fishing off the stern, but then Captain Ira asked Pike if he saw anything on the pipeline while he was working that afternoon.

"Crabs," Pike said. "The pipeline was crawling with crabs. You got to be careful with them. I once got pinched so bad I had to leave the job."

"Really? Are you a mama's boy?" Captain Ira joked.

"It got infected. My thumb was the size of a cantaloupe."

Captain Ira nodded and smiled.

"I'll admit I was a mama's boy once in my life, a very long time ago," Pike said. "But I was cured with a belt strap one Thanksgiving."

"Yeah!" Seed snorted, suddenly joining the conversation. "My folks cured me also. Horse whippings and cigarettes!"

Everyone looked at Seed now. His voice was louder than anyone else's. He was almost yelling.

"Looky here. These little scars I got all over me." Seed raised his arms and turned them so everybody could see. "I got these from my folks trying to make me a man."

"What are they?" Captain Ira asked.

"Cigarette burns and lighter burns from the car. I was their human ashtray. Said it would toughen me up! They burned me every day. All over my body." Seed laughed strangely, like it hurt him to do it.

Jonah looked at Seed's face. His mouth was smiling, he made a sound like laughing, but his eyes showed pain. There was something unnerving about the guy, as if inside himself he was in constant turmoil. Sometimes he seemed like a lonely, distressed outcast who talked too much and tried too hard to fit in. But other times like a wild animal that had been severely abused and starved, pushed way past its breaking point and capable of almost anything.

"I'm all man now," Seed said. "Thanks, Mom! Thanks, Dad!"

The room went silent for a moment.

Pike sat back and looked down at his plate.

Seed looked around the table, smiling awkwardly and nodding to everyone. He seemed to need to be acknowledged, to be understood a little bit. But one after the other, Pike, Captain Ira, and the deckhand looked away from Seed's eyes. What Seed had said was too raw and too ugly.

Then Seed looked at Jonah.

Feeling for him, Jonah made eye contact and nodded back. As a small boy, and also after his grandmother died, he had lived in foster homes. He knew firsthand what it felt like to be alone in the world and how badly Seed needed to connect. It was a small kindness.

CHAPTER EIGHT

NIGHT FISHING

After dinner Jonah borrowed fishing gear from the deckhand: a stand-up belt, a gaff, and a thick rod with a 6.0 hook on a ten-foot steel leader. The deckhand warned him that big fish hunt around oil platforms, especially at night, that he might hook something big enough to drag him overboard. The deckhand smiled and said, "Don't lose my rod overboard unless you plan on divin' tomorrow an' git it back."

Jonah baited his hook with four shrimp he had saved from dinner. Standing upright he latched on the stand-up belt then cast out his line. He stood on the fantail, looking at the ocean. A long feathered cloud settled over the moon like an eyebrow.

He felt the weight of the line and wondered what was swimming around the platform, if anything was looking at his hook.

Suddenly Jonah had something on the line. It was pretty big and very fast but was overpowered by the heavy rod. After a few minutes he pulled to the surface one of the largest barracudas he had ever seen. The fish looked at him for a second, then took off down under the boat. At first, he hadn't even recognized the long, thick body as that of a barracuda. Everything, including the scales, looked too large, more like a tarpon. But he had caught a glimpse of the fish's sinister expression and stiletto-toothed mouth. The small platform's warning horn and nightlight suddenly startled him because he was concentrating so hard on the barracuda. Jonah wanted someone to help him with the gaffing the next time he wrestled the fish to the surface, and yelled for the deckhand. No reply.

He yelled again and began reeling the fish back up. Nobody could hear him; he'd have to do it alone.

He stepped up as close to the black shiny water as he could, being careful, because there was no railing. The gaff lay on the deck by his feet.

His rod dipped as the barracuda fought. Abruptly, the fish splashed to the surface within gaffing range.

Jonah crouched over, reaching for the gaff, and then his wound opened up, began to burn.

Suddenly something huge thrashed and exploded in the water in front of him. He jumped back in panic, raising the gaff and fishing rod to defend himself. An enormous broad black back flashed out of the water, then sank back. A predator as big as a car.

Foaming waves slapped together, filling the gap where the creature had been. The line pulled hard, squealing through the reel with a steady weight, then popped slack.

He reeled in his line. When he lifted it from the sea, only the thin lower jaw of the barracuda dangled on the hook. What the hell kind of creature had done that? A shark? Maybe a killer whale? It was black like a killer whale, but killer whales weren't common in the Gulf of Mexico. Whatever it was, it was big and fast and strong.

Jonah's chest was on fire. He put the fishing rod, stand-up belt, and gaff back where the deckhand kept them, then touched the bandages under his tee shirt. His blood looked shiny black in the moonlight.

Below deck, Pike was still telling tales of his youth and debauchery in the red-light district of New Orleans. Jonah, clutching the side of his chest, went straight to his cabin. He re-bandaged his wound and fell exhausted into bed. He lay on his rack and his mind drifted. The propeller blades had almost shredded him, but he was past that, and now he feared the strange black creature that had taken the barracuda. He wished he'd seen it more clearly. The *Falstaff* tugged gently on her hawsers, then nudged up against the platform's fenders, rocking him, cradling him, rocking and rocking until he fell asleep.

CHAPTER NINE

THE OCTOPUS

Jonah didn't get back into the sea for three days. The dive station was nearly all broken down and tied fast for the trip to the next pipeline-crossing inspection. Pike interrupted the Tenders' work to send Jonah into the sea on a simple task. Jonah was to cut free the yellow downline tied to the small oil rig they were anchored next to. He stripped to his underpants and tee shirt. As he removed his dirty work clothes he noticed the cut on his chest had turned into a nine-inch-long scab. A nonstrenuous dip in the ocean wouldn't hurt it at all. Jonah put on a mask, snorkel, gloves, knife, and fins. He jumped off the boat and dropped into the waves. He only needed to swim down 20 feet to cut the downline with a stroke of his knife.

Seed tended the safety line tied around Jonah's waist. He unspooled the line as Jonah snorkeled the twenty feet to the oil rig's corner leg.

⚓ ⚓ ⚓

The water felt cool at first, then soft and lukewarm as Jonah got used to it. His hair fluttered around his ears. A large school of gray spadefish crossed near him, then glided between the legs of the oil rig. Half an inch of water puddled in his mask, tickling his nose. He cracked the lower seal of his mask and blew the water out while following the yellow downline with his eyes. It led slanting to the corner section of the cross brace where it had been tied at the beginning of the job. He took a deep breath, then jackknifed, pinching his nose and diving downwards. He kicked with his fins and entered cooler water.

Above him the oil rig's support legs towered up through misty blue, the girders and I-beams encrusted with sharp barnacles, feathery stinging hydroids, and bright crimson and fiery orange soft sponges. Jonah kicked closer to where the downline had been tied. A multitude of forms and streaks of parti-colored fish scattered away from the intruder, then circled around the nearest girder and re-settled at a safe distance on the oil rig's mini-reef. A pugnacious damselfish rose up and pecked at the lens of his mask. Barely the size of a silver dollar, the glittering blue fish with a gold tail crossed and pecked at Jonah again as he neared the fish's coral home.

With one sideways slash, Jonah cut the downline free. He began to loosen his grip on the cross brace to swim back to the surface, but stopped when something curious caught his eye. Tucked between marine growth on the corner section of the bracket, he saw an algae-covered conch shell, a little smaller than an American football, and he moved laterally over to the shell and touched it. He tipped the conch upwards to peek inside. A pair of slit-like pupils looked sharply back at him. Jonah plucked the shell free from its unlikely perch. They could have conch chowder tonight. Halfway back to *Falstaff's* ladder, he held it triumphantly over his head for Seed to see.

"What is it?" Seed shouted from the fantail of *Falstaff*.

"Conch chowder!" Jonah shouted back.

Pike appeared at Seed's shoulder.

"What's happening?" Pike asked.

"Nothing. He found a conch. He's bringing it back for the cook to make chowder."

"Hey!" Pike yelled.

"What?!" Jonah shouted, treading water with one arm.

"Did you find that conch by the downline?!"

"Yep!"

"That's not a conch!" Pike yelled, grinning.

"Sure it is!" Jonah said, holding the shell up. "I can see his eyes looking at me right now!"

Suddenly an octopus slithered out of the conch shell. It landed with a wet slap on Jonah's shoulder and sat there for an instant like a small ugly wig with eyes. It gripped his flesh with the suction cups along its tentacles.

Jonah was too shocked to scream. The octopus slid lower into the saltwater, looking for a crevice to hide in. Jonah and the octopus both flushed dark red with distress.

The frightened creature wedged itself into the crevice of Jonah's upper thigh and crotch before he could react, tightly gripping him with all eight arms.

Now Jonah screamed, and dropped the conch shell. He began whirling and splashing in a circle as he tried to pull the octopus off. The water around him turned lacy with white foam where he slapped it.

Pike doubled over in laughter. Seed laughed but pulled on the safety line to keep Jonah's head above water. All the time, Jonah was gasping and shouting obscenities.

The octopus at last came free of Jonah's crotch and thigh. But the animal, in its panic, now suctioned itself to his hand, and Jonah shook his arm to get it off. But now Jonah started to laugh, and calm down.

He lowered the octopus into the water and held his arm and hand completely still, then put his mask into the water and watched as the octopus relaxed its grip, and turned from red to light blue. Finally, the traumatized octopus let go and swam rapidly backwards spurting ink, its body inflating and deflating like an umbrella to propel itself away.

Moments later, at the top of the ladder, Jonah said to Seed, "I could only think of its damn beak!"

Seed couldn't talk. His body convulsed with laughter and tears were running down his cheeks.

CHAPTER TEN

A SMALL ACCIDENT

arly the next morning, the dive team on board the *Falstaff* was diverted from its next scheduled job. Instead of another pipeline crossover inspection, they were instructed by the company dispatcher via radio to help, on an emergency basis, with a blowout on a drilling rig and the recovery of any missing persons. As it turned out, by the time the *Falstaff* motored alongside the blown-out drilling rig, around noon, the fire had gone out by itself, which made the divers' work considerably easier. Instead of using explosives to extinguish the fire, the divers only needed to cap the well at the sea floor. Also, there was only one body to search for undersea.

The crane operator lowered the conical-shaped personnel net down to the deck of the *Falstaff* to bring up the dive crew for a meeting and a complimentary lunch in the oil rig's cafeteria. The personnel net was hooked by the ring at its point to the crane and consisted of four sections of rope ladder that several men at a time could hold on to while standing on the round base. Pike and Captain Ira were hoisted onto the drilling rig first, to have the meeting with the superintendent.

Next Jonah and Seed crossed the *Falstaff's* deck. Clinging tightly to the outside of the rope ladder, Jonah stepped on the net's rim, opposite Seed. They distributed their weight this way so as to keep the net balanced and level in the air. The crane operator hoisted them up into the sky and over the sea. They swung heavily left and right like a pendulum. As they lifted up, Jonah looked at the massive legs of the oil rig and how they went down into the ocean.

Straight below, Jonah could see small brightly colored fish moving underwater around the rig's legs. The *Falstaff* grew smaller as they lifted higher.

Up above, on the platform, the derrick tower was charred black and the top of it had burned off or blasted overboard during the explosion. Smoke still rose from the remains and the wind brought an acrid, burnt smell to Jonah's nose.

The crane operator brought them twenty feet above the drilling rig's main deck, still swinging like a pendulum from one side of the deck to the other. Without waiting for the pendulum motion to slow sufficiently, the crane operator quickly lowered the personnel net to the deck. On the way down, the personnel net swung over and touched against the guardrail on the second floor of the control tower. Seed's back hit the guardrail just before the personnel net set down safely on deck. A light whack on the back.

"Hey! What the fuck is that!" Seed shouted. He jumped off the personnel net and waved his arms, challenging the crane operator to come down on deck in front of him.

Jonah looked over and saw the man in the crane's control booth looking down at Seed. He was big and had glasses and a mustache. He shrugged his shoulders and turned his hands up apologetically. Then he mouthed the word, "Sorry."

The rig foreman came over. "Sorry about that, men. Our crane operator is not himself today. He meant nothing by that. You're okay, right?"

"Yeah, but he could of broke my back," Seed said. He looked angrier the more he thought about it.

"It was an accident," Jonah said, trying to help Seed let it go.

"That's right," said the foreman. "Understand, it's his cousin that is dead in the ocean. The one you are going to search for. Give the man a break."

Seed looked at the foreman, then up at the crane operator, and by his expression Jonah could see that Seed was not persuaded by their arguments. He appeared on the verge of doing something rash. His face was red with anger and he worked his jaw like he was chewing food, but there was no food in his mouth.

Seed turned and looked at Jonah. "There ain't no accidents," he said, and spit on the deck.

CHAPTER ELEVEN

THE BODY SNATCH

D uring the pre-dive meeting between Pike, Captain Ira and the drilling rig Superintendent, it was decided, out of decency, that the divers ought to try to recover the body before capping the well on the sea floor. Only Pike had the skills and experience to cap a well, so the job of locating and retrieving the body was assigned to the next most senior member of the dive team, Seed. It was hoped that Seed could find the body quickly somewhere underneath or around the platform's legs, or officially report the body lost. Then Pike would cap the well. The divers would work from the deck of the Falstaff, because it was easier to dive from the boat than from the platform ninety feet up. All told, the dive crew expected to finish the work and be on their way aboard the Falstaff by dinnertime.

⚓ ⚓ ⚓

It took Seed only twenty-eight minutes to find the body. He reported that the corpse was hanging upside down, tangled in fishing line around one of the rig's legs, at a depth of nearly eighty feet. As soon as Pike informed the rig foreman over the CB, a crowd of men gathered at the edge of the oil rig. Jonah looked up and saw them looking down at him as he tended Seed's umbilical hose. There were almost twenty men watching him. Over the communication box Seed called for the recovery basket to be lowered to him in the sea. Pike relayed the message to the rig foreman, and the crane lowered a steel basket big enough to hold the body of a large man, lying down, and two lengths of rope to tie the body in place. After a few minutes, when Seed told them to do it, the crane began raising the body from the sea.

⚓ ⚓ ⚓

Jonah pulled in and coiled Seed's umbilical hose until Seed surfaced and started up the side ladder of the *Falstaff*. Seed was on deck and had removed his dive helmet and dropped his weight belt by the time the recovery basket rose dripping out of the waves.

"There's no body in the basket," Jonah said.

The empty basket slowly turned and dripped seawater as the crane took it higher.

"Keep watching," Seed said.

A taut rope hung down from the basket into the water.

Suddenly, the head, ghastly and leaning to one side, poked out of the waves. Then the shoulders, the torso, and the whole body came out of the sea. The body dangled by the neck from a perfect hangman's noose and the jeans were pulled down so the naked ass hung out in a disgraceful way.

"Jesus Christ! What are you doing?" Pike said in angry disbelief, looking from the corpse to Seed.

"You've done it now, boy," Captain Ira said. He ran to the wheelhouse.

The crane operator hoisted the body all the way up to the deck ninety feet above. Jonah heard angry voices shouting on the oil rig but could not make out what they were saying. After a few minutes, the voices stopped and a big man appeared at the edge of the deck above them. He had glasses and a mustache and looked like the crane operator. He looked down at Jonah and Seed with what seemed to be binoculars.

Seed looked up at him and waved his arms to make sure he had the man's full attention. Then, with dramatic exaggeration, Seed shrugged his shoulders and turned his hands up apologetically. Then he mouthed the word, "Sorry."

⚓ ⚓ ⚓

"You're going to get us killed." Jonah stepped back from Seed.

"Nah, they're pussies," Seed said as loud as he could.

Jonah looked up and saw something small dropping at them. "Heads up!" He shouted.

The mallet fell ninety feet and struck the deck with deadly force, denting the steel deck and missing Seed by just inches. It bounced ten feet up in the air, spinning like a small propeller, and ricocheting over the starboard gunwale into the sea. Jonah looked to see what else was dropping down at them, but all he saw was the row of men and the big man watching them with binoculars. It probably wasn't him who dropped the mallet; he was using both hands on the binoculars. Jonah had the feeling a lot more was about to drop down on them.

Suddenly, Captain Ira blasted a shotgun in the air. A warning shot. Then he pointed it at the men on the oil rig. All the men disappeared from the edge of the platform.

"I'll be damned if they're gonna damage my boat!" Captain Ira cursed.

Seed laughed. "I told you they were pussies."

"Seed!! You're done. This is your last job working with me and my crew. Getting your head split open is what you deserve," Pike said, angrily.

"Is that right?" Seed said.

"That's right," Pike said.

The two men stared at each other like they might fight, until Captain Ira said, "One of us needs to talk to the Rig Superintendent."

Pike went to the wheelhouse to use the CB and talk to the Superintendent of the oil rig. When he came back down on deck ten minutes later Jonah heard Captain Ira ask Pike, "How'd it go?"

"I apologized, and made it clear the hanging was the work of Seed and nobody else."

"What did he say to that?" Captain Ira asked.

"He understood, but he said he wouldn't want to be us right now. He said some of the roustabouts are hot as hell over it. They might pay us a visit on the beach. You too."

"No doubt." Captain Ira shook his head. "Shit."

"And he wanted to know the name of every diver on board."

"Did you give him our names?" Jonah asked.

"I did. It's already on the paperwork anyhow."

"We still doing the job?"

"Of course. In the end, it's always about the money."

Then Pike turned to Seed, who was now in a very good mood, whistling and smiling, like he'd won a contest. "Seed, you're on very thin ice. While I decide whether to have you fired outright, you'd better impress me with some hard work. Because as it stands right now, you're finished at Abbott Divers."

"Yes boss," Seed said, unfazed.

Then Pike told Jonah and Seed to get the dive station ready. He was going into the sea to cap the well.

All afternoon Jonah did his work, but kept looking up, waiting for something else to drop on them.

CHAPTER TWELVE

THE OLDEST LANGUAGE

S ix days later the *Falstaff* returned to its Houma port. Pike drove off, but Jonah and Seed stayed behind. As Tenders they had to unload the compressors and equipment, then load it onto the flatbed truck that was supposed to arrive any minute.

Jonah and Seed sat on a bench in front of a dilapidated shed made of rusty corrugated steel and waited for the flatbed to show up. The docks were empty except for a shrimp boat lazily bobbing several slips down from the *Falstaff*. A shirtless bronze-skinned young man sat spraddle-legged on the deck, methodically mending a shrimp net. From the tall thicket of reedy grass lining the gravel parking lot a nutria rat scurried out, twitched, then ran back.

Without Pike around Seed was in a very talkative mood, full of swagger and high spirits. He was proud of hanging the corpse and kept laughing about it, saying he wished he could have seen the crane operator's face when the body lifted out of the sea. Jonah asked Seed if he'd done it as a joke.

"Sort of, but not really. I ain't easy meat is the main reason," Seed said.

"What do you mean by that?"

"It's like this," Seed explained. "Me and the crane operator was having a kind of conversation. He started it off by asking me a question." Seed glanced at Jonah like he was checking to see if he understood. "And then, a little later, I gave him an answer to his question. It's as simple as that, really. But he didn't like my answer, so now there are hard feelings between us. Too fucking bad."

Jonah thought about what Seed said for a few seconds, remembering the sequence of events up to the hanging.

"Do you get what I'm saying?" Seed asked.

"Yes," Jonah said. Seed could not see that the crane operator's bumping him was just an accident. Then, not sure what to say, Jonah tried to put a little humor into the conversation. "What language were you guys speaking? Klingon?"

Seed laughed. "You're funny, Jonah. You make me laugh. No, it's not Klingon."

"What the hell was it then?" Jonah said.

"WHAT?? The oldest language ever spoke. Before Greek. Before anything. The original, true language that is going on, mostly without words, all the time right up to this very minute. And everybody still speaks it, whether they know it or not. They speak it in Angola and they speak it in the White House. And any animal with teeth speaks it."

"Bullshit," Jonah said.

"It's not bullshit. It's the language that decides everything important. Who gets the best piece of meat. Who gets the good view and the fresh air. Who gets the cream and sugar in their coffee. The softest pillow. Who sits by the warm fire and who sits out in the cold. Who gets to joust the sweetest pussy. Who hides and cries. Who gets on their knees and opens wide just to survive. Everyone talks to each other all the time about these things. Most free people pretend they don't. They talk fancy and civilized, but really they're just fooling themselves, playacting, because they can't admit to themselves they're just low, hungry animals like me. Fucking girls, getting rich, sizzling hot steak, cold beer. That's what it's all about. Best I can tell, the main difference between me and regular people is that I'm more honest about what I am and more direct about what I really want. That's why I like you."

"You do?" Jonah asked, a little alarmed. Seed was trying to claim him as a friend, but Jonah wanted to keep his distance.

"You don't act like you're better than me. You might be better, but you don't act it. Plus you're one funny son of a bitch. As long as I live I'll never forget that day with you and the octopus. That's the only time in my whole life that I laughed so hard I cried. That was truly beautiful. Something else."

"Yes it was," Jonah said, getting to his feet. The truck had arrived.

⚓ ⚓ ⚓

The flatbed truck drove in and parked by the dock near the *Falstaff*, and a slow cloud of dust followed it. Jonah and Seed went to work with the crane operator and offloaded the dive equipment from the workboat onto the truck.

"That's it," the truck driver said after everything was chained down. He hopped from the flatbed and landed on the gravel in a delicate manner, as if the jump hurt his legs. He wiped sweat from the side of his cheek and exhaled loudly as he turned to face Jonah and Seed. He had curly gray hair and a tired-looking goat face that made him look a lot older than he was. He drew a cigarette from a pack in his breast pocket and offered it.

"No thanks," Jonah said with a wave of his hand.

Seed took a cigarette. "Thanks."

The truck driver lit his cigarette and inhaled with great relief, then lit Seed's.

"I'm glad you got here when you did," Jonah said. "A couple more hours and the mosquitoes would've sucked us dry."

"I know it," the truck driver agreed. "It's bin a long fuckin' day." The sky had turned dark gray and it began to rain.

Jonah and Seed got into Seed's Bronco to leave.

Seed drove, and the whole way to Jonah's apartment in New Iberia he tried to convince Jonah to go out partying, hunting cunts with him. That's how he put it, *hunting cunts*. Jonah said no, he just wanted to lie down in his own bed and sleep for a day. Seed told crazy stories about girls he'd had sex with to change Jonah's mind. He said he liked to record his sex encounters with a hidden video camera and could show Jonah movies if he doubted what Seed was telling him.

Jonah said no thanks. Most of the stories were nasty and some were pretty funny, but they didn't change his mind.

By the time Seed dropped him off it was nearly eleven at night. Jonah was exhausted and glad to be off work. Glad to be away from Seed.

CHAPTER THIRTEEN

THE SINGING SEA MONSTER

When onshore, Jonah lived in a room over a bar-restaurant called the Yellow Catfish. It came with a dresser, a small bedside table, and a cot, and cost $100 a month. Musty floorboards sagged near the middle, the wood marked and scuffed with stains by previous occupants. No curtain on the shower, no telephone, no air conditioner, no TV. Callers had to leave messages with the cook or bartender downstairs. The only decoration he put in the room was a color photograph of a humpback whale breaching.

The picture came from the pages of a dive magazine; and he had tacked it on the wall in a prominent place, as a sort of goal—to see a whale underwater in the open ocean. As a boy of six he had watched a scientist and a group of college students trying to rescue a stranded humpback whale on a beach in Rhode Island. At the time, Jonah didn't know anything about whales. He'd come to the shore with his grandmother to see the ocean for the first time. The baby whale was maybe twenty feet long, sunburnt, and helpless. Seagulls had pecked a bloody wound on its back. To Jonah, the creature seemed like a lumpy sea monster, something that smelled like seaweed and would eat a little boy.

He hid behind his grandmother's legs. Out of the water, sagging like a giant bloated serpent, it looked like nothing Jonah had ever seen before, and even his grandmother didn't know what it was. The baby whale had long white-mottled flippers and flukes, his face had lumpy knobs with bristly hairs sticking out, and his entire body looked like a giant peach pit with grooves and ridges. The calf lay gracelessly on the sand, dying, but his eyes were alive. The eye facing Jonah and his grandmother moved and looked their way.

"What is it?" Jonah asked, clinging to his grandmother's leg.

"A baby humpback whale," one of the college students said.

"A humpback whale?" Jonah's grandmother asked. "Aren't they the ones that sing?"

"Yes, ma'am," the college student said.

"Do they really sing?" Jonah asked. Looking at the whale, he imagined a loud sound like the organ music he heard played in church, especially the deep notes he could feel with his whole body.

"Yes," his grandmother said. She took his hand, squeezed it, and looked down at him. "This kind of whale sings underwater songs. Ocean songs."

The college students dug a trench in the sand between the ocean and the whale to bring the water up quickly, and Jonah watched as the waves rolled closer and closer. One of the college students emptied buckets of seawater on the whale's back to keep him wet and cool. The giant creature breathed, the blowhole opened and shut with a popping sound.

That night at dinner Jonah asked his grandmother if they would go back to see the whale the next day. She told him that it had died and that the men had taken the body away.

The next day they went to the beach, but found no trace of the whale calf. Jonah had hoped there would be something left, flipper prints in the sand, but the high tide had swept everything away. The sea appeared calm and friendly that morning, but Jonah knew better. He knew the ocean was really a wild, dangerous place, full of magic and singing sea monsters, and it swept everything away, no matter how big.

Jonah learned something more from the encounter, something that over the years he'd always kept to himself. He had been afraid of the whale, thought it an ugly monster, and even though his grandmother had been there to protect him and told him the calf was harmless, he had secretly wanted the whale to die, and when the whale died, he had been happy about it. When he turned eleven, he read his first book about whales and it chilled him to the bone. He felt ashamed of himself and shocked that he had been so cruel. He also felt guilty, because he wondered if he'd killed the harmless whale calf with his thoughts. He had wanted it to die and it died. As he got older he forgave himself the reaction of a frightened six-year-old. But what stayed with him was the grim understanding that ignorance and fear in anyone is a powerful and dangerous combination.

Back in his $100 room, Jonah pulled his knife from his hip pocket and put it on the dresser. The room was airless and stuffy, and he wiped at the small beads of sweat on his brow. He unlaced his steel-toed Red Wings, kicked them off, and thought about unpacking his offshore duffel bag, but decided against it. He felt dead tired. He shucked off his clothes and got into the tiny shower stall, walls so narrow that his shoulders touched the walls. Using a piece of soap as thin as a sand dollar he scrubbed his face and washed his hair in ice-cold water until he began to shiver. He walked to the cot without drying off, turned out the light, and lay down naked on the mattress. The warm air felt cool on his wet skin. When he closed his eyes he saw translucent underwater blue and drifted off into it.

CHAPTER FOURTEEN

HUNGRY, AWFUL SMILES

Jonah slept all day. When he woke up he went straight into the taproom to eat a sandwich and check for telephone messages. There was just one message. A retired diver named Porter had called to say the tiger shark head Jonah had ordered a month earlier had come in. Like many divers, Jonah liked to collect souvenirs from the sea. He planned to cut the jaws from the shark's head and make them into a trophy.

Still in the taproom, Jonah called Porter and arranged to pick up the tiger shark head straight away.

He went upstairs to his room to get his car keys—a rusted-out Chevy El Camino with bald tires. A young woman he had noticed before was sweeping the walkway in front of his door. The last time Jonah saw her she was carrying an armful of books to a red Volkswagen in the parking lot, and then drove off in a hurry.

Today she wore jeans and a white flowered blouse and had her dark hair combed into a glossy ponytail. She could be a relative of the old woman who owned the Yellow Catfish and ran the kitchen, but more innocent. Clear-eyed and fresh-faced, she looked as if she had never lit a cigarette or set foot in a bar.

"Sorry," Jonah said, sidling by in an effort not to step in the dust she'd swept into a pile.

She leaned back against the railing to let him pass.

"That's okay," she said pleasantly.

Jonah drove to Porter's cabin to pick up the tiger shark head. The cabin was the last of three dwellings down a narrow gravel road on the edge of a bayou. Jonah switched off the engine and stepped out of the El Camino. The sound of frogs and insects rose in his ears like a wordless chant, something from a million years ago. The sun began to set and mist drifted over the bayou.

Jonah knocked on the front door of the cabin and Porter let him in. Porter seemed half drunk and unsteady on his feet. The old diver carried himself with an attitude of surly intolerance, unshaven and gray-haired, but he acted glad to have a visitor. Jonah had only met him twice before but didn't really know the man. They went into the living room. Although Jonah had seen it once before, it still impressed him.

Porter had an enormous collection of shark jaws mounted on the walls floor to ceiling with mouths wide open, ferocious and ready to bite. There were at least thirty, all of various sizes and different species and many with evil-looking teeth. The cabin's cypress floor and walls made it feel like the inside of a giant hollowed tree; a tree haunted by a host of hungry, awful smiles and memories of abyssal blue. Jonah reached out and brushed the edge of one tooth. The jaw was labeled *oceanic whitetip*—the most dangerous open-water shark in the ocean. The tooth stung, and there was a thin line of blood on his finger.

"It's in the kitchen," Porter said. "Follow me. We need to drink to the shark." Porter got shark heads from a commercial fisherman and cut out and cleaned the jaws himself. He got the tiger shark head for Jonah from the same source.

The two men stood in the kitchen holding teacups one-quarter full of whisky. Between them on the kitchen table like an alien creature lay the enormous half-frozen head of a twelve-foot-long tiger shark. The head had been roughly severed with a chainsaw. Jonah gazed at the shark head with pure admiration. It was beautiful, perfect. He didn't try to hide his delight and couldn't quite believe the head was his.

The tiger shark head rested spotless and intact down to the beginning of the first gill flap. On the two black trash bags it had been delivered in, it looked like a heavy blunt piece of gray meat. They drank to the shark.

The whiskey burned Jonah's throat, and his eyes watered.

Porter rolled the shark head over with a scraping thud, turning the white underside and curved mouth up to the ceiling. Blood leaked slowly from the middle of the raw end. It was very fresh. Leaning close, Jonah could just see the tips of the teeth behind the rim of the lips. A whiff of urea reached his nose.

"This was one serious mother in her world," Porter said patting the shark on the nose. "The tiger jaws I've got through there came from a fifteen footer but this one is real nice also. There's not even a mouth wound. See. She must have been gut hooked."

"Yeah," Jonah agreed.

"Feel it," Porter said.

Jonah put his hand on the shark.

"This is one solid animal," Porter said. "Thick muscle and hard cartilage. Skin, rough and sharp against the grain, like some kinda abrasive chain mail. Nothing fat or soft on her. The only place where there's some give on a shark is in the gills and the eyes. Besides that, they're perfect for the ocean. Wild and perfect."

Porter went on to describe in detail how the jaws should be removed and cleaned. He showed Jonah where to expect difficulty cutting and how to cut around the occipital lobes of the upper jaw rather than through them. He gave Jonah a sharp carving knife, a scalpel, three spare blades, and a large sealed white bucket containing industrial-strength hydrogen peroxide diluted by half with tap water. At the end of the lesson, they rolled the head over the right side up. Even with frozen eyes, the austere fish seemed to regard them with contempt. Again they raised their teacups to the shark.

Jonah carried the tiger shark head and the large bucket of hydrogen peroxide out to the El Camino in two trips. Bear-hugging the shark head, he placed it in the carryall. He set the bucket down inside the car on the floor of the passenger's side. Looking back past the dark silhouette of Porter's cabin, Jonah noticed a stand of young cypresses growing crookedly by the swamp's edge. They looked like black gnarled scarecrows hovering above the thin mist stirring over the bayou. The air hummed with mosquitoes, and he tried to wave them away, but they were tireless.

Feeling light with whisky but happy to have such a great set of shark jaws, Jonah walked back across the loose gravel and inside. He felt charged up and meant to clean the jaws as soon as the head thawed, even if it took him all night. He thanked Porter a second time and collected the carving knife, scalpel, and extra blades that Porter was lending him.

On the way to the car, Jonah looked back into the living room window. He saw Porter crossing the room with a fresh beer held like a prize. The old diver put his beer down on a table, then walked up before giant shark jaws and stood with his arms akimbo. His head wagged in conversation. Alone in the room, the old diver talked to the shark jaws. And drank to the shark.

CHAPTER FIFTEEN

ABUSE OF A CORPSE

Back at the Yellow Catfish, Jonah parked in the only open slot in the parking lot. He took the shark head, the carving knife, the scalpel, and the bucket of hydrogen peroxide up to his room. He put the shark head, still in the black trash bag, on the floor and the cutting implements next to it. Then he went downstairs into the taproom to have a beer while the head thawed. He also needed to get some old newspapers to spread on the floor beneath the shark head when he carved out the jaws later.

Tuesday night, the taproom was packed, even this late. Jonah worked up to the bar, edging around throngs of sunburnt dirty-nailed laborers. The air in the dark room hung thick with cigarette smoke, and the boisterous sound of zydeco music blared from the jukebox. In one corner, below red lights, two couples shuffled in a drunken two-step. Behind the bar the manager danced clumsily while tending to customers. Jonah waved him over, and the manager seemed glad to see him again.

"Hey bud, someone is looking for you." Without his apron, the manager looked like one of his customers. He wore a tight-fitting plaid shirt and dungarees with a large boar's head belt buckle below the swell of his stomach.

"Who?" Jonah asked, almost yelling to be heard.

"That guy. Over there." The manager pointed across the room.

Jonah turned and looked. Seed was near the jukebox talking to a couple of girls. Seed saw Jonah. He said something to the girls, and one of them made a disgusted face and shook her head no. Seed came across the room toward Jonah. In the dim light he looked like a monster. Both of his eyes were black and swollen and his nose looked like it had been broken. There were plugs of bloody tissue in each nostril.

"What happened to you?" Jonah said.

"I got into a fight with a couple of guys," Seed said.

"Was it about the hanging?"

"No. A woman." Seed was very drunk, but he was smiling at Jonah. "They broke my nose and I had to set it myself."

"Where did this happen?"

"At the Rusty Nail in the parking lot," Seed said. "But never mind that shit. I came here to find you. I'm running a tab. Let me get you a beer!" Seed swatted Jonah on the back.

"Okay," Jonah said.

Seed waved to the manager. "I'm buying him a beer."

The manager shouted to Jonah, "What are you drinking?"

"Dixie beer," Jonah said.

"And a shot of the house whisky," Seed added.

The manager nodded and said, "If you order two shots, you get a free shot of house wine."

"Well, give us two then!" Seed shouted, striking the table with the heel of his fist. The manager mopped his sweaty brow with a napkin.

"You got it." He grinned.

Seed turned and faced Jonah. His high spirits were suddenly gone. Now he looked troubled. "Jonah, I'm in deep shit."

"What?"

"I hear they're going to press charges against me."

"Who?"

"The relatives of the dead guy I hung."

"What law did you break?"

"Abuse of a corpse. It's a charge they usually use against undertakers who have sex with corpses or people who chop up dead bodies after they've killed somebody."

"Damn," Jonah said. "You didn't do any of that."

"It's serious. It will violate my parole. I'll be sent back to Angola."

Seed seemed to want Jonah to help him somehow. Jonah was a little drunk and feeling good about the world. He thought for a moment, trying to figure a way to help Seed, then said, "What if I testify or give a statement that you were just reacting to how the crane operator nearly broke your back? Maybe they'd drop the charges. Or not file them."

"You think that would work?"

"I don't know. I'm no lawyer, but I saw it with my own eyes. You overreacted, but you were provoked first. You shouldn't go back to Angola for that."

"You'd testify to that?"

"Yes," Jonah said.

"I'd owe you," Seed said.

"No, you wouldn't. It's just the truth."

"You'll do that for me and you don't want anything in return?"

"That's right," Jonah said. Seed looked genuinely surprised, touched even.

"Could you tell Pike?"

"I'll tell it to anybody. It's the truth. The guy was careless."

"I need you to tell Pike," Seed said, adamant.

"All right, I'll tell Pike." So he'd tell the lead diver, Pike, big deal.

"I saw that bastard earlier today. He said if the cops come to him for a statement, he'll say I did it. He cussed at me and said that I should never have been let out of Angola in the first place. Said I was human trash."

Pike's and Seed's animosity toward each other seemed to be growing stronger every day.

"Yeah. The dumb motherfucker threatened me," Seed said. His face turned serious and cold as he thought about Pike.

The manager put the beers and shots of house whisky in front of them. Seed smiled and clicked his shot glass against Jonah's.

"To the only honest man in the world," Seed said.

Jonah threw his shot down and chased the cheap whisky with beer. Seed did the same. The manager, moving with the music, grooved over and unscrewed the lid on a jar of bright red-hot sausages floating in marinade. With a tumbler he scooped some of the fetid-looking oily pink vinegar and stirred the sausages that bobbed like little logs on water. "Here's your free house wine," he said, setting the tumbler in front of Seed.

Seed smiled slightly and the manager arched his eyebrows and folded his arms expectantly. Seed raised the tumbler in a silent toast and tipped the liquid into his mouth and gulped it down. His face constricted and he reached for his cold beer.

"Hot," he whispered.

The manager smiled. "I'm real impressed. The last three guys to try the house wine got sick."

"No more wine," Seed said, putting down his beer. " Hey, Jonah, I'm righteously fucked up. Can I sleep on the floor of your place? Not right now. Later after the bar is closed. I want to talk to those girls again."

Something in Jonah's mind said no. But he didn't want to disappoint Seed. "All right."

"Thanks, buddy. You're in room three, right?"

"Yes. I'm going upstairs now. I've got a shark head up there. I'm going to carve out its jaws."

Seed nodded but he looked confused, like he didn't understand what Jonah said. Then he went across the room toward a group of girls.

Jonah was tired of alcohol, and his stomach felt queasy. He wanted to work on his shark jaws, and he needed to drink water and sober up to do it properly.

"Do you have any old newspaper?" Jonah asked the manager behind the bar.

"Not here. Go around to the side door outside and ask Olene."

"Thanks."

Outside, the warm humid air felt like a wet cloth on Jonah's face. Around the corner of the building, wisteria crept up the side of the wall and over the doorway.

Jonah went to the side door and rapped on the wood above the doorknob. He listened for sounds of someone moving inside, but the music from the taproom next door was all he heard.

The door suddenly opened and a wedge of light spilled out. The clean-faced young woman he had seen sweeping earlier looked out at him. This must be Olene. Somehow her face seemed fuller and her forehead higher with the light behind her. Her hair was pulled back and tied with a pink scarf.

"Excuse me for bothering you so late, but the manager said to ask you if there was some old newspapers I could have. He said you would know." Olene wore the same white blouse with the flower print as before but had changed into a pair of blue shorts. She looked doubtful. "I'm Jonah. I live upstairs," he added.

"I know who you are. The newspapers are in here," Olene replied. Barefoot, she led him through a room with sofas and a desk with a reading light. The light was on and textbooks were stacked on the right side of the desk. One book lay open under the light. She took him to a closet-sized coatroom where old newspapers were piled up two feet high.

"Help yourself," she said. Over her shoulder he saw a clock on the wall. It was 10:05.

"I'm sorry it's late," he said.

"It's nothing. I usually stay up, studying. I have to clean up when they close."

Jonah picked up a handful of copies of the *Daily Iberian* and tucked them under one arm. When he turned he found himself face to face with Olene. She yawned and brought her hand up to cover her mouth. Again he was struck by her resemblance to the old woman who owned the place.

"What are you studying?" Jonah said. He glanced at the books on the desk.

"Business administration with a minor in marine biology," Olene said.

"How do they fit together?"

"I don't know if they do. I have a pipe dream about making a fortune growing shrimp. I'd like to figure a way to establish the world's first commercial indoor shrimp farm and patent the system." Olene smiled like she was telling a joke.

"You'd be rich," he said.

"Hopefully. But I'll probably wind up just running this place." Olene shrugged.

Jonah looked at the books on the desk again. One had the title *Legal Studies*, another *Accounting*, and another *Chemistry*. They looked like hard work.

"Where do you go to school?" he said.

"University of Louisiana, in Lafayette."

"That's pretty close," Jonah said. She obviously went to college during the day because she worked at the Yellow Catfish at night.

"A short drive," Olene said.

He looked at her thin, sinewy legs as she led him back to the door. She had a large brown birthmark on the back of her right thigh and walked with a certain graceful authority. At the door he asked, "Are you related to the old lady who owns this place?" The liquor was making him bold.

Olene smiled, apparently pleased by the comparison. Her face brightened, more pink in her cheeks.

"Yes I am," she said. "My *grandmère*."

Jonah looked at her for a moment. She was pretty.

"What do you need the newspaper for?" Olene asked.

"I've got the head of a tiger shark. I'm getting ready to cut out its jaws. I need the newspaper so I don't get my room all bloodied up."

Olene's brow furrowed and her almost transparent eyebrows moved closer.

"Really? Are you just saying that to make fun of me?"

"No, I honest to God have a shark head up in my room."

"Well, that'll stink up the place," she said.

"For a little while maybe." Then, "If you want I can show it to you. It's just upstairs."

Then he thought of Seed showing up in the middle of the butchery, dumb idea.

She looked at him, and he saw that she knew he was drunk.

But not too much of a jerk.

"No thanks."

CHAPTER SIXTEEN

THE TIGER SHARK'S HEAD

Jonah dragged his bedside table to the middle of the room and left it near the foot of his bed. He unfolded two newspapers and placed one on the floor under the legs of the table and the other on the tabletop. On the front page of the newspaper he saw an article about the recent Breaux Bridge Crawfish Festival with a black-and-white photograph of a couple eating crawfish from white Styrofoam containers. He pulled the tiger shark head out of the trash bags and placed it on the couple eating crawfish.

The head was still partially frozen but thawing fast. Jonah let it sit while he laid out the carving knife and scalpel.

Suddenly the room was oppressively hot, and his head reeled. He drank cold tap water from the sink and it hit his stomach like a lump of ice. He wiped his mouth and moved over to the wall nearest the shark head. He slid down the wall, sat on the floor with his legs splayed out, killing time, while the shark head thawed.

He pictured himself from a point high outside his body and saw a young man sitting alone in a room late at night with a large shark head.

Most people wouldn't understand what he was up to, but his grandmother would have, and he still missed her. It was a curious thing, but when Jonah thought about his childhood, most of his memories came back to him in black and white, without sound. The past he lived with was sad, like an old movie about a kid who grows up in a crowded foster home where nobody notices or pays attention to him—early memories that were fuzzy and hard to feel, as if they belonged to somebody else.

Only the years after his grandmother adopted him seemed real, the years when he lived by the ocean with her—when he felt loved and wanted. His memories of the ocean were always vivid and in color: the awesome blue of the Atlantic; the roar of the waves crashing onto the beach; seagulls shrieking and laughing; the iodine smell of drying seaweed; the wiggly feel of wet sand between his toes; the cold sea rushing around his naked legs and sucking the sand from beneath his feet; his grandmother holding his hand so he wouldn't fall over. She was right there in all of his ocean memories, teaching him how to swim, taking care of him, standing on the beach behind him when he went out on his own. Always keeping him safe.

Their last year together she had given him a special hardback edition of *Moby-Dick* for his twelfth birthday, and she signed it:

To J,
A young Ishmael, because you love the sea.

Gran

Jonah sat on the floor, his eyes level with the shark's eyes, losing track of time as he watched the head thaw. By degrees her eyes unclouded and ultimately turned a shiny black-brown. Blood seeped from the raw decapitation, forming a small pool on the newspaper. Yet the shark looked so fresh, returned Jonah's gaze with a visage so near life, that he wondered drunkenly, if by some miracle, she was still alive.

He leaned wearily back into the wall and breathed deeply; a tranquil reverie settled over him. A faint splash of salt spray touched his ears, a pelagic wilderness opened before him, and with a deep sigh, he closed his eyes and saw the shark as a living creature, bodily whole and robust, the free-swimming and supreme predator she had been.

Forward she glided—always forward and deep down beneath it all—propelling herself through and over layers of blue, piercing the waters nose first with heavy sweeps of her crescent tail, taking into her broad mouth and breathing through her gills the life-sustaining seas. Between rows of sharp white teeth passed the fluid substance of deep canyon ridges, ravines, and yawning blue. The undiscovered whereabouts of shipwrecks and priceless treasures were hers to drink up. Effortlessly she navigated the treacherous currents and tides of coral atolls, mangrove shallows, turquoise cays, and glittering lagoons. From the Mozambique Channel to the waters of New England and on and on . . . Jonah imagined her even dropping into the midnight depths, probing the planet's darkest places: a chasm of crushing darkness with underwater mountain ranges and plateaus unseen and unvisited by man.

His eyes still closed, he saw the tiger shark cruising among schools of squid, passing incredible and grotesque fish of every shape and size: misshapen chimaeras, lampreys with suctorial mouths, inflated pufferfishes, sawfishes with rostrums rounded by teeth, and huge iridescent jellyfishes. And feasting and feasting, with powerful jaws and snapping teeth, consuming and devouring carrion and all manner of living flesh, from great dead leviathans to scanty brine shrimp.

In some far region of his mind, Jonah envied the shark for being born to the water, for having so clear a purpose, such a free life. He envied the shark for her sheer potency and vigor, and her complete mastery. Suddenly his eyes came open and he stared at the shark's head, at the bluntness of her snout and the contrast of her gray-ocher skin with her cream colored underjaw. He followed the line of the labial furrows extending toward her eyes and was struck with a sense of perfection in her design.

A slurred voice said, "What a fish, what a fish," and he realized he was talking aloud.

He pushed off the floor, gathered his legs under him, and walked over to her. He crouched, resting a hand on the shark head. He wanted to go where she'd been. To see what she'd seen, to swim in her world. To *live* it.

Jonah forced open the single window and pushed the door ajar to let in fresh air. Moths and mosquitoes came into the room, and their shadows flickered on the ceiling near the naked lightbulb. Jonah started cutting out the shark's jaws.

Two hours later, Seed staggered upstairs poisonously drunk. The room reeked of urea, and the mangled jawless shark head lay unrecognizable on the newspaper spread on the floor. Blood smeared Jonah's hands and forearms red as paint.

He sat at the table on the foot of his cot, bent over in concentration and sliced with a scalpel at a long shred of meat hanging from the jaws.

Seed walked into the room. "Looks like you killed somebody."

"It's like peeling an orange," Jonah said. "You want to work long strands so you have leverage."

"Fucking smells." Seed almost fell on Jonah.

Jonah raised an arm to fend him off and the slippery jaws snapped shut on his right hand.

"Goddammit!" Jonah cursed. "That's the third time that's happened." His hands and fingertips were slashed and cut from working with the cockscomb-shaped teeth while drunk. The disembodied jaws were slimy and hard to hold on to. They bit him whenever he mishandled them, as if defiant even in death. Carefully, he once again worked his hand free from the shark jaws.

Seed swayed but made his way to the bathroom. Jonah heard him urinate, drink tap water, then fall down. Then Jonah heard him vomiting. A lot of oilfield divers were falling-down drunks onshore. After weeks swallowing their fear and risking their lives underwater, the urge to get drunk built up in some men like a volcano getting ready to blow. Jonah let himself drink the first two nights ashore, but that was it. And sometimes he didn't drink at all. Just wasn't in the mood. Other divers drank every day and every night when they weren't working. And the boozing got so bad with some divers that it cut their careers short and ruined their lives.

Seed looked to be one of that kind. Easy to understand, easy to forget.

Jonah, following Porter's instructions for cleaning the jaws, used the knife to slice off the large pieces of flesh. Then with the scalpel, he painstakingly whittled away all the remaining meat. He carved off strips of the slippery, pinkish flesh until the cartilage, pearly and moist underneath, lay fully exposed. Bit by bit, the contours of the jaws emerged like a sculpture from clay, thick curved ribs with row upon row of fantastic sharp teeth. Somehow, when he was done, the jaws looked even bigger and gloriously wicked.

He held them up to the light and examined his work, turning them around to all angles. He saw no more tissue to cut: the jaws were defleshed enough. He pried off the bucket lid and lowered them into the hydrogen peroxide to whiten. Jonah dipped his hands in the bucket to push the foaming jaws all the way under, and the cuts on his hands stung.

When Seed staggered out of the bathroom he pulled off his shirt and bunched it up, revealing his scars and tattoos. He stretched out on the floor in the corner of the room with his shirt under his head. Resting a forearm across his eyes, he said, "Thanks, Jonah."

Jonah nodded.

"You're all I have," Seed said. He started to snore.

Jonah watched a mosquito land on Seed's chest. Seed was in a dead-drunk sleep and felt nothing.

For a time, Jonah stood in the open door frame and listened to the voices below in the parking lot. The sky had become clear and starry and the men across the street working in the fabricator warehouse had finally finished welding for the night.

When Jonah turned around he was startled to see Seed looking like he belonged in a hospital ward. He had turned on his side and was now curled up facing Jonah sound asleep. Naked from the waist up, Seed lay on the hard floor like an unwanted dog in an animal shelter. He had no pillow and no blanket and his burn scars appeared somehow unhealed in the dim light—a permanent reminder of the unspeakable cruelty of his childhood. His eyes were swollen black and blood had crusted around the nostrils of his crooked, broken nose. A small spot of vomit drooled from the corner of his mouth. Yet most shocking and upsetting of all, was the way Seed, a grown man with big calloused hands, sucked his thumb like a small child comforting himself. While in his other hand he gripped his knife. Ready, even in his sleep, to fight to the death to stay in the same loveless world that had by all accounts tortured him, scorned him, driven him insane, all but killed him.

The sight of Seed filled Jonah with an old sadness. And brought up his own bad memories. Why did people do this to each other? How could parents do this to their own children?

But the sight also made Jonah wary and afraid, and he did not want to sleep with Seed in the room. Better to stay up all night.

At dawn Seed sat up, pulled on his shirt, and walked out of the room without saying a word. Birds were making a racket in the trees when Jonah finally shut the door, locked it, and turned out the lights. In the darkness he lay down on his cot and instantly fell asleep.

CHAPTER SEVENTEEN

THE SNAKE EATER

A t the stroke of the hammer the stunned cottonmouth sprang to life, coiling and lashing its fat serpentine body wildly side to side. Renoir, a tall gaunt man, had driven the ten-penny nail through the snake's nose into the tree.

Renoir stepped back to take in the reptile's agony. He had practiced nailing snakes through the head without killing them for years, starting when he first began eating them for their magic.

After a few minutes, the cottonmouth struggled less and started to hang under the weight of its exhausted, stinking body—they always gave off the strongest smell near the end.

With his fillet knife in hand, Renoir cut the full circumference of the serpent's neck and throat, taking great pains not to cut too deep and kill it. Again he stepped back to enjoy his work, and his Adam's apple bobbed as he grinned and swallowed.

Renoir's filthy jeans stuck wet to his thighs, and his knee-high boots were full of marsh water that sucked at his legs when he walked. Dark hair hung down on his neck in a greasy short ponytail, and his eyes were red-rimmed from crystal meth. With chipped and muddy fingernails he tugged on the seam of cut skin around the cottonmouth's neck. The serpent wheezed and in a frenzy tried again to thrash free of the nail.

"No, no. You en't goin nowheres," said the man, enjoying the snake's agony. When Renoir got a good hold, he yanked the scaled integument downwards, skinning the cottonmouth alive. The stinking black skin came away with a wet tearing sound, in one long piece, like a sock peeling off a man's foot. Moving quickly, to do it before the animal stopped suffering, the gaunt raw-boned man began carving the meaty flanks from the ribs and dangling viscera. Even though crank killed his appetite, he knew he had to keep up his strength, and cottonmouth meat was the only thing to do it.

Renoir was well-known and appreciated for his maniacal work habits and sleepless nights on the barges and oil rigs of certain companies. It was commonly said he performed the work of two good Riggers—offshore topside laborers who did all the gruntwork. He could never be found idle, even after his shift. Most of his co-workers knew the source of his unnatural energy.

Renoir was a Cajun outcast from the Atchafalaya Swamp Basin. His parents lived in an old cypress house in Butte LaRose. He hadn't seen them in the twelve years since he became the leader of an infamous ring of thieves who relentlessly robbed families all over the basin. His gang had caused terrible hardship and aggravated the mistrust among the fishermen and trappers in the swamps. Renoir and his gang had stolen more than a thousand nets, crawfish traps, cypress lumber, outboard motors, and anything else they could sell.

When his father found out Renoir was responsible for the thefts, the old man leveled a shotgun to his son's chest and told him to clear out of the woods for good. His father cursed him for bringing shame on the family and told him that if he ever came back home he'd kill him even before the others could. "You en't my boy no more. You en't my boy no more," he'd said. Renoir's mother stood crying on the porch by her husband. Wordlessly, she nodded.

Renoir ran off to Texas for the next eight years. His last year in Texas, he spent locked up in the substance-abuse felony-punishment facility in Huntsville for selling crystal meth. As soon as he returned to Louisiana, he got himself sent to Angola for a two-year stretch for assaulting a man in a bar.

Now that he was a free man, he'd come back to Louisiana for good, but he never went far back in the woods, except sometimes at night. Mostly he paddled his pirogue along the outer regions of the basin after the sun had risen enough to bring out the water moccasins. The cottonmouths were everywhere, sitting on branches in the Spanish moss, laying out on logs, or coiled up in the mud on the banks. They never tried to run from Renoir. Sometimes one came straight for him, especially at night, if he put a flashlight on it.

Renoir had been bitten three times: once as a boy and twice as a man. He'd gotten sick enough to die each time, but the venom never quite killed him. His mother blamed the cottonmouth that bit him as a boy for turning him vicious. Whenever someone lived through a snakebite, copperhead or cottonmouth, she said it changed him. Everybody ever bitten by a venomous snake that she'd known was different afterwards. She believed that the cottonmouth venom had settled in Renoir's heart, that it had rotted his goodness out.

He walked quickly, his face shiny with sweat and spotted with mud where he'd scratched his chin and temple. He emerged from the shaded stand of slash pine behind his trailer. In one large bony hand he carried the raw snake meat and in the other he carried the hammer, the burlap sack, and his snake stick.

What remained of the dead cottonmouth he left nailed to the tree amid the riotous buzzing of flies. The trees nearby it were studded with nails and clean snake skulls.

Barefoot inside his squalid trailer, Renoir curled back his lips in a grimace to check his decaying teeth in the mirror. He didn't mind if they hurt a little; he only wanted to see if they looked worse. Renoir had no trouble getting around routine urine tests, but it was a paranoid worry of his that his bad teeth would cost him his job. He rarely smiled, but when he did, he tried not to expose them.

After dropping the snake meat on the skillet he checked his answering machine for messages. There was an advanced job call-out leaving from Port Arthur, Texas, sometime in the next several weeks. The dispatcher needed to assemble a standby relief crew for a deepwater pipe-lay barge operating far offshore. They were laying a new ninety-mile pipeline in 590 feet of water. Sounded like a big job with a big paycheck.

The second message came from Seed—he needed to talk. Renoir had heard about the hanging and had a big laugh over it.

He knew Seed from Angola and it sounded like Seed was up to his usual tricks. Seed could be more fun than a rabid dog eating its own tail, but after hanging a corpse in front of his friends, guys would want payback. Renoir expected Seed wanted him to put the word out that Seed belonged to his crew. That he was protected. Renoir and four ex-cons from Angola were friends and looked out for each other in situations like this. Although Seed was the only diver in the group—Renoir and the other three were Riggers—he was still a member, and willing to do almost anything to stay a member. Some people referred to them as the Angola Club.

The Rigger sat down in a chair by a sour smelling pile of dirty laundry. He thought a minute if there was anything important he had to do the next day but nothing came to mind. He returned the work call to confirm he'd be there and with a pencil stub wrote down the details. Then he called Seed and told him to stop by anytime.

Even though Renoir hardly noticed it himself, he knew he stank of cottonmouth musk, crank sweat, and rotten breath. He didn't care, but he decided to shower anyway and put on his cleanest clothes, so he could go into some of the better bars and clubs. He cooked and ate the snake before getting wired because he knew that he surely wouldn't eat anything afterwards.

On the glass of an old picture of his dead sister, he cut the ivory powder into two neat lines. He cut generously, taking more than he really wanted. There was no shortage. He had several dime bags stashed away. Before his time in Huntsville, Renoir used to run a meth lab himself and cook it up in his own bathroom.

He snorted up the powder. With burning eyes and stinging sinuses, he raised his face from the glass, then thrust an eyedropper up each nostril and moistened the powder. He breathed deep, with teary satisfaction, feeling the raw energy and fresh rage coursing through his veins.

⚓ ⚓ ⚓

Jonah slept until the sound of someone sweeping outside woke him. His watch read 11:32. He got out of bed, put on a pair of shorts and a shirt and went over to the bucket with his shark jaws.

He pulled the jaws from the bucket. They felt spongy and had turned white all over. Then he propped them open with an empty long-neck beer bottle. He set them in the position for drying, and left them on top of the dresser he didn't use. When they were dry, they would become hard and rigid. The sweeping outside grew louder.

Jonah opened the front door and saw Olene with a broom. She had her back to him and was humming a tune he couldn't recognize. Something pretty.

"Olene," Jonah said.

She turned and looked at him. "Yes?"

"Look." Jonah pointed to his shark jaws.

Olene squinted a little, like she wasn't sure who he was, or what he was showing her. She set the broom against the railing and stepped into his apartment for a better look. It came to Jonah that she needed glasses. "You weren't teasing me," she said.

"No."

"They're pretty nice. What kind of shark?" Olene stepped closer, and Jonah thought he could smell shampoo in her hair. Her face relaxed and her gray eyes seemed to smile. He liked her.

"A tiger."

"So many teeth. Amazing." She looked Jonah in the eyes. "Sometimes I see sharks when I go fishing, but nothing like this. Just little sandbar sharks. They snatch the bait and break the line." She looked at the photograph of the breaching humpback whale he had tacked to the wall.

"You like whales?" Olene asked.

"Yeah. One time when I was a kid I saw a stranded humpback whale. Ever since, I've wanted to see a whale underwater—where it lives, where it's the boss."

"Is that why you're a diver?"

"Well, a little part of it," Jonah said. "But not really. Being a commercial diver isn't a good way to see a whale. When we're at work we make too much noise. The best way would be to go out in a private boat and find a pod of whales, then slip into the water real quiet, with a scuba tank or snorkel, and ease up to them."

"It would be a little dangerous," Olene said.

"I don't think so. Not if you were careful not to get too close, especially if there was a mother with a calf."

"That would be something to see." Olene's face took on an amused expression as she seemed to imagine what it would be like to see whales underwater.

"Where do you go fishing?" Jonah asked.

"My brother has a Boston Whaler down in Dulac. I go out with him and his wife mostly. Sometimes I go alone. Fish near one of the small rigs close in to shore."

"You ever dive or snorkel around those rigs?"

"No, I wanted to once, but everyone else was chicken. My old boyfriend wouldn't even touch the water."

"I'd go with you," Jonah said brightly, hoping she'd say yes.

"I'm not certified. I've never been scuba diving, let alone hard-hat diving like you-all."

"I meant snorkeling."

A pickup pulled into the parking lot and Olene looked to see who it was. "Okay, Jonah. Let's go snorkeling. When?"

"Tomorrow. Can you use the boat tomorrow?"

"I think so."

CHAPTER EIGHTEEN

WATCH YOUR BACK

After Olene left, Jonah went down to the taproom. In the daylight the place looked completely different. Fresh air and sunlight streamed in the open windows and the room looked bigger because the partiers were gone. The only trace from the night before was the faint smell of spilled beer and cigarette smoke. Jonah ordered a gumbo omelet from the bar menu and got up to use the payphone by the bathrooms. Time to call the old man Pike and tell him about the whackjob Seed.

Now that he was sober, Jonah hated having to make the call. But he'd given his word.

He dialed Pike's number, and Pike picked up on the third ring.

Jonah said hello and asked if they could talk.

"I'm glad you called," Pike said. "I was going to call you."

"What about?" Jonah asked.

"Seed's conduct has brought repercussions."

"What?"

"Somebody nearly killed the captain of the *Falstaff*. He's in the hospital," Pike said. "I can't talk about it now. I'll tell you tonight. Watch your back."

Pike said to meet him at a bar-restaurant called Sweet Onion.

"Okay," Jonah said. He hung up the phone and felt almost sick, a mix of adrenaline and fear. He didn't want to be put in the hospital himself, and even more than that, he didn't want to lose his job. If he was seriously injured it could end his career. Without diving, Jonah had no future, had nothing. Absolutely nothing.

He'd put everything he had into becoming a commercial diver, and he'd fight like hell to keep it.

⚓ ⚓ ⚓

The Sweet Onion bar was one mile past Lake Peigneur on Jefferson Island Road. From the outside it reminded Jonah of a dog kennel—a long, narrow building with cinder-block walls and slat windows. Plywood paneling, three dim ceiling lights, and several neon beer logos decorated the small front room. Red checkered tablecloths covered the tables. Over the bar hung three polished turtle shells from alligator snappers. The smallest shell was big as a washtub. Two pool tables stood in the back room, and out front in the dripping rain a large wooden sign over the entrance said SWEET ONION. Jonah saw Pike sitting at a table alone and went over to join him. He nodded as Jonah sat down.

"Thirsty?" Pike asked.

Jonah just nodded. He felt like somebody was hunting him. All because psycho Seed hanged the dead Rigger.

"Well, tonight's on me," Pike said. "When you break-out to diver, then you can buy me drinks."

"Okay," Jonah said. He was flattered to be drinking with Pike. Most divers thought it beneath them to fraternize with Tenders.

A small, delicate-looking waitress in a pink sleeveless shirt and cut-off jeans came to the table and forced a smile. She was young and tan with straight brown hair and there was something determined about the way she moved and chewed her gum.

"What are you having?" Perfunctory cheerfulness.

"Dixie beer," Jonah said.

"And you?" she asked Pike.

"Tell the bartender that his friend Pike is here and I want a glass of that special sauce *romagosa* he keeps behind the bar and gave me once before; and we need an ashtray and two plates of boiled crawfish."

The waitress leaned on one leg and arched her eyebrows skeptically. "Are you sure about that *romagosa*? If you drink that moonshine, it'll roll you over blind. I've seen it happen to guys before. You'll be stuck in your chair; you won't be able to move."

"Well, at least I can yell for help," Pike said.

"But whether anybody'll understand you is a different matter," she replied.

"I want what I want," Pike said.

She placed the order at the bar. Her cut-off jeans were very short, just covering the cleft of her buttocks. Pike studied her brown shapely legs. He said with sincerity loud enough for her to hear, "She's got a real nice pair of legs."

Her head lifted, then shook sideways, but she didn't turn to look their way.

"She liked that. I meant for her to like it. I've been here plenty times before and she likes to flirt. She looks delicate, like a little sparrow, but she's really a full-on woman." Pike put a cigarette in his mouth and held a lighter up to it. His face momentarily brightened in the flame. Several Riggers wearing company shirts walked in. One of them turned and stared straight at Jonah, then at Pike. They knew Jonah and Pike were involved in the hanging. One muttered, "They've got balls coming in here after what they done."

The Riggers ordered beer at the bar then disappeared into the back room to play pool. Pike blew smoke toward the ceiling.

"Those Riggers noticed us," Pike said.

He didn't like that they knew.

Why would he?

"It's going to be a long season because of Seed. A long season with Riggers at our throats more than usual. We're safe here, though. I know the bartender and he doesn't tolerate any fighting. He's got a gun under the bar."

In spite of what Pike said, Jonah braced himself for trouble; the Rigger who stared at him looked like he wanted something.

"What happened to Captain Ira?" Jonah asked Pike. Captain Ira had worked the live-boat job with them on the *Falstaff.* After Seed hanged the drowned Rigger as a sick joke, Ira had threatened the crew on the oil rig with a shotgun to protect his workboat. Now he was in the hospital.

Pike looked around to be sure nobody else was close enough to hear. "Someone jumped him outside his house. His skull is fractured, he's got a broken collarbone, and the orbital bone around his left eye is cracked. He said he's got a permanent migraine. Feels like a knife stabbing in both his eyes he said."

"And this was payback for the hanging?"

"Ira thinks so. The guy didn't say anything Ira can remember. But he was knocked out cold and could have forgotten." Pike lowered his voice and was now more serious than Jonah had ever seen him. "Ira says this guy surprised him right after he got out of his truck. Hit him with something like a stick or a pipe. He thinks it was just one guy, and didn't see him coming. Either the guy followed him home or was waiting for him. You and I need to grow eyes in the back of our heads. The way I figure it, we're next."

Jonah sat up straight.

All at once he was wide awake. Like someone had poured cold water over him.

"You'll be lucky to breathe, let alone walk after this," the waitress said returning with the drinks and an ashtray. Jonah took his beer, drank half of it straight down, but didn't feel any better. Pike, beaming, looked up and gave her his best smile.

The waitress carried her round tray—serving drinks, delivering checks, clearing and wiping tables—and was the smallest person in the room. Numbly, Jonah watched her work and it came into his mind that she drifted around the oil field workers and beefy bikers like a tiny, nimble cleaner shrimp picking parasites out of the teeth of barracudas—her services were more than welcome, but she was always in danger of being accidently swallowed.

The ZZ Top song "I'm Bad, I'm Nationwide" finished on the jukebox, and the place slipped into a momentary silence. The neat click of pool balls came from the back room, and from above a soft patter of rain started on the galvanized tin roof. A new song started playing and filled the room with the rollicking sound of accordion, frottier, fiddle, and drums. Pike slowly swished the moonshine around his glass. He gazed at the clear spirits, almost affectionately, then took a gulp.

"That's the ticket," he gasped.

"I talked to Seed last night," Jonah said. "He's worried that the relatives of the body he hung are going to press charges."

"He told me that too. I think it's a crock," Pike said. "I haven't heard anything except they plan to kick our asses. Maybe someone is trying to scare him. I'll tell you what though, if he did that to my brother, I'd press charges—after I cracked his melon." Seed had really gotten under Pike's skin.

Jonah felt awkward and a little foolish as he tried to get Pike to understand how the crane operator had accidentally swung Seed into the guardrail on the control tower before Seed lost his cool. That he hung the body as retaliation. The gravity of the subject caused both men to speak in lowered voices.

"That's no excuse," Pike said. "Seed wasn't even hurt."

"That's true," Jonah said. "I'm just saying that in his mind he had a reason for what he did."

"Look, kid. I'm going to be blunt about this. You got to wise up. Lots of guys have had a tough life, and they don't act like our jerk. I've looked at Seed's file. The court report is in there. And press clippings. Do you know what he did to get put in prison?"

"He told me he beat up his girlfriend because she was screwing another guy."

Pike laughed. "Well, first of all, she wasn't his girlfriend, just some girl who he wanted to make his girlfriend. He tried to pick her up a few times and she said no. Anyway, Seed must not like girls who say no, because he beat her into a coma, carved his name on her back with a knife, and left her for dead. Somehow she lived. Lucky for her and lucky for him."

Jonah felt oddly unsurprised.

"He's a liar. He's a bad guy. You don't want to be taking his side on this or getting mixed up with him in any way. I shouldn't tell you this, but I tried to have him fired. The owner, Abbott, said no, not right now. In my opinion Abbott is making a big mistake. He figures we're getting swamped with work and Seed is a pretty good diver. Divers are scarce right now, so he's keeping him on, but I won't have him on my crew."

Jonah nodded.

"If you hang out with the wrong people it can ruin you. You've got a future as a diver and you need to protect that. They should've never let Seed out on parole. He should be rotting in prison as far as I'm concerned."

"Yeah," Jonah said. Pike was obviously right.

"By the way," Pike said. "Our crew is broken up. In a few days you're being sent out with a new crew on a liftboat."

"What's the job?"

"Installing risers." Riser pipes connected oil rigs to the pipeline systems on the sea floor. Riser pipes rose vertically off bottom—like the drainage pipe of a gutter on the corner of a house—bringing the oil or natural gas in a pipeline up to the surface of an oil rig. "You'll be tending the divers and running a decompression chamber. If you're lucky, you'll get some handjetting dives." Tenders often did the handjetting, sinking undersea pipelines by digging a trench under them with a pressurized water hose.

"What's Seed doing?"

"He'll be stuck in the shop taping hoses and pulling weeds."

"Indefinitely?"

"No. A week, or two, or three. Until he's needed offshore."

"He's not going to like that," Jonah said.

Pike smiled and nodded.

CHAPTER NINETEEN

THE LIDLESS EYE

The next day Jonah drove to the dock at Dulac to meet Olene for their snorkeling date. Her family's fishing boat was an eighteen-foot Boston Whaler. The young woman stepped on board carrying a bag with suntan lotion, snorkeling gear, a large red beach towel, and a six-pack of diet soda. Jonah paid for the gas and brought sandwiches. It was a cool morning. The fiberglass surface of the boat felt mildewy and damp.

"You drive," Olene said, moving to the bow of the Whaler.

The outboard Evinrude engine growled to a start then quieted to a steady rumble.

The Whaler pulled away from the dock, easing past the slips of fishing trawlers and charter vessels. Some of the power boats, running their engines, puffed smoky exhaust from their transoms, while a couple of paying tourists stood patiently on the dock waiting to go fishing. A brown pelican ruffled its wings and settled on a piling and looked out over the morning harbor. Another casually paddled around in the oily water. As the Whaler left the mouth of the harbor, Jonah accelerated. The Whaler began to bounce over a short chop of waves as they turned clear of a channel shoal. Looking ahead Olene said, "Go straight out."

"How far?"

"Out to a rig where it's real deep. I want to see where you work. And who knows . . ." She smiled coyly. "Maybe your wish will come true."

Jonah felt his face get hot. "Which one?"

"Maybe we'll see some whales," Olene said with a little laugh. She said *see some whales* in a playful, suggestive way, and it seemed that she might really be talking about making love. Either way, she was getting to him, and as they looked at each other he felt a brief spark, a moment of sudden connection.

The lovely woman stood with her feet square on the deck, holding the bow line and leaning slightly back, like a water-skier. She wore a red bikini bottom and a sweatshirt with UNIVERSITY OF LOUISIANA printed across the chest. The wind lifted her hair and shook her sweatshirt. They hit the wake of a fishing boat a little too fast and the hull bounced hard. Olene bent her knees to absorb the bounce but somehow lost her balance and landed on her bottom.

Jonah stopped the propeller and went forward. He felt horrible and embarrassed.

"Are you okay?"

Olene was laughing. "I'm fine." She saw his worried look and teased him. "You did that on purpose just to give me a big bruise on my ass."

"I'm sorry, I'll be more careful." He gave her a hand up, pulling her to him, and as she got to her feet he had the sudden urge to kiss her. She went to the bow as before, and Jonah drove the boat farther out into the Gulf. With the sound of her laughing still in his mind, he could see her shoulders through the sweatshirt, her naked legs, the roundness of her bottom through the bikini, the birthmark on the back of her right thigh. She stood gracefully, concentrated on the feeling of the boat moving across the gentle surface of the water, adjusting to each dip and rise. Except for the occasional bump of a small wave, the ride seemed to make her peaceful. On the horizon floated the pristine white profile of a large cruise ship on its way to New Orleans.

The Whaler carried them over a startlingly clear and shallow sea where the water was turquoise and radiant as a meadow of fine opals. They passed a dozen small oil rigs, and as they traveled further out from shore, the ocean grew deeper and darker but without losing its gemstone light.

"Right there," she said. "That's the oil rig where we usually fish."

Two boats loaded with fishermen were already anchored next to the oil rig.

"Too crowded," Jonah said. "Let's go farther out."

The girl nodded, and he hit the gas.

Barely within sight of land, he killed the engine and the Whaler glided to a stop.

Jonah pulled off his tee shirt.

The propeller scar on his chest stood out purplish-pink and ugly.

"What happened to you?" she asked.

"Propeller on a shrimpboat." Almost three weeks had passed since he'd been cut, and the wound was healing nicely.

"That's bad. You're lucky to be alive."

"I know it."

"Can I touch it?" Olene asked.

"Sure." He wanted her to touch him, and moved closer.

"It's weird," she said, tracing the scar with her fingertips. Her face softened and looked thoughtful. "But it looks ugly and somehow pretty at the same time."

She paused.

"It says something about you," Olene said. "Like you're rough, you're not afraid."

"Is that good?" He looked at her face when she answered, at the delicacy of the skin beneath her gray eyes.

"Yes." Olene took her hand away, and her cheeks turned red.

Jonah didn't know what to say, and he began to feel awkward.

"Do you have any scars?" he finally asked, kidding.

"No." She laughed and looked up at him. Her eyes were moist and bright.

The boat rose and fell with the easy roll of the sea. Waves gently slapped the hull and fell softly away with silvery gurgling. Nearby floated a large patch of sargassum weed.

"You think we should snorkel right here?" she asked in disbelief. Her eyes narrowed.

"Yes. You study marine biology. Don't you have to do stuff like this?"

"No. It's mostly working in a lab. More than half the class get seasick and have to wear a Dramamine patch just to go out on the bay. Be serious. I don't mind swimming around oil rigs, but this? There's nothing here; it must be hundreds of feet deep." She stood up and leaned over to peer down into the blue.

"Maybe," Jonah said, working on a pair of swim fins. "Come on Olene. It'll be fine."

"I don't know," she said. She thought for a minute, then looked apprehensively at the water, and back at Jonah, at the scar on his chest. She fingered a strand of hair near her face.

Suddenly, she pulled her sweatshirt over her head and gracefully tossed it to the bow. She did it so quickly that for an instant he thought she was taking everything off. Her breasts bounced as she sat down to pull on her fins and the sheer fabric of her bikini top hid very little. It was almost as if she had painted her breasts red. Her skin looked smooth and soft, with a delicate pink glow, and a line of nearly imperceptible downy hairs grew just below her navel and led innocently downwards into the triangular front of her bathing suit. And somehow, now that she was almost naked, she looked bigger, more formidable, more womanly, and she seemed to know it. Olene gave Jonah a funny smile that said, *I know what you're thinking.*

"Okay," she said, "let's do it now, before I change my mind."

Jonah watched as Olene shuffled and scraped with fins on her feet to the side of the Whaler next to him. She put the snorkel in her mouth and paused a moment.

Then she pointed down into the water at the reflection of them next to each other on the smooth surface shaded from the sun. He waited while she stared, mesmerized by the peculiar image of them wearing masks on their faces and holding snorkels in their mouths. An eddy passed through the reflection, making it stretch and twist.

"Ready?" he asked.

They broke through their own images into indigo blue and bubbles.

⚓ ⚓ ⚓

A wave of vertigo briefly touched her. Olene quickly scanned the water all around, fearful, expecting anything. But nothing came. The cavernous blue dimension underneath overwhelmed her. She blinked, trying to gather some resolve.

She surfaced and blew water clear from her snorkel. Then turned around three times, feeling distinctly alien to the watery and unresisting environment, hardly noticing the coolness on her skin. Jonah floated parallel to the surface next to her, staring down into the depths.

Olene fought off the urge to climb back into the Whaler, took a deep breath, and lined herself up next to him. She forced herself to gaze downwards for a proper look, the way he did. Suddenly she breathed rapidly and had the urge to pee.

Columns of sunlight pierced down through the lustrous blue water, phantom wisps of creatures among them, visible only from the corner of her eyes—evasive shadows. Tiny specks of plankton floated by like electric blue dust.

She turned several times to face the motion of the phantoms and came each time to rest her panicky eyes on the shifting sunlight. Like a lidless eye, the awesome blue deep stared up to meet her gaze at every turn.

Under the hull of the Whaler, she pressed her back and legs against the comfort of its solid surface; a little less exposed.

She looked down again, but the view still spooked her, maybe because of the great empty space beneath her.

Jonah looked at her through the glistening motes and she bravely signaled she was fine.

Gradually, as the minutes passed, her fear began to give way to amazement; the shafts of sunlight seemed to diffuse and soften with accumulating depth into a deep, rich blueness that had no solid object.

Looking down, she suddenly thought of a mouse she had once seen dropped into a glass tank for a python to devour.

Then her hands were intertwined with his.

She pressed the lens of her mask against his and shut out the ethereal light. She could see Jonah was smiling.

Holding his hand, she followed him toward the patch of sargassum weed.

She eased over the surface of the sea. The sun warmed her back in between the waves lapping gently over her.

Olene put her hand out to touch the sinewy dense tendrils of the sargassum weed. Among the holly-shaped leaves there were bubbly growths that looked like grapes. She squeezed one between her thumb and index finger and realized the curious bubbles contained air. Looking even more closely, she saw a tiny crab retreating from her intrusive hand. The whole weed thrived with life like a little floating city, an *Alice in Wonderland* world.

The brightness of colors and tiny sea life exhilarated them. Without warning, Jonah dived downwards, trailing bubbles, and she watched him grow smaller and smaller.

Olene began to fear that he was going too deep, that he would drown down there. She watched as he stopped and turned in a circle, looking all around, then up at her. He waved to her, then turned downwards and incredibly went even deeper, until his figure seemed only a dot in the immense blue eye of the sea beneath.

Miraculously, just when she thought Jonah would drown, his figure grew a little larger, then a little more, gathering momentum with his rise from the deep, headfirst, his mask lens opaque with surface light. Olene thought he swam too slowly to make it, and it frightened her, but then he came closer. His head was shrouded in bubbles as he exhaled just before breaking the surface.

Then his head broke the surface.

She grabbed hold of him and, putting her head out of the water, spit out her snorkel.

"You scared the hell out of me," Olene said. "I thought you were going to die."

"Oh . . . sorry." He seemed surprised.

She took his hand and gave him a squeeze.

He gave her a squeeze back.

She looked up out of the water and realized that they'd drifted some distance from the Whaler. She swam back to the boat, arriving just ahead of him, and climbed aboard.

While they ate cucumber-and-bologna sandwiches, the water dried on their bodies. Her salty wet hair stuck out in all directions and he said there was a red oval mark around her eyes and nose from the mask.

"Thanks for bringing me here." The clear deep blue had scared her but it was beautiful.

"Maybe next time we can swim around a reef or an old oil rig. Something full of life."

"That'd be great." And she meant it.

By the time they returned to the dock and unloaded the Whaler the late-afternoon shadows crossed the ground. Olene smiled when he asked her to dinner later that night. Somewhere besides the Yellow Catfish.

"I wish I could, I really do, but I have a ton of schoolwork I have to do, and I also have to work at the Catfish tonight," she said. "Thanks for asking."

"Maybe next time." He seemed to pull back into himself.

"Definitely." That made it better. "Hey, if I write a letter, how do I send it to you?" she asked. This question seemed to touch him. His face lit up.

"Mail it to me care of the dive company and they'll get it to me on a supply boat or a personnel chopper. Even if I'm there only a couple of days. But I figure I'll be gone a lot longer. Maybe the rest of the summer." Jonah suddenly looked around the harbor, a little anxious.

"Is something the matter?" Olene asked.

"No, I just felt like someone was watching us," he said. Then he kissed her goodbye. Olene was caught off-guard and hardly reacted. She worried that he might think she didn't like him, so she kissed him goodbye and set the record straight. He tasted delicious and salty, like the sea.

As Olene watched Jonah walk across the parking lot to his El Camino, she liked how he moved and how he looked. He had sturdy, broad shoulders, a certain confident roughness, yet kind, intelligent eyes and an honest smile. But there was something deeper she liked about him, something that she couldn't quite put her finger on—a good kind of strangeness, something about him and the sea. Jonah was a good man, and she would see him again if he asked.

CHAPTER TWENTY

OIL PATCH SCUM

When Jonah drove up to the Yellow Catfish the parking lot looked dark and almost empty—just two pickup trucks. The partiers hadn't yet arrived. He went up the stairs to his apartment. He planned to pack his duffel bag to go offshore the next day and get to bed early. He reached into his pocket for the key to his room, but stopped short. He thought he heard a sound come from inside. A small bump or creak, like somebody inside. But he couldn't be sure. Maybe the sound had come from the bar downstairs.

Jonah unlocked the door.

As he turned the handle and pushed it open the bad feeling grew stronger.

A different smell.

He entered the room and suddenly ducked.

A steel pipe swung at him and barely missed his face.

The man was tall. He had very pale skin, short red hair and dark shadows under his eyes like he hadn't slept in a month. A swastika covered with a three-leaf clover was tattooed on his right biceps. He held the steel pipe in his right hand. The man looked frustrated that he'd missed Jonah with his first swing. Now things might get messy.

The man rushed him again, swinging the pipe.

In a sudden move Jonah shot in on the big man's left leg like he'd done for years against opponents in wrestling tournaments.

A second later he stood up holding his leg.

The man grunted and his eyes widened like he knew he was in trouble. Off-balance, he swung the pipe at the top of Jonah's head, grazing the scalp.

Jonah quickly stretched the man's leg straight and locked the ankle tight under his armpit.

In an explosive move, he spun under the man's outstretched leg, torquing the lower leg and destroying the man's knee. The tendons ripped with a distinctive twang, and the cartilage tore with a sound like a pepper grinder.

The man screamed and dropped the pipe.

When Jonah let go of him, the man's left foot and lower leg faced backwards.

"You got one minute to crawl outta here before I do your other leg."

Groaning with pain, the man tried to get up, but he couldn't. He dragged himself out of the room and collapsed on the walkway in front of the door.

Jonah grabbed the man's shirt to drag him further away from his room but the man's shirt ripped off in Jonah's hands.

Across the man's bare chest was a tattoo in dark blue letters:

THERE'S A NIGGER IN MY FAMILY TREE.

Below the words was the tattoo of a dead black man hanging from an oak. The tattoo was so realistic it could have been drawn from a photograph. The black man was bare-chested, his hands were tied behind his back, and his mouth was open like he had died trying to scream.

Jonah had never seen anything so hateful. A sick sensation rose in the back of his throat and his eyes began to itch.

Jonah stepped over the broken man and went downstairs to the manager of the Yellow Catfish. This piece of shit was his problem now.

The manager apologized. "Oil patch scum. He must have picked the lock. I'll call the police."

While waiting for the police to arrive the man sat in agony and begged Jonah to give him a shirt. He didn't want the wrong people seeing his tattoo.

"Tough shit."

Jonah stood by the entrance to his room making sure the man didn't crawl away before the cops arrived. "Who the hell are you?"

"A friend of the dead man you boys hung."

When the police car pulled into the parking lot the man saw one of the cops was black. The man's face became desperate and sweaty. He licked his lips as he watched the police go into the taproom to talk to the manager.

"Just give me a shirt and I'll make sure you don't disappear. Accidents happen, man, specially when yer a diver."

"Are you threatening me? I can still do your other leg."

The police came out of the taproom and started up the stairs.

"Gimme a shirt!" The man pleaded.

"Sorry. Honesty is the best policy."

"Do you know how easy it is ta kill a man offshore and make it look like an accident?" Now the man's face flared bright red with anger. "I want you ta think a me when the crane operator crushes you under a load. I want you ta think a me when you catch fire in the decompression chamber, when yer air gits cut off, er poisoned. When a gang of Riggers breaks yer arms and legs, and throws ya overboard in the middle a the night."

The policemen walked up.

"Why don't you shut up," the white cop said.

"Nice tattoo," the black cop said.

The cops stared at the man's knee, at his tattoos. Then they glanced at each other.

Something bad passed between them.

The man also saw it, and his face turned pale.

"I need a ambulance," he moaned. "I need ta go ta the hospital."

"Don't you worry, son, the ambulance is here. You're in good hands now. We're gonna take special good care a you," the white policeman said in a calm, professional voice. "I'm nurse Betty, and my partner here is nurse Wilma."

"Where does it hurt? Here?" The black cop hit the man's bad knee with his nightstick.

The man screamed, then started crying.

"I thought that was the spot," the white cop said.

They handcuffed the man's arms behind his back and dragged him sobbing down the stairs, his backwards foot bouncing on each step.

Then they loaded him into their patrol car, shoving him roughly in the back.

Before they left, the police took a statement. Afterwards, the black cop told Jonah, "You did good, but next time, break his neck and claim self-defense."

"Yeah, put a blade in his hand after he's dead," the white cop said. "You'll be doin us all a favor."

As the police car pulled out of the parking lot Jonah had the feeling the man with the tattoo wasn't on his way to any hospital. Anyhow, not right away.

⚓ ⚓ ⚓

At work the next morning a truck, ready for loading, pulled up outside the company warehouse. Jonah hand-cranked the two compressors tagged for the job for one last check. The machines coughed and started, and he let them run a minute. He shut them off and the crane operator began placing them one at a time on the flatbed trailer.

On the ground Jonah slipped the crane hook into each compressor's padeye and back out, once the compressors rested securely on the flatbed. He finished loading the truck at eight o'clock. The dispatcher came out of the warehouse with a clipboard and paperwork.

"That's it. Good job," the dispatcher said. "Be in Freeport by midnight tonight."

"Okay," Jonah said.

The workers assigned to stay onshore and work in the warehouse started to arrive in the parking lot to begin their day. Seed arrived with them, and when he saw his friend out by the loaded truck, he walked over.

"You going offshore?" Seed asked, walking up.

"Yes."

Jonah and Seed walked over to the yard. "Pike got me stuck here in the warehouse," Seed complained. The yard contained an array of white-painted decompression chambers, air compressors of different sizes, and a dive bell on a pallet. The air looked hazy now and began to feel Louisiana hot. Sweat made Jonah's work shirt stick to his skin.

"Did you talk to Pike?" Seed asked.

"Yes. I told him how the crane operator swung you into the guardrail."

"Thanks, man." Seed smiled and looked a little relieved. "Do you think it worked? Did you persuade him not to blame me if he gives a statement?"

"I don't think so."

"Why not?"

"Pike doesn't see it your way."

Seed stared at him. "You sound different to me. Are you on Pike's side now?"

"I had a guy break into my apartment and come at me with a steel pipe last night. Because of you. Captain Ira is in the hospital, and he might never be right again. Because of you. You brought all this trouble on us, and yourself. So yes, I'm on Pike's side."

"I thought you were different." Seed kicked a stone in the dirt. And for a minute he looked like he would crumble to pieces. He seemed to be connecting this moment to events in his life that Jonah knew nothing about. Events that cut him to the bone.

An awful expression crossed Seed's face. A human expression Jonah had never seen before. Like pain and terror and rage, all at the same time. "This ain't right. You're better than this," he gasped. "I know it."

Jonah shook his head to disagree.

"Don't shake your head." Seed's voice turned cold and strangely calm. "I know you understand what I'm talking about."

"You don't know me." Jonah was suddenly very angry.

They'd worked together for one job and now the guy acted like they were brothers or childhood friends. Seed was lowlife scum, dangerous and out of control. All sympathy for Seed had dried up.

"So that's the way it's going to be?" Seed's voice held a threat.

Not sure what to say, Jonah looked around the yard. Cowbirds sat silent in the shaded branches of a willow. A truck went down the rutted dirt road at the end of the yard and disappeared behind a stand of oak trees hung with Spanish moss.

"No," he said. "That's the way it *is*."

All emotion drained from Seed's face and he gave a look that made the hairs on the back of Jonah's neck prickle up.

"Then I'll see you around." Seed turned quickly and walked away.

For a moment Jonah stood and watched Seed going back to the warehouse. He felt uneasy and his heart pounded in his ears.

What did Seed just show him? It felt worse than the threats the man with the steel pipe made before the police took him away. The man with the steel pipe said it was easy to kill a man offshore and make it look like an accident.

And, then it came. Seed didn't just take rejection badly.

Seed would kill him for it.

⚓ ⚓ ⚓

Jonah began the long drive across Texas for the riser-pipe job off a liftboat. The crew was scheduled to shove off from Freeport at midnight. He headed north along flat, sandy backroads bordered by shallow drainage ditches, past the flooded rice field crawfish farms of Terrebonne Parish. Gleaming and thick with cereal grass, the farms stretched on a low plane to the tree lined horizons. Further inland the road hugged algae covered sloughs and bayous where glistening water turtles sunned themselves on logs near cypress knees.

As he sped along the wet green country Jonah glanced out the window and suddenly thought about Olene. Going offshore put money in his pocket, but he wished he'd been able to spend more time with her. They shared a last-minute lunch together but had to rush the meal because she needed to get to class and he needed to start driving. She kissed him goodbye and said, "I hope you get to see a whale."

CHAPTER TWENTY-ONE

THE LIFTBOAT

little before 1 a.m. Jonah came up to the dock at Freeport, the first one there from the dive company. He felt wide awake from the gas station coffee he'd forced himself to drink. The truck carrying the equipment for the job hadn't arrived yet, so he got out of the car and went down to the water to see the vessel that would be his home for a month. The harbor lights cast a pink glow that attracted clouds of bugs.

His short sleeves didn't cover his arms and he walked along the quay at a fast clip.

The mosquitoes followed in his wake.

In the dark, the port looked vacant except for a class 229/38 Atlas liftboat moored by the quay. Liftboats were the workhorses of offshore service vessels. Tough utility boats that jacked-up out of the ocean on hydraulic legs to create stable work platforms. The one by the quay had an ugly barge-like platform-hull, three towering legs, and a crane. When the massive vessel moved, the legs had to be retracted out of the water. A squat, three-story tower loomed over the deck. The top floor housed the control room, the second the bunkrooms and the bottom floor the galley. Down a short stepway the engine room huddled in the belly of the vessel.

Out of water, the legs of the ship stood like three massive black pillars. One jutted up from the center of the afterdeck and the other two from the port and starboard foredeck, each standing roughly two hundred feet in the air.

When a liftboat arrived at a worksite, the legs would be lowered until they pressed the sea floor and raised the work platform thirty or more feet up out of the water.

In place, a liftboat looked like an H.G. Wells Martian attack robot come to life. But, when in transit, with legs high above the deck, they looked so top-heavy, it was hard to imagine that these vessels didn't flip over in every sort of sea except one that was glassy smooth. Actually they did. The year before, one flipped over in stormy seas and drowned eleven men. They were the most unstable ships in the Gulf.

The truck arrived around 2 a.m. and circled to a stop at the edge of the quay next to the loading crane. Then a Toyota pickup arrived and parked next to Jonah's car.

A tall gangly Tender, an apprentice diver called Escargot, got out. His co-workers called him Escargot because he walked with a slow, oily gait and didn't eat meat. The name stuck and most divers no longer knew his real name. Jonah had never met him, but had heard plenty.

Escargot was an eyesore. Unless he had become incredibly filthy he wouldn't wash. He considered showering an exercise in futility, because it took mere seconds to become grimy and sweaty again when you were working offshore. Escargot also chewed tobacco twenty-four hours a day and habitually placed his cud in the front of his lower lip, making it bulge open, revealing black tobacco that hid his lower teeth. No diver ever let Escargot borrow his dive helmet without first making him scrub out his mouth.

"You must be Jonah?" Escargot said in a slow drawl.

"That's me."

Jonah slapped a mosquito stinging his eyelid. Bugs were starting to swarm and he wanted to get to work and finish quickly. Then he could go inside and get away from them. *Where the hell was the port crane operator?* He looked at the empty cab of the crane then at the port office trailer. Blue light and the faint sound of a TV came from within.

A three-hundred-pound fat man who had been watching TV inside came out of his air-conditioned oasis, walked slowly across the yard, and grunted as he climbed into the cab of the loading crane. Finally, they could start work.

Jonah stood on the deck of the liftboat, receiving and guiding the equipment swinging from the crane. Escargot moved around on the flatbed of the truck unfastening chains and hooking the crane hook to pieces of gear ready to be hoisted.

When they started to sweat from their work, the zinging fibrillations of tiny wings filled the air. Omnipresent and countless, the mosquitoes came in droves to drink blood. Jonah slapped at them and swore, and worked even faster.

They loaded three compressors, a full 350-pound tool locker as big as a sarcophagus, bound umbilicals, different hoses for the handjet and impact wrench, a decompression chamber, and other assorted gear.

A pair of topside Welders came aboard and went straight to the choicest of bunk rooms to sleep. The forty-foot joints of riser pipe they were going to weld on the job had been loaded earlier and stacked on the starboard side of the deck.

The Dive Supervisor and the three divers also boarded while the Tenders worked.

Once they unloaded the truck, Jonah and Escargot lashed everything to cleats and steel bollards on the liftboat with yellow nylon rope, then double-checked every knot and every piece of gear. They were ready to get underway.

The engines of the liftboat rumbled and clanged and the deck shook like an earthquake. The captain lowered the platform hull down into the oily water until the hull floated and the liftboat's three legs were fully retracted. They looked like massive steel redwoods jutting into the sky. The vessel was now an upside-down tripod, angling away from the concrete quay and pink lights of the port.

Jonah came out the door of the living quarters. His watch read 3:52 a.m. and he was going to be up all night. He'd had too much coffee to sleep, and they'd be at the worksite in only two hours. He stood on the catwalk landing and watched the lights of Freeport recede into darkness. It felt nice to be moving.

The long, thin purple scar on his chest itched, and he rubbed it through his shirt. This made him think about how Olene had touched it; then he stared out at the dark sea. The mosquitoes and heavy dank air were left behind for the clean, breezy air of the open Gulf.

⚓ ⚓ ⚓

The sky brightened with dawn, revealing fair weather and the sea dipping and swelling with glassy foam. The liftboat had arrived at the first work location. The steel deck vibrated and groaned underfoot while the gearbox engines lowered the black pillar-like legs into the waves.

Standing on deck, Jonah felt the supports hit bottom and the platform-hull of the boat began to jack-up into the air above the sea. Dripping torrents of saltwater, the awkward square vessel rose on its three legs like a gigantic mechanical insect. At the height of thirty-five feet, the captain locked the tripod rig in place. They were securely elevated thirty yards from the small oil platform—swimming distance for the divers. For a few short minutes the only sound was that of the waves rinsing and whorling around the liftboat's legs. Then the work began.

The job was not unusual. Install riserpipes on the side of the oil rig and connect them to a pipeline on the sea floor. The oil came out of the earth, ran through an offshore drilling rig and was pumped ashore. Then refined. Most went to motor vehicle gas tanks across North America, part for home heating oil. The world went on without a hitch because divers worked at the bottom of the sea.

Half the bolting and welding would be done topside, half underwater. That's where the divers came in.

Jonah and Escargot set up the dive station. With help from the deckhand operating the crane, they moved the decompression chamber out of the way. Jonah carefully positioned the air compressors so that the intake valves wouldn't suck in carbon monoxide exhaust from any of the engines and poison the diver's air supply. He set the umbilicals right by the dive station and connected the deck pressure hoses called whips running from the decompression chamber to the compressors.

Next they prepared the decompression chamber. It looked like a horizontal cylinder set on a pair of skids. Painted white to reflect the sun and made of stainless steel, this was the standard crawl-in, two-chamber, pressure vessel large enough to allow two men to recline inside for hyperbaric treatment. There was one round pressure-sealed door on the end and another halfway inside, dividing the two chambers. The antechamber and the main chamber each had a small viewing port and a two-way telephone to talk to the Tender just outside.

Jonah unlaced his Red Wing boots and, hunched over, entered the chamber in his socks to clean the interior. He put fresh sheets on the mattress, swabbed the oral/nasal oxygen masks with vinegar-moistened Kleenex, and checked the seal on the inner and the outer hatch. Escargot cut four lengths of rope and suspended a tarpaulin over the chamber to shade it and keep it as cool as possible.

The morning sun had risen one-quarter the way up the eastern sky with puffy white clouds from horizon to horizon, when Jonah saw the lead diver step overboard for the first jump.

Back in a makeshift dive control shed with a tarpaulin roof, Troy, the Dive Supervisor, sat on a stool smoking unfiltered cigarettes. He had a black beard flecked with gray and a confident voice reassuring to hear underwater, particularly if the job turned dicey. Taciturn and pragmatic, he approached the job without any trace of sentiment or enthusiasm. Jonah had seen him once before in the shop and knew he had an excellent reputation.

On the coffee stained desk in front of Troy were notepads, pens, procedure manuals, the engineering blueprints for the job, a slim booklet containing the complete U.S. Navy decompression tables, and the telephone communication box. He had already looked over the dive station to be sure the Tenders had set up everything correctly. During the check, he asked Jonah, "You're the one who swam through a spinning propeller and lived?"

"Yeah." Everybody knew everything out here.

"Promising." That was all the Dive Supervisor said, and more than he said to Escargot.

Troy reviewed the engineering blueprints with the Lead Diver before the first jump. The Lead Diver had to reconnoiter the exact distance of the pipeline-end on the sea floor to the base of the platform. Jonah stood by to operate the decompression chamber at the end of the jump. Escargot tended the diver's umbilical. With a depth of 141 feet, the jump was shallow and the diver breathed surface-supplied air delivered through his umbilical hose into his helmet.

The work would continue twenty-four hours a day with a diver in the water and another decompressing in the chamber in ongoing succession. Jonah, Escargot, and a third Tender worked sixteen-hour shifts: rotating from tending the diver in the sea, to decompression chamber operation, to finally getting wet themselves.

At night Jonah hung floodlights over the side of the liftboat to illuminate the submarine work area. The lights attracted nocturnal sea life that splashed and stirred to the surface. Beneath the interface of water and air, the floodlights changed the dark aquatic world to a weak eerie blue.

The propeller wound had finally healed enough for Jonah to work at depth again. When he got the chance to dive, nothing seemed real to him but his breathing. Working undersea by the lights at night seemed like working in gray vapor. Sometimes, if visibility was very bad, the ocean enshrouded him in blue-gray gauziness and gave him the feeling of a small space. Perched just above the ocean on the liftboat's steel legs, the dive crew lived on the threshold of two worlds. The feeling of being a creature exclusive to either place blurred and vanished once the diving started.

The primary variation marking the passage of days was the sun and its steady heat, or its conspicuous absence.

In this state of limbo Jonah worked and lost track of time. The fall of night brought relief, cooling the deck and soothing his sunburnt face and arms. Like a breezy veil enclosing him in gentle weariness and whispering solitude. During the day the deck grew scorching hot and the sun unbearably bright. The white splash and sinuous swell and curl of the encircling ocean were the only constants.

The days ran together and the weather did not change for a month.

Early in the job Escargot re-earned his reputation for moving slowly. Jonah happened to be on deck when Escargot failed to turn quickly enough, although the Supervisor yelled to duck. The tag-line steadying a joint of pipe swinging through the air off the crane tapped Escargot across the shoulders. It knocked him overboard.

Pinwheeling his arms, he fell, and cussed like a convict the full thirty-five feet to the waves. Jonah heard Escargot's body hit the surface of the ocean with a great *slap*! Then Escargot disappeared.

Troy, the Dive Supervisor, was about to begin rescue procedures when Escargot surfaced. He swam jerkily to the long ladder, embarrassed and aching from the thirty-five foot belly flop. The ocean left a big red mark on his chest and stomach— like he'd been slapped by a giant.

CHAPTER TWENTY-TWO

THE SWAMP

By the edge of the Atchafalaya Swamp, Renoir, the snake-eater, stepped inside his trailer and shut the door. He carefully put the burlap bag on the kitchen table. The burlap flattened out, moving and bulging, as the cottonmouths tried to find a way out. They were agitated, and that was good.

Renoir picked up the phone and called Seed. After three rings Seed picked up and, by the excitement in his voice, Renoir could tell that everything was turning out perfect.

"It's gonna be a big night," Seed whispered urgently.

"That's right," Renoir said.

"You catch any?" Seed said.

Renoir was supposed to bring the cottonmouths; Seed was supposed to bring Pike, the fuckhead Dive Supervisor.

"Yeah, two good ones. Real pissed off," Renoir said. "The little one tried to nail me twice before I got 'em in the sack. What about you?"

Seed said yes, that he'd grabbed Pike coming out of a restaurant.

"Good, keep him quiet. Make sure nobody sees you."

"I got it covered." Seed laughed.

Renoir looked out the window. Getting nice and dark.

"Don't you do it till I get dere."

"I won't. I'm waiting for you."

Renoir hung up the telephone and looked at the bag. One of the snakes was moving and hissing.

Insects splattered on the filthy windshield and made it hard for Renoir to see. He reached over and patted the burlap bag of cottonmouths on the passenger seat. It was a shame he couldn't eat them when it was over, but they had a job to do.

Renoir followed the dirt road nine miles down to the meeting place by the swamp. He pulled over and left his headlights on, waiting for Seed's signal. There it was. Headlights from a vehicle parked back in the woods flashed, then went out.

Renoir turned the wheel and drove up to the green Buick Seed had stolen for the job. He parked and switched off the engine.

Renoir stepped out into woods that were darker than the night sky. The smell of moist wet earth wafted over from the swamp and mingled with the scent of pinewoods. Cicadas chirred and a cloud of winged insects whirled around the dim little lantern Seed lit.

"Don't make it too bright," Renoir said. Even though they were in the middle of nowhere, you couldn't be too careful.

"We got to see what we're doing," Seed said. He led Renoir to the trunk of his Buick and opened it. Pike lay inside with his hands tied behind his back, duct tape over his mouth. The side of his face was bloody and he smelled like he'd already pissed himself. He squinted up at Renoir and made a groaning noise that rhymed with the word *please*.

"All right. Up you get, cocksucker," Seed said.

Together, Seed and Renoir dragged Pike out of the trunk. He fell to the ground, then struggled to his knees. He moved awkwardly, like bones on his right side were broken.

"He's pretty gimpy," Renoir said.

"I beat him good," Seed said, smiling. "Used a tire iron."

"I'll be right back," Renoir said. He went back to his truck and grabbed a can of gasoline and the sack of snakes.

When he came back Pike was sitting on his heels. His eyes shifted, looking at what Renoir was carrying. Once more he made the groaning noise and tears started down his cheeks.

"Tip him forward so his head is down," Renoir said. He untied the rope that held shut the sack of cottonmouths.

Seed pushed Pike forward so he fell on his chest, grunting and sobbing, his face in the dirt. With his hands tied behind his back Pike was absolutely helpless. Seed grabbed a handful of hair on the back of Pike's head and pulled his face off the ground. "I'm not going back to Angola," Seed said.

Renoir dragged the snake bag under Pike's face, quickly opened it, and pulled the sack over Pike's head. As Renoir tied the sack tight around his neck it seemed like the cottonmouths started biting. There were spasms of motion inside the sack.

Pike screamed, but the sound was muffled by the duct tape and sack. Somehow he stood up and began violently shaking his head.

Seed and Renoir burst out laughing.

"He's like a chicken with his head cut off," Seed said.

"Look at that boy go," Renoir said.

Pike tried to run, but tripped and fell to the ground. He struggled back to his feet and tried to run again. This time he hit a tree and bounced to one side, staying on his feet. Frantically, he spun around and around, shaking his head, and trying to scream. Gradually, he slowed down, laboring hard to breathe, on the verge of collapse.

"The chicken cain't breathe too good," Renoir said.

Pike stumbled and fell right in front of Seed, thrashing and rolling in the dirt. Soon he stopped moving, except for his hands, which twitched and shook with a life of their own. Then Seed doused him in gasoline and set him on fire, but was disappointed. Pike was already too far gone. He hardly reacted to the flames.

CHAPTER TWENTY-THREE

BLOOD ON HIS BOOTS

A week later, out in the Gulf of Mexico, Jonah watched as a diver climbed up the long ladder onto the liftboat's deck, then walked several paces inboard. Escargot, who was tending him, coiled the umbilical hose on the deck. The diver unclamped his neck dam and Escargot took his helmet. The diver needed to enter the decompression chamber within five minutes of leaving the water—or start getting the bends—so he shed his gear as fast as his Tender could take it from him. After a speedy hosing off with fresh water, the diver entered the horizontal cylinder completely naked. He was a hairy, well-built man, trimmer than many divers. Jonah dogged the hatch shut.

Jonah pressured the chamber to forty feet and the compressed air hissed loudly and abrasively as it blasted inside. He followed the treatment schedule prescribed by Troy, the Dive Supervisor. It was the Dive Supervisor's very great responsibility, before the decompressing of any diver, to determine the correct treatment. Factoring in the depth and duration of the dive, the Supervisor on any job consulted the diver's bible: the U.S. Navy decompression tables. He transcribed the applicable sequence of pressures on a form sheet and initialed it. Then he handed it to the Tender operating the chamber to follow exactly. At the end of the chamber run, the Tender returned the form sheet to the Dive Supervisor who then filed it. In this way, records were kept of each dive and each decompression.

Hour by hour, dive after dive, Jonah stared at the pressure gauges on the instrument panel. Using levers controlling the intake and out-take of pressured air and the flow of oxygen, he treated the chamber occupants to a series of depth stops gradually ascending to zero feet. Routinely he vented the chamber, flushing out excess oxygen to guard against the possibility of a flash fire. He regularly peered in through the viewport to check on the recumbent diver inside and to signal when to start or stop breathing oxygen from the oral/nasal mask.

After every diver's treatment, Jonah cleaned the chamber and placed dry clean clothing and a towel on the mattress. The next man expected to find these things after entering wet and naked. Usually, the next diver, immediately before his jump, would hand over to the Tender operating the chamber the clothing and other articles he wanted while being decompressed. Sometimes requests were made for a cup of water and frequently divers put paperback novels or skin magazines folded in with their clothing.

Jonah stood attending the chamber with his hands on his hips. The sun glancing off the steel platform hurt his eyes and made him squint, but he didn't care because he'd received via a passing supply boat a nice letter from Olene that morning.

He read the short letter three times, almost memorizing it:

Dear Jonah,

I didn't want to let too much time go by without thanking you in writing for showing me your "workplace." Even though I was scared at first and scared when you went deep, I had a great time. When I looked down it was like looking into the eye of God, and the whole time I had the feeling that the eye was watching us. Anyhow, let's snorkel again when you come back home. Maybe I'll learn to scuba dive and we can see some whales!

In other news, work has been crazy. It's been raining like Niagara Falls the last couple a days and last night the bar cat brought inside a baby alligator. And the alligator was still alive believe it or not! So the cat jumped on the bar top and all hell broke loose. The gator went snapping and thrashing in the cat's mouth, spilling beer and glass everywhere. A woman tried to push the cat off the counter and got scratched by the cat AND bit by the baby gator at the same frickin time! You should have seen her face. My God, I couldn't stop laughing. It was like a hybrid monster with cat claws, two tails, two heads, fur, gator teeth, and a bad attitude. I finally chased the monster back outside with a broom! And got a round of applause when I came back inside. Write me back if you find the time. And be real careful. I don't want to see any more scars on you!

She drew a little heart and signed her name. Jonah couldn't help dwelling on Olene and her letter. In his mind, he began composing a long enthusiastic letter back. How he was getting deeper dives on this job than he ever had before. How he was going to "break-out" to Diver-Tender this summer.

Jonah vented the decompression chamber. He looked in to check on the diver—not having seizures or any other symptoms of the bends. Decompression affected different men in different ways: some bent like pretzels, while others never experienced so much as a skin tingle. The diver formed an "O" with his thumb and index finger. He was okay.

Seeing his own reflection in the viewport, Jonah noticed his hair had turned almost white and his face burnt umber in the sun. His features looked different to him, sharper and older. The sun and sea had changed him quickly, in part because the Dive Supervisor didn't insist as mandated by the company's insurance policy that they all wear hard hats and life vests. On steel decks under the full sun nobody wanted to wear anything more than plain work clothes and steel-toed boots.

Jonah turned the lever releasing pressure from the chamber at the end of the diver's decompression treatment. The needle on the gauge reading in depth seawater, moved gradually from 10 feet toward 0. The escaping air loudly blew out the exhaust opening.

Suddenly blood sprayed out the vent and splattered on Jonah's boots.

The diver began shrieking and pounding on the chamber walls.

Jonah immediately halted the escape of air and looked in the viewport. Through the mist within, brought on by the dropping pressure, he could barely see the diver on the mattress thrashing and squirming in agony. Leaving the decompression chamber, he sprinted across the deck of the liftboat to Troy, the Dive Supervisor, sitting in the control shed.

"The diver has an embolism!" Jonah shouted. "I brought the chamber to 3 feet on his final ascent and blood sprayed out the exhaust and he began screaming and convulsing."

"Did you fuck up the schedule I gave you?" Troy gave him a hard look.

"No. I followed it exactly."

"Are you sure?"

"Yes."

"You'd better be."

"One of us should get in there with the first aid-kit while the other runs the chamber on table 1A," Jonah said. "If that doesn't work we should go to table 5."

"Do you want to go in?"

"Sure, I can handle it."

"You know what to do?"

"Yes. Keep him on his left side. Be sure he doesn't swallow his tongue. Watch his breathing and for symptoms."

"Good." Troy looked at the blood on Jonah's boots.

"Let's go," Jonah said impatiently.

"Slow down a minute."

"Why?"

"Why don't you taste that blood on your boots?"

Jonah realized instantly that he'd been tricked. He bent down and wiped a smear of the red liquid off the toe of one boot. He tasted it. Ketchup.

"You did real good. If he really had an embolism, the diver would have lived. You got a cool head. Cool heads save lives. Sometimes even your own."

After Jonah brought the chamber up the final 3 feet, he unlocked the chamber door. The diver stepped out. In his hand he held a plastic ketchup bottle.

"Just testing you." He grinned.

CHAPTER TWENTY-FOUR

BROCKMAN AND THE *NEZ PERCE*

Hundreds of miles southwest of the liftboat in the direction of the abyssal Sigsbee Deep, another kind of offshore vessel moved slowly in calm seas. The *Nez Perce*, a deepwater pipe-lay barge, was pioneering new ground, laying pipe that would connect an underwater wellhead to a new production platform on a tract of seabed completely isolated from the rest of the offshore industry. Despite the fact that it was August, the middle of the official hurricane season, the weather was calm and the owners of the *Nez Perce* were not worried. The Gulf of Mexico region produced almost forty percent of the nation's domestic supply of crude oil and ten billion cubic feet of natural gas a day. With hundreds of billions of dollars at stake, as well as the nation's economy, the danger to human life on the rigs and vessels was a negligible part of the cost of doing business.

So far out to sea, it would be difficult, perhaps even impossible to evacuate the barge if a tropical storm or hurricane hit. Such weather normally served as a boon to the commercial dive industry, creating millions of dollars worth of repairs and inspection work on damaged oil rigs and undersea pipelines. But if you were caught in the storm, chances were good you wouldn't live to see another payday.

The *Nez Perce* worked far outside U.S. waters, in a region of the Gulf where the continental slope declined from 590 feet of dark sea to over 10,000 feet funereal depth. It was a very deep and dangerous job for the dive team. And the company had reached all the way to Scotland to hire Aleck Brockman as the Dive Supervisor.

Holding a sheaf of papers, Brockman walked across to his dive control shed. He wore no badge or hat indicating his position, but everyone knew who he was.

To Renoir, the snake-eater, Brockman moved slowly like a cagey, hoary bear: his body worn out and slightly hunched from a life spent under the weight of oceans. He had a large freckled head half-encircled with coarse, graying red hair, and he spoke differently from anyone Renoir had ever heard before.

Renoir stood near a stack of secure pipe across the barge. He watched the Dive Supervisor go up the steps into his dive control shed. In the square entrance the man suddenly turned and looked straight at Renoir. Brockman had hard eyes and gave an unfriendly smile, almost like he knew he was being watched by an enemy.

Renoir knew that was impossible, but he looked away involuntarily. He had been extremely cautious in watching Brockman, like he would stalking cottonmouths near a gator nest. The Supervisor, with his eyes still fixed on Renoir, raised his chin defiantly, then disappeared into the darkness within the dive control shed. Renoir had heard that Brockman worked longer shifts than any other Supervisor in the business and would not come out of the shed for many hours. Brockman was hard-core.

Indeed, Brockman's dive team lived and worked under the deadliest of conditions and relied on the Supervisor for direction and protection. The work site was at a depth of 590 feet. When not working on the sea bottom, the divers lived on deck inside special pressurized living quarters. They entered through a round hatch like a decompression chamber door at the very beginning of the job, but would not be released until the end. For the entire duration of the job they remained trapped inside the living quarters compressed to a holding pressure slightly less than the depth of the work site. In this way their bodies became fully "saturated" to working depth. Saturation jobs were called "sat jobs" for short.

The saturation divers used helmets, umbilical hoses, and wetsuits like any other commercial diver, but the job was different in two important ways. The worksite was very deep, and the men would not decompress after each dive like they would on a shallower assignment. On a saturation job divers decompressed only once, when all the work was done.

The saturation chamber living quarters consisted of a large three-compartment deck decompression facility with an attaching dive bell. The divers rode to the worksite at the bottom of the sea inside the dive bell, then were brought back and returned to the living quarters the same way. The system looked like a giant decompression chamber but with compartments and a detachable dive bell mounted on top.

Every man on the barge, even Renoir, knew that if for any reason the divers were suddenly released from the holding pressure to sea level (by a blown seal or a bad weld on the sat unit living quarters) the divers would die an awful death as the pressured gas absorbed in their flesh and cavities would violently expand.

Safe decompression from a deep saturation job required the slow ascent rate of six feet an hour and frequently took the better part of a week. Aside from pressure related risks, anyone working undersea was at the mercy of treacherous currents, foul weather, hypothermia, the motion of the waves affecting the stability of the suspended pipeline, the rack operator controlling the mix of breathing gas, the possible recklessness of the crane operator lowering dangerously heavy objects down to them, or accidently on them, and more. When the divers were in the water, the Barge Superintendent necessarily forfeited control of topside activities to the Dive Supervisor who was the intermediary between the upper and lower worlds. In him alone rested the responsibility of coordinating the topside lowering of various objects with their undersea reception. When the divers were in the ocean Aleck Brockman, the Dive Supervisor, was the supreme authority of the barge city. He let no one forget it.

Renoir, the snake-eater, felt drawn to Aleck Brockman; the man's authority and infamous reputation set him apart from all other men on the barge. But there was more than his being the Dive Supervisor or the rumors about him that made him different. Brockman had a strange accent and a reclusive manner. Even the eccentric, the hardened, and the criminal sorts who work offshore were aware of an indefinable hard quality about the man; something in the way he moved, something in his eyes when he looked at you.

While the men were wary of him and did not like him, they had never encountered a more professional or competent Dive Supervisor. With ruthless thoroughness and with great frequency Brockman personally inspected all dive systems, from the seals on the saturation unit living quarters to the accuracy of the gauges on the gas rack's manifold. He checked everything, but most of all took a special interest in the dive bell and its proper attachment to the lifting cable used to lower and raise the vessel in and out of the sea. Once Renoir even saw him at night seemingly transfixed with an air of somber puzzlement, inspecting the dive bell.

Brockman reached out to test the clevis pin and cotter key that shackled the dive bell to the lifting cable. If the clevis pin and cotter key weren't rightly engaged, the dive bell with its cargo of men could be lost forever to the ocean deep.

The Tenders, like everyone else, stayed clear of Brockman as much as possible. He had a bullying manner with them and constantly tested their attentiveness and alertness. Anyone or any equipment he found in the slightest state of disarray or in poor maintenance, he immediately ordered corrected. Not only did he demand a state of high readiness and reliability in everything related to diving, but also the scrupulous neatness and order of all equipment and systems.

Curiously, but in keeping with his aloofness, Brockman did not take as companions any of his fellow divers or even the barge foremen and the superintendent. On rare occasions, to the surprise of all, he would converse in a friendly way with a lowly galley hand or an idiot Rigger. Brockman was also distinct in that no other man on the barge had lost three fingers. Index finger through ring finger had been sheared off during a dive when a section of pipe unexpectedly dropped on his hand.

Renoir gazed at the dive control shed and the empty square of blackness at its entrance, and he imagined how Brockman would scream with a sack of cottonmouths tied over his head. "Louder . . ." he finally muttered to himself.

CHAPTER TWENTY-FIVE

KIP

Kip was a greenhorn Tender newly arrived on the *Nez Perce*. He had finally escaped the drudgery of shallow dives in muddy swamps that all new hires had to endure. He had scruffy hair, a slight build, and looked too soft to work offshore. This was his first time out at sea and nothing seemed right; everything looked far different than he had imagined. On the crew boat he wondered what he'd gotten himself into.

Even though the idea of diving in the open ocean frightened him, he had to do it. He had boxed himself in. He told himself that after he forced himself through it a few times, he wouldn't be afraid anymore. The truth was, Kip was more interested in being thought of as a deep-sea diver than actually *being* a diver, and now after all of his bragging and big talk to his friends he had to try to live up to the cocksure face he presented to the world.

Kip first saw the *Nez Perce* in the bright morning light after an eighteen-hour crew boat ride. Unsheltered from the sea's raw elements, the steel factory worked night and day, a sun scorched, salt blasted little city with more than a hundred citizens: X-ray technicians, Riggers, Welders, mechanics, cooks, various assistants, electricians, and deep sea divers.

The men worked twelve-hour shifts—except for the divers who were on call round the clock. Everyone did their jobs despite the deafening, metallic roar of all kinds of engines, the bitter smell of hot tar, rough language spoken by rough men, and the hiss and sputter of welding and burning steel; all set against miles of heavy-rolling, wind blown ocean.

When Kip reported to the barge clerk, the man didn't say "hi," didn't even look at him. Suddenly he knew that out here he was lower than whale shit. Which for anyone who doesn't know— is at the bottom of the sea. A pang of dread came to him and seemed to settle in his bowels. He looked out the window on the control tower hoping to see the crew boat had not left—maybe he could ride back to land. No luck. All he could see was the *Nez Perce,* the huge floating factory, and then beyond: the vast deep, surging and heaving with menace, as far as the eye could see.

Kip took in the staggering sight—a barge 550 feet long and 150 feet wide. Deck cranes at bow and stern, four davit cranes port and starboard for handling the pipeline. A three-story control tower topped with a helicopter pad.

The vessel pulled itself forward with anchor winches in forty-foot increments when the men rolled freshly assembled pipeline overboard. Kip knew this much: that the barge relied on a twelve-point anchor system with heavy steel cables coiled on large iron wheels mounted to the deck. Whenever the foreman pulled the anchors on board, or the seas grew too violent, anyone with half a wit went below to avoid being cut in two if an anchor cable snapped.

Below deck Kip found a maze of air-conditioned stairways and narrow corridors leading to various quarters and rooms with double bunks. Like catacombs, the workers' rooms were pitch dark and cold. The men used every ounce of energy on deck and went below only to eat, shower, and sleep dead tired.

The second floor had a large bathroom with twenty shower stalls. A mechanic's room with cluttered shelves full of tools, spare parts, and machines took up half the available space on the bottom floor. In the adjoining laundry room the self-serve washers and dryers rarely sat unused. Through the next door a brightly lit cafeteria-kitchen served food twenty-four hours a day.

The barge complex consumed huge quantities of forty-foot long pipe sections, welding rod, tar, cement, sand, fuel, and food. Provisions and mail and fresh work crews were brought out as needed by crew boat or tugboat several times a month.

Occasionally, if the weather permitted, oil company officials, invariably wearing Stetsons and cowboy boots, flew in by helicopter to inspect the work, insects flying in from hives unknown, to inspect another hive.

The Day Foreman told Kip the rules of the barge. Fighting, any kind of fighting on board was a federal offense and forced an immediate return to the beach and arrest at the dock. Drugs and liquor were strictly prohibited, and those found in violation were summarily fired and discharged to land.

The focal point of every citizen on board the *Nez Perce* rested 590 feet down, at the bottom of the ocean. They were anchored above a preexisting, completed, large-diameter pipeline carrying oil to U.S. land based refineries. The barge crew had for weeks been lowering the first half of the new ninety-mile pipeline to its place on the ocean floor, but had now stopped. The new pipeline had to be connected or "tied-in" at a ninety degree angle to the preexisting large-diameter pipeline before extending fifty miles past it to a production rig.

"This job puts pressure on every man to do his work quick and straight," the Foreman said. The team of saturation divers that Kip would tend had to burn and weld, or connect and bolt the two pipelines' flange faces together on the ocean floor; Kip was glad that he was only tending the divers, working topside *on* the barge.

If the flow of oil pumping through a pipeline had to be shut off, for whatever reason, every passing day cost the oil company tremendous money in lost production. When this occurred, it always brought a sense of urgency greater than usual in all phases of the work, from the superintendent's oversight of barge operations down to the cook's assistant frying potatoes.

Everyone on board had an incentive driving him: the bonus to be earned for finishing ahead of schedule. At minimum, many workers wanted the work to progress swiftly for no other reason than because they'd developed "channel fever" and greatly missed their wives, families, and the freedoms of the beach. If, as often happened, a delay was caused by the real or imagined ineptitude of one work crew or another, the offending parties were ostracized and treated with bitter contempt. Just no fighting.

Kip looked at the ocean and imagined how deep it would fall away under his feet when he had to jump in. The thought alarmed him. However, three other Tenders also worked on the barge and maybe he wouldn't be picked to dive. He hoped so, he really hoped so.

⚓ ⚓ ⚓

One morning Brockman called Kip to the dive control shed and ordered him into the sea to perform a routine inspection of the stinger. Brockman stared at Kip as he gave the directions and didn't seem to notice or care when Kip turned white with fear.

Jutting out 180 feet under the waves off the starboard rear part of the barge, the stinger was a ramp-chute with buoyancy-controlled pontoons and sets of rollers that supported the pipeline like a playground slide supporting a line of children. Every inch of the new pipeline had to pass over the rollers of the stinger. The stinger arced downwards underwater and served to keep the pipeline from bending too much, or buckling, as it was lowered to the sea floor. The entire weight of the stinger and its very heavy load floated with gigantic steel fingers locked and controlled by hydraulic rams to the pontoon hitch on the stern of the barge.

Brockman told Kip that it would be a non-decompression dive. The Supervisor warned the Tender to avoid the dangerous area where the pipeline rolled down the wave-pounded ramp and first entered the water. He was to swim directly out into the sea, calm at the moment, and pull himself along underneath the stinger to check the proper lay of the pipeline on the rollers. In truth, nothing was amiss. With the decent weather and the delay in saturation operations, any Supervisor would judge it a good time to break in a virgin Tender on a relatively simple job.

⚓ ⚓ ⚓

Of the four Tenders on the *Nez Perce*, one remained by the saturation deck chamber and plied the four divers inside with food. Another Tender stood ready as a standby diver for Kip. The duty of tending the new man on his first jump therefore fell to the other new hand, Seed.

Seed was well known for hanging a Rigger's corpse, but he was also part of the Angola Club, a group of four ex-cons who were on the barge with him. Renoir, the snake-eater, was the leader. The Angola Club made Seed untouchable.

Seed quickly learned that on this job, clandestine ridiculing of Brockman brought acceptance and popularity. For the amusement of Riggers and Welders, Seed performed mocking, derisive pantomimes of the hated and feared Supervisor. He wanted them to laugh, and they laughed and cursed.

⚓ ⚓ ⚓

Kip stared anxiously at the open ocean. Its waves were gray and austere under a dreary gray sky. He had rehearsed for this moment countless times: first in a shallow swimming pool with dirty Band-Aids and hair clumped on the drain screen, then in the company's diving simulator tank. Still, he felt unready. It bothered him that the bottom was 590 feet down and that he wouldn't be able to see that far. He wished it was only 100 feet deep and that he would be working on the ocean floor, with something solid under his feet.

Seed helped him snap the helmet to the neck dam. Kip nervously gave a thumbs-up, and Seed returned the gesture.

"All set?" Brockman asked over the dive telephone. His hard voice sounded distant and unreal through the speakers inside Kip's helmet.

"Yes, sir," Kip answered, trying not to sound nervous.

"You don't need much lead on your weight belt to work near the surface. You don't want to sink," Brockman cautioned.

"I know. I'm ready."

"After you jump, head out well away from the barge before swimming under the stinger. You got that?"

"Yes, sir, go well away from the barge before going under the stinger."

"Good. And keep your arms and hose outside of the pipeline and rollers. If they bounce apart in a swell you can get sucked in and crushed to death. Stay on the guideline and don't let go of it."

"Roger that." Kip's rectum and balls tightened at the words *crushed to death*.

Brockman gave him the go-ahead to jump.

"Going in," Kip said.

He closed his eyes and forced himself to jump overboard.

He landed badly in the water, on his front, instead of feet first.

When he opened his eyes, he had to fight his panic.

A nervously shifting school of silver baitfish poured into itself to get away from him. The shoal shimmered like a mass of sequined leaves fluttering under the barge.

Kip forced himself to look nowhere else but at the pontoons of the stinger supporting the pipeline. They declined at a gradual angle through the dusky blue water until out of sight. If he looked down he knew that he would freeze, because the blueness moved like it was alive, especially below.

He'd left too much lead on his weight belt, so he swam awkwardly. He was negatively buoyant, and a spasm of anxiety hit him. He forced himself not to curse out loud.

He pressed on, too embarrassed to report his error and restart his dive. He frog-kicked and muscled himself through the water.

After struggling past the dangerous area where the waves pounded and swept up the ramp, Kip clutched desperately at the guideline on the underside of the stinger and felt tremendous relief when he took hold of it.

He hung below the stinger a minute with his back to the deep, his eyes looking up at the stinger, and paused to catch his breath. Then began pulling himself slowly along, while looking up through the trellis work to inspect each set of rollers supporting the concrete-encased pipeline.

The pipeline slowly lifted and fell onto the rollers. Above it the surface undulated like a enormous canopy of liquid silver.

⚓ ⚓ ⚓

On the outside of the dive control shed hung a loudhailer connected to a microphone on the Supervisor's desk inside. During dive operations Brockman communicated with the Tenders in a loud biting voice in order to be heard over the array of engines running on deck.

"Slack off the diver," he instructed over the amplifier.

Seed threw out several coils of Kip's umbilical then stopped.

"Keep slacking off the diver. He's going out at least a 180 feet."

Seed paid out more umbilical. He looked over to the dive control shed then back at the waves below, jumping and sinking.

A minute passed.

"Slack it off! You're hanging him up! Can't you feel him?" warned Brockman. There was a shade of anger in his voice.

Seed was uncomfortably aware that one of the Riggers had heard Brockman's tone and now looked Seed's way to learn who was screwing up. To silence Brockman, Seed quickly fed out more umbilical.

It worked. For a while he heard no more from the Supervisor. Thankfully, the Rigger no longer looked his way either. Seed did not want to be blamed for causing a delay in barge activities.

Brockman made him feel rattled and nervous, and in this state, Seed could not tell the pull of an undersea current from the tug of a diver needing more slack. In his determination not to be admonished over the loudhailer, he paid out more umbilical hose without being so instructed, then a lot more. When he stopped, he stared vacantly for several minutes at the ocean while holding Kip's umbilical loosely in one hand. He fished a packet of pistachios from his back pocket then deposited a pinch in his mouth. With the skill of a parrot he cracked the shells between his teeth, extracting the meat with his tongue, and spit out the shells.

"Pull it in. There's too much slack," Brockman said.

Seed pulled roughly forty feet back in then stopped.

"I said pull it in. There's too much slack!" Brockman barked in an increasingly angry voice.

Seed began pulling the umbilical quickly hand over hand onto the deck. The Rigger was watching him again.

"Pull him up! What the hell are you doing?!" Brockman boomed, suddenly amazingly angry. "You! Go help him!" he shouted to the Rigger. "Standby diver, get your hat on!"

The Rigger ran over to Seed and together they began with wild energy pulling the umbilical in. It piled up in a great wet tangle on the barge deck behind them. The standby diver put on his dive helmet in case Kip needed rescuing.

Undersea, only ninety feet from the barge, Kip had lost his grip on the stinger's guideline. He had foolishly tried to dislodge a small piece of tar caught in a roller. His dive umbilical was not taut as it should have been. There was so much slack in the hose and so much lead on his weight belt that he sank like a skydiver in a free fall.

Kip was so stunned he forgot to clear his ears. His eardrums began bending painfully inwards under the increasing pressure. He became confused and disoriented. Everything happened too quickly for him to respond.

Pain, like ice picks stabbing into his ears, made his eyes water.

The shimmering surface receded like fast rising clouds, then became blurry gray and indistinct.

Dusky blue rushed up past him.

His ears somehow cleared by themselves with a sharp squeak and he felt incredible relief. His panic subsided, and in his light-headed state he thought for a pleasant instant that he was really asleep, that he was just dreaming, and in the dream he was swimming in the sky and would wake up at home in his bed in a few seconds.

Then Brockman's voice saying something about his weight belt brought him back, and he became terrified.

His ears began to hurt again. He believed that somehow his dive hose had been severed; he could think of no other explanation for his rapid fall.

He looked out at the ocean with wild eyes.

Down, down, he sank with increasing speed.

Kip screamed and groped frantically for his weight belt. Inside his wetsuit he felt his bowels loosen, then void.

With tortured ears he heard Brockman's voice repeatedly saying to no avail, "Calm down, Kip. Clear your ears, Kip. You're going to be all right."

Kip knew he was dying, could even see his body dead on the sea bottom. Everything grew darker around him. He did not know if his eyes were failing him because he was now dying, or because he'd traveled so far from the sunlit world above. He imagined the dive bell with its floodlights lowering into the gloom like an alien spaceship landing on a strange planet to retrieve his body. The divers would drop out the hatch like subterranean miners with lights on their helmets. They would search in the haunted blackness for his body then place it, cold and pale, in the basket to be drawn to the surface.

Unbelievably, Kip jerked to a stop.

A current pulled him sideways and with incredible relief he felt his connection to the surface tugging at him once again. The umbilical was still attached to his harness.

"Calm down, Kip. Stop screaming and listen," Brockman said sternly. "The Tender has screwed it up badly. You've dropped to 200 feet. You're going to have to make decompression water stops. How are your ears?"

Kip began ascending as Seed and the Rigger pulled in the umbilical above.

"I can't hear well. I think I split my eardrums. I couldn't clear fast enough," he said miserably.

Hanging from his harness for his first decompression stop, Kip felt glad to be alone.

He stared at the pelagic wilderness around him and quietly wept.

CHAPTER TWENTY-SIX

THE DEMOTION

Once Kip completed his decompression water stops, he climbed up the short ladder onto the barge.

The ocean fell off him and puddled at his feet.

Miraculously, he hadn't ruptured his eardrums. Seed helped him out of the dive helmet and harness. Seed waited until Kip stripped off most of his dive kit then said, "That son of a bitch Brockman kept telling me to slack off the hose. He did this on purpose, man. That ornery bastard don't like any one, not even divers. I tried to stop given out slack but he kept yellin over the loudhailer to *slack off*. Ask any one, ask that Rigger there."

Kip's eyes were puffy and red from crying. He looked at Seed doubtfully.

"I swear, man," Seed insisted. "I *know* how to fucking tend. Brockman set us up to make us look bad to the Riggers. He'll blame me to you and blame you to me to split us up. Don't believe a word of it. He's a sly bastard."

Kip, still upset and bewildered from his ordeal, didn't know what to say.

"We'll talk more later," Seed hissed.

Kip shook his head, *whatever*, and went below deck to change his shorts and shower. He would wash out his wetsuit later.

"Seed," Brockman said in a commanding voice over the loudhailer. "Report to the dive shed." Brockman standing in the entrance of the dive control shed stared down at him from half a football field away. Brockman. Shit

⚓ ⚓ ⚓

The Rigger who had witnessed Seed's debacle stood near the dive control shed with two Welders. They looked at Seed with amused expressions then broke into mirthful, gap-toothed laughter. Seed ignored the trio; he walked by them and ascended the three steps to the dive control shed. On the threshold he stood blinking to adjust his sight to the darkness within.

Brockman, standing behind his desk, was filling out a form sheet on a clipboard. The ballpoint pen looked very small in his hand. Brockman's squat body occupied most of the space in the small room and Seed, after entering, felt trapped by the much larger man.

"I want to verify a few facts," Brockman said without looking up.

"Go right ahead," Seed said trying to sound agreeable.

"You haven't tended much, have you?" Brockman asked, taking a seat by the desk. Even sitting, Brockman was a big intimidating presence.

Seed absentmindedly moved his right hand near his knife.

"Sure have," he said. "Before I broke out to Diver-Tender, I did lots of tending."

"And where was that?" Brockman asked quietly.

"What do you mean?"

"Where did you work before here?"

"What is this? Some sort of test?" Seed laughed, trying to lighten the mood.

Brockman stared at Seed with gimlet eyes, waiting for an answer.

"Out of Texas," Seed said.

"What company?"

"Oceaneering."

"Like hell you did." Brockman looked about to spit. "They wouldn't hire trash like you to sweep their shop. Who at Oceaneering do you say you worked for?"

Outside the Rigger and Welders laughed.

"What do you mean? The whole company of course," Seed replied angrily.

"Sure you did," Brockman said sarcastically. "Who broke you out from Tender then?"

"I forget exactly. It's been a couple years. They changed Supervisors halfway through the job. John something."

Brockman smiled and made a fist with his good hand. "Can you even name a single employee of Oceaneering's? Or for that matter, anywhere else?"

"Yeah," said Seed emphatically. "Like I told you, John, the guy that broke me out. I'm sure I could remember if you'd stop yellin at me. Call them up and check it out . . ."

"You are a piss poor Tender," declared Brockman, cutting him off and pointing with his mutilated hand. It was like shoving a crab in his face. "Do you understand the responsibilities of your job? Men will die if you betray them with sloppiness. There can be no excuse, no apologies. If you Judas a diver in the water like that again, you'll be done." Brockman paused, apparently caught up by a thought. Then he leaned forward still pointing with his two fingered-hand and repeated, "If you Judas a diver in the water like that again, you're done . . . and as of now you are demoted from Diver-Tender to plain Tender with the corresponding cut in pay. I'll file a report to the personnel department for gross incompetence. Now get out of here."

"You can't do that," Seed said.

"If you don't like it, get on the next crew boat."

"Wait a minute," Seed said. "I can explain . . ."

"Get out of my sight." Brockman stood up.

With startling quickness the Supervisor moved toward Seed, confronting him closely, face to face. In Seed's eyes Brockman's features in motion blurred, then came solid with hard contempt.

Seed, expecting a blow to the head, flinched and raised one arm to protect himself.

The Dive Supervisor moved closer.

In the heat of the moment, when Brockman moved so close, Seed didn't know what to expect. Seed, the inferior, backed down, said nothing and retreated backwards. The only place he could go.

⚓ ⚓ ⚓

Outside, Seed raised his fist to the shed and extended his middle finger.

"You want to play with me, fine," he swore under his breath. "This is just the beginning, motherfucker, just the beginning."

The Rigger and Welders laughed at him. "Watch out for the little girl," the Rigger said. "She's angry now."

Seed flipped them his finger also.

He marched off enraged, not knowing where to go. He wanted to get as far from the dive control shed as possible. He was off-duty but didn't want to eat or sleep. Not in the mood to joke or entertain, even in passing, Seed avoided the handful of off-duty men loitering on deck. Aimlessly, he paced the port side of the barge until he found himself alone at the center stern in the long shadow of the control tower.

From starboard the harsh sound of the ocean repeated, pushing in and sucking out with terrific force against the pipeline ramp declining into the sea. Seed watched the waves pounding up over the ramp where the stinger connected to the massive pontoon hitch then rush away foamy white. The huge steel incline gently rose and fell with the barge, bouncing the descending pipeline with more than enough force to crush a man between the two.

"This is just the beginning," Seed repeated out loud. "Just the beginning."

"He can sure git under your skin, that ole boy," said a dry voice from behind. "I know. I know all about it."

Seed swung around. Renoir, the snake-eater, leaned perfectly motionless against a steel bollard. He looked hungry and intense, like a vulture waiting for his meal to die. He held a smoking cigarette clamped between long bony fingers.

"I ain't in a funny mood," Seed said.

"Me neither," Renoir said, grinning without parting his lips. "Whut happened? He git to you too? Git inside yer head? He plays head games."

"Nothing I can't fix," Seed said with a dismissive wave of his hand.

"You ever seen him at night?" Renoir asked. He squinted.

"No. I'm on the day shift. Why?"

Renoir inhaled deeply from his cigarette.

"Probably nothin. Just sometimes he don't move right."

"How do you mean?"

"I've trapped plenty animals. His legs don't work right. You can see it at night when he leaves the dive control shed. Sometimes he moves real quick, and other times slow and uneven. I think he's hurt worse than anyone knows and tries to hide it."

Seed thought of the way Brockman had just moved on him in the shed.

"You after him?" Seed asked.

"No. Just watchin him. He makes me curious. Something about him reminds me of that bastard prison guard, Roundtree." Renoir exhaled an enormous amount of smoke. Seed had never seen anyone else hold so much in their lungs.

"I know what you mean," Seed said. Roundtree was the worst guard at Angola. He was brutal and tricky, and you couldn't intimidate him.

"We've got to keep cool, though" Renoir said. Keep our heads down, right?"

"I know," Seed said. "But the fucker just cut my pay and gave me a demotion."

"For whut?"

"Hardly anything. I think he's messing with me or trying to run me off. He looks at me strange, like he suspects me of something."

"He's not stupid. He's got to know about the hanging. And he probably heard you imitate him and make him out to be some kinda clown fool in front of the Riggers and Welders."

"That's true." Seed considered this a moment. "But after what he did to me just now, I've got no choice but to push back. But after the job. Plus, first I got to find something that'll really talk to him where he lives, if you catch my meaning."

"I do, bud, I do," Renoir said. He slipped off the bollard and started to leave. "But not out here. Not on this job. Don't do nothin stupid. We've got to lay low. Not be seen together too much. Right?"

"I know. I got it." Seed headed to the cafeteria, even though he was too angry to eat.

CHAPTER TWENTY-SEVEN

BROCKMAN AND THE SNAKE EATER

J ust a week earlier, Renoir had made the daylong brutal crew
boat ride in heavy seas to the *Nez Perce* deepwater pipelay
barge and the hard-ass Dive Supervisor Brockman. He was
part of a work crew of Riggers brought out to replace men
returning to land. Welders and a couple of Tenders for the dive
team made the trip as well. One of them was Seed—Renoir and
Seed pretended not to know each other during the long ride out.

Over the years, as the quest for more fossil fuel pressed the oil
companies to search for virgin oil and gas fields in deeper seas,
they sent their work crews farther and farther out into the Gulf
of Mexico. With the development of 3-D seismic imaging, it was
cheap for geologists to use sound waves to discover and survey
deeper subsea hydrocarbon formations, including those hidden
beneath layers of salt beds. The new pipeline being installed was
to service the most recently tapped deepwater field.

These new coordinates represented the latest outpost, a dot
of floating humanity more remote, more cut off from the world
than any worksite of Renoir's prior experience. The crew boat
ride seemed to have gone on and on forever. Wind and high
waves battered the boat and rattled the bones of all men on
board. Some of the men didn't know it would be a full day's ride
and did not bring food to eat and went hungry. Renoir bit the tip
of his tongue during one heavy yaw and tasted blood most of the
way. None of the men had ever worked this far out on the ocean.
They were used to horizons broken by neighboring platforms

and service-vessel traffic. If something went wrong here—a life threatening injury, an explosion, a hurricane—help would be too far away to save them.

Renoir perked up from the hellish crew boat ride when he learned that Aleck Brockman supervised the dive operations. Brockman's presence caused a stir among the men and Renoir wanted to see what all the fuss was about. And after ingesting several lines of crystal-meth he felt fully restored. That very first hour aboard the *Nez Perce*, Renoir set for himself the task of closely watching the Supervisor's every action. The rumors were that Brockman had killed men before. Some workers were afraid of Brockman. Renoir wasn't, and he didn't believe any of the stories.

Every Rigger Renoir asked about the Dive Supervisor reported that Brockman couldn't perform physical work because of a spinal injury he'd suffered in an underwater accident overseas. Brockman's powerful build and harsh manner couldn't hide the fact that he was too old, too lame, and too slow. At the end of his first full day Renoir was convinced that Brockman only looked dangerous.

But after several days had gone by, with Renoir lurking around the barge at night, high on crank, he wasn't so sure. He didn't know what to make of Aleck Brockman.

With so many men living on the *Nez Perce*, all working various schedules and sleeping and eating every hour of the day, it was virtually impossible for one worker to fully learn the habits of another. Yet the insomniac Rigger had only once observed Brockman eating and sleeping. In fact several times, once in broad daylight and twice by moonlight, Renoir would have sworn the Dive Supervisor had left the *Nez Perce* altogether—he could find the man nowhere. But anytime Brockman's expertise had been needed for dive operations, the Supervisor miraculously appeared on deck. And one eerie night, while Renoir stalked Brockman from a dark corner by a rack of gas cylinders, the man traveled from the dive control shed and came into view right behind Renoir without the gaunt Rigger seeing him take a single step. Either the man had somehow snuck out of the dive control shed or Renoir was losing it.

Brockman turned his head slowly as with great effort and stared quizzically at Renoir, who stood absolutely still and taken aback. Then Renoir braced himself for the worst, thinking Brockman caught him spying. But the Supervisor, with an odd smile, merely asked, "What's your name?"

"Renoir."

"Mr. Renoir, get the hell away from my dive station," Brockman said.

Renoir walked away without saying another word.

Sometimes when Renoir snorted too much crank and had not slept for several days, he saw tiny dots wriggling before his eyes and at the same time he heard an ominous sawing. The dots twirled in front of him like a kaleidoscope, and the sawing sound in his head, seemed to come from the past, from a time when woodsmen were crosscutting giant cypress trees in the swamps of his youth.

As a young boy he had camped out with his grandfather and uncle along Catahoula Lake before the levee was built, before any trees were protected. While the men sawed giant cypress for the timber company, he and another boy set out bush lines and fished. Every day they heard the crosscut saws droning like enormous cicadas as the lumber crews cut down one ancestral cypress after another. The buzzing of the wood's death came to Renoir whenever he ingested too much crank. The sound of saws set his mind back to the cut, pillaged places where he'd played as a boy: the Red-Eye Swamp, the Sibon Canal, and Bayou Benoit.

⚓ ⚓ ⚓

At midnight a day later, after Renoir had spent an hour searching the barge without finding Brockman, he suddenly decided to check the helipad. He still didn't know where Brockman disappeared to when he wasn't working. Without expectation he mounted the steel switchback stairway outside the control tower. The windy stairway went up four flights and had a large landing at each level; it led to the broad helipad perched high over the barge. The helipad was posted off-limits, but it was possible that Brockman went up there. Maybe this would explain everything.

Renoir eased up the stairway on tiptoe. The higher he ascended, the windier it became. The barge city, like a toiling pit with its work lights, turning cranes, white saturation chambers, and scores of laborers shrank below him as he climbed. The growl of engines faded, and the smoky scent of burning steel thinned into clear air. The blinding electricity of the Welders' arcs at their workstations dazzled on and off in the night from bow to stern like miniature bolts of lightning. On the third landing a sign was fastened to the railing:

NO UNAUTHORIZED PERSONNEL BEYOND THIS POINT

Renoir clenched his fists and started up the remaining stairway. He stopped when he could just peer over the crest of the helipad without being seen.

There, in a silver pool of moonlight Brockman sat facing the ocean to the port side. He was eating a sandwich and had a thermos next to him. Renoir crept a little closer, taking a sideways vantage of the scene. Brockman looked out over the ocean and incredibly his face had taken on a gentle, friendly appearance. Renoir exhaled softly in disbelief. Brockman sat but inches from a fatal precipice, and looked to be completely distracted by the ocean in front of him. If Renoir wanted to push the Dive Supervisor to a death that would look like suicide this was the perfect moment.

Brockman suddenly turned his head an inch toward Renoir, almost like the Dive Supervisor was looking at him with peripheral vision.

Renoir froze, until a minute later, when Brockman went back to watching the night ocean and eating his sandwich. The Dive Supervisor hadn't noticed him. With tremendous relief, Renoir went back down the stairs. Now he knew Brockman's routine.

CHAPTER TWENTY-EIGHT

MOLA SUNRISE

Since being hired by Abbott Divers, Jonah had made steady progress as an apprentice diver: first in shallow bayous, then off oil rigs, then from the live-boat job aboard the *Falstaff*, and now off a liftboat. Each step of the way he'd quickly learned to handle unfamiliar and dangerous tools in difficult circumstances, and he'd been getting more and deeper dives, especially lately. Troy, the Dive Supervisor on the liftboat, told him the company was happy with his work and that if he kept it up he would break out to Diver-Tender in the near future.

The liftboat now stood next to the final oil rig of the job, the worksite at a depth of 180 feet. Still groggy from sleep, Jonah drew his legs out from under the blankets. He put his bare feet on the floor of the Tenders' quarters. The room was frigid with air conditioning and completely dark. The only light was a dim glow from the deck lights outside. It leaked in around the edges of the window blind. He stood up, feeling a little stiff, and glanced at the other bunks in the room—they were empty. The job was nearly over; in fact it might already be over. They were close when Jonah had knocked off last night and they could have finished up the handjetting while he slept.

In his underwear he padded hopefully across the room to look out the window. He pulled back the blind to see what the others were doing.

Down on the deck of the liftboat everything glistened wet and glossy with dew. Troy, as always, held a lit cigarette while he sat in the dive control shed. At the far edge of the rig, Jonah could barely make out Escargot silhouetted against the night.

The riser-pipe job on this third oil rig had gone well. The days had been marked by good weather and a gentle, extremely clear sea. Jonah checked his watch. It read 3:02 a.m. He had twenty-eight minutes to eat breakfast before work.

Outside in the muggy dark he walked up to the dive station to start his shift.

"Hey, man," Escargot said. "You've got a dive."

"Me?" Jonah asked.

"Yep. A night jump."

They set up for the dive. But just as Jonah began pulling on his wetsuit, Escargot discovered a tear in the seam of the hand-jet hose—equipment needed on the dive. Irritated by the delay, both Tenders worked hastily to change out the torn section.

The hand-jet hose consisted of half a dozen segments of hose mated together to a length determined by the depth of the worksite. It looked like a fireman's hose, and delivered water pressured to 500 psi down its length. The pressurized water blasted powerfully out both nozzles of a weighty steel T-bar fitted on the working end. The diver underwater controlled and steered the T-bar's water jets to carve trenches in the seabed to sink a pipeline. The tear in the seam that Escargot had found would have reduced the pressure and had to be repaired for the system to work.

With pipewrenches Jonah and Escargot unmated the hoses and disassembled the fitting on the damaged one. They moved the fitting down past the tear, then tightened it. Methodically they reconnected the entire length and finished the repair. Finally, just one hour before dawn, Jonah was ready to dive.

⚓ ⚓ ⚓

The sky above loomed clear with sparkling starlight and a bright moon. Below, the ocean darkly chopped and pulled between the liftboat and the oil rig. The lights of several distant oil rigs shone out on the black horizon like far off campfires on an open prairie. A shoal of fish eluding a predator broke the surface with small, urgent splashes then slowly moved off, carrying their struggle beyond Jonah's sight. As he watched the splashes move away he wondered what hunted them.

Jonah tugged on his harness to assure its fit. Like a snug turtleneck, he pulled the neck dam down over his ears. Eagerly he accepted the helmet from Escargot and locked it over his head to the neck dam's stainless steel ring. He began drawing air from the oral/nasal regulator and now looked out at the predawn world from behind a clear Lexan viewport.

Every time he dived the feeling of surreal frozen time started at this moment, just before entering the sea. The sense of profound isolation and the resumption of a mysterious journey beyond any possible description came over him each time, but at no time more so than at night. In the darkness the ocean writhed, a vast and secret otherworld.

Once Jonah had donned all the necessary life-support gear, he checked the communication system by talking to Troy, the Dive Supervisor, and told him he was ready. Troy told him that all systems were go, he could jump. Jonah stepped into open air and dropped to the ocean.

Hitting the water, feeling the cool fluid enter his boots and wetsuit, brought on hyper-alertness. The swell of a wave lifted past him.

"Going down."

"Roger."

He felt free immediately. As he started to sink away from the upper world the discomfort of the wetsuit, the awkwardness of the helmet, and the drag of the lead weights were relieved. Underwater the outfit made sense. He could move and sink and breathe.

He followed headfirst the hand-jet hose away from the meddlesome chop and turbulence of the interface. Pressing the helmet's small padded T-shaped device to his nose, he cleared his ears. Jonah had the good fortune of being able to easily equalize the pressure in his sinuses to match the increasing pressure of depth—the more quickly one could descend the sooner one started to work. Time made the difference between good commercial divers and bad ones.

The sea that rare morning was clear as gin, and even in the dark Jonah could see the bottom nearly 200 feet down. Buried beneath the limpid fathoms the small-diameter pipeline ran pale green across a seabed of floury brown sediment originating from far up the Mississippi River. Lunar rays instilled the marine environment with an unearthly, almost supernatural energy. Never before had Jonah seen so clearly on a night dive without artificial light.

He pulled himself lower and in the deepening sea his wetsuit compressed and his weight belt grew looser around his waist and seemed heavier. Silver bubbles purled over his helmet and shoulders, rising behind his body with each exhale.

Jonah began to fly down to the seabed. Chest first, spread eagle, he plummeted. The faster he flew, the more frequently he grabbed the hand-jet hose to retain control. Sometimes at night, when he was falling asleep, he wondered how many seamen, women, and children had dropped like this from sinking ships— not on the way to work, but to drown.

Jonah sank lower and lower into an enchanted scene, a scene like the glass globe of water that he'd played with as a child.

Descending past 150 feet he felt mildly intoxicated and aware of the dropping temperature. Nearing the bottom he gripped the hand-jet hose to slow down, swung his legs under him and landed. His booted feet pressed into the soft mud of the ocean floor, and a silty cloud puffed up to his knees.

"On bottom."

"Roger."

180 feet under the sea, beneath more than 5 atmospheres of pressure, Jonah scrambled half-swimming half-crawling along the pipeline. Under it lay a three-foot-deep trench dug by divers before him. The trench started at the base of the riser pipe on the oil rig and ran out thirty feet.

The oil rig legs, imposing and alive with fish, stood like the frame of a phantom house, reaching upward. Beyond it, the ocean was murky and deeper. Anything could be watching from out there.

Jonah followed the pipeline away from the oil rig legs to where the trench ended. The T-bar of the hand-jet lay slung by its hose over the pipeline where the last diver had left it. Jonah picked up the weighty T-bar.

"Topside, I'm on the hand-jet."

"Roger. You ready for power?" Troy said.

"Roger. Ready for power."

"Stand by."

"Roger. Standing by."

Jonah carefully hugged the device so that one pipe nozzle of the T-bar pointed harmlessly out from under his armpit and one pointed down into the trench. He sat atop the pipeline with his legs and left arm locked around it to hold himself on bottom. When a hand-jet's power is turned on, all air trapped in the system comes out first. The hose straightens with pressure and becomes so buoyant that it will rip an unwary diver to the surface.

"It's on," Troy said.

"Roger that."

Like a giant serpent the jet hose trembled, jerked, and coughed behind Jonah, then sprang solidly to life.

Jonah held on tightly to the pipeline. The jet hose tried to yank him upwards, then the pressure leveled off.

Very carefully, he adjusted his position. He unstraddled the pipeline and put his legs back on the sea floor next to the trench. He began directing the twin jet nozzles so that one carved into the trench end-wall and the other pointed out into open water. Jonah knew that the water jets could blow his helmet off.

Muddy sediment billowed up in a large black cloud and blocked his view of everything but the lengthening trench in front of him. Sweeping left and right, he blasted into the sediment with one jet cutting four feet down.

He edged forward, clinging to the pipeline with his left arm for stability, as he extended the trench. The sea around him fluttered and swirled with the turbulence of the hand-jet.

"Slack me off," he said, whenever his umbilical grew taut and impeded his progress.

For more than an hour he worked in the silty dark.

It felt after a while as if he were in a pitch-black closet wrapped in a heavy sponge blanket and not really at the bottom of the ocean. His arms grew tired from controlling the powerful hand-jet, his pupils dilated from the blackness, and he felt warm from the exertion.

"Time's up," Troy said at the end.

"Roger."

Topside, Escargot turned the water pump off.

Underwater, the jets stopped flowing and the hose deflated lifeless in Jonah's arms. He draped it over the pipeline then started back the way he'd come.

Escargot, standing on the edge of the liftboat's deck, looked down at the waves. The Dive Supervisor gave Escargot the signal and the slow man began pulling Jonah up from the sea floor by his umbilical.

Jonah abruptly lifted off bottom.

His umbilical pulled him upwards from the dark sediment cloud and the water effloresced into clean, radiant blue. The luster of it was startling, and proved the sun had risen. The blueness was incredibly fresh, intense, and huge—a fluid universe pressing on him from all sides.

The ocean's molten color poured into his helmet. It shone through his lens onto his face. It flooded into his eyes, filled his face and mind with concentrated blue until that's all there was to know. The hue was so sharp through his open pupils, it was as if he'd just been born and was seeing color for the first time. Then it poured in more.

The brightness moved Jonah with a contagious feeling of joy. Blinking, he had the disorienting sense that he had journeyed very far, and been away for longer than he could reckon. And he was glad for it. He was also glad because in the back of his mind he knew that the small matters were going his way as well: he had earned depth pay and finally they were going ashore.

Jonah rose up through the ethereal brilliance, through its vital body, its viscid weight, that washed over him. He rose into warmer layers and more dazzling light. The splendor penetrated him, his heart beat invincible, and his blood surged hot with the life of the sun.

Turning in a circle he watched the jeweled and magnificent creatures with fins living about the oil rig legs. Fanciful and variegated ocean triggerfish, parrotfish, and swarming wrasses milled and danced over the coral encrusted supports. Schooling crevalle jacks raced into sight. They pooled and thickened, a protean flow of silver briefly lingering by the oil rig. Then their mass spilled over. The school lengthened and thinned into a fast stream pouring into obscuring blue. Jonah watched them all in a state of happy amazement just at being there.

As he neared the surface he saw the bizarre image of three large molas gracefully hovering overhead. The giant fish lay on their sides, basking in the morning light. Jonah had never seen creatures as odd. They were antediluvian, with disklike, oblong bodies at least seven feet long. Oblique shafts of sunlight played through them. Like sentries painted silvery white, the molas guarded the threshold to the azure sky blazing just above.

Jonah looked down between his feet. Below, the sea floor and pipeline shrank away. He felt as if he was dangling from a tether over a powdery moonscape. Then he looked up. Above, the ocean's ceiling rumpled, puckered, and stretched as a fluid mirror.

Like a ghostly carousel, the molas righted themselves and began to circle with slow serenity, each flapping its tall dorsal fin and single anal fin at once one way, then the other. They did not scatter as Jonah emerged exhaling bubbles among them, but with large, soulful eyes gazed at the man in deep-sea dress. They looked on him with mottled faces and gentle, patient expressions, as if they had been waiting for him a long time. Gamboling about their moonish, headlike bodies flitted tiny striped fish, nipping parasitic copepods from their pale flesh.

The molas gathered before Jonah with a considered gentleness and a peacefulness that made him think of three monks. Maintaining their vertical equilibrium, the three monks slow-fluttered closer, flapping their dorsal and anal fins like the wings of a bird flying sideways. They seemed curious and ready to communicate.

But try as he might, he could learn nothing from their inscrutable faces. He had no time. In a cloud of bubbles he broke through.

⚓ ⚓ ⚓

Dripping saltwater, Jonah pulled himself out of the ocean. Gravity sucked at his arms, bobbled his helmet, and yanked at his weight belt. He climbed hand over hand into the humid heat of the day on a long crude steel ladder made by the Welders. He felt smothered in his gear and for the first time that dive, wet.

On deck, near the decompression chamber, he emptied his boots of water and sand. He stripped off his wetsuit and discarded it. Naked, he turned around, arms up, while Escargot hosed him down with fresh water.

With a towel wrapped around his middle Jonah entered the decompression chamber. Escargot swung the outer hatch shut with a clamorous bang and dogged it down. The inner lock had been prepressured to 80 feet. Escargot, turning a lever, quickly equalized both compartments to 40 feet.

The inner lock unsealed with a soft pop and Jonah entered. He turned around and leaned into the round door to reseal the inner hatch as Escargot, with the rush of released air, lowered the outer lock to 0 feet, sea level.

Now safely sealed within the inner lock, Jonah pulled on his shorts and lay back on the mattress to receive pressure treatment. He thought of the chamber as nothing more than an overlarge scuba tank with two compartments and two viewports. The hissing sound of pressured air piercingly reverberated inside the small space as Escargot brought Jonah to his first stop at 50 feet. The chamber air felt dank and smelled faintly of the vinegar used to wipe out the oral/nasal oxygen masks. He signalled his well-being to Escargot through the viewport.

Jonah put on the oxygen mask as instructed. Like the din of a train arriving in a subway, the chamber blasted with screeching air, then quieted still with cloying mist. He looked up at the curved white ceiling of the chamber and the large gentle molas swam back into his mind, the way they had circled about him like an undersea carousel. He could see the look of their faces and the peculiar way they had approached him. A weird thought came to him, that their ghostly presence had been purposeful, maybe important. The more he thought about it the more it seemed undeniable to him that the strange fishes had brought a message or a warning, but he couldn't comprehend it.

CHAPTER TWENTY-NINE

BEGGING FOR A RECKONING

Renoir, the snake-eater, walked across the deck of the *Nez Perce*, feeling great. He'd snorted so much crank the last few days that he could hardly sleep or eat anymore. His cheeks and eye sockets had become even more sunken and pronounced, and he notched his belt two holes tighter. Renoir had just spent six hours at the tar station and another six at a welding station. The drossy fumes of burnt welding rods and the smell of tar clung to his greasy hair and grime-stained work clothes.

The Night Foreman approached him. The Foreman held a plastic container used for urine drug tests.

Inclining his head up to the taller man, the Foreman asked, "Rigger, are you sick?"

They stood near one of the welding stations. The electric arcs of the night Welders at work cast a milky shine on Renoir's forehead and skeletal face. He looked almost dead.

"No, not really. I et somethin that don't agree with me," Renoir said in a dry voice. He patted his stomach and grinned without smiling. He stood poised and perfectly still, almost hovering. He stared silently at the Foreman.

"It's cause you eat snakes. That's what I heard," the Foreman said.

Small welding arcs the size of staples reflected in the Rigger's eyes. He slowly blinked and turned his head away from the Welders across the barge.

"I do eat snakes, cottonmouths, especially," Renoir said. "That's good meat. Gives you plenty a energy. As a matter of fact, I sure could use a cottonmouth about now." Again, he pursed his closed lips into a sort of grin.

The Foreman stepped back. "Well, you look sick. You look like a cadaver in the morgue. Your breath stinks rotten. I seen you up all night, Renoir. What you doin all night? What you up to all night?"

Renoir did not answer.

The Foreman became frustrated.

Renoir just grinned in his closed-mouthed way.

"Are you on drugs?" the Foreman asked.

"No," Renoir said.

"Well I need you to piss in this cup. Okay?" the Foreman said.

"Why? I work harder than anybody else. I haven't done nothing wrong."

"Just piss in the cup."

"What if I don't?"

"Then you're fired. And headed back to the beach on the next boat in," the Foreman said.

"When's the next boat in?" Renoir asked.

"In two days."

"This is bullshit! I've worked for you guys before and I do good work," Renoir said. Somebody must have complained. He'd worked several jobs for this company while high on crank and nobody said anything before.

"Yes you do, but you are one walking, talking safety hazard on drugs. You know the rules. You are shit-canned effective right now," the Foreman said.

Renoir watched the Foreman walk away. Brockman must have filed a complaint. *It must have been Brockman.* Renoir was sure of it. He shook his head and closed his mouth tight to conceal his rage.

That King Shit was begging for a reckoning.

⚓ ⚓ ⚓

Most of the time Brockman remained in the shadows of the dive control shed, like a bear in a cave. He normally worked the night shift, but frequently worked the day shift as well. By choice he had essentially removed himself from the rest of the barge and all the other men. With telephone and charts he oversaw the underwater work taking place 590 feet below. He was not a physical laborer. He was an intelligence, a voice of experience that gave direction. Very rarely, and only during the nights, did he step outside his shed. During the day, if he was on duty, he was always inside the shed, and the sunlight turned its bright exterior into such a frosty brilliant white that it was impossible to see him within the inner gloom.

One could hear his odd, briny voice, even outside, and from several feet away, giving peremptory commands to the divers over the communication box. Any other Supervisor might stroll outside for a little exercise or to survey the far sweep of the sea around them. Not Brockman. With his misanthropic temper he claimed and was given a wide berth. Most workers knew him more by the sound of his voice than his physical appearance. He was odd, but so long as a man did his job little else mattered.

Renoir was so enraged about being fired he decided to risk nosing around the Supervisor's cabin. And if he got the chance again he would push Brockman off the helipad.

⚓ ⚓ ⚓

Renoir waited for just the right hour, on the afternoon of his last full day on the barge, when the Supervisor had started his shift and sat in the dive control shed working. After the dive bell had been let down to the seabed for the saturation divers to resume work and Renoir could be certain that Brockman's attention was fully occupied, he went below deck. Silently he made his way through the dark. He walked along the frigid air-conditioned hallways and stairways to the private cabin designated for the Dive Supervisor. Renoir had peered in on occasion, but never entered. With the utmost caution he turned the door handle as he had several times before. He saw no one was within and silently entered.

For a second in the semi-darkness, he thought that he'd entered the wrong room. It looked almost empty, except for a single cot. He closed the door quietly behind him and switched on the light.

In this small chilly space he saw the single neatly made up cot, a desk, a desk lamp, and a closet. At the foot of the cot stood an old wooden sea chest. The padlock hung loose from the hasp.

Renoir quickly and methodically began searching the room. In the closet he found foul-weather gear and one very heavy woolen sweater unsuitable for the Gulf of Mexico. Beneath the hanging garments lay a pair of scuffed Wellington boots. On the floor by the desk an accordion file contained neatly handwritten records detailing the day-to-day activities of the ongoing dive operations. There was nothing under the bed or the pillow.

Renoir investigated the sea chest last. Its old hinges creaked as he opened the lid. Inside the trunk a polished wood case protected an exotic, rare-looking helmet. It was a custom-made bronze-cast dive helmet somewhat similar in design to a Miller hat, but much larger to fit Brockman's ample head. It felt heavy and shone like gold as the Rigger turned it under the light. Next to the wooden case lay a pristinely maintained diver's harness and a scabbard sheathing a large jackknife with one sharp blade and a marlinespike. The handle of the jackknife bore the initials AJB. Folded near the harness rested a wide-cut, well-oiled, leather weight belt. It was an old time diver's belt, the nicest Renoir had ever seen, with gleaming bronze rivets and rings, and a shiny brass buckle.

Renoir's heart picked up a beat. Wedged flat behind the helmet case he found an artist's medium-sized sketchpad. Perhaps, he had found a way to understand Brockman better. It felt soft and worn as the Rigger prized it free. He threw it open, and unexpectedly found its ivory sheets completely filled with nicely drawn ink and pencil sketches, drawings of seabirds and seascapes. Renoir, in a rush, leafed through the entire pad. He looked closely at one picture framing a gloomy rock islet, whose hilltop summit was blanketed in clouds. Nothing depicted in any of the drawings was familiar. Even the many sorts of seabirds, drawn in detailed close-up were strange.

One sketch was of a weird-looking whale swimming underwater and had the title "Spade-Toothed Whale." It looked animated and alive, as if it might swim off the page. It was clear that Brockman had studied how the whale moved. At the bottom corner was a simple outline of the creature, diagramming the length and proportion of its fins, beak, flukes, and body. Renoir found the drawing fascinating—no human being had ever seen a living Spade-Toothed whale before.

At the bottom of the trunk was a small collection of old hardback books. One book had the title *The Iliad*, another *The Odyssey*, written by a guy with a single name, Homer. Most of the other books were written by Joseph Conrad: *Lord Jim*, *Almayer's Folly*, *The Nigger of the Narcissus*, *Typhoon*, *The Collected Tales*, etc. The books were meaningless to Renoir.

Then he noticed a leather-bound book that had no title. He opened it and saw that it was Brockman's *personal* log. The pages contained notations on a variety of work-related subjects: technical details about diving, anecdotes about marine life, mathematical computations, decompression times, weather, and comments about jobs and personnel. The book covered several years of Brockman's working life. Renoir skipped to the most recent daily entries and quickly skimmed the pages for any mention of himself or Seed:

Dive bell in good order . . . equipment superior to the old days. No signs of pressure-related illness among saturation divers . . . visibility a hundred feet in upper sea. Sounds of a whale at night . . . undersea thunder spooking the divers . . . like a ghostly leviathan.

Job delays adding up . . . time slipping away . . . tension between work crews grows by the minute . . . think Seed feeds it. Dive team falsely blamed . . . Riggers threatening violence . . . nothing solid, no action to report.

Withholding names for now.

Yesterday whale returned to the area . . . unearthly great noise . . . distinct blue whale sound . . . right through the walls of the dive bell. Topside dive crew grows more divided. Black-hearted Seed and yellow Kip against two decent Tenders . . . not sharp enough to handle . . . Job a mess . . . engineer plans wrong . . . may have to do it myself.

Renoir flipped to the last page and his eyes widened as he read the final entry:

Seed knows Renoir? Prison buddies? Swamp scum meth-head still watches me . . .

Shark food.

Renoir took a breath and, for a second, closed his eyes in shock. He felt sickened and sweaty. Like he'd been bit by a cottonmouth again. *Swamp scum still watches me.* How could Brockman know? Did he have eyes in the back of his fucking head? He also knew about Seed.

Renoir ripped the last page out of the log, folded it twice, and stuffed it into his breast pocket. Again he asked himself, *How could Brockman know so much?*

For a moment Renoir felt afraid, but he reminded himself Brockman was a lame cripple. Still, things weren't adding up right. A kind of confusion, like a headache, settled over him. Then he turned angry as Brockman's insults sank in. Renoir continued his search.

On the upper-left hand corner of the chest were two wood inlaid drawers. The Rigger unlatched each with a flick of his finger. One contained a King James Bible, the other drawer a spool of thread, two needles, an ivory comb, a fat packet of old letters, and several black-and-white photographs of Brockman's family.

A little smile came onto the Rigger's face. Here was something Brockman cared about.

Suddenly a sound came from outside the door. Renoir stopped and stood perfectly still. Somebody walked down the hall. Two slow minutes passed and no other noise followed. Cooler now, the Rigger resumed his search.

With long bony fingers he picked out a formal family portrait that showed a much younger looking Brockman standing next to a serious looking wife. Cradled in her arms, she held a baby girl with a frilly bonnet. Next to her stood a small boy wearing a kilt and sporran. The family had assembled near a fireplace in a low-ceilinged living room. For the photograph Brockman had dressed in his church clothes and hid his mutilated hand in his coat pocket. The family stood close together, and Brockman smiled proudly.

Renoir then examined another photograph. The date on the back was six years later than the first and showed Brockman's smiling daughter wearing a frock dress. She was missing a baby tooth in front, and she clutched a china doll. He found this picture within an envelope over a twig of dried plant. It sessile leaves were crowded together like an evergreen and it had tiny pinkish-purplish flowers. A thin pink ribbon had been tied about its stem. The Rigger sniffed it, then shrugged with indifference.

Not really having a plan, the Rigger pocketed the photograph of the girl. He sensed that she was important to Brockman. Feeling better, he carefully replaced everything to its original position and slipped out of the room.

CHAPTER THIRTY

FISTS AND BOOTS

Seed worked hard to restore his standing on the barge. Brockman's humiliating public reprimand and demotion hurt Seed's reputation. Consequently, he went out of his way to mingle with key sets of Riggers and Welders and tell crazy stories about his time in Angola and screwing girls. During his brag-fests he skillfully foisted all of the blame for his debacle on Brockman and the two Tenders who worked a different shift than him and Kip, the greenhorn Tender; for his audience, though they pretended otherwise, actually knew little of dive procedures. Kip worked on the same rotation as Seed and hoped to enjoy a little acceptance with these same topside workers. Even though it was Seed's incompetence that caused Kip's dangerous free fall into the deep, the experience ironically brought them closer.

When the topside crews began to think the dive team was intentionally dragging out the work to get more days earning top dollar at the bottom of the sea and putting at risk the topside crews' bonus pay, Seed shrewdly deflected all blame. He used his popularity with Riggers and Welders to both validate the rumors and make sure that all the harassment and invective were placed exclusively on the two Tenders on the other shift. Steadily, the hostility directed at the two isolated Tenders escalated, while Seed and Kip were left alone. Seed didn't care who got hurt or killed—this was fun.

His lies worked superbly. Twice, the two unlucky Tenders found small effigies of themselves hanging from nooses over their bunks. Then one day bad news circulated across the ranks of the steel city. The pipe-lay operations had fallen so far behind that earning bonuses for finishing ahead of schedule would now be almost impossible. A rumor sprang up that the saturation divers had caused delays by making a mistake in their measurements of the "tie-in" distance between the new pipeline and the complete one, and so the dive crew was now blamed for missing the bonus. This raised tensions to the breaking point. The two unlucky Tenders were attacked by a pair of angry Riggers.

⚓ ⚓ ⚓

Past midnight, the same evening as the deck fights, Renoir, the snake-eater, retired to the Riggers' unlit quarters. There were eight curtained double bunks in the room, and from half of them he heard Riggers snoring.

His hands trembling, Renoir reached into his locker closet for a dime bag, his mirror, eyedropper, and short straw. His long, wide hands trembled even more as he picked the items up. He dropped the mirror, then cursed and crawled around like a blind beggar on the floor, searching anxiously for the mirror with his hands. When he found the mirror, he kissed it.

Renoir sat heavily on his cot. He could hear the deep steady breathing of exhausted men above the continuous whisper of the air-conditioning vent. He knew his body was emaciated, and felt his prominent ribs and too-pointy pelvis and joints; he had once been a large man. Renoir thought idly about not getting high.

Suddenly, a spell of lucidity dawned on him, and he now knew that he was much overdue to eat and rest. He began to persuade himself it was time to sober up. Besides, he was leaving tomorrow and had a long, rough ride ahead of him. Some sleep would do him good.

Then, like a burning insult, the thought of that son of a whore Brockman sitting on the helipad lashed him again. He couldn't let go of the notion that the Supervisor sat there for no other purpose than to torment him with temptation. It was all too perfect to be a coincidence—if Brockman fell on that particular side of the barge, there was a good chance that no one would find his broken body until morning. There was no better way to kill him and have it look like an accident. He thought about asking Seed and the other members of the Angola Club to help him kill Brockman, but decided it was better to do it alone. If he asked for help, there'd be more risk and he might come across as weak. Brockman was, after all, a cripple. With unrelenting insanity, Renoir had thought of little else lately, and he was now utterly incapable of resting, even his usual one hour a day.

"Bad crank," he whispered. "Must be bad crank."

⚓ ⚓ ⚓

The bathroom was empty and silent except for the drip of a leaky faucet. Renoir entered with his usual stealth. He walked along the row of sinks to the last one. The mirror above each sink leaped with his phantom image as he passed. He stood still at the last, and pulled back his lips before the looking glass to inspect his carious teeth and swollen gums. He smiled to his ghastly reflection.

At last he walked into one of the stalls, shut the door behind him and sat on a toilet with the lid down. He pulled the photograph of Brockman's daughter from his shirt pocket and stared at it, trying to imagine what she looked like as an adult. Then he stuffed it back in his shirt pocket with the page he'd torn from Brockman's journal.

On his small mirror he divided neat lines of crank with his knife blade. With a dry wheeze he snorted in a line through the straw and snapped up straight. He wiped his eyes with the back of his hand, then quickly pinched his nose. Renoir inserted the stem of the eyedropper up his burning nostrils and squeezed water in. Without pausing he prepared more lines.

The wasted Rigger ingested far more crank than usual during the session. Near the end, the eyedropper no longer relieved the fiery sting in his sinuses. He didn't give a shit. In a murderous rage, he continued cutting lines and didn't stop snorting until tears streaked his cheeks and his glazed eyes were bright red. There would be no turning back tonight.

Renoir next found himself standing on deck at the base of the stairway. Tiny dots swam in front of his eyes and he could plainly hear the sharp buzz of men crosscut sawing the old cypress forest. This time he imagined there were thousands of lumberjacks pulling on saws, the sound was so dense and loud. Tonight, they would surely cut everything down. The wasted Rigger's eyes searched the dark barge to be sure nobody would see him going up the stairway. He stared briefly at the ocean. Something sinister seemed alive there. Dark convolutions formed a human face, then a black dorsal fin. Then it was gone.

After a minute Renoir turned from the waves. He patted his breast pocket to be sure the photograph of Brockman's daughter was still there; it was. He was going to give it to Seed. He would be pleased to know that Brockman had a daughter.

Noiselessly, Renoir started up into the wind to murder Brockman. Tonight. No question about it.

CHAPTER THIRTY-ONE

BORN OUT OF THE SEA

M iles away on the liftboat, a balmy breeze passed under the moon. The gusts soon increased in strength and began driving rolling scud clouds across the sky. As a cold front pressed closer, black thunderheads gathered to the southeast like an ominous mountain range of pure coal. The divers worked quickly, racing against the darkening weather to finish the job. By the wee hours a full-blown storm moved over the sea with a loud rustling.

Jonah watched slate-gray waves crowned by white horses leap high and streak the ocean with frothy spume as dawn broke hard and ugly. The anvil-shaped thunderheads cracked thick branches of blue-white lightning, and sporadic rain fell in great sweeping sheets. Millions of dimples sprinkled across the convex watery disc encompassing the liftboat. A smoky perimeter rose up around the elevated boat, cutting the crew's view in half with its wispy curtain.

At lunchtime Jonah sat in the galley eating bread and waiting for chicken soup to be ready.

The cook switched on the radio and turned the dial to a news channel. A man was talking about the stock market and the Dow Jones Industrial Average. After that a female radio reporter talked about a blue whale that had been sighted several times during the previous month in the Gulf of Mexico.

Jonah leaned forward to hear. The reporter said all the usual stuff: that blue whales are the largest animals to have ever lived on Earth and are now virtually extinct, that this whale was one of the very last of its species. She also said the sightings of this rare and apparently distressed animal had become a national media story, with a TV crew following a team of scientists to photograph the endangered mammal.

Then a marine mammalogist came on and said that this blue whale was starving and disoriented, suffering from a respiratory infection; she had large ulcers on her head around her blowholes. The marine mammalogist suggested the whale was sick from feeding in polluted water: PCBs, heavy metals, human sewage, and petroleum slicks from the oil industry. He said healthy whales come every winter to the Gulf of Mexico to mate and calve in the warm water, then in the summer they leave the tropics for the food-rich polar waters. He said there aren't usually any whales in the Gulf during the summer months and that this blue whale was clearly very sick and confused.

The scientists wanted to examine her and, ideally, to recover her body and perform an autopsy if the whale died. They would continue to track her because they believed that it was only a matter of time before she died and added that the National Science Foundation greatly appreciated the numerous fishermen's reports of her whereabouts.

Jonah had read in one of his whale books that for all practical purposes blue whales were already extinct. There were so few left that the chances of two mature adults of opposite sex actually meeting was small. Jonah hoped that she would swim by the liftboat, and if she did he would ask Troy, the Dive Supervisor, for permission to snorkel over to her for a look. The cook said he'd heard reports about it on the radio the last two nights.

"I'd like to see a blue whale before they're gone for good," the cook said.

"That's for sure." Jonah wondered how big the whale was. Some blue whales were a hundred feet long.

Suddenly the galley's oval door swung inward, letting in a loud squall wind and spattering rain. Troy, the Dive Supervisor, in bright yellow foul-weather gear stepped out of the noisy downpour and shut the door behind him. His cheeks were wind-burned red, and rain dripped from the bridge of his nose and over his beard. He threw back his hood and announced merrily,

"The job's done. The last diver is out of the water. The captain says the weather is supposed to break in an hour. The worst has already passed. Then we'll jack down and head for land."

Jonah wanted to jump for joy but didn't show it. He was going to see Olene.

Troy took off his wet yellow rain slicker and hung it on a hook near the door.

"As soon as you're done, Jonah, get back out there and tie-off everything with the others," Troy said.

Jonah nodded. He'd just got off-shift but didn't mind going back to work if it would speed up their departure.

The cook ladled soup into bowls and passed them around. Troy crossed the galley and sat down. He tore open a packet of crackers for his soup.

"We ought to be back on the beach around midnight," the cook said, reading his wristwatch.

"Yeah, we'll see," Troy said skeptically. He rubbed his large thick hands together, wiping off cracker crumbs. One of his knuckles was scraped and scabbed with dried blood. He sat quietly, looking at his steaming soup bowl for a second. Jonah watched him and thought he saw the Supervisor's lips move in an inward prayer. Then with great deliberation Troy dried the rain from his face and beard with a paper napkin and wiped his eyebrows, before starting to eat.

The radio chattered and rain and wind beat unsteadily against the galley door.

The cook said, "You fellahs heard about that new Dive Supervisor, Aleck Brockman? You know. The North Sea guy."

"What about him?" Troy's pale green eyes glanced sideways. He held his full spoon halfway to his mouth. Yeah, he knew the man. Knew the reputation. Everyone did.

Jonah slowed down eating so as to hear what Troy would say. The Supervisor rarely spoke, but when he did, he usually said something interesting.

The cook said, "They say Brockman killed his dive partner over in the North Sea. Locked him outside the dive bell and let him freeze to death."

"Really?" Troy asked.

"Yes," the cook said from over by the sink. "I heard all this weeks ago, before we started out from Freeport."

"Brockman killed his partner?" Troy said.

"That's what they say." The cook smirked.

Jonah knew the cook was full of it. The man liked attention and would say anything to get a conversation started.

"That's bullshit," Troy said. "The truth is that Brockman was down nearly 500 feet in the North Sea working in a dive bell. His partner was outside and Brockman was inside the bell tending him. They were right on bottom. Some fuck-up Tender assigned to the bell didn't check the clevis pin and cotter key on deck pre-dive. The shackle opened up and the bell dropped off the lifting wire.

"It was an older, cruder-type bell that sank into the bottom closing off the entrance hatch and trapped Brockman's partner outside. The hot water to their suits and power cut off when the incompetents topside tried to lift the bell by only its umbilical. With no buoyancy device or dumping weights on this old bell, the divers couldn't lighten the bell and it was stuck. They sat at the bottom of the North Sea until the diver outside froze to death and Brockman slowly ran out of breathing gas inside.

"Topside heard them communicating for a while. Apparently Brockman's partner pounded on the bell walls with a pipewrench to signal to Brockman inside that he was still alive. Eventually the knocking got softer and softer. Before the end, they tried to lift the dive bell one more time and the umbilical broke off. They lost the bell and both divers. No heat, no power, no gas supply from the surface, no communication, and a limited supply of breathing gas. Brockman sat in the detached dive bell, at the bottom of the sea, listening to his buddy die outside in the deep black, and then waited the rest of the day for a rescue team to arrive. At some point his breathing gas ran out.

"By the time the rescue team got to the dive bell, Brockman had suffocated. He was stone dead, lying on the floor of the bell. But as they raised the bell with both corpses inside, one of the rescue divers miraculously was able to revive Brockman, but not the other diver. Nobody knows how long Brockman was dead, but they say his body was as cold as the North Sea. That's probably why they could bring him back. They say he came back to life just before the dive bell came out of the waves."

"How can a man get over that?" the cook said.

"Yeah," Troy said, glancing at Jonah. "He isn't exactly a sociable guy. Who can blame him really? There are experiences and emotions a man can have, that simply can't be put into words or shared with another human being. That mark you for the rest of your life. Imagine it—dying on the ocean floor with your buddy, then being revived. One moment you don't exist in this world, then the next, your heart is beating and your eyes open, just in time to watch yourself rise from the waves. It must have seemed like he was being born again. Except this time he was being born out of the sea—not from between a woman's legs. Brockman is a strange man. A different kind of diver. He's gone deeper than anyone I know—and even died down there—and yet somehow he keeps coming back to the surface."

"He still dives?" Jonah asked.

"No. Not officially. His back is shot," Troy said with a little smile. He thoughtfully dabbed the edge of his mouth with a napkin. With a look of perfect equanimity he said, "It's hard to get to the truth of things out here sometimes. And bringing it back to the beach is even harder."

⚓ ⚓ ⚓

Wailing wind rattled the rain-streaked window and weak gray light poured in the Tenders' dim quarters. Outside, the storm was dying.

Jonah sat on the bottom mattress of a bunk bed. Straining his eyes, he reread Olene's letter and wondered if she'd gotten the letter he sent her on a passing crew boat a week earlier. The humid sea air made the page feel as delicate as rice paper. He looked at the date on the letter and realized a month and a half had passed since he'd seen Olene.

Escargot lay on his back on the top bunk. Any minute Jonah expected to feel the jarring rumble of the liftboat's gearbox engines as it retracted its legs and lowered down into the rough seas to head back to Freeport.

Troy walked in wearing his wet slicker. He switched on the light.

"Hey, I'm trying to sleep," Escargot said before he saw it was the Dive Supervisor.

"Bad news," Troy said. "You two aren't going home."

"What?" Jonah lowered the letter to his lap.

"You're going out to a deepwater pipe-lay barge," Troy said. "A crew boat is on its way to pick you up right now." And just like that Jonah wasn't going home, wasn't going to see Olene anytime soon.

"Damn!" Escargot cursed, striking the mattress with a fist. "What's the job?"

A sinking feeling started in Jonah's head and dropped down into his chest. All of a sudden he felt tired. He rubbed his eyes. Tenders had to pay their dues, and he was paying his now by going from one job to the next without time off.

"The *Nez Perce* barge. *Brockman's barge*. It's the new ninety-mile deepwater pipeline," Troy said. "They've gone fifty miles and are hung up on a tie-in. There's a saturation team out there now. You'll be working with them at first, but they won't be there long. Basically you'll be diving off the stern of the barge and checking the stinger once the pipe-lay operations start up again."

"That the Supervisor with the missing hand?" Jonah asked.

"Fingers. Brockman."

"The same guy the cook just talked about?"

"Yeah. The same guy," Troy said. "And I hear it's been pretty squirrelly out there."

"What do you mean, squirrelly?" Jonah asked.

"There was some fighting and they need to replace two Tenders and two Riggers. The company called the control room hoping we hadn't left yet. We're closest to the barge, and they need men pronto. The barge is being delayed because the saturation team is now undermanned."

"They ought to fly someone else out in a chopper," Escargot said.

"Not in this weather," Troy said.

"What the hell." Jonah exhaled heavily. "What the hell." Restless anger made him stand up. He walked over by the window to see if the crew boat was within sight.

Jonah looked out the window. He saw only the gray empty ocean, heaving and rolling, and a wall of mist. The mist eddied and stirred as if something gigantic were trying to take shape and get out, but only waves emerged. Jonah thought maybe the sick blue whale was nearby, but he shook his head. He was only wishing.

⚓ ⚓ ⚓

Wearing rain slickers and orange life jackets Jonah and Escargot crossed the liftboat's deck to the personnel net attached to the crane. Jonah pulled aside a section of rope ladder then shoved the duffel bag inside onto the round base next to Escargot's.

The crane operator hoisted them up into the rainy sky and swung them out over the gray heavy waves roiled up by the storm. Jonah's rain slicker flapped like a broken kite, and needles of rain stung his eyes. Clutching the net, trying to keep his weight balanced, and flying in this chaos of sky and sea, he felt very small indeed.

Below, the crew boat pitched and rolled in the froth. The captain fishtailed his vessel into position to receive the Tenders. To achieve a safe landing for the men, the crane operator timed the placement of the personnel net with the fall of the crew boat in a wave trough. Jonah and Escargot stepped off the net the instant it touched down on the unsteady vessel's canting stern deck and quickly yanked their duffel bags clear. The personnel net slapped once on the bounding deck then lifted away.

Waves swept the length of the crew boat and spindrifts broke over her sides. For a second Jonah saw the square flat hull of the liftboat looming large above him, then the captain pressed the gas and they motored away.

As Jonah looked back at the shrinking form of the liftboat, the world seemed different. The horizon had changed. It was closer now because of the storm and the smallness of the crew boat. The sound of the wind grew suddenly more plangent, and the throw of waves underfoot dominated his senses. The waves rolled and bucked with a power he had not felt minutes earlier on the liftboat, and standing upright on the crew boat took everything he had. He grabbed his duffel bag and went below.

Sitting grimly on rigid plastic seats inside the crew boat were a medic, two replacement Riggers, and a federal officer with a pistol holstered at his waist. They had all taken separate corners. One Rigger sat with shut eyes but the other men cast cursory glances toward Jonah and Escargot as they shambled into the room. The replacement Rigger who was awake fidgeted with a makeshift pillow, trying unsuccessfully to make himself comfortable. The medic looked seasick. The federal officer, a sallow-faced man with a stern countenance sat awake and alert. He was traveling to the barge to arrest the men involved in the fighting and to retrieve a body. His manner was austere but he seemed to notice everything.

Jonah stuffed his duffel bag between a row of vacant seats, pulled off his rain gear, and took a seat near Escargot.

Escargot put on the headphones of his portable cassette player and listened, as usual, to the heavy metal band Judas Priest. Jonah tried to lean against the side of the crew boat and sleep but could not. The seas in the wake of the storm were too rough. He kept banging his head as the vessel jolted and shook. He gave up trying to rest and after several hours pulled his rain gear back on and went out on deck for some fresh air.

A light rain still fell from whirling clouds and the hard gray sea tumbled and broke. Its color seemed dead. Jonah scanned the horizon and saw nothing but open ocean.

He strode up the gangway around the deckhouse. Ahead on the blank horizon the clouds were thinner and brighter. The waves rose up, crested with pearly foam, and dropped back as far as the eye could see. Jonah breathed deeply and a fine sea spray fizzed across his face. It felt warm. He licked the salt from his lips and wondered how much farther they had to go.

Looking up into the drizzle, he noticed a white egret blown out to sea by the storm. The hapless shorebird, far from home, flew zigzag as if tired in the wind and seemed to be following the crew boat. Jonah could have sworn that she looked directly at him.

An hour later a veteran deckhand, chewing on the stump of a cigar, walked up near Jonah. The deckhand wore a shirt dirty with oil stains and old paint smudges, and he surveyed the sea off port and starboard, then chose the less windy port side to lean against. Casually watching the water, he smoked his cheroot to a nub and tossed it over.

"What's that way if we keep going?" Jonah pointed straight ahead.

"Another few hundred miles you'll hit the Yucatan Peninsula, I think."

The egret crossed low over the bow then held itself at a steady altitude above them. The deckhand gazed up at the snow-white bird.

"Looks like you found a friend," he remarked.

THE TOILING CITY ON
THE OCEAN

The rain broke suddenly and Jonah noticed a black speck far off on the horizon. A rainbow formed in the intersection of trailing rain clouds and advancing sunlight. Soon the pipe-lay barge, *Nez Perce*, stood out on the distant blue curvature as a remote steel island, a world unto itself, glinting in the widening gap of fair weather. Everything took on sharp color as the sun came clear of the clouds: the sea glittered deep blue and the parting clouds revealed a clean blue sky.

As they drew nearer, the *Nez Perce* looked raw and dangerous, with stacks of pipe and steel scaffolding, a little like the construction site of a new building when only the girders are starting to go up, sharp rods of rebar are exposed, and lethal accidents are waiting to happen. Two cranes tilted into the sky, machines clattered, and dozens of laborers wearing hard hats clambered about the complex.

Jonah could see where the pipeline went down the ramp into the sea at the back of the barge, as well as the pontoons of the stinger jutting down underwater cradling the pipeline and where it disappeared into the depths.

As the crew boat prepared to moor alongside, the Day Foreman of the *Nez Perce* appeared on the stairway of the control tower. He wore a bright red work shirt and came down to meet the boat. He was a medium-sized man with a spit-and-polish manner and a strawberry nose with a brown melanoma spot on the tip.

Jonah hardly set foot on the toiling city before receiving his first instructions. The waiting Day Foreman roughly ordered him and Escargot to fetch a dead body and load it on the crew boat. Clearly the man was angry and agitated by all the setbacks of the previous evening.

"They've got a dead man," Jonah whispered to Escargot.

Escargot looked surprised. "That's what it looks like."

They dropped their duffel bags on the deck and somberly followed the Foreman to where the body lay wrapped in a faded canvas tarpaulin. Blood had soaked through in several maroon patches but there was none on the deck around it, which glistened with a sheen of rain water.

"How did he die?" Escargot asked.

"The crazy son of a bitch jumped off the helipad last night. Guess he thought he could fly," the Foreman said callously. "Looked like raw hamburger this mornin."

Something bright moved overhead. Jonah looked up. The egret, frosty white and numinous against the azure sky, circled the barge in a wide arc, as if she were hungry or watching for something.

Jonah and Escargot bent down and seized the bloody canvas by the folded ends. The body felt surprisingly light as they lifted it.

"Who is this?" Jonah asked. He couldn't believe he was carrying a dead man.

"Renoir, a snake-eating son of a bitch," the Foreman said, putting his hands on his hips.

The Foreman stared as the two new Tenders secured the body between them. He wiped the melanoma spot at the end of his strawberry nose and said, "You two better git on with the other men on this barge. If you can't control ya-selves, you git right back on that crew boat. There's been more personnel trouble on this snake-bit job than I ever seen in my life. You hear me?"

"Yes," Jonah answered stiffly.

"Well, then get that dead Rigger off a my barge." He waved them on.

Jonah and Escargot carried the body like a slumped rolled carpet from the control tower toward the crew boat, stepping carefully on the slippery deck. The Foreman walked behind them. The ring of keys hanging from his belt jingled until he adjusted them with a sweep of his hand.

Jonah was alert to the distrustful and unfriendly eyes of workers watching them from all points across the barge. Looking about for the dive station or some friendly sign of the dive crew, Jonah's eyes came to rest on the dive control shed down the barge. A large fierce man stood motionless in the entrance watching them carry the body.

"Is that the Dive Supervisor?" Jonah asked.

"That's Mr. Aleck Brockman," the Foreman said.

Escargot slipped and nearly dropped his end of the corpse.

"Watch ya-self! I don't want that Rigger splashed across the deck again," the Foreman shouted.

Escargot steadied his legs under him and repurchased his hold on the body. He could not turn to look at Brockman and instead, he looked questioningly at Jonah. Not knowing what else to do, Jonah shrugged. When he glanced back at the dive control shed, the Supervisor had disappeared from the dark entrance.

CHAPTER THIRTY-THREE

HELL JOB

The crew boat captain watched with a displeased expression as Jonah and Escargot loaded the dead Rigger onto his boat. He refused to allow them to stow the body below, so they placed it on the deck. They tied it like a piece of equipment with timberhitch and bowline knots to the base of the steps leading up to the wheelhouse.

Jonah wanted to handle the corpse with care, but to tie it properly meant he had to treat it roughly. He looped a piece of rope around the canvas just below where he guessed the shoulders might be, and then looped the rope around a stanchion and tightened it using his body weight for leverage. He knotted the first rope and put another rope around Renoir's waist.

Escargot did the ankles and knees, and when they were done, the canvas was pressed tightly to the dead body and Jonah could see the shape of a tall, gaunt man.

Jonah could tell, even through the heavy canvas, that the dead Rigger had broken his legs so that the tops of his shinbones overlapped his femurs, making him seem to have an enormous set of knees.

In the background Jonah overheard the federal officer conversing with the Foreman in scornful commiserating tones about the suicide and the fights. The Foreman referred to a "damn idiot" several times and said Renoir's breast pocket had somehow been torn open down to his stomach in the fall. Then one of them made a remark and they both laughed.

Soon the two victorious fighters were presented for arrest. A group of men at the nearest welding station cheered and whistled. The Rigger waved to his friends then pranced and goose-stepped, thrusting his arms over his head like a prizefighter being declared the winner. His friends applauded loudly and howled at his histrionics. This prompted the Foreman to walk over and silence the gang at the welding station with threats of immediate dismissal.

The victorious Tender stood quiet with head high.

The federal officer with cold authority placed the victorious Rigger and Tender under arrest and read them their rights. The Tender and Rigger glared at each other from opposite sides of the officer until he gave one a shove and threatened to handcuff both of them on the spot—if they behaved they would only be handcuffed when they reached the dock.

The seasick medic had walked with his doctor's bag onto the barge to examine and redress the wounds of the badly injured losers. Jonah watched as he now came back with his patients.

The Tender had been carved and stabbed with a rigging knife. The wounds were across his chest and stomach, and he moved stiffly and held his arms across his front as if afraid his guts would spill out.

The Rigger's face and teeth had been broken with a lead weight belt. His face was black and blue where Jonah could see it and his head was swollen and lopsided with bandages.

Both men, sullen and defeated, wore clean gauze bandages.

The medic gently assisted his patients, one at a time, down onto the crew boat.

"Those sorry sons of bitches are gonna have a long, hard ride to shore," the captain said. "They're gonna wish they'd waited a little longer for the weather to finish clearing for a chopper."

The federal officer, asserting his jurisdiction, again warned the able-bodied Rigger and Tender to stay away from each other or he would handcuff them right then.

Jonah finished his grim task, wiped his hands, and went with Escargot back onto the *Nez Perce*. He stood watching the federal officer as he led the fighters onto the crew boat. The men who had been beaten wouldn't look into the eyes of the men who had hurt them.

It was late afternoon and the sun was very bright and the ocean a crisp cobalt blue. Jonah still couldn't believe he'd carried a dead man. He felt numb, like he'd taken a narcotic just as he stepped on board the *Nez Perce*.

The Tender who had won his fight stood alone out on the stern. He had a black eye and a long scratch on his forearm. The dead Rigger, who ate snakes, lay horizontal against the deckhouse behind him, of no more significance than a few logs of wood wrapped in canvas, except for the maroon stains.

"What the hell happened here?" Jonah asked. He hoped the sound of the Tender's voice would puncture the bubble of unreality he felt.

The Tender gazed up at him from the crew boat. "You guys watch your backs. This is a real hell job. The Riggers will be out to shank you."

⚓ ⚓ ⚓

Jonah located the Tenders' quarters at the end of a dim corridor. These rooms were always the same: as dark and cold as a tomb. The bunks had individual curtains around them and there was a tall locker for each cot. Waiting for Jonah was an effigy hung by a noose over his bunk. Unimpressed, he yanked the figurine down and tossed it roughly into the waste bin and then unpacked his duffel bag.

Ready to work, he and Escargot walked the length of the barge to the dive control shed. The sun by this time hung low over the sea. Riggers moved about, panting on the still-hot deck, hauling and moving their loads. A horn blasted from the control tower to signal that a section of pipe was rolling off the ramp into the waves. The section would lengthen the pipeline toward the tie-in.

Jonah could smell burnt welding rods and hot tar as he passed a welding station next to the pedestal mounted rollers of the pipeline ramp. Suddenly a Welder threw off his face shield; he had burned himself. He shook his hand and furiously cursed God.

The dive shed, elevated by three short steps, bore a recent coat of white paint that glared and hurt Jonah's eyes in the sunlight. The shed had been strategically positioned facing starboard so that from its entrance the Supervisor could look out on both the stern dive station near the stinger and the davit crane at midbarge that lowered the dive bell undersea. At the steps of the dive shed Jonah and Escargot looked at each other to see who would lead the way. Jonah went ahead.

"Aleck Brockman?" he called at the dark doorway.

"Come in," said a hard voice.

Jonah entered and Escargot followed.

Although the inner shed wasn't in fact very dark, coming from the brightness outside it seemed like a cave.

Facing the man, it struck Jonah plainly and instantly that Brockman was indeed very dangerous. The Supervisor sat before them as a marine authority representing vast untold experience. He was a commander unlike anyone Jonah had ever encountered, the exact personification of an old-time deep-sea diver, a manifestation of countless dives and a life shaped by and consumed within the depths of oceans. Brockman had intelligent eyes that turned on you as if he would be your final inquisitor and judge. His body was hard and thick. He had a broad chest, a bulging forehead, and his face had the unmerciful ruthlessness of an old warhorse. It was impossible to tell if he was evil or merely pitiless.

"Good afternoon," Brockman said with an odd accent. He sat straight-backed behind his desk opposite the new Tenders and regarded them each, one at a time. His pupils seemed oddly shaped, not quite round, and his irises were a color between smoke gray and blue. The wall to his right had three large-diameter gauges mounted on it to monitor pressures: the first for inside the saturation chamber, the second for inside the dive bell, and the third for the dive bell's exterior. An elaborate manifold of crisscrossing pipes, valves, and gauges controlling various banks of gasses and breathing mixtures covered one wall.

Jonah glanced at Brockman's hands. He almost grunted in surprise when he saw three uneven stumps on the Supervisor's right hand; the ring, middle, and index fingers had been severed close to the base knuckles.

Brockman caught Jonah's curiosity with the hint of a smile.

"Reporting for work. I'm Jonah." Extending his hand, he somehow expected Brockman to clasp it with the mutilated one. The Supervisor ignored the gesture and leaned back from the desk, shifting in his chair. He did not take his eyes off Jonah until the Tender withdrew his arm. Then Escargot introduced himself.

"Have you both tended on a saturation job before?" the Supervisor asked. For a second he seemed amused by the pair.

"Yep," Escargot said.

"No. I began tending four months ago," Jonah said.

Brockman leaned back. "The worksite is at 590 feet and I've got four divers living in the sat chamber and riding the bell to work every day. Either of you boys ever seen what a diver's corpse looks like after being at 590 feet for six days and coming to the surface without decompressing?"

Both Jonah and Escargot said no.

"Well, you don't ever want to. Now one of these divers might make a mistake and cause his own death or get crushed by the crane operator or poisoned with the wrong gas mix by me. But what will not happen is that the divers get hurt or killed because one of *you* fucks up. Taking care of the divers is job one. Job two is checking the stinger twice a day. It's not very deep, but it is very dangerous. If you get between the rollers and the pipeline, you will be crushed to death. Do you understand?"

Both Jonah and Escargot said yes.

"Also you should know we've been hung up tying in the new pipeline to an old pipeline under us right now. Some of the other crews are blaming the dive crew. They think we've made a mistake and cost the whole barge their bonus pay because it looks like we're going to blow the deadline. That's bullshit. The truth is the engineers screwed up the blueprints, but we're being blamed anyway. So welcome aboard."

"Are we on a twelve-hour rotation?" Escargot asked.

"Mostly," Brockman said. "You say you've worked sat jobs before, so I'll expect you to show Jonah what's what. I'll be watching." There was a warning in his voice.

"There's one thing," Escargot ventured. "We just got here and already someone's hung dolls of us off our bunks."

Brockman scowled. "I just told you the other crews are blaming us for the delay. Cry me a river, lads. If you can't look after yourselves why are you out here?"

"I'm just telling you," Escargot said.

Brockman bluntly dismissed them by lowering his face to the paperwork on his desk.

⚓ ⚓ ⚓

Walking toward the sat chambers, Escargot asked, "So what do you think?"

"Nothing good," Jonah said.

"How do you mean?"

"Every hell job needs a devil to run it."

"Well, he and the sat divers are only out here on a temporary basis. Brockman will be gone in a week. Two at the most," Escargot said. "We just got to stay out of his hair and he'll be out of here before we know it, soon as the saturation work is done."

"I'm for that," Jonah said.

Both Tenders stopped and looked upwards at the helipad on top of the control tower. It was the highest point on the *Nez Perce* and towered above everything like a castle turret. Something white had moved or waved up there.

"What the hell?" Jonah remarked.

"Maybe someone waving a shirt."

They both squinted, trying to see what had moved on the helipad. Jonah lowered his gaze and noticed a Welder glaring at them.

"Escargot, have you ever worked a job like this?" Jonah asked.

"No," Escargot said.

As they walked the barge, Jonah saw the other two Tenders maintaining the divers in the saturation deck living chambers, and one of the Tenders was Kip, the yellow Tender. Everyone knew he'd defecated in his wetsuit when he dropped into the deep. Kip, using the control switch fixed outside, flushed the chamber toilet for a diver inside who had just used it. The other Tender was Seed. He was washing dive suits used during the last bell dive.

Jonah's chest and arm muscles tightened in warning, and he became suddenly very alert, like he did before a fight. In an uncanny way he wasn't surprised to find Seed on this barge. Without thinking, Jonah balled a fist and clamped his jaw tight.

As Jonah approached, he heard Seed telling Kip how to get more oral sex from his girlfriend: get her drunk enough that she'll snort cocaine—the cocaine will make her horny—then use a can of Reddi-wip so his cock is like an ice cream sundae for her. Seed had his short sleeves rolled up so that all of his biceps muscles and some of his shoulder muscles showed.

Kip was a foot shorter than Seed, smaller-framed, and seemed weak and obsequious next to him. Adding to this impression was the way Kip gratefully accepted Seed's sex advice as the gospel truth.

Seed turned from what he was doing; his face went cold and his eyes darkened.

"Look what we have here."

Jonah felt like anything could happen.

Seed stepped back and suddenly spread a broad, friendly grin and held it. A fake smile on a frozen face. Seed seemed on the verge of laughing.

"Buddy, let's start fresh," Seed said. He talked slowly, almost patronizing, "If we go at it now, we both get fired. If you still want to bring it on after the job, we'll do it on the beach. So what do you say, how about a truce?"

Jonah couldn't take his eyes off Seed's face.

"All right," Jonah said, playing along. He didn't believe Seed wanted a truce. The man seemed different, strutting and full of swagger, almost gleeful. He liked being on the *Nez Perce*.

"So I hear this is a bad job," Escargot said.

"Not really," Kip said. He blinked nervously, and Jonah noticed he had long, blond eyelashes.

"Them other two couldn't make friends. I guess for them it was a hell job," Seed snorted contemptuously. "And Brockman is a real cunt."

Kip's face twitched nervously at Seed's insulting of the Supervisor. He looked worriedly behind him and around the saturation unit to be sure Brockman wasn't standing near. "What job are you-all coming off of?" he asked quickly, before Seed could go on.

"Riser pipes, off a liftboat," Jonah said. "We've been offshore for six weeks now."

"Hell, that's too long without a woman," Seed said. "I was on the beach two weeks ago, and you can bet, I had me some *good* honey." Seed winked at Jonah and smiled.

"So Brockman's real bad?" Escargot asked.

"Oh yeah," Kip said in a discreet voice. "We're liable to get cussed out any minute on his frickin loudhailer if he catches us being distracted by you." He glanced toward the dive control shed.

"If you want to get along with Brockman, you better learn to play poker or tonsil hockey," Seed said with proud venom. "He's already won the paychecks off his only two pals: a galley hand with false teeth and the dumbest Rigger on the barge."

Again Kip checked the entrance of the dive control shed for Brockman's presence. Jonah could see he was frightened.

"You'd better go before he starts bitchin over the loudhailer," Kip said.

"Yeah, I got to make a phone call anyway," Jonah said.

"You're going to make a personal call?" Seed asked in a way that made Jonah instantly regret having said a word about his private business. Seed smiled meaningfully and his eyes smiled as he picked up from the deck a dive suit lathered in soap.

"No . . . my stockbroker. Gonna short oil pipe."

Seed hung the dive suit from the line and rinsed it down with the freshwater hose. "Well you ought to know they've got a radio down in the kitchen that picks up the satellite phone in the control tower. There's a fat-mouthed cook who listens to guys calling home."

"Really?"

"Yep. You won't get any privacy here. He turns it up real loud so everyone in the grub hall can hear whoever is whining home or getting sweet on their woman. I got a standing ovation when I went into the dining room after making one of my girls beg me not to ditch her. I even broke her down to where she promised to roll over and gimmee her ass, which she's never let me have till now. I'm gonna take that honey to a whole new level when I get back, let me tell you." Seed lewdly raised his eyebrows twice in quick succession to emphasize his meaning.

"I'll have to take my chances then," Jonah said.

"Yep, just trying to warn you. Save you some humiliation," Seed said.

"Thanks," Jonah said in a neutral tone, but felt Seed had tricked him into saying it.

⚓ ⚓ ⚓

Jonah climbed up the stairway to the control room to call Olene, and Escargot went to the cafeteria to eat. Jonah wanted to tell Olene that he'd been sent to a barge and wouldn't be able to see her for a few more weeks, at least. He went up the first flight of stairs and paused a moment on the landing. Grabbing the railing, he leaned over and peered down where the dead Rigger's body had lain in canvas. He half expected and sort of hoped to see an outline or some kind of mark, but there was nothing.

Jonah went up the next flight of perforated stairs to the second level of the control tower. The third flight of stairs went up to another landing, then a fourth flight on up to the helipad. He entered the control room on the second floor.

"I need to make a phone call," Jonah told the barge clerk, who wore a shirt with the name SMITTY embroidered over the left breast pocket.

"Have you signed in yet?" Smitty asked. As the barge clerk, one of his responsibilities was to keep track of who was on the *Nez Perce*.

"No, I haven't."

"Here," Smitty said as he passed a ledger.

Jonah wrote the date, his name, and then Escargot's name in the "IN" column. He noticed that the dead Rigger's name, Renoir, had been written in the "OUT" column.

"Let me have the numbers for the phone call." Smitty talked on the telephone to a marine operator and gave the numbers as Jonah said them.

Smitty said, "All right." He handed over the receiver.

The telephone rang and Jonah looked out the tall, wide window. The *Nez Perce* barge spread out below him, a massive, dirty-gray rectangle; a cluttered factory city without a roof or walls, with welding stations, the pipeline assembly ramp, machines, cranes, davits, and exhausted, sunburnt men. All around, the immense open ocean wrinkled and swelled slowly, alternating a mirror surface with the bright reflected glare of the setting sun and another surface marbled with veins of purple and cobalt blue.

Jonah's eyes focused on the saturation deck living chambers. They looked clean and stood out like white bubble-shaped petroleum tanks. He could see the small figures of Seed and Kip in front of them. Then Jonah looked to the left and focused on the dive control shed, Brockman's office.

"Yellow Catfish," an old woman's voice. It must be Olene's *grandmère*. So where was Olene?

"Hello, this is Jonah. Is Olene there?"

"She's not talking to anyone now."

"I'm the diver in room three. I'm offshore on a barge . . ."

"Olene's not well. And she especially don't want to talk to no diver on no barge."

A dial tone buzzed indifferently in Jonah's ear. Olene's *grandmère* had hung up.

Jonah pressed a button to disconnect and handed Smitty the receiver, then marched off. He went down the stairs and entered the door leading below deck. He meant to try to sleep off his frustration.

In the Tenders' quarters, Escargot lay prostrate on his bunk still awake with the privacy curtain open. He turned his head and gave Jonah a drowsy look.

"Did you get through?" he asked.

"Her grandmother hung up on me. Said Olene was sick or something. I'll try again in a few days."

"You want to hear something weird?" Escargot's eyes woke up a little.

"Not really," Jonah said reflexively.

"One of the Welders said the sick blue whale has been sighted swimming around this barge. She's been around for almost two weeks now. He said you might see her spout if you watch the ocean. Especially in the morning."

"I hope she's still around." It would be good to see a whale in the ocean, maybe touch it. Whales reminded him of his grandmother and the time she showed him the stranded baby humpback washed up on the beach in Rhode Island. Whales and his grandma . . . connected somehow.

"I got more."

"What?"

"Some guys don't believe that Rigger, Renoir, committed suicide."

"So? What do they think happened?" Jonah was starting to feel uneasy, like something around him was out of control and he didn't know what.

"They think Brockman killed him," Escargot said.

"Did they know what they were talking about, or were they just bullshitting?" Jonah remembered the story about Brockman killing his dive partner in the North Sea. Now it was two guys Brockman had supposedly killed.

"Who knows," Escargot said. "And I also found out why Seed has got that big grin on his face."

"Why?"

"He's got friends with him on this job."

"Who?"

"Ex-cons he knows from Angola. There were four of them, but the dead Rigger was one of them, so now there's just three. They're called the Angola Club."

"That's nice," Jonah said. He stared blankly up at the cross braces of the bunk above him and wondered if Olene was really sick or was her *grandmère* just pulling his chain. He saw the dead Rigger, Renoir, wrapped in canvas, then the outside of Brockman's dive shed, and finally Brockman himself, his mutilated hand on the desk. The Tender who had won his fight warned them, "You guys watch your backs. This is a real hell job. The Riggers will be out to shank you." Jonah thought about Seed and how satisfied he seemed to be. Maybe he had something up his sleeve with the Angola Club, but Jonah was exhausted now and wanted to go to sleep.

CHAPTER THIRTY-FOUR

THE MIDNIGHT DEPTHS

A few hours later Jonah prepared to dive. His helmet viewport fogged again. He turned the free-flow valve to blow the lens clear.

"Going down. Keep slacking me off," Jonah said.

Now underwater, he climbed down the rig's leg headfirst like a spider. Hand over hand, through fish hovering about the marine growth on the underwater structure, he penetrated deeper and deeper layers of increasingly darkening, chilling sea. His throat felt parched and cold from the helium oxygen gas mix he had to breathe in order to work at 400 feet. This time he brought a dive light. He climbed downwards toward the embracing gloom, toward the endmost limit of the sun's reach.

Jonah checked his depth with Brockman over the telephone and remembered that blood looked dark green at this depth. A current, bitterly cold and deadly, rose up from the black abyss. Icy tendrils wormed into his wetsuit and leached the warmth from his body.

"Next time I want to wear a hot-water suit," Jonah said.

The dark river churned over him.

"You on bottom yet?" Brockman asked.

"No."

"Then quit talking and go."

Jonah couldn't see anything. He switched on the Super Q dive light duct-taped to the handle on his helmet. No light came on. If anything, it seemed darker. The battery had died. The flashlight was useless. His wetsuit felt packed with ice and he began to shiver. Still, Jonah pulled himself deeper into the midnight depths. His fingers went numb. His arms began losing their strength. Every other time he reached for the next handhold he missed and clawed uselessly into the blackness. Finally he collided with the unseen bottom. He jammed his neck and tipped over on his head. His body gave out.

He couldn't move; he lay on his back as if in a grave looking up and seeing nothing. The whole weight of the ocean above pressed down on his chest. The gas came thin and shallow.

"Jonah, come back up. You sound weak," Brockman said.

"I'm dead," he said with nearly his last breath.

"Where are you?"

"I can't see. Like a tomb," Jonah gasped. "No light. I'm suffocating. Pull me up."

"We'll start you up. There's some light up here and we've got something special for you to see," Brockman said in cold voice.

⚓ ⚓ ⚓

Someone else began talking again.

"Wake up." Escargot jostled him. "We're on shift in twenty minutes."

Jonah sat up from the nightmare, his heart pounding. He sprang halfway out of his bunk. His watch read 6:41 p.m.

A residue of the nightmare lingered like a bad taste in his mouth.

Escargot opened his locker across the room to get a pouch of chewing tobacco from his duffel bag. He took a pinch and inserted it in his cheek.

"You want a taste? You look like you need it." Escargot held the open pouch out for him.

"No thanks."

The two Tenders grabbed some coffee in the galley then went on deck to work. Their first task was to help the saturation divers go undersea in the dive bell.

The saturation chamber system stood out in the night like a strange set of large connected igloos. Slowly chewing his tobacco, Escargot apprised Jonah of his duties and how specifically to perform them. Jonah knew generally what to do but had never had to do it until now.

He studied the saturation deck decompression chambers, which looked like the standard decompression chambers he'd used for shallower jobs, except there were three connected chambers instead of one and they were much larger. Because the saturation chambers had to sustain higher working pressures, they also had thicker walls. Through a viewport, he could see the spare, cramped living quarters with ceilings just high enough for the divers to stand upright. There were sleeping bunks, seats, a toilet, a table, a shower, and a transfer lock large enough to pass and receive dive gear, tools, and food.

On the outside of the main chamber stood a weatherproof console with atmosphere control systems to regulate the temperature, humidity, and breathing mixtures. Four divers sat inside the chamber living quarters, waiting for their next shift. The divers worked in teams of two, and while one team was lowered to the sea floor in the pressurized dive bell to work, the other two remained in the chamber resting for their next rotation.

Next Jonah and Escargot manually checked the levels of emergency gas stored in the cylinders mounted to the dive bell, tested the hot-water systems heating the dive suits, and made dead sure the clevis pin and cotter key on the shackle that locked the bell to the lifting cable were in place.

After carefully going over each item on the predive checklist the two Tenders went over to the dive control shed and reported to Brockman.

The Dive Supervisor stood alert and expectant in the doorframe of the shed. His arms were folded and he looked down from the top step. Unblinking, he listened fixedly to Escargot's report. Compressor oil and fuel levels were checked, the dive bell lights checked, emergency systems checked, hot-water pump ready, dive bell attachment to the lifting wire locked tight, and the divers were suited up. The Dive Supervisor asked Jonah if he understood what he'd been told.

"Yes," Jonah said.

"Good. If you don't understand anything ask questions immediately," Brockman ordered.

Jonah found himself studying the Supervisor. Brockman had the trick of looking either dumb and vicious or wise and meditative, depending on the angle of his face. The contradiction was baffling.

The Dive Supervisor sent the Tenders to top off the fuel tanks and make certain the oil levels were high enough in the hydraulic tank and air compressors. He also told them rather sharply to recheck the clevis pin and cotter key. It was time to lower the saturation divers to the sea floor inside the dive bell to work.

Jonah watched as two divers climbed through the saturation chamber living quarters and into the dive bell. The two Tenders removed the lug nuts locking the dive bell onto the chamber. As the davit crane lifted the round vessel up it resembled a massive egg with windows. The churning clash of the hydraulic engine and other engines on deck made it hard to hear without shouting at the top of their lungs as they began launching the bell into the sea.

The round white dome swung slightly from its gallows-frame davit. With a slight jerk it began to descend. Brockman, using control levers near his shed, dropped the bell sharply to break through the surface, then slowed its descent so that it sank controlled and evenly. Jonah saw one of the divers gazing out a viewport as the white bell lowered under the dark waves. The thick lifting cable and heavy umbilical began to pay out steadily. The crest of the bell's head glowed greenish blue under the sea, then was swallowed up in black.

As Brockman controlled the bell's descent to 575 feet, Jonah and Escargot stood near the water managing the bell's thick umbilical. All the time Brockman spoke over the loudhailer keeping the Tenders in line even when they were beyond his sight.

During routine operations the round door on the floor of the bell opened so the divers could enter the sea below. One man remained in the bell, feeding out and pulling in the umbilical of the other diver outside working in the sea. Eventually they would trade positions. After they both worked their shifts on the seabed, they would ride inside the bell back to the surface and reconnect to the saturation deck chamber and crawl into the living quarters. Then the other two divers would ride undersea in the bell.

To prevent hypothermia, the divers wore special wetsuits heated with hot water pumped through attached hoses and breathed heated gas through oral/nasal regulators in their helmets. They also had floodlights on the dive bell and headlights on their helmets, because of the deep dark at 590 feet, a freezing, nightmare black.

Jonah worked alongside Escargot through the night, feeding and caring for the bleary men incarcerated in the main chamber. When the saturation divers weren't diving, they mostly rested on their bunks or read books. They always returned from the deep exhausted from the underwater labor and wanting something hot to drink and eat. Whenever Jonah peered into one of the viewports, the divers inside always looked languid and miserable to him, like caged animals in a zoo.

While the dive bell made three undersea journeys and Jonah drank too much coffee, a foggy sleepiness eased over everything. The engines' discordant growls softened to a dull hum. A gentle breeze secretly lulled him if he stood motionless too long, and at times it was easy to imagine this starry night would continue for an eternity. The dark figures of other laborers walked by as work crews switched in the small hours of the new day. Their voices and laughter sounded soft and friendly against the engines.

Jonah looked out at the sea, and the waves rolled black and endless. He wondered if the blue whale was anywhere nearby— he watched for her spout. At one point he thought he saw an enormous dark shape surface near the barge, but when he pointed a flashlight on it, there was nothing but water.

Somewhere below . . . the divers, fathoms beneath the upper world, slipped out of the dive bell into the endless thick night on the deep ocean floor. Groping in the darkness, they trudged across the silty bottom on their way to work, dressed like astronauts on a sunless mud planet. In his mind, Jonah could see them as they worked on the new pipeline's tie-in to the pre-existing pipeline. With shovels they dug trenches under the two pipelines so that they could slip slings under them. Working with Riggers topside, they lifted the pipelines using separate davit cranes and tried to bring the two flanges close enough to mate and bolt together. Repeatedly they tried and failed. The two pipelines were still too far apart.

Topside, the Tenders stood ready to deliver down an assortment of tools and gear as the divers needed them: a pneumatic impact wrench, davit chains, snatch blocks, extra wrench sockets, flange studs, and flange nuts.

Brockman's gruff foreign voice did not amplify over the loudhailer very much to the Tenders after the first deployment of the bell. When he did speak, it was only to give essential directions. Once, between launches, Jonah caught sight of the Supervisor outside of the dive shed, examining the clevis pin and cotter key on the dive bell's top. With his crippled hand he reached out and tugged on the shackle. Brockman apparently sensed eyes on him and turned, and Jonah was shocked to see the tragic dignity in his face. The man appeared disturbed. His attention was turned inward. He seemed wholly absorbed by an old problem and some great regret. With a faint nod he finally acknowledged Jonah, then moved off.

⚓ ⚓ ⚓

Dawn came with a flaming pink like the inner lip of a queen conch shell. Jonah felt less tired in the growing brilliance of the day as night fell away. He released the chain stops holding the bell's umbilical to the lifting cable and watched the dive bell come back up. In the morning sun and just under the blue water, it looked like an enormous egg, maybe from a prehistoric sea creature. It broke the surface, lifted clear of the ocean, and gradually rose to the full height of the gallows-frame davit. Streams of seawater poured off its round walls and spattered the deck.

Jonah looked curiously at the round lid, like a manhole cover underneath, plugging shut the only way in or out of the dive bell. The divers inside were still pressured to 575 feet. Through a viewport you could see them like fish in a dry aquarium, sitting motionless, exhausted from hours of hard labor. One of them clutched his dive helmet. On the dome's crown hung a tendril of seaweed.

The two Tenders mated the bell back onto the saturation chamber and bolted it in place. The divers left the bell and went through the narrow entrance trunk into the saturation deck chambers. Inside the chambers they showered and passed some of their gear out through the transfer lock for the Tenders to wash and dry. Then the divers lay back on their cots in the cylindrical prison and waited for breakfast.

"You're off shift," Seed said close behind him.

Jonah turned and stepped back to put a little space between them.

"Did we connect the pipelines yet?" Seed asked. He was different, not laughing or gloating inside. He acted familiar and made an earnest and friendly face.

"Not yet."

"Not yet? This whole fucking job is being hung up by this tie-in. The barge can't lay pipe until we get past this. Once the pipelines are connected, Brockman's out of here with the saturation team. I want that."

Jonah did not reply. Seed was trying to ingratiate himself. Creep.

"Did old Brockman give you hell last night?" Seed's face had a scornful look, like they were discussing a mutual enemy and could talk confidentially.

"Not really."

Brockman's orders sounded over the loudhailer to the Tenders from a distance across the barge, and there was never any opportunity to talk back even if they wanted to. The Dive Supervisor had no contact with any men except, it was said, an idiot Rigger and Nelson, a galley hand with false teeth, both of whom he'd been beating in an ongoing card game.

"Wait and see. He's one sly bastard. He'll get to you. I don't know how he does it. But he does it. He'll get to you," Seed assured. He stepped close and said softly, "He killed his dive partner in the North Sea. And I think he killed that crankhead Rigger. You and me got to be careful."

CHAPTER THIRTY-FIVE

THE EGRET

Jonah walked toward the door on the control tower leading below deck. With tired eyes he saw something inhuman move ahead of him: a flash of frosty white.

Whatever it was, it seemed to have floated low across the deck. The white glided out of sight between a pair of heavy dive trunks and a rack of empty gas cylinders. It was the same blink of evasive white that Jonah and Escargot had seen up on the helipad just after arriving on the barge.

Curious, Jonah went over to investigate and to his amazement found the snowy white egret, the one blown out to sea by the storm.

Jonah's approach alarmed her. In a panic she spread her wings, causing no more sound than a puff of wind. She held them outstretched and aloft, threatening to fly away if he came any closer.

Jonah stooped down to her level. The egret gazed at him with the helpless expression of a creature caught out of her element. She stood nobly on bright yellow feet and had thin black legs that bent backwards like the elbows of a man. The radiant purity and gentle whiteness of her plumage were astonishing.

She positively glowed.

With sinuous grace the egret turned her long, slender neck. She cocked her head sideways, displaying in profile a sharp beak blackened to the base like a quill pen stained with ink. She fixed a small, yellow, sagacious eye on him.

In this stance the two scrutinized each other for a full minute. He edged discreetly closer.

Unfooled, she blinked at him and with awkward elegance stepped backwards to reclaim the distance.

After a moment, the beautiful bird folded her wings to her sides and moved into the shade. She no longer acted threatened but seemed quiet.

Against the backdrop of the barge city and the concrete-encased pipes and steel, the egret made Jonah think of a beautiful, rare flower. He edged a little closer, so he could almost touch her.

Again, she unfolded her wings as if to fly off.

He edged back again until she folded her wings. He did not want to disturb her.

"Out here! Iffin you git hurt, you git hurt permanent!" declared a simple-looking laborer. He had tousled, wispy black hair, and his eyes were set too far apart. The man was distinctly bowlegged and smiled vacantly. Jonah looked up and guessed that this was the Idiot Rigger.

"Look at her!" the Rigger exclaimed, pointing to the egret. He clicked his tongue and shook his whiskered face, agreeing wordlessly with him in his attention to the majestic bird. He took a deep breath and slapped his thighs with the palms of his hands. "Good, good," he muttered, then said something in French to the egret: "*La grâce de Dieu.*"

"What did you say?" Jonah asked.

"God's grace," the Idiot Rigger said, smiling. He looked at the egret a moment longer, then strode away with a jerky gait on his bowed legs.

The egret and Jonah eyed each other for a few moments, then he left her in the shade in peace and went below deck to rest.

On the way to the Tenders' quarters he passed a large, brutal-looking man without a shirt and nearly bumped into him coming around the turn at the bottom of the stairs. The man's face was pockmarked; his shiny head was shaved and very brown. His hairy torso and arms were covered with scars and multi-colored tattoos: voluptuous women, a devil, a raven, a snake, a belt and bracelets of barbed wire, and too many others to catch at a glance.

The man had obviously lifted a lot of weights, probably in a prison yard. His muscles rolled and swelled under his skin like thick water snakes coiling to strike, his shoulders were huge, and his deltoids rose to a peak halfway up his neck. He looked at Jonah with an expression of jeering hate as he walked by and said, "Fucking diver."

No doubt a member of the Angola Club.

In the Tenders' quarters Jonah found new effigies hanging over his bunk and Escargot's. None over Seed's and Kip's.

Jonah decided to keep his effigy this time, and hung it on the outside of his bunk as a trophy.

The next day, an hour before his work shift started, Jonah visited the egret again. She allowed him to get closer but still recoiled and raised her wings whenever he stepped too near. It was early evening and the sun lay at the horizon under a mantle of black clouds like a glowing half orange. The flaming disk hovered above the shoulder of the earth and cast a coppery sheen over everything. Among the waves and white caps the refracted color flickered in the moving water like so many fires. The heat of the day ebbed, and the egret ventured out from her shaded place between the tall, empty cylinders and dive trunks. Her steps were smooth and light despite the gawkiness of her stride.

A breeze ruffled the feathers on her nape.

She glanced at the Tender and suddenly flapped her wings into a blur of white and leapt into the sky.

The bird rose and flew off and up against a luminous firmament streaked with lavender and scarlet. He watched her until she became a small dot, a delicate white creature threading her way through the windy air and above the coppery sea. Flying somewhere toward Olene.

⚓ ⚓ ⚓

It was nearly 2 a.m. and Jonah smelled rain coming. He stood alone where the dive bell's umbilical went down into the waves; the bell had been undersea nearly four hours. A deck light illuminated his immediate vicinity, but there was darkness between his station and the next deck light in either direction. You couldn't tell who was coming your way until he walked up close. Escargot worked over next to the saturation chambers, adjusting the oral/nasal regulator and polishing the fiberglass exterior of a diver's helmet.

Jonah caught on quickly to tending a saturation job. In some ways he thought tending a saturation job was easier than tending off a liftboat, where he had to pull the diver up by his umbilical and had to help the diver put on his gear. On a saturation job the divers dressed themselves inside the chamber, and the davit crane—not human muscle—raised and lowered the divers to work.

After the saturation divers were safely back in the living quarters between dive bell trips undersea, Brockman asked Jonah questions about standard diving procedures and protocol. Like a test. The Tender answered every question correctly.

"After I leave the barge at the end of the saturation job," Brockman said, "whichever of you Tenders are most senior will have to step up and supervise the inspection dives off the stinger. That might be you, Jonah," he said with a smile.

Then the Dive Supervisor taught him how to operate the bank of mixed gasses so that he could deliver a variety of gasses—heliox, nitrogen, pure oxygen, or plain surface-supplied air—to an umbilical dive hose and down to a diver in the sea. Surface-supplied air and different gasses became toxic at certain pressures, so divers had to breathe specific gas mixes at different depths, or die.

The Dive Supervisor seemed to be preparing him for something much more challenging than routine inspection dives of the stinger. It was almost as if Brockman were training him to run a mixed-gas dive from the surface. The Dive Supervisor was a good teacher, and Jonah absorbed everything he said. Afterwards, the Tender stepped outside and prepared to launch the dive bell again.

Suddenly Jonah heard an angry shout from somebody walking the barge behind him. The warning popped into his head, "*Watch your backs. The Riggers will be out to shank you.*"

He turned quickly to see who was coming.

A form beyond the nearest deck light moved toward him. Abruptly, the bandy-legged Idiot Rigger came out of the darkness and across the deck, cursing angrily about something. He spoke quickly, raising his voice from loud to an outright yell, then dropping back to loud again, but Jonah could barely understand him.

The man waved his hand and pointed a finger, and when he stepped fully into the deck light, you could see that his face was bright red and that there was a drop of spittle on his lower lip. He complained vehemently about someone and confessed that he had a bad back. "And I'll tell you whut. I don't know who he knew or who he blew to git on with dis company, but he is de laziest sombitch I ever did see." He grunted indignantly as he turned to leave. Suddenly, he stopped and called, "Wait a minute, you. Where is de bird?"

"Flown away," Jonah said.

"Flown away?"

"Yes. Probably back home in the swamp by now."

"When she fly?"

"Earlier, around sunset."

The Idiot Rigger put his hands on his hips and grunted again. It was hard to tell in the dark, but Jonah thought he was troubled by the information.

"Tonight?" the Idiot Rigger asked.

"Tonight."

The Idiot Rigger walked off in the same direction he'd come.

Brockman's booming voice sounded over the loudhailer and told Jonah the divers were ready to work.

⚓ ⚓ ⚓

In the morning a soft, pale light and tepid wind fanned over the ocean. The waves were now clear and distinct; blue disorderly ridges surged up and dropped, some hissing and white, some with filaments of seaweed, and some with moon-shaped jellyfish.

Time for Jonah to go off duty. He walked wearily along the *Nez Perce* toward what had formerly been the egret's shaded resting place. Tired of standing, and below deck he would shower, eat, and sleep. A group of Welders carrying face shields walked past him followed by several Riggers, shirts already soaked with sweat.

Jonah went to the egret's spot and suddenly saw a flash of white. She was back! And he nearly walked right by without noticing her.

He squatted down for a close look. Yep, the same egret. The bird looked identical, but ragged, and she acted unthreatened as if familiar with him. She had, he thought, turned back from her flight home in exhaustion. Her feathers had lost a little of their luster, and her yellow eyes seemed less clear. Now too weak to fly. Jonah worried over what to do: the sun would soon make the deck scorching hot.

He decided to fetch a cup of fresh water from the cafeteria and place it at her feet. When he returned from the galley he held the water out toward her so she could see what he was offering her. He placed the cup by her scaled yellow feet. He spoke to her in gentle tones and tried to coax her to drink. She eyed the cup suspiciously, then turned her head away.

CHAPTER THIRTY-SIX

THE PROMETHEUS DIVE

That night, Jonah returned from the galley a few minutes past midnight with a cup of coffee. He came out on deck from the south door nearest the dive control shed. The night looked clear and the air felt heavy with humidity. The constellations looked unnaturally close overhead, almost reachable, as if fixed inside a dome and not in the high, distant heavens. Escargot sat perched on an empty drum in front of the saturation chamber holding a Styrofoam spittoon. Brockman wouldn't allow him to spit tobacco juice or Seed to spit pistachio shells on the deck near the saturation system. The divers inside the chamber were restless, trying to ignore the vibrations of the engines on deck and sleep.

Jonah started toward Escargot then stopped involuntarily. The wind blew up the barge and he faintly heard a commotion over the engine din. He looked down toward the control tower and saw by a deck light a group of off-duty laborers being entertained by Seed. They were laughing.

Jonah had heard that Seed told funny sex stories and acted them out, but he'd never seen one of Seed's shows. He looked at their weathered faces—there were nine or ten men—and recognized a few. The Angola Club, three ex-cons, stood watching. Kip, the yellow Tender, was also there and Jonah recognized an electrician and an X-ray technician.

The group had gathered by the dive trunks and empty cylinders where the egret went to avoid the sun during the daytime. Seed was in the middle of recounting one of his escapades, cavorting and acting it out in X-rated pantomime. The audience loved him and Seed exerted his influence on them like a foul, dancing magical puppet.

Around the corner came the Idiot Rigger, almost walking straight into Jonah.

"There you is. *HE* is looking for you. Told me find you."

"Where is he? In the dive control shed?"

"Yes." The Rigger waved.

"Okay."

Jonah walked rapidly to the dive shed, went up the steps to the entrance, and stepped inside.

The Dive Supervisor Brockman sat on the edge of his desk, dressed and ready to dive. He had on a broad leather weight belt with a shiny brass buckle, a patched and faded hot-water dive suit, an antiquated harness, and he held on his knee what appeared to be an old-school dive helmet with two headlights. A measuring tape, an underwater writing tablet, and a pen hung from his harness. In his other hand he held a fishnet sack.

"I need *you* to tend me," the grizzled old diver said.

Jonah looked at him. Had Brockman gone mad? He was crippled and couldn't dive.

"Why?" he asked, addressing not so much Brockman's statement but the idea of his diving.

"You, I can trust. This has to stay between us."

"I thought you had nerve damage in your back. We need a standby diver. The dive bell isn't ready."

Brockman's eyes sharpened on Jonah and seemed to look straight into him. "I'm not using the dive bell."

"It's too deep not to. I don't know mixed-gas ratios. I could kill you."

"No you won't. Everything is set up. I've mixed the gasses and planned the dive and laid everything out so you don't have to think or calculate. I've got my own depth gauge so you don't even have to take pneumo readings. You just have to tend me." The Dive Supervisor stood up, ready to go. "Let out slack when I tell you and pull me up when I tell you. And switch gasses when I tell you. When the umbilical is too heavy, get Escargot to help you and use the winch if you have to. I've already put him on notice that we're doing this. It'll be quick and easy."

"Quick and easy? It's almost 600 feet deep," Jonah said.

"I'm going down to the worksite, taking some measurements, and coming straight up. I'll make decompression stops in the water, and I'll tell you when to switch from surface-supplied air to heliox and when to switch to the heliox-nitrogen mix, then reverse the sequence as I come back up. I'm taking O2 near the end of my decompression. Just do what I say. And tie this mesh sack to the downline. I'm taking it with me." Brockman's voice was suddenly impatient. "Let's go."

"What the hell."

The Dive Supervisor stared at him. "The Russians have a saying: *The legs feed the wolf.*"

"I need to see the decompression tables."

"Not for this dive. This is outside the boundaries. Prometheus territory."

Jonah shook his head. This was unbelievably dangerous.

"Diving is still an emerging science. I wrote this out. It's my own gas-mix recipe and decompression schedule," Brockman said. "It's not from any table. I know deep water, and I know my body." The old diver handed the Tender a piece of paper. On it was a handwritten decompression schedule about two and a half hours long. "I estimate eighteen minutes on bottom. Then two-plus hours of decompression water stops with the right gas mix and I'll be on deck before sun up. Before the Barge Superintendent is out of bed."

"I've never worked a dive like this," the Tender said.

"Nobody has," Brockman said, suddenly smiling.

"It would be smarter to make a dry run in daylight."

"Not possible. It's a bastard jump."

They went outside next to the ocean. Brockman had tagged and labeled the levers and switches to make everything as simple as possible for Jonah. The Dive Supervisor also showed the Tender the small portable communication box he'd set up and the voice unscrambler—this made it possible to understand a man talking while breathing helium.

"Do you understand what to do?"

"Yes," Jonah said. "But I still don't like it. If something goes wrong..."

"You were just following orders."

The old diver placed his helmet over his head with the fluid ease of a veteran and snapped it to his neck dam and started breathing surface-supplied air. He switched the light on his helmet on and gave his Tender a thumbs-up.

Jonah hesitated, then returned the gesture.

The Dive Supervisor jumped into the sea, and the Tender fed out the umbilical and hot water hoses as fast as he could.

The old diver went down fast.

The line tied to his fishnet sack went out equally fast, its spindle spinning quickly.

After a minute Brockman's voice spoke over the communication box.

"Stop giving me slack. I'm ready for heliox."

"Roger that. Here it comes." The Tender turned the lever for the helium-oxygen mix and waited.

The old diver spoke, but his voice was distorted by the helium. He sounded like Mickey Mouse.

Jonah turned on the voice unscrambler so he could understand Brockman.

"Say that again."

"Give me slack and turn on the hot water," the old diver said. "I'm going down."

"Roger. Here comes slack. Here comes the hot water."

Brockman descended very quickly, and Jonah threw out coil after coil of the big pile of umbilical and hot-water hoses.

Somebody tapped the Tender on the shoulder and startled him. He turned to see who it was.

"Where is *HE*?" the Idiot Rigger said.

"Check the dive control shed," Jonah said, covering for Brockman.

The Idiot Rigger started to say something but stopped. He briefly watched the Tender throwing the umbilical and hot-water hoses into the ocean, then stared at the spindle of the fishnet sack line, spinning out line. "I know where *HE* is," the Idiot Rigger said as he walked off.

"Stop giving me slack," Brockman's voice said over the communication box several minutes later. He was breathing heavily. "Switch me to the heliox-nitrogen mix."

The Tender switched the gasses and listened to the old diver's breathing. The man sounded ragged.

"Are you okay?"

"Fine," Brockman said. "Going all the way down."

Jonah threw more hose overboard and the old diver went to the bottom of the ocean.

The Tender stood in the dark holding the umbilical steady for about twenty minutes. He watched the waves undulate and splash and a bright corona form about the moon. What he was doing didn't seem quite real—tending Aleck Brockman in the middle of the night on a dive to 590 feet. The old diver's breathing didn't sound human over the communication box. It sounded more like somebody shoveling icy snow: a slow, rasping scrape followed by a release of weird gurgling bubbles, then another slow, rasping scrape and another release of bubbles.

Jonah looked around and the only person nearby was Escargot. He still sat on his empty drum in front of the saturation chamber.

"I'm coming up. Get Escargot to help," Brockman said. He sounded exhausted.

The two Tenders pulled the old diver up.

They stopped ten times for decompression stops.

The decompression lasted two and a half hours, and Jonah changed gas mixes as Brockman instructed.

At 5:07 a.m. the old diver came out of the ocean.

He climbed slowly up the ladder and stumbled onto the deck. Jonah helped take off his dive helmet.

When the helmet lifted off Brockman's head the old diver's face looked white-blue, like sculpted marble. Except there was blood on his lips and a look of pain on his face. The writing tablet hanging from his harness was filled with numbers.

"You don't look good," Jonah said.

"I'm fine," Brockman said gruffly.

"I'll get the first-aid kit," Escargot said.

"No you won't," the Dive Supervisor snapped.

"You've got blood on your lips. I think you have an embolism," Jonah said.

"I'm fine. My body always does this to me," Brockman said. He shivered as if cold, but he was starting to sweat. Small beads appeared across his forehead.

Brockman swore under his breath and limped into his dive shed, leaving a trail of wet footprints.

Jonah followed him. "Do you need help?"

"No," Brockman said angrily. He began changing out of his dive gear and back into his topside work clothes. The old diver's hands visibly shook as he took off his harness.

Jonah stood in the entranceway to the dive shed watching him. The Dive Supervisor looked vulnerable, almost delicate, but still himself. Like a grizzled old man who'd once been an Olympic wrestling champion.

"You gonna leave me alone, or what?" Brockman said testily. Like he didn't want anyone seeing him in this condition.

"Not until I'm sure you don't have decompression sickness."

The Dive Supervisor sighed with frustration. "I appreciate your being professional. Doing your job properly and to the detail. But at my age, after all the deep dives I've done, after all the times I've had the bends, it takes my body a while to recover from any dive, regardless of how deep. I always tremble, and I always aggravate my back. Sometimes I lose feeling and some control of my legs for a while. But it comes and goes even on the best days, whether I'm diving or not. So this is normal for me. I'll be back to my usual singing and dancing tomorrow. So don't give it another thought. If I have a real problem, I'll send for you and you can decompress me. Okay?"

"All right," Jonah said, still staring at Brockman. His limbs still trembled and his face dripped sweat.

"See what you have to look forward to," the old diver said with disgust. "Now get back to work."

Jonah left the dive control shed frustrated. He wanted to talk to Brockman about the dive, but it was out of the question. Did he get done what he needed to do? What did the ocean look like at 590 feet? Did he see anything?

The old diver confided in nobody.

Soon after sunrise Jonah saw the Dive Supervisor walk away from the control shed towards the doorway that led to his private quarters. He limped and staggered like a drunk and yelled at the Idiot Rigger when he tried to help him.

Moments later the Idiot Rigger walked up to Jonah. "Hey, *HE* said for you to give me dat net sack."

"What?"

"I have to git dat net sack, me. I lose cards. *HE* said I could have back my paycheck if I clean it, me. And Nelson. Make us a good deal, him." The Idiot Rigger was now happy.

Jonah went to the yellow line he had tied to the handle of Brockman's net sack and hauled it quickly to the surface. If there was anything in it, it was too light to notice as he pulled it up. With a splash he pulled the sack out of the sea. At first the dripping mesh appeared empty, but Jonah abruptly cried out and dropped the sack. Something had hurt the back of his hand. It had bitten or stung him. His hand felt on fire.

"What the hell is that?" he asked angrily to no one in particular.

"Don't know," the Idiot Rigger said. "*HE* wants it. I clean it, me and da galley hand, Nelson. Git our paychecks back. Mail to him. Be rich."

The Idiot Rigger bent down on one knee and untied the line to the sack. He cautiously grabbed the handle of the sack and started off with it.

"Wait a minute," Jonah called. He jogged over and looked in the sack. Three blood-red sea urchins lay at the bottom. He had never seen their type before. Their bodies were the size of grapefruits and their needle-thin spines were long and white at the tips. The urchins were feebly trying to rotate their venomous spines through the mesh. Jonah held his hand up in front of his eyes. The tip of an urchin spine was embedded in the back of his hand. He could see the long barb under his skin. His hand would throb for two days until the urchin's venom wore off.

CHAPTER THIRTY-SEVEN

LA GRÂCE DE DIEU

As the new day passed, Jonah brought the egret fresh water every time he came on deck after a meal; to his amazement he discovered that he was not alone. Other workers had also noticed her and harbored some silent affection for her. First only the Idiot Rigger joined his attempts to aid the wasting bird. Then, surprisingly, other men revealed a tacit admiration and a desire to save her. A few Welders, a few Riggers, and a galley hand surreptitiously began placing silver baitfish caught off the barge and bits of shrimp donated by the cooks at her feet next to Jonah's cups of water.

Through the shared cause, he met and became friendly with some of the other men. Besides the Idiot Rigger, who had taken it upon himself to latch on to Jonah, he met a paunchy galley hand named Nelson, the one with false teeth. Nelson had the disconcerting habit of removing his denture plate in mid-conversation to scratch a silvery scab of psoriasis on his shoulder with his front teeth. He would casually squint and inspect his false teeth for scales, then pop the denture plate back into his mouth without missing a word.

However, the egret would not accept any of their offerings all day, no matter how fresh the fish or how large the container of fresh water. Jonah had even found a bucket and put it at her feet full of water, and Nelson had given her fish still flopping. She continued to fast and decline, growing weaker with dehydration and hunger. Her plumage lost its sheen and became soiled. By the third day she stooped disheveled instead of proudly erect and no longer raised her wings in readiness to flee at the approach of a man. The men believed she would certainly die.

Then, according to the Idiot Rigger who was the only witness, something strange and completely unexpected happened. In the middle of what would have surely been the egret's last earthly night, Brockman approached her. She allowed him to get closer to her than anyone ever had before. At first the Idiot Rigger thought the Dive Supervisor would take her by the neck and kill her, but he did not. Brockman merely whispered something in her ear and withdrew to his dive control shed. The egret stood motionless after he left, but seemed to perk up. Then she suddenly dipped her head and drank water from the bucket Jonah had left at her feet hours before. The Idiot Rigger also saw her eat the fish that Nelson had set down.

Oddly enough, as the egret slowly recovered, the pestilent mood on the *Nez Perce* began to lift, as if her well-being somehow had an influence on the hearts of the men. The work crews did not exactly become friendly, but the sharpness went out of their eyes and the anger eased from their voices. Jonah and Escargot noticed that looks from certain Riggers and Welders were no longer as hostile. And whoever had been hanging the effigies at their bunks suddenly stopped. The new attitude passed from one man to the next like a benevolent wave of the hand. Within twenty-four hours of the white bird's return, the change was conspicuous. The different work crews worked harder at their tasks and left each other alone.

After several days, the Idiot Rigger approached Jonah when he was washing a diver's boots. He mumbled some nonsense in Cajun French, which he had done more and more, usually finishing his pronouncements in rough English accented with the soft patois of the Cajuns. This time Jonah understood him to say that it was a better place because "La grâce de Dieu" had come for a visit and because HE was happy. The Idiot Rigger scratched at his peeling nose and said "HE" with emphasis and a nod toward the dive control shed.

⚓ ⚓ ⚓

The improved morale certainly seemed to coincide with the egret's return to health, but also with the resolution of a harsh disagreement over how to best remedy the divers' engineering problems and complete the tie-in to the pre-existing pipeline. Whether the men ascribed the better mood to the bird or not, it was a fact that during the passing hours the dive crew made up lost time to a degree previously thought impossible. Finishing on schedule now seemed quite likely, and finishing ahead of schedule within long reach—but only if the work continued at this new fast pace. The laborers talked hopefully of bonus pay once again.

However, with the two steps forward, they slid one step back. The Barge Superintendent, the Lead Saturation Diver, and the Day Foreman had all argued bitterly with Aleck Brockman on how best to connect the new pipeline to the existing one. They disagreed with him completely, and the dispute became hot. A great deal of money, as well as personal reputations were at stake. The Superintendent said he was going to call the oil company and have an executive fly out in a helicopter to solve the impasse. But in the end Brockman, in his fierce and resolute way, won out. With an uncanny mastery of facts, he persuaded the others. In fine detail he described the exact solution to the complicated engineering problems: providing the many precise measurements, the angles of the pipelines needing to be joined, the proper sequence of steps, and the man-hours required down to the last minute. The Lead Saturation Diver went down as a skeptic to sound out Brockman's plan, but speaking from the sea bottom he was a believer. He was astounded by the Dive Supervisor Brockman's perfect accuracy.

Everyone involved in the decision stood in the dive control shed listening to the report. The confounded Lead Diver, his voice distorted over the voice unscrambler, said, "I never seen anything like this. You bin down here Brockman? You know this site better than I do."

The Barge Superintendent jumped up from his chair and said, "You're the man, Brockman!"

However, the tension in the shed did not abate, for the Dive Supervisor Brockman sat motionless, unmoved by the conciliatory flattery. He looked straight ahead, pulling on the stubs of his missing fingers, almost as if he sat alone in the room, meditating on some distant matter.

The Barge Superintendent shook his head ever so slightly. No matter what positive occurrence took place, he would never feel comfortable around him. Something about this Dive Supervisor made him feel inferior.

The Barge Superintendent had dingy gray hair that clasped his skull like a cloth of steel fibers. He had a large head and ears, and brownish-pink cheeks scored with deep vertical furrows. He was a scrupulous man with years of experience, an engineer with a high reputation and an unflappable demeanor; and yet he had personally avoided Brockman as much as possible. Now the Barge Superintendent felt genuine relief even though the old diver had proved him wrong, because they would need to see each other less. However, he felt shame in this reaction; he was a man in the habit of seizing and maintaining control, and he realized that because of a feeling of inadequacy, he'd lost it in regards to Brockman.

Again, he hoped that the saturation diving would soon be done and Aleck Brockman would leave the *Nez Perce.*

"Maybe we'll make that bonus after all," said the Day Foreman.

"Maybe," the Barge Superintendent said looking at Brockman across the table he used for a desk, "but if we do get a bonus, it's all Brockman's doing."

"Amen to that," the Day Foreman said.

The Dive Supervisor still didn't respond or even look at them. He was brooding, now with evident hostility. It was clear to the men they were no longer welcome in his dive control shed and they got up and filed out.

The Tenders and Riggers went to work lowering a freshly built twenty-foot long welding hut undersea. It was fitted by the divers over the gap of space between the two pipelines' butt ends the divers were trying to connect. The airtight hut, once secure, was pumped full of mixed gas to create a dry rectangular welding room at the bottom of the ocean housing the pipeline ends. Then a twelve-foot, three-inch section of pipe was cut on deck true to Brockman's specifications and lowered into the sea.

The divers on bottom unhooked the crane slings and brought the pup joint under the dry welding hut and up inside. They fitted it snugly between the two pipe ends, thus joining them, and locked it in place with lineup clamps. After the pipes had dried enough for a good weld, the two divers certified as Welders entered the dry hut and welded it all together. The saturation divers performed this complex and laborious tie-in job at a depth of 590 feet in record time. The new pipeline was at last connected to the preexisting one.

Brockman had amazingly anticipated and nullified each possible setback before it could occur. Now, if the saturation divers' work tested true, they would start their long decompression and, along with Brockman, would soon be leaving the barge.

All this while, Jonah and his friends continued to feed and water the egret. She was now tame and healthy and becoming radiant in her whiteness again.

⚓ ⚓ ⚓

Just before their shift, Jonah sat having a supper of catfish, rice, and carrots with Escargot. News about the sick blue whale played on the TV screen mounted on the wall in the galley. A reporter was interviewing a marine biologist. The scientist, a man with a beard and glasses, said: "The whale is behaving in an increasingly strange manner. There have been reports that the blue whale has been circling oil rigs, almost as if looking for something. Her behavior is atypical and unprecedented. Blue whales go north to polar waters in the summer. The whale has a respiratory infection and is disoriented . . ."

Seed swaggered into the galley and looked their way. He flashed his gameshow host smile at them, and after getting a cup of red fruit juice he joined them. Jonah had noticed that whenever Seed approached anybody, he always seemed to be looking for a way to unite them with him against others, always angling for something. Also, lately his eyes looked red and sometimes he acted jittery—like he'd started snorting meth.

Today the psycho munched his pistachios, sipped his fruit juice, and pressed his idea that if there was to be a break-out dive, he was the most experienced Tender and therefore should take it. Escargot was already a Diver-Tender, so Seed directed his conversation to his only competition, Jonah.

"If that bastard Brockman hadn't demoted me, I'd still be senior to you. So if one of us gets promoted, it'll be *me*. No offense, but I've got seniority. He screwed me over."

"If I'm picked, I'm taking the dive."

"I'm sorry you feel that way," Seed said, striking a false tone of fairness and patience. "We'll talk again later, when you're feeling more agreeable."

Jonah suddenly had the feeling he was being played. Sometimes the psycho's cheeks were rosy and his eyes shiny like he was about to burst out laughing. What was so damn funny?

Seed smiled and stretched, his face full of fun. There was a pink line across his upper lip from the red fruit juice.

"Hey, boys, I'm thinkin of puttin a party together when this damn job is over. I reckon a bunch of us ought to whoop it up on the crew boat going in, then head over to Orleans and find us some whores. How bout it?"

"I don't pay for sex," Escargot said.

Seed's eyes narrowed. Then an idea appeared to please him. "I've got a sweet new girlfriend. Either a you ever share a woman with a friend? She ain't really used to a bunch a men in line, but she'll learn to like it after she gets more practice. I'm looking for recruits. I need some guys like you two to help me." Seed smiled. "You guys want in?"

"No," Escargot said. Not everyone was a perv.

Jonah ignored the conversation. He didn't know exactly what the psycho was talking about, but it sounded like he meant to gangbang some girl he was seeing.

"Come on. You boys bin out at sea for months now. Don't tell me you ain't hornier than hell."

Jonah suddenly felt like fighting. "Are you looking to get hurt? Or are you just stupid?"

The psycho laughed and slapped his hands on the table. Like everything he'd said was only a joke he'd been playing on pals, just to get a rise out of them, and Jonah had just said the punch line. "But you're my pal!" he said with melodramatic glee.

Jonah looked back down at his plate. The food had lost all attraction now. He was trying not to lose his temper and smash Seed in the face, but everything seemed to be speeding up.

"Sorry, I don't mean nothin by it. Just foolin with you boys," Seed said.

"Get the hell out of here."

Escargot, chewing carrots, smiled orange.

"What did you say?" The psycho's face darkened. He leaned closer. His eyes widened.

"You need me to write it out for you? But then you'd have to read."

Seed seemed barely able to restrain himself. Jonah watched him carefully in case he took a swing. He really wanted the ugly prick to try. The psycho seemed to notice that, and his face took on a false smile.

"Here I am, just havin fun with you-all. And you tell me to get out?"

"That's right, sunshine."

Escargot guffawed and sprayed a few carrot pieces. He was enjoying the moment.

A queer look: a mix of sudden recognition and incandescent malice bloomed on Seed's face. A new line had been crossed.

He stood up. "Friends are hard to come by. One day I might have to save your life down there in the blue. Remembering how you shucked me off might affect my skill."

Then Seed slithered out of the room.

"Man, that boy's crazier than a shit-house rat," Escargot said.

Jonah couldn't eat now and pushed his plate aside.

Activity on the *Nez Perce* had ceased for hours as everyone waited anxiously to see if the pipeline and tie-in were good. If they were, then the barge could move forward into shallower seas and lay the next forty miles. If not, the laborers would have to go back and fix whatever was wrong, and would certainly fail to earn bonuses.

A few tables down from their table, men began arguing. "No, you git it! I bin out at sea on different jobs now for nearly two fuckin months. All I want is a nap and a piece a ass, and not necessarily in that order!" a Welder said.

"If you wanna put food on da table, and feed yo kids, you do what da man says. You do it as long as he says. And you like it," said someone else bitterly.

The Day Foreman with the strawberry nose and melanoma spot walked in through the cafeteria door. All eyes went to him and everyone stopped talking. Someone's fork fell to the floor and rattled still.

"Back to work," he said to the Welders. "The pig come out of the trap!" Which meant the Divers and Welders may have actually accomplished their tasks.

The Welders burst out in whoops and high-fives, and Jonah felt a surge of energy.

"All right!" Escargot said.

So the job was closer to being done. A sizing pig—a special plug usually made of polyurethane foam or steel—had been pressured miles through the entire length of the new pipeline and through the tie-in and into a pig trap. The men knew that their work on the pipeline up to this point and the tie-in was sound. The test told them that the pipeline's internal diameter had not been compromised by a buckle, a dent, or a dangle of welding bead which could hang like an obtrusive steel icicle inside. Now the barge could start laying pipe again, and bonuses were once more within reach.

CHAPTER THIRTY-EIGHT

BONUS PAY

The deck erupted with activity. The jackhammer cacophony of engines fired up, sweaty Riggers rushed about hauling pipe, cranes pivoted and their swing horns sounded. All three welding stations crackled with blinding light and smoke, and the *Nez Perce* resumed its determined crawl across the waves, creaking and pulling itself forward by its anchor winches. The barge moved slowly into shallower water—now 422 feet—and lowering the pipeline became less difficult.

While Jonah worked he watched a pair of swarthy Riggers fix slings around a pipe joint. This done, they stood back, one man holding the tag-line. Turning carefully on its base, the crane reeled the pipe skyward, then lowered the joint into position on the pipeline assembly ramp running down the starboard side of the *Nez Perce*. Two other Riggers accepted it and loaded the forty-foot-long sections of pipe flush on the pipeline ramp's large rubber-covered rollers, called "shoes." Welding crews standing at three different stations, spaced forty feet apart along the ramp, then went to work.

The ends of each pipe joint measured twenty-four inches in diameter and were beveled and left bare for welding. The rest of every pipe's forty-foot length had been previously painted with a green anti-corrosive known as the "dope coat" and encased in a three-and-a-half inch shell of concrete. Each section of pipe weighed twelve tons.

The two Welders at the first station on the *Nez Perce* deck, on opposite sides of the pipeline, brought their face shields down with sharp downward shakes of their heads. They told their helpers to turn on the power, then leaned into the pipes in concentration. With the tips of their welding stingers they struck blue electric arcs to begin welding the pipes together.

Acrid smoke rose from the blinding blue light and crackling heat. After the men welded together the entire circumference of the pipe ends, they cleared the scoria off with peanut grinders until the seam buffed clean. They raised their visors over sweaty faces and looked to be sure that they had each laid a perfect steel bead: one resembling silver pennies resting sideways and evenly spaced in the fashion of fallen dominoes all the way around.

After the first weld, or "root pass," the joined pipes were rolled aft along the *Nez Perce* to the next station, where the second set of Welders put on the filler bead.

At the last welding station workers welded the capping bead. The point of union of the two pipe ends, now called a field joint, next had to be X-rayed for cracks or imperfections. Once approved, men rolled the field joint further aft to the last station at the stern.

At the dope station, dope hands painted the field joint with the green anti-corrosive, then wrapped sheet metal around it and poured hot tar inside the sheet metal. Now the joint was ready to be rolled down the stinger into the ocean.

The laborers would build and install the whole ninety-mile pipeline in this painstaking manner, one forty-foot joint at a time. And before oil could be run through it, the pipeline had to be checked internally for blockages or cracks by pressuring a sizing pig through its entire length.

Jonah looked up as the horn on the bridge tower blasted once again with a shrill call that marked the pipeline's progress every forty feet. The men laid into the job to win their bonuses.

Jonah checked on the divers in the saturation unit. They had begun a decompression treatment that would continue for almost a full week before they could be safely released from the musty, crowded chamber. One of them read a paperback on his cot, two played cards, and the fourth stared with profound boredom at the curved white walls of the saturation chamber.

Jonah felt like a prison guard.

⚓ ⚓ ⚓

The Tenders continued looking after the decompressing saturation divers but now had the additional responsibility of routinely checking the 180-foot-long stinger. The stinger lowered the pipeline undersea and looked like a steeply angled, trellised conveyor-belt.

Once in the morning and once at dusk, one of the Tenders dived into the ocean and swam and pulled himself through the everpresent school of silver baitfish living under the *Nez Perce* and down the stinger's length. First he checked that the giant steel fingers holding the stinger to the barge were all engaged, then that each of the hydraulic and air hoses properly connected to the pontoons, and lastly that all of the rollers on the ramp were working. If the stinger didn't correctly support the pipeline, it would buckle or break. The strong ocean current made the work exhausting.

Kip, the yellow Tender, wasn't yet ready to dive again, particularly at the same site where he'd dropped out of control and defecated in his wetsuit on his first dive weeks earlier. Everyone remembered how he panicked and nearly died in the cold darkness. The memory wasn't lost on the man either, and he stared at the ocean with a mixture of loathing and ambivalence. This place had bad karma.

Seed happily took every twilight dive at the end of the day shift. More money for him, and nobody would notice that he was cranked.

Jonah and Escargot alternated in the mornings at the end of the night shift, and days went by.

CHAPTER THIRTY-NINE

FIREWORKS IN THE SEA

Two hours before dawn a steady salt breeze blew in from the oceanic darkness and over the *Nez Perce*. Seconds after discovering the problem, Brockman called Jonah and Escargot to fix the stinger. The underwater rollers on the stinger weren't supporting the pipeline evenly. One of the vent valves at the end of the pontoon had jammed open and flooded its compartment.

Jonah had to swim out and close the valve with a crescent wrench.

Cloud cover blotted out all the stars. The sea's surface rolled opaque black but randomly flickered with bioluminescence as patches of intense color broke out, near and far, in short, magical bursts like winking blue embers. The phenomenon, caused by light-emitting plankton, made the impervious black ocean fleetingly lucent as you looked downward.

Jonah put on his weight belt. The waves crashed loudly onto the pipeline ramp, and the concrete-encased pipeline bounced up from the ramp then came back down with crushing weight. The massive steel fingers locking the stinger to the barge held fast against the rushing power of the sea.

The spindrift lit up with a glowing spray of greenish turquoise. In slow motion the spray dropped from the air, with an after-flash on the men's retinas, and landed on the foam receding down the pipeline ramp, which also sparkled green. The plankton in the waves flashed back and forth, and their small blasts of brilliant color in one area seemed to trigger responses all over the water like competing marine fireworks shows.

Jonah put on the helmet and checked the Super Q flashlight mounted on top. Then he turned the free-flow valve and blasted air into the helmet to clear a slight fogging. He felt for his knife and the crescent wrench to be sure they were tied to the D-rings on his harness.

Escargot stood ready to feed out the umbilical hose.

"I'm set," Jonah said into the microphone in his helmet. He had checked the stinger several times in the morning light, but never in the dark and never in a sea alive with the flashing glow and dazzle of millions of light-emitting plankton.

"Remember, stay away from the ramp and keep track of your umbilical hose. You don't want to get sucked between the pipeline and stinger," Brockman warned.

"Roger that," Jonah said. "I'm jumping." He switched on the headlight on his helmet.

"Okay," Brockman said.

Jonah jumped and immersed downwards.

He arrived with a rush of coolness and bubbles in a fantastic pelagic cosmos where he could touch the stars. The ocean ignited cold molten blue with his entry.

Each stroke of his arms and kick of his legs caused the plankton to fire. A multitude of flashes broke out near him, then far off as if in answer, patterned like fluid constellations.

He swam immediately away from the strong suck and push of the waves near the lethal pipeline ramp. Blue-green flashes raked through his fingers, pressed up against the lens of his helmet, and rolled over him. He concentrated hard not to lose his bearings in the wonder and dazzle of the bioluminescence around him.

"It's incredible down here."

"I know," Brockman said.

When Jonah at last held the guideline in his hand, he paused. The surreal flashing slowed and stopped, and now the ocean flowed utterly black all around him. Below his dangling fins a black abyss waited. He started down underneath the declining stinger and the bioluminescence started again.

Facing upwards, like an insect crawling on the bottom side of a tree branch, he pulled himself deeper along the guideline.

Above him the pontoon and rollers waved with the current. He watched to see that the pipeline was riding steady on each set of rollers, that there was no space between them.

The marine lights, the bioluminescence, kept shooting off around him and the stinger as it moved with the sea. Because he couldn't see it, Jonah could ignore the drop under him.

"I'm on it," he said having reached compartment 19.

"How's the pipe riding?" Brockman asked.

"Looks all right up to here. The pipe isn't sitting on the rollers here. The compartment is definitely flooded."

"Close that vent and move back," the Dive Supervisor said.

"Roger."

Jonah felt across his harness for the lanyard tied to his crescent wrench. Before turning the valve, he positioned himself safely behind and down current of the vent. In deep water all vents are capable of sucking the flesh off a diver's hand or trapping him to it. He wrenched the valve shut and told Brockman.

On the barge the Dive Supervisor turned a lever on the control console and blew the flooded compartment full of air.

The compartment became buoyant and that section of the stinger floated upwards. All of the stinger's rollers pressed back up under the heavy pipeline, once again evenly cradling and supporting it on its way to the sea floor.

"It's set back down on the rollers," Jonah reported.

"Good," Brockman said.

"Take in my slack. I'm coming back."

"Roger that."

Jonah started back up. Again, the plankton gave off their cold, flameless fire as his passage disturbed them. Every little motion, from his turning the valve with the wrench to the flick of a fin, set them off.

A small medusa-like jellyfish knocked softly against his lens. A blue glow revealed its gelatinous body and threads of cilia-like spun glass. He approached the point on the stinger where he would let go and have Escargot haul him safely past the banging at the ramp.

The baitfish living under the barge suddenly closed around him in a skittish confusion of silver bodies and crazy light.

Jonah instinctively stopped moving. The school of fish hovered still, and the spangles around them slowly went out.

The sweep of a vortex hit him as something large swam by. A hunting shark?

A flurry of silver and blue-green coruscations broke out and the school of fish bolted in a contagious panic that even he felt.

The school of fish raced over him and the stinger and pipeline, wheeling in a big circle, back under his feet, thousands of fish, and round again. Like an unearthly Ferris wheel in the black deep, sparkling bioluminescence.

A flaming blue javelin chased the fish from below.

Racing past his feet.

He gasped.

"What's wrong?" Brockman asked.

"Something's feeding."

"Did you see him?" the Dive Supervisor sounded oddly enthusiastic.

"Yes." Jonah could feel his heart beating.

"You're not a fish, don't sweat it. They only eat fish unless you're dead or in a chum slick."

The dazzling maelstrom left him and whirled deeper, perhaps 50 feet below.

The confused cloud of flashing blue-green scattered like chips of sapphirine mica then reunited.

The long, wide javelin of blue flame ripped through the darkness into them, turned sharply and circled.

It moved with powerful lateral sweeps of its tail. The plankton glowed brightly around the roil of baitfish and the prowling javelin.

Then the darkness closed in again.

"You all right?" Brockman asked. "You're breathing fast."

"I'm fine."

The javelin, trailing wisps of bioluminescence, shot by again, diving deep. It disappeared like a meteor, gone in a sudden streak.

⚓ ⚓ ⚓

After breakfast Jonah brought a fresh bucket of water for the egret. In the mornings she usually stood in her favorite shaded spot. At night she wandered about the *Nez Perce* and sometimes flew up to the helipad. Now friendly enough to take fish from a man's hand.

In the late afternoon Jonah worked out with the weights on the second landing and ran up and down the tower stairs for thirty minutes. He planned to call Olene and wanted to clear his head with fast blood and oxygen. He needed the feeling of liberation, of being set right and steady, which came from good exercise. And he needed to stay ready for Seed. Never know what the psycho would do.

Afterward, Jonah went up the stairs to the bridge to make the call. Fresh sweat trickled over his face and stung his eyes as he held the receiver. The telephone rang four times.

"Yellow Catfish," Olene's *grandmère* said.

"Hi, this is Jonah. Can I talk to Olene, please?"

"No, she's not taking phone calls."

"I sent her a letter. Do you know if she got it?"

"If she did, she'll probably write you one back."

"Is she sick?"

"Goodbye." The old lady hung up.

Leaving him to stare into the dead phone.

CHAPTER FORTY

YELLOW TROLL

The last day of the saturation divers' decompression, the Inspection Team following the *Nez Perce* ran into trouble. These men worked for a separate company and never set foot on the *Nez Perce*. The Inspection Vessel had followed the pipe-lay barge from the beginning of the job to visually inspect the on-bottom pipeline for any cracks or buckles that might have occurred during delivery to the ocean floor. To do this, technicians used a small, sophisticated, unmanned submarine, a Remotely Operated Vehicle—or ROV. It was the size of a man and looked like a swimming eye. The inspectors called it Yellow Troll. The technicians, seated before a TV monitor, operated the submarine using joysticks. As Yellow Troll glided over the undersea pipeline, it transmitted a live image from its electronic eye.

Aside from the submarine technicians, the inspection crew consisted of two divers who were needed in case the very long umbilical hose caught on something undersea. On this day the long umbilical attaching Yellow Troll to the ocean surface had become tangled with an unidentified sunken wreck next to the pipeline, and for the second day in a row both inspection divers were sick with the flu.

Rather than waste time flying out another diver, the inspection team asked to borrow the best Tender on the barge to free up Yellow Troll's umbilical. The wreck rested at a depth of 293 feet, which was too deep for an entry level Tender.

Brockman intended to give Escargot the job because he was already a Diver-Tender and the most senior. A quick call to the dive company back onshore cleared the way—turned out the company needed more qualified divers.

The Dive Supervisor promoted Jonah.

Brockman called Seed into the dive control shed over the loudhailer. The Tender strutted in, then struck a pose of seriousness and readiness.

"What's up, boss?"

Brockman looked up from the paperwork on his desk. He fixed his eyes on the Tender. "Wake up Jonah and Escargot. There's a job on the inspection boat."

"Jonah's breaking out?"

"Yes," Brockman said.

"What the fuck?" Seed angrily scuffed his boot heel on the shed floor.

"Don't stand there like an idiot. Wake them up." Brockman got slowly to his feet.

"Hey, boss, I'm senior to Jonah. Let me take the jump." Seed smiled and showed his teeth.

"Not you." Brockman pointed at him with his mutilated hand. Like sticking a crab in his face again. Seed kept smiling, waiting.

The Dive Supervisor looked for a long moment at the pyscho. He shook his head sideways, then moved quickly towards him. "Get out."

Seed stopped smiling and rushed out of the shed. He was furious that he had not been picked for the break-out dive, not even for the backup position. He had suffered a lowering in status ever since Renoir died and Jonah and Escargot arrived. Even the number of topside laborers chummy with him had dropped off. As the barge made headway on the job and the work crews got along better, his popularity had declined. Most would rather sleep or go fishing than listen to his obscene stories.

Brockman had screwed him over again.

Seed turned the lever and opened the oval door leading below to the living quarters. He trotted down a set of stairs and turned right at the first passageway. A dark, shabby hall. Before he went into the Tenders' quarters, he touched the knife in his pocket. Maybe it was time.

"I don't know what kind a shit you pulled, Jonah. And you, Escargot, but I'll even up sooner than later," he said while shaking Jonah awake. The room was pitch dark. The two off-duty Tenders had been asleep for four short hours.

Seed leaned over Jonah.

He could cut the son of a bitch's neck.

He shook him again, harder this time.

Jonah woke up with the psycho's hands near his throat.

He kicked his feet in front of him and nearly busted Seed's jaw.

The psycho jumped back.

"What are you talking about?" Escargot asked groggily from above.

"You, Jonah, have been picked to break-out." Seed said bitterly. "A heliox jump to 293 feet. The ROV's hung up and their divers are sick or something. You know if Brockman hadn't screwed me over it'd be mine. I'm warnin you, don't take it. You go out and tell Brockman it's mine!"

Jonah pushed the psycho back from the bunk, almost ripping off the privacy curtain, and punched Seed in the mouth.

Seed grunted and fell to one knee. He spit one tooth out, then another.

"Musserfucher," Seed slurred.

The psycho came swinging back and threw a savage right that missed.

Jonah shot in on him like a wrestler. He grabbed Seed by the torso and jammed him up against the bulwark with his shoulder.

The psycho tried to work his right hand into his hip pocket for his knife, but Jonah tightened his gut-wrench hold on him and trapped that arm.

Seed clutched and twisted Jonah's tee shirt, trying to push him off.

Escargot, naked except for green underwear, jumped down from his bunk with a slap of bare feet and switched on the lights.

The sudden glare stopped the fight.

Jonah had one of the psycho's arms trapped to his waist, about to hip-toss him face first into the floor, but stopped.

They wanted to fight, but neither wanted to lose his job and be arrested.

Jonah pulled himself back in. "Wait until we hit the beach you dumb bastard."

The psycho relaxed his hold on Jonah's tee shirt.

"If you make it to the beach, you sorry son of a bitch." Seed spat through the gap in his front teeth. His mouth was full of blood and it dripped over his lips and chin.

Jonah pushed him away.

Seed spit blood on the floor, then crouched down to pick up his teeth. They were perfectly intact, roots and all.

"Nice punch," Escargot said. "You must have nailed him right on the gumline. Is your hand messed up?"

Jonah looked at his scraped knuckles. They were beginning to swell. "No."

Escargot couldn't resist slapping Seed on the back of the head and laughing at him as he left the room. "Don't forget to brush your teeth tonight."

CHAPTER FORTY-ONE

A COLOSSAL FACE

A line squall formed as Jonah and Escargot rode on the tugboat back to the Inspection Vessel. A gale stirred up high waves and low dark clouds blanketed the sky; the wake at the bow broke in a glassy blue "V," and behind the tugboat Jonah saw the *Nez Perce* ringed with foam. The clouds burst open in a downpour, thrashing the surface of the sea into white froth and fresh water, and the inspection vessel bounced in the squall now two miles behind the *Nez Perce*.

Jonah borrowed a blue SuperLite dive helmet and a full half-inch wetsuit from one of the sick divers on the inspection vessel. The sick diver, a mustached man named Withrow, sat hunched forward in a chair at the vessel's dive station. He had a pained expression, but still managed to smoke a cigarette. His face looked green and he held a bucket between his knees. Apparently the other diver was worse off and lay below suffering in his rack. Supposedly they had the flu, but Jonah thought Withrow smelled hungover.

Jonah didn't care if the man was half drunk—Withrow could talk coherently and Escargot would tend and serve as the standby diver—because his moment had finally arrived. His *break-out* dive, his promotion to better work and more money for deeper dives: *depth pay*. He would willingly risk a lot more than usual to see it through.

Still smoking cigarettes, Withrow briefed Jonah and Escargot on the situation. "Follow the ROV's umbilical straight down. You'll find the robot near bottom. Looks like a big eye with headlights on either side. We call it Yellow Troll. Don't touch the propellers. It has handles on it. Grab it that way." He finished the meeting by saying, "It's your lucky day, pal. This is a gravy dive. Down and back, no sweat."

Jonah dressed in the pouring rain for the deepest dive of his career. He pulled on the borrowed wetsuit—his own was only a quarter-inch thick, and it would be cold down there. This one would keep him warm. Escargot duct-taped Jonah's boots to the wetsuit legs. He might need to walk on the wreck.

Next, he put on his harness and Escargot tied an extra flashlight and knife to the D-rings; the Inspection Team wasn't exactly sure what Yellow Troll's umbilical hose was caught on, and Jonah wanted to be sure he had a good cutting blade. He put on the borrowed helmet and fit his face into the oral/nasal regulator—it smelled of cigarette smoke. He tested the communication system, and it worked fine.

It was still raining hard when Jonah jumped.

The bubbles mushroomed and clouded past, as always, and the ocean swept in and gathered under him. This time he wasn't swimming at a declining angle as on the stinger, but going straight down.

Jonah pulled himself down Yellow Troll's umbilical hose into the turbid emptiness.

Bellied out in the current, the remote control submarine's umbilical slanted down out of sight only 40 feet away. Yellow Troll was tangled far below, on the bottom of the ocean, and he could not see it or anything else. Just open water.

Poor visibility today.

"Stop up. You're at 50 feet. Time for gas," Withrow said. "Turn on your free flow."

"Roger. All stop." Jonah turned the valve on the side of the helmet and air began rasping into the helmet. "Free flowing," he reported.

He hung off Yellow Troll's long snaking umbilical hose to the surface and waited. He looked up at the surface, a silvery canopy blurred and convoluted with wave action.

He was going to 293 feet and would certainly suffer Nitrogen Narcosis unless he breathed mixed gas.

"Okay, give me a count," Withrow said.

"One, two, three, four, five, six, seven . . ." The mix of helium and oxygen came gushing through the umbilical. Coming through the hose it sounded different: lighter, and tasted thin and strange. Jonah's voice became high-pitched and cartoonish because of the helium. "Eight, nine, ten. All set," he squeaked. Topside put his voice through an unscrambler to understand him.

"Roger that. Go ahead if you're ready," Withrow said.

"Going down."

Below 40 feet, the depth filtered out red wavelengths of light and the sea looked bleak and grayer blue.

While descending, Jonah swallowed to make his ears pop and clear.

The nether world rose up to his lens with cathedral quietude and solemnity.

For what seemed a long time he heard absolutely nothing but his own breath. His regulator hissed as he sucked in gas and rumbled with bubbles as he exhaled: a familiar and repeating *hiss* and *whoosh*.

The cold murk seemed to upwell into him faster than he could sink, so that at times there was an illusion of hovering, but he dropped lower and lower.

Bright color steadily drained away to dim twilight.

Suddenly, it seemed like dusk.

Jonah continued down Yellow Troll's umbilical.

For a little while everything looked the same, but then he reached a new level, a new kind of color blue that he'd never seen before. Perhaps it looked that way because his eyes were adjusting and becoming more sensitive, but it was an eerie, darker blue, and dense. He flew into it and through it, and felt its chill.

The blue-black layer smothered over him, it came at him and into him, swallowed him up. It was so peculiar and intense, that Jonah didn't know where he was for a second and stopped descending.

He gripped Yellow Troll's umbilical hose and hung in an incomprehensible place: a blue-black vacuum, a shuddering abyss. He looked up and could only tell it was up because it was faintly brighter in that direction and his bubbles rose. He squeezed the umbilical in his hand and feeling it triggered him into action. He'd better get back to work.

Jonah continued down and watched the blue darkness coming up to his lens, charging like the blackness in a subway tunnel. Then everything changed again.

The ocean seemed to thicken below him and cloud up, becoming even darker all of a sudden.

Suspended in the sea were fragments of slowly sinking specks of plankton, diatoms, fecal pellets, sand granules. The deep seemed enshrouded with one filmy layer after another; gray billowy curtains filigreed with flakes and dots; gelid curtains that parted and closed behind him like whirls of snow in a blizzard.

"Are you good?" Withrow asked and his voice sounded as if he were talking to Jonah from a satellite in orbit.

"Yep."

"Let me know if you start to feel weird. Anything at all, no matter how slight."

"Okay. I feel fine."

"Do you see Yellow Troll?"

"Not yet. Visibility is bad. It's snowing down here."

He dropped further and broke out of the cloud he'd been coming down through. Suddenly he could see space below him: a milky-gray liquid column thrown up by the underwater robot's dim lights. It was a small pocket of visibility surrounded by darkness.

Jonah glided down Yellow Troll's umbilical toward the light. It seemed like a porch light left on for an expected night visitor in the middle of a barren wilderness.

The shadowy outline of the wreck came gradually into view, slanting on a hump of silty ocean floor. As Jonah came down on it he could see the pipeline off its port side. He recognized the wreck as a workboat.

Yellow Troll's umbilical was ensnared between a stern davit and its rusted pulley block. The underwater robot looked like a yellow trunk with a large mechanical eye and headlights in the front. It had propellers and rudders on the back end.

"Topside, I'm on Yellow Troll." He hung vertically in the water next to it. His feet dangled just a few feet above the deck of the wreck.

"What's it hung up on?"

"A davit and pulley block on the stern."

"Take a depth reading."

"Roger."

Jonah stuck the depth-measuring hose at the end of his umbilical down as deep as he could reach.

"That's it," he said.

"You're at 278 feet. Congratulations. You're now a Diver-Tender."

Jonah felt a surge of happiness. He could handle anything right now.

"What kind of wreck is it?" Withrow asked.

"Looks like an old workboat."

The wreck sat swathed in coralline algae and a giant elephant ear sponge bloomed out from its stack like a goiter. The brownish-gray sea floor around the wreck and over to the pipeline had formed into parallel ripples and even cusps. The water was so icy it numbed Jonah's gloved fingers. The dense fall of marine snow continued very slowly, taking more time to land than Jonah could spend watching it. The flakes had piled up over centuries, forming smooth drifts across the soft swale.

"See any skeletons?" Withrow asked lightly.

"No, the deck is clear. Do I have time to check it out?"

"No. Just clear your umbilical and free up Yellow Troll."

"Roger." He tugged on his dive hose making as sure as possible that it arced away from the robot's umbilical hose. "Topside, I'm about to free it up."

"All right," Withrow said.

With one hand on a grip handle of Yellow Troll and the other on its umbilical hose, Jonah yanked it down and out from the davit and hanging pulley block.

The buoyant sub swung free.

He let go of it, and Yellow Troll floated swiftly up out of sight.

"It's clear and coming up fast," he said, now hanging from his harness.

"Good. We're bringing you up."

Escargot began pulling in Jonah's umbilical. His harness tightened and he rose. Only as he ascended from the snowy bottom did he realize how cold he had become despite the half-inch-thick wetsuit.

He made an underwater decompression stop at fifteen feet.

He swayed gently in the open water and could tell when the sun came out from behind the rain clouds. The whole ocean lit up.

Shafts of sunlight revealed layers of blue color that pulsed and moved, beating with a solar heart. The water felt strangely alive.

He sensed an awesome presence.

Just 40 feet away, the blue whale's enormous head suddenly appeared, a mythical creature from ancient seas.

Her small eye, dark and strangely beautiful, seemed to stare at him and the declining angle of her mouth made her look painfully shy. Her head was flat across the top like a massive wedge. A colossal face in a cathedral of light.

Jonah was struck dumb—he could hardly believe it.

The leviathan swam silently. The sunlight played on her titanic back and she glowed, luminous blue-gray against the dark blue sea.

The whale seemed to acknowledge Jonah.

The colossal face slowly nodded as she swam past.

How could such an enormous creature move so swiftly and so quietly?

He wanted to touch her, and extended his hand, but she wasn't close enough. The leviathan was so big that he could not see her whole body at any time—just parts of the whale. Visibility had improved to 50 feet with the sunlight, but she was much longer than that.

Her jutting pectoral fins and grooved body went flowing past, like an avalanche sweeping along. She flexed her whole body like one long, sinuous, jumbo jet-sized muscle, driving her massive self through the sea past the insect-sized diver. The largest species to have ever lived on Earth.

Finally, her flukes, nearly thirty feet tip to tip, gracefully fanned past like huge wings.

She disappeared without a trace.

Vanished as quickly and mysteriously as she had arrived.

Like a great spirit.

"Jonah, you've stopped breathing. Are you okay?"

"I just saw the blue whale." He felt numb and stunned.

After he climbed on the deck of the inspection boat he crawled into a decompression chamber for the rest of his treatment. Even though he had been underwater less than twenty minutes, the decompression time would take roughly an hour and a half, but Jonah didn't care how long it would take. He had punched through, his career was starting to take off and he'd seen the blue whale! He felt on top of the world—*if only he could talk to Olene.*

CHAPTER FORTY-TWO

A VOICE IN THE DEEP

Back on the *Nez Perce*, the saturation divers had been released from the chamber after their weeklong decompression. All four of them stood joking on the barge deck. They had emerged from the clammy saturation chamber squinting and sucking at the fresh air like prisoners coming out of solitary confinement. One of them wore a gaudy Hawaiian shirt and they all smoked cigars. They stood in the sun chatting amiably about the job.

Immediately upon release, the divers had gone to shake hands with Aleck Brockman for doing such a fine job in directing them, but were disappointed.

They could not find him.

In the beginning they had not trusted Brockman or known him. They had only met him once, very briefly, just before entering the saturation complex at the start of the job. They remembered a large intense man, standoffish and stony-faced. They knew about the Dive Supervisor's background in the North Sea and had heard the rumor that he once killed a dive partner. They had entrusted their lives to Brockman with great reluctance. Now that the end of the job had arrived they still didn't know Aleck Brockman, but they trusted him absolutely.

Over the course of the job, when they were incarcerated and under tremendous pressure, the Dive Supervisor had entered their minds constantly. He sounded in their ears all the time as a companion, as a peculiar intelligence. His was an uncanny voice that spoke in their helmets, in the dive bell, and in the saturation chamber; a deceptive rough voice that they could now only associate with the darkness of the ocean floor.

While the saturation divers had traveled up and down in the dive bell and scampered and crawled in the absolute and unending night 590 feet beneath the ocean, Brockman talked continuously to them, his voice always penetrating their isolation. It had directed them: cajoling them when exhausted, admonishing them when they were careless, but most of all deftly explaining things to them in a rough manner that made them understand. His all-knowing voice had been there throughout the weird nights and had taken on a surreal quality. No other Dive Supervisor in their experience had ever described for them with such expertise, let alone guessed at or understood, the peculiar visions and sounds of the deep, or given instructions as precise as his. Brockman had been able to warn them of unforeseen dangers, and his voice spoke out of the darkness with an astounding knowledge of what the darkness hid.

On a personal level, Brockman somehow understood each of their dispositions. He handled each diver differently and they all grew to respect his authority. He detected their private fears, their personal hurdles, and defused and rested them without once causing embarrassment or even seeming to raise the subject.

He made them all better divers, and they knew it. Most of all, more than any other Dive Supervisor, Brockman gave the impression that he really was down there in the midnight depths with them. They never felt alone.

So they were very disappointed to find Brockman's quarters empty. The Dive Supervisor had apparently cleared out the minute his job was done, without saying goodbye to anybody and without signing "OUT" with the barge clerk to indicate his leaving. Although this was not a irregular occurrence offshore, Brockman's departure started a spate of rumors and speculations. A supply boat had left the *Nez Perce* early in the morning and most workers believed that the Dive Supervisor had gone aboard. A few superstitious men quietly believed that he had never really been aboard the barge at all, that he was supernatural, a ghost, and thought he was as nearby as ever.

Unbeknownst to Jonah, many of the Riggers knew that he had tended Brockman on that clandestine night dive. The Idiot Rigger had mentioned it to a co-worker, and another story circulated among the topside laborers that Jonah had special knowledge about the Dive Supervisor.

CHAPTER FORTY-THREE

A WICKED GLITTER

O n the day after he broke out, the air felt fresher to Jonah, and the ocean rippled and undulated like a blue jewel sparkling in the sun. Brockman was gone and the saturation divers were free. The *Nez Perce* barge proceeded across the waves at a terrific clip, laying the pipeline twenty-four hours a day. The job would soon be over and bonuses were well within their grasp.

Jonah felt great, and he wanted to call Olene and tell her about the blue whale and his promotion. As a Diver-Tender on future jobs he would get more deep dives—with a $1-per-foot depth pay the money would add up—and an extra $112 a week working topside. He went up the control tower stairs.

As he walked onto the second landing a white bucket over by the barbells and weights caught his attention. It glowed in a spot of sunlight.

He went over to it.

The bucket sat full to the top with fresh water. Inside, at the bottom, rested Brockman's three sea urchins, lifeless. Most of their long reddish needles had fallen off and lay scattered like thin chopsticks about them. Their venomous spines and blood-red flesh had fallen away to reveal amazing white domes with intricate markings.

Jonah remembered the Idiot Rigger telling him that he and Nelson, the galley hand, were going to clean the urchins for the Dive Supervisor and mail them to his family. Brockman had won their entire paychecks in a game of Cajun poker and all he wanted in exchange for them were cleaned urchins.

Jonah shook his head impressed. For the first time, he saw that beneath the bristle and sting, the sea urchins were beautiful.

Smitty, the barge clerk, swiveled in his chair as Jonah walked into the control room. He rubbed an apple on the midriff of his work shirt.

"Hey, Smitty, I have to make a call," Jonah said.

Smitty tipped his baseball cap back and rubbed his forehead. "Give me the numbers." Smitty talked to the marine operator and set up the call.

Jonah pressed the receiver to his ear and waited.

The telephone started to ring.

Through the window Jonah looked down at the dive control shed. Seed stood nearby with his three Angola pals. Kip, the yellow Tender, was also next to him.

Seed broke into a dancing pantomime. He gave the finger to the dive control shed. He gave the finger to the control tower and then to the sea and the sky.

Jonah knew he would fight Seed again, and looked forward to it. He'd fix the psycho's knees so he couldn't walk for a long time.

The saturation divers with their cigars looked over at the show.

The Angola Club laughed. Seed continued his performance, and Kip clapped like an organ grinder's monkey.

The horn blasted on the tower, and the *Nez Perce* plowed forward.

"Yellow Catfish," a woman's voice said.

Was it Olene? The voice sounded very small and very soft, but a little like Olene's.

"Is that you, Olene?"

"Yes. Jonah?"

"Yes, it's me."

"Hi." Her voice grew stronger, more like herself. "Thanks for your letter. I haven't written you one back yet. I haven't been well."

"Your *grandmère* wouldn't let me talk to you when I called before."

"I was sick," she said softly. "I was raped."

Jonah started to tingle all over like he'd been hit with the bends.

It barely registered when he saw Seed grab the egret roughly by the neck.

The psycho hoisted the bird off the deck and she began trying to fly. He laughed as she frantically worked her wings. Her body was above him and her long, delicate neck was stretched down like the line of a kite.

The egret struggled to get loose.

"My God. I'm so sorry."

"It happened last month."

Jonah felt a rush like he was going to faint, then went numb and clear.

Seed pulled the egret down from the air and Kip stepped in to help subdue her.

The egret struggled wildly, flapping white wings and kicking her thin black legs. The Angola Club laughed and egged their man on.

Kip took hold of one leg and clutched for the other.

Jonah shifted anxiously, but he couldn't hang up on Olene.

"Do you know who did it?"

"No, they kidnapped me from the parking lot." Olene started to cry. "They were going to kill me, but one of them changed his mind at the last minute. He talked the others into letting me go."

Seed stretched out the egret's neck. He was hurting her.

Kip grabbed at her other leg but she kicked him in the nose with a scaled yellow foot. He let go of her and covered his face.

Jonah could not take his eyes off the horror, yet he could not leave Olene.

"They left me naked on the roadside," she said.

The flash of a dive knife, a wicked glitter in the sun. Seed meant to cut the egret's head off. He held the bird's neck with his left hand and the knife in his right.

The egret flapped up in front of him, scratching at his face with her feet.

Seed let go of her neck and grabbed a wing. He swung her down into the deck, trying to maim her.

The Angola Club clapped and shouted.

Small white feathers floated to the deck.

Now the egret waved her free wing and scrambled in a circle around Seed. He slashed at her with his knife—and bloodied the nearest wing.

Jonah wanted to cry out, but he said, "Olene, I'm so sorry. I wish there were something I could do to help you."

Kip joined in, chasing the egret with his knife, red-faced and laughing.

"Thanks for calling, but I just wasn't up to talking."

"I understand."

"I'll write you a letter," she said. "I have to go now. I've got work to do."

"Bye."

"Goodbye."

The egret suddenly broke free of the men with knives. She left two large, white feathers—tinged with blood—in Seed's fist.

The egret flew up against the wind, rising high in the sky over the barge, glowing in the sun. She turned south and raced away over the sea.

In the distance, the blue whale suddenly surfaced. A huge, long body glinted in the waves. She spouted a white jet that flared thirty feet into the sky. The spout shimmered like a rainbow in the sunlight, then evaporated into nothingness.

The egret seemed to fly right over the whale.

In seconds the majestic bird was gone.

Jonah stared out the window in disbelief and growing rage.

Seed rubbed his hands together to wipe off a bloodstained feather and did a little dance.

The sun ducked behind a cloud, and the choppy sea suddenly looked gray.

The blue whale slowly raised her flukes as she began to sound. The enormous tail hovered over the sea, dripping water, for an extended moment, almost like an omen. Then the blue whale disappeared underwater.

Kip took the egret's feathers and duct-taped them to his hard hat as a trophy. He pranced around like a fool, and the Riggers laughed and cheered.

Jonah floated down the stairs, step by step, holding the rail, moving like a sleepwalker with open, vacant eyes. He was numb; nothing had meaning to him. Near the bottom of the stairs he stopped and leaned on the rail.

Laughing voices drifted toward him.

Kip's face bobbed up before him with an idiot grin. The cowardly Tender leaned forward, tilting his hard hat down so Jonah could see the feathers.

Jonah punched him in the face, knocked him flat.

Kip's hard hat fell off and he shouted.

Jonah picked up the hat and threw it bouncing across the deck.

The barge seemed to flow and splash with sunshine like crashing waves on a beach, and somehow Jonah was seeing himself from outside of his body, from up high, but remote. Who could hurt Olene like that?

Sunshine swept over the barge and he closed his eyes against the brightness. When he opened them, Seed and the Angola Club were in front of him.

Jonah went straight for the psycho, but one of the convict Riggers tripped him up. He fell on his knees and they started kicking him.

He tried to get up but Seed, whooping with joy, kicked him in the testicles. Pain ripped through him and he nearly fogged out.

A boot came into his face and he felt somebody kicking his stomach. He had the taste of blood in his mouth.

"That's enough," Seed said. "This was just playing. We'll get him for real on the beach."

Seed looked down into Jonah's face and smiled. His gums had two scallop-shaped indentations where his teeth used to be. "How you like them apples?"

Then he felt their hands on him. They dragged him to the edge of the barge and shoved him overboard.

He fell forward and landed flat on his belly.

The ocean shot up his nose and into his mouth.

When he surfaced, Seed and the Angola Club were looking down at him and laughing.

Jonah's groin was in agony; he could barely move his legs to tread water.

"What the hell is going on!" the Day Foreman with the strawberry nose shouted as he came on the scene.

"Nothing, just fooling around," Seed said. Kip stood next to him with a big black eye growing. The trio of ex-convicts walked away.

"You-all's been fightin," the Day Foreman said to Kip.

"No sir, just roughhousing."

"My ass," the Foreman said. "How did you lose your teeth?" he asked Seed.

"I slipped on the stairs," Seed said.

"That's bullshit! What about you? You bin fightin too?" he called down to Jonah as he swam along the barge to the side ladder at the stern dive station.

"No sir, just trying to get out of their way, and I accidently fell over." There was no way in hell he was going to lose his job because of the psycho.

"Well, if I catch any a you roughhousin again, I'm citing you for fighting and sending you in."

⚓ ⚓ ⚓

Jonah climbed slowly up the ladder out of the sea. He limped down the barge in soaking wet clothes, his groin throbbing from the kick. Painful bruises were already forming on his thighs and stomach, and he had a red abrasion on his forehead.

Escargot walked into view, shaking his head. "It was real shit, man. The cook had you on the radio. Everybody heard." Then Escargot saw he was wet and roughed up. "What happened, you fall overboard on some barnacles?"

"I had some help."

"Seed and the Angola boys?"

"Yeah, I was an idiot. Tried to take them all on."

"By yourself?"

"Yeah. They tried to kill the egret."

"Oh man, what *bastards*!" Escargot shook his head. A moment later, "You want some chew?" He offered Jonah his open pouch of tobacco.

"No...well, yeah. Why not? Might as well," he said. Attacking Seed with his convict friends next to him was the dumbest thing Jonah had ever done in his life. But he knew it came out of a huge frustration and rage that Olene had been raped and that there was absolutely nothing he could do about it. He also wanted to deck the cook for eavesdropping on his conversation.

He reached into the tobacco pouch that Escargot offered. Pinching a moist lump of it between his index finger and thumb, he raised the chew to his mouth.

"That's a lot, Jonah, especially if you never chewed before. It's pretty strong stuff."

"Good." He needed to cut through the numbness.

He tucked it into his mouth, over to one side, in the trough of his left cheek.

"Thanks." It felt lumpy and uncomfortable and tasted sour.

"Yep." Escargot patted him on the shoulder and went off to work.

Jonah headed toward the Tenders' quarters to put on dry clothes.

Around the corner of gas racks and empty drums he found Kip clog dancing and prancing like Seed had done.

Kip had put his hard hat back on and found the Idiot Rigger. "How do you like my new hat?!" he asked, almost hysterical. His black eye had partially closed from the swelling. Kip saw Jonah and backed away.

The Idiot Rigger winced and turned his face. He cast his wide-set eyes down. He shook his head and looked angry, but also bitter as if he could have predicted this outcome, as if he had been forced many times before to deal with blatant evil. He glanced around, and Jonah couldn't tell whether the Idiot Rigger looked more at Kip or at the blood-tipped feathers on his hat, but his face had an expression of profound sadness.

The look came on small at first, but quickly enlarged like a bubble rising to the ocean surface, expanding and gathering dimension all the way up, defining and reshaping his reddening face and moistening eyes, then altogether evaporating into air. The Idiot Rigger contained himself and strangled the source of that expression.

CHAPTER FORTY-FOUR

A BOIL IN THE SEA

Jonah and Escargot scrubbed and cleaned the saturation chambers. Then they began burning off the welds holding the chambers to the deck. The whole system needed to ship out with the saturation divers on a crew boat that night.

The two men went back to work like everyone else, with the icy veneer of hardened professionals. After a silent hour passed, Jonah suddenly put down the burning torch and walked over to the edge of the barge. He bent over at the waist and vomited into the sea. The tobacco had made him sick.

At sunset the wind stiffened, and night rose from the east and blackened the sky. A foreboding disturbance broke out in the waves next to the *Nez Perce*. Several Welders paused at their workstations to look at the thrashing boil in the water.

A school of great barracudas encircled the baitfish living under the barge. The 'cudas drove the small fish out from under the hull and trapped them in the open. In slashing flurries the predators tore into them and devoured the small, skittish fish. The surface broke and splashed with the chase. Whatever fragments the barracudas did not eat sank like bloody tinsel to the hungry mouths of circling neighbors. The feeding continued until the predators slaughtered and devoured all the baitfish. Escargot, the diver next in line to check the stinger, discovered the school of barracudas still lurking under the barge.

Near midnight a black hammerhead shark swam along the entire length of the *Nez Perce*. It swam down the side next to the pipeline ramp and workers. Its dorsal fin stuck straight up, tall and luridly glistening under the work lights. Ten feet back was its tail, like a trailing baby. It pressed its thick body and back as high out of the sea as possible, as if trying to display itself to the men. Its powerful tail beat from side to side and churned the ocean white. Only the men on the night shift saw him.

Unlike the normal passing of an occasional shark, this giant began returning every night. Some of the Welders were so disturbed by its nagging presence that they argued over who would work on the seaward part of the pipeline. They thought the lobes of its head looked like the horns of the devil, and everyone who saw the hammerhead agreed that it was as black as the night and as long as a train.

So the black hammerhead became known as Night Train.

Jonah and Escargot hadn't seen Night Train yet and didn't believe that a black hammerhead haunted the barge. They suspected the other work crews had made it up to harass them.

Since Seed and Kip tried to kill the egret, hostilities between Tenders and Riggers had resumed. Effigies were hung from their bunks again, and Jonah found on his bunk an inflatable sex doll with the name Olene written on the forehead. And now it seemed everyone spoke about a giant shark.

⚓ ⚓ ⚓

Two days following the egret's departure, Kip stepped forward to dive. He had finally mustered the courage to try again. Jonah helped him in his decision by telling him that if he didn't have the nerve to do it, he was in the wrong profession and ought to quit.

Now that Brockman had left, Jonah and Escargot took turns supervising the dives. Ranked as Diver-Tenders, they had seniority over Seed and Kip, who were ranked as mere entry-level Tenders. The dives were simple, non-decompression inspection checks of the underwater pipe-lay ramp called the stinger.

Kip put on his helmet. The scared Tender seemed as prepared as he ever would. He had the right amount of lead on his weight belt and he knew to expect the school of barracudas under the barge.

Escargot tended the umbilical hose; Jonah stood ready as the standby diver.

Kip's job was pretty simple: a routine check of the stinger. The stinger was a submerged pipe-laying ramp, a half-open metal chute started off a few feet below the surface close to the barge. The ramp-chute then slanted down towards the sea floor like a seven-story slide, and ended abruptly. The oil pipe would fall the rest of the way to the sea bottom by itself.

Just before Kip entered the waves, the horn on the tower blasted again and more pipe was rolled aft into the sea. Oil pipe would be sliding right by him along rollers, never interrupted. Pipe after pipe, linked like a vast length of concrete intestine sliding off into the deep; with every foot sunk meaning more money in your pocket. Pipe after pipe. Get it done on time and everyone gets a bonus in his paycheck.

"It's all clear. Jump when ready," Jonah said. He had done this dive so many times that he knew exactly what Kip would experience and see moment to moment. As he sat in the dive control shed, he listened to the yellow Tender's voice and breathing through the speaker in the communication box and pictured every detail of the dive.

Kip hopped overboard.

The sea and bubbles now rushed across his lens and a great vacuum opened below. A surge of anxiety raced through him, but he would ignore it as best as he could and flounder over to the guideline.

Once he took the rope in his hand, the man wouldn't release it for anything. More than a lifeline, that string became the diver's life.

Jonah imagined Kip going down the guideline under the pipe-lay ramp, his hands aching because he was squeezing the rope so tightly. The scared Tender gazed upwards like a mechanic sliding under a car to inspect the undercarriage. Above, the pipeline occasionally lifted off and dropped back down on the steel rollers of the ramp to the rhythm of the waves.

Below, the blue deep waited.

Suddenly Kip started breathing faster, a quick rasping that came clearly through the speaker of the communication box. He was afraid of something.

Jonah pictured a delegation of barracudas silently staring at the diver.

"You doing all right?"

"Yeah, I'm figuring it out," Kip said, trying to sound confident.

The barracudas would study him with spooky, dead eyes. More of them, in single file, would glide down through the blue to watch him. Large ones, with bright silver flanks. Most of the school would remain bunched like a gigantic shimmering cloud under the barge. A mass of eyes and saber-like teeth.

"How's the pipeline look?" Jonah asked.

"Fine. A lot of barracudas down here."

"Don't worry about it."

"I'm not," he lied.

Kip grunted and pressed on. He was 42 feet deep, and halfway down the 180-foot-long stinger. Like a spider halfway down the underside of a children's playground sliding board.

A few minutes later, Jonah could tell when Kip suddenly reached the end. The diver's breathing slowed, and he sounded relieved. The pipeline had to be resting nicely on the rollers. Now all he had to do was get back to the barge.

"Topside, I'm on the end. It looks good. I'm starting back."

"Roger," Jonah said. "Good job."

Suddenly Kip held his breath.

"Shit," he whispered.

"What's wrong?" Jonah asked.

"These barracudas won't move. They're getting squirrelly on me."

"Ignore them. Push through them."

"Okay."

Kip started breathing harder.

"Get out of my way," Kip said. Talking to the barracudas. "That's right, go!"

Then Kip gasped. He started gulping air, his breathing out of control.

"What's wrong?" Jonah asked.

"*Something's* coming!"

On deck the shriek of the emergency siren blasting brought all pipe-lay operations to a sudden halt. The emergency siren meant someone had been maimed or killed.

The Barge Superintendent ran across the deck to the dive control shed. Every Welder, Rigger, Tar-Man, X-ray technician, Crane Operator, and Assistant put down his tools and stopped working.

The factory fell still.

Idle men opened their mouths in confusion or muttered quietly to their neighbors.

Except for the sounds of wind and sea, a strange silence spread over the deck of the *Nez Perce*.

Only the men in the dive control shed could hear Kip screaming and begging for his life underwater.

With every ocean swell the pipeline lifted and fell on him. Each forty-foot concrete-encased joint weighed twelve tons. The force of it brutally ground him into the set of rollers like a maw. Somehow he'd gotten himself snagged. Now the stinger and the pipe and the rollers were slowly chewing him to bits.

Something had terrified Kip. Something had terrified him so bad that he had tried to climb on top of the stinger and pipeline for safety. That must have been it.

He had clawed with both hands at the top of the pipeline for a hold and had perched his knees precariously on the ramp, when a swell rolled by. His fear was about to kill him. The pipeline lifted off the steel wheels with the surging wave, and the suck of the ocean pulled Kip into the slide.

As the seconds became minutes, Kip died pinched between the steel rollers of the ramp and the concrete-encased pipeline. His chewed-up corpse literally jammed the cogs of the factory and shut it down. While they worked, at first to save him, then to extricate his mangled body from the stinger, all other work stopped for seven hours.

So the barge city blew the deadline.

No Kip.

No pipeline installation.

No bonus.

On his way down for the rescue, Jonah saw nothing but barracudas and blood. The pipeline lay on Kip's entire body except for one arm and his helmeted head. His hand twitched and shook, and his blinking, terrified eyes were fixed on Jonah the whole time he worked to free him.

They tried to rescue Kip by yanking him loose at the same instant a swell lifted the pipeline from the rollers. Escargot and a Rigger took a hard strain on the dying Tender's umbilical topside, and Jonah pulled on Kip's free arm.

"Now!" Jonah shouted innumerable times as the pipeline lifted up with a wave. Each time they pulled with all their strength, but nothing happened.

It was no use.

The dying Tender had been mashed like cookie dough into the ramp's cross braces and his right arm shattered and crushed through a wheel slot.

Each wave pulverized the Tender's body a little more. His eyes went dead and bubbles ceased to rise from his regulator. Jonah hadn't noticed until that moment that Kip had blue eyes.

"He's stopped breathing," the Barge Superintendent said. He'd taken over as Diver Supervisor while Jonah tried to save Kip.

"I know."

"Come back to the barge."

"How the hell are we going to get him out? He's really stuck in there."

"Get back on deck and we'll figure that out."

Jonah moved through the cloud of blood, while the knifelike silhouettes of a dozen barracudas floated above him in the crimson fog.

What had frightened Kip?

Jonah again searched all around, but past the blood there was only the blue wilderness.

Nothing moved except spicules of marine dust and plankton in the shafts of sunlight.

As Jonah clambered up the side ladder he caught sight of Seed leaning against a bulwark. At first glance he appeared to be his same menacing self, nonchalantly spitting empty pistachio shells on the deck.

But when Jonah looked more closely there was something different about Seed's face. He had a new look.

The man was terrified.

⚓ ⚓ ⚓

The Barge Superintendent called a meeting with the dive team. Seed and Escargot went inside the dive control shed.

Jonah, still in his wetsuit, stood in the entrance to keep the shed floor dry. The room was grim, the men's faces set. Outside, topside laborers gathered to find out what was going to be done. Jonah heard them talking in low tones behind him.

"What the hell happened?" The Barge Superintendent turned his large gray head and scanned the room; years of being accountable for multi-million-dollar deadlines and thousands of lives gave him sharp eyes. The man always kept his voice level; he was manifestly competent and everyone in the room respected and deferred to him.

"He saw something," Jonah said.

"What? A shark?"

"I don't know," Jonah said. "He didn't say shark and I think he would have if he'd seen one. He said there were barracudas, but he was all right with them. He just started cursing and screaming."

"What the hell are you saying?" the Barge Superintendent asked.

"I'm saying nothing. I wasn't down there. I'm just telling you what I heard."

"What did you *see* down there when you went to save him?"

"A dead man and barracudas."

The Barge Superintendent kept his eyes on Jonah like he was noticing something about him for the first time and making a mental note. The Diver-Tender met his gaze and didn't blink.

The laborers behind him heard his comment and repeated, "Dead man and barracudas," like a whispered echo.

"It had to be a shark," the Barge Superintendent insisted. "What are they calling that hammerhead that's been around here this last week?"

"Night Train," Seed said vacantly. He seemed baffled by the conversation. He'd been sleeping in his bunk when everything happened.

"What about you?" the Barge Superintendent said, turning to Escargot. "You were his Tender. Did you see a shark?"

"No," Escargot said. "I saw nothing at the surface."

"All right. Mention the shark in the report anyhow," the Barge Superintendent said. He spoke in a disarmingly equable tone, as if they were discussing a trivial or mundane matter. "Next question. Can we get him out?"

Everyone looked at Jonah again. The Diver-Tender thought for a moment. "He's stuck in there pretty good . . . but I think so." He pictured Kip dying, and the mangled look of his body on the stinger. "The main trouble is his arm is smashed through the wheel slot on one of the rollers."

"Maybe you'll have to cut it off," the Barge Superintendent said casually.

The room went quiet.

"Let's think this through," the Barge Superintendent said. "If we swing around the stern crane and put some slings on the pipeline we can lift it off the stinger. It's going to move a lot more without the pipeline's weight on it. Are you boys really going to risk your own asses going under the pipe to dig him out?" He sounded so dispassionate he could have been asking them what time it was. "He's dead now. It'd be smarter if we left him and keep laying pipe over his body. This crap job'll be over in two fucking days. We can pick him out then and no one else will get killed doing it."

"Let's try and get him now," Jonah said. It didn't seem right to leave the body. It might come apart or disappear if they left it. The men seemed to agree.

Reluctantly, the Barge Superintendent nodded. For a long moment he stared at Seed nearly sniveling in the corner as if to wonder what a useless POS was doing on his barge. Then he looked down at the desk and forgot the man ever existed.

Seed conveniently came down with a sinus cold, which he claimed made it impossible for him to clear his ears undersea. He could not dive but he could tend, he said. Nobody believed him but there was nothing anyone could do about it. And Seed managed to avoid the water for the whole rest of the job.

⚓ ⚓ ⚓

Escargot took the next dive. He risked his life setting the crane slings as far down the pipeline as he could get them. Seed tended him and Jonah sat on the deck in his wet dive gear as the standby. The Barge Superintendent took over as Dive Supervisor for the duration of the emergency. Workers gathered on the stern deck to watch the only activity on the barge. Many wanted to see Kip's body come up, and many cursed him for losing their bonuses.

The crane's engine chugged and rumbled. It turned and boomed down, extending its neck over the rear of the *Nez Perce* and out over the stinger. Its long black shadow dropped across the deck.

Jonah stood near the brink of the barge in his clammy wetsuit watching waves play across the ocean. Five flying fish broke out of the water, all silver ambition, and glided surprisingly far before slipping back under. They leapt again, another distance, the pattern of their lives seemingly unaffected by all that was happening on the barge city. Jonah saw Kip's terrified face again and heard Olene's soft, hurt voice saying, "I was raped."

Oddly, a great many seagulls began to fly in from the southeast, the direction of the Caribbean Sea, where the sky was darkest. Jonah watched them coming, a line of dots at first, appearing suddenly at the curve of the earth, racing along purposeful and urgent. The gulls pumped their gray wings just a few feet over the waves as if they were following something below them, perhaps a school of fish near the surface. Not likely, because the school of fish would have had to have been swimming very fast.

There were hundreds of the black-headed gulls—more than Jonah had ever seen near the barge before, and when they arrived they rose up high and began to circle the control tower.

After an hour and a half of dicey maneuvering, Escargot, down in the sea, rigged the crane hook to the slings on the pipeline. Exhausted from lugging heavy slings and shackles through the water, he made underwater decompression stops and finally came in. When he took off his helmet he looked up at the dense cloud of seagulls rotating in the sky above.

"What the hell is goin on with those damn birds?" Escargot asked.

"I don't know," Jonah said. He looked up, but it made him dizzy to watch them circling and circling.

The crane's engine grew louder and began to smoke as it took a slow strain on its massive load to test the slings before a diver went under the pipeline. The pipeline lifted and the cables did not break, so the crane operator set it back down.

CHAPTER FORTY-FIVE

NIGHT TRAIN

J onah had the next jump. The sun dipped near the horizon and the light in the ocean was starting to ebb.

After he entered the sea, the water seeped into his wetsuit and felt cold for the first few minutes.

He swam out to the guideline gushing bubbles behind him and began pulling himself down the stinger.

A silver fish the size of a fingernail raced in front of his lens and Jonah wondered what in the world it was doing so far from a sheltering reef or patch of sargassum weed.

Barracudas flanked him all the way to the body, where the blood had stopped coming in clouds. However, when the pipeline lifted with a swell, dark rosy tendrils of blood curled up like smoke from a smoldering fire.

Jonah felt glad Kip had on a wetsuit, something to hold him together. It would have been horrible to try and pry him free if he was coming apart. Like roadkill glued on train tracks, the coward Tender was now part of the stinger. And the pipeline would scrape across his dwindling corpse like a slow-moving train.

"I'm next to him," Jonah reported via the microphone in his helmet. "Go ahead and lift the pipe."

He swayed in the current below the stinger.

Kip's hand and forearm were above him. They had been squashed through one of the roller slots. The pipeline lifted.

"It's lifting. Tell us what you see," the Barge Superintendent said.

There was only four feet between the pipeline and the rollers.

"Not enough room. Take it higher," Jonah said. He didn't want to get crushed like Kip.

"Okay. Taking it up."

The pipeline lifted ten feet off the rollers of the ramp. Like a giant concrete tree, endlessly tall, dangling horizontally above an industrial-strength sliding-board-like chute with wheels.

"How's that?" the Barge Superintendent asked. "We can't do much better from this angle."

"Not sure."

"This is it. We can't lift it anymore," the Barge Superintendent said. "If you can't do it, we're leaving Kip there."

An ocean swell surged by. The stinger swung upwards maybe three feet then sank back down. It moved more without the weight of the pipeline on it.

"Okay. I'm going to try. Give me some slack." Jonah hauled himself onto the stinger.

The first thing he felt was an increase in the force of the sea because he had put himself in a bottleneck space. The water rushed between the pipeline hanging above him and the giant pipe-lay ramp under his knees. He held on tight. If the pipeline fell, it would crush Jonah to death right next to Kip.

"I'm on it."

"Watch your ass. If it gets dicey, jump out the way you came on. Don't leave your hose across the stinger."

"Roger that."

Jonah crept over Kip's mangled body. It was pressed flat into the braces of the ramp-chute and one of his arms had been hideously jammed through one of the wheel slots. It looked like every bone and joint in the arm had been broken. Only one leg and one arm waved free.

Jonah locked his fingers around Kip's harness. He tried to yank him upwards and back but there was no give at all. The body was horribly smashed and the underside was stuck in some way Jonah couldn't see.

"He's not coming loose."

A plume of blood clouded into his face. The barracudas were watching. The water was growing darker from blood and a setting sun.

He pulled as hard as he could and almost fell into the rush of the current.

"He's really stuck."

The concrete pipeline dangled above his head, a death trap poised to mash him.

The water suddenly seemed rougher. A storm?

"Hurry up," the Barge Superintendent said. "If you don't get him quick, I'm calling you in."

Jonah grabbed Kip's helmet by the handle grip on the top. He leaned back and pried at the body headfirst. The neck arched back. He cringed as it snapped. The head gave more, but the body still didn't follow. He couldn't dislodge it.

"Shit."

"Get off the stinger right now," the Barge Superintendent said.

"Let me try again."

"I said *get off the stinger right now*!"

"Roger."

Jonah dived headfirst over the pontoon.

"I'm off." He caught hold of the guideline underneath.

The pipeline came down suddenly, bouncing onto the rollers.

"You all right?"

"Yeah, I'm fine."

"Good. One of the slings snapped. We were losing control. Start coming in."

"Roger. Do you want me to cut loose his umbilical hose?" Jonah asked. "I can't unscrew the fitting. Some of the hose is stuck under the pipeline with him."

"No. If the body comes loose we can drag him in. We got to show something to his mother. Good job."

Silence for a moment, bubbles and barracudas . . .

"Hey, buddy. You've been down there a while," the Barge Superintendent said. "You need to make a decompression water stop."

"Roger." Jonah suddenly pictured Kip's mother at his funeral. She would never know what a screw-up her son had been. Just as well.

He swam to the side of the barge and took hold of the bottom rung of the side ladder, ten to fourteen feet underwater depending on the motion of the barge.

Jonah dangled like a piece of bait under the *Nez Perce* for his decompression stop. The current sucked him under the hull, swaying like a sea fan.

Barracudas hovered around him in great numbers, too many to count. *Hey, maybe I'm their mascot.*

Exhausted, he hung limply and watched the twilight darken the ocean to dusky blue.

The *Nez Perce* pulled forward and began to lay the last ten miles of pipeline. They would slide the pipeline over Kip's flattened body and on down the declining pipe-lay ramp to the sea floor, towing his corpse with the barge until the end of the job. Like a dead animal stuck on train tracks, the yellow Tender was now part of the stinger. And the pipeline would grind across his dwindling corpse like a slow-moving train ten miles long. Would there be anything left for his mother once all the pipeline was laid? He had to stop thinking about Kip.

Jonah sensed motion and lowered his eyes.

Something stirred out there.

In the blue space beyond the stinger a spectral darkness was gathering and taking shape.

In a flash the barracudas spooked and packed defensively together under the barge.

Jonah squinted; something fearfully large slipped out from behind the blue shroud of the deep and swam his way.

Night Train.

Like a nightmare the black hammerhead emerged silently from open water. He grew inexorably larger and more vivid with each sweep of his tail and each sinister oscillation of his great black head. He glided across columns of water, rising and rising, awesome in his approach. His skin was pure black, his back humped with thick muscle. The dorsal fin jutted up thin and tall, like a scythe, but most fantastic were the wings on his wide, flat head and his mighty jaws.

He swam effortlessly and with exquisite grace. Thronged about him a fast horde of pilot fish raced like striped courtiers to a dark king.

Jonah nearly lunged up the side ladder onto the barge, but hesitated for no reason, except perhaps that he did not feel directly threatened. The black hammerhead swam generally in his direction, but did not seem focused on Jonah. What had Brockman said? *"You're not a fish. They eat fish and won't mess with you unless you are dead or in a chum slick."*

From this distance he could see Night Train all too well. A huge shark, an animal of enormous proportions, much longer than twice a man's height. A fat remora, a suckerfish—clung to his white belly.

The hammerhead came up next to Kip's cadaver, slowing like an airplane about to stall. For a few seconds he lingered, nosing around the body and sustaining his precarious position with gentle measured strokes of his tail and minute adjustments of his pectoral fins. Abruptly he gave in to gravity and slid under the stinger.

Angling with the lobes of his head, the shark circled around below the very end of the stinger and came up to Kip again. This time the giant deftly seized Kip by the arm sticking out from under the pipeline—the same arm Jonah had pulled on when trying to save him.

Night Train yanked and jerked his head sideways. The arm came off like a toy in the giant's mouth. The pilot fish darted in, flashing silver and black stripes, looking for scraps.

The shark dropped under the stinger again. Turning sharply, he carried his prize away.

Jonah saw a curious round eye move on the side of his winged head, then the shark yawned and devoured Kip's arm in a flash of teeth.

It was the animal's ability to vanish and reappear that was most frightening. Sinking and gliding, he dropped from sight.

Jonah twisted around in his harness to look for him but he was gone. He had simply vanished.

The Diver-Tender looked back at Kip's corpse, halfway expecting the shark to materialize again, but saw nothing.

He spun again and saw only blue in every direction.

The school of barracudas under the barge turned nervously, maintaining their defensive posture.

He knew Night Train was near—he could feel his presence like a current.

From nowhere the black hammerhead crossed under the stinger, now swimming with incentive. The shark aggressively sniffed around the body for several minutes and approached both sides of the stinger repeatedly, but could find nothing to bite onto. With an opaque but evident frustration, he circled widely into the distance several times, each time fading like a phantom.

After a lull, Jonah began to think he had left for good, but the black hammerhead approached one final time. His wide crescent mouth was open and his gill flaps billowed out with the flow of water. He searched again for a way to get at the meat he had tasted. His pilot fish crowded around Kip's corpse. The shark poked against the pipeline and stinger, working his jaws like a hog rooting for truffles, but he could not close his mouth on flesh and at last gave up.

The pilot fish, sensing imminent departure, rejoined their king, who swam away with casual yet savage power. His winged head passed Jonah first, then the muscled heavy body with triangular fins, and lastly the crescent tail, dissolving into the magnificent folds of blue twilight.

⚓ ⚓ ⚓

By the time Jonah climbed out of the ocean most of the wandering seagulls had landed on the helipad and control tower stairway, but a few still circled the *Nez Perce* in the dark sky. If one went up the stairway, the noisy gulls could be heard even over the heavy chugging of the diesel engines. Throughout the night their cries and caws sounded like mocking laughter.

Demoralized and haunted, the men on the *Nez Perce* went grimly about their work to end the job as soon as possible. All hope of bonuses and any sense of camaraderie were gone. Most were listless and dispirited, stripped of all mischief and macho grit.

Night Train continued to visit the barge, and the Idiot Rigger told everyone that Brockman himself had sent the black fish to reap bloody vengeance for trying to kill the egret and driving the white bird from the barge. Standing on deck, with seagulls shrieking in the sky overhead, the Idiot Rigger wailed like the town crier, "Look what happened to Kip! Look what happened to Kip!"

Nobody wanted to admit it, but the idea stuck in everyone's minds. Many men had now seen the black hammerhead and knew he was real. They also knew that Kip's corpse was jammed up in one of the wheel slots on the stinger and that he had tried to kill the egret. How could they forget? Every new joint of pipe the Riggers hoisted onto the pipeline ramp and every bead the Welders laid would pass over him. The horn on the tower blasted all day and all night and each time reminded them of the dead diver and they still had to lay ten miles over his cursed body.

⚓ ⚓ ⚓

The seagulls left in one great flock early the next morning and a grease fire broke out in the kitchen. The automatic halon spray over the grill wasn't working so the fire charred part of the wall in the dining room before a galley hand could put it out with an extinguisher. The cafeteria food became as awful as the morale. Sugar was mistakenly put in the salt shakers and vice versa. These mishaps occurred in large part because the cooks had found the last bulk jars of peaches one of them had illegally preserved in Louisiana moonshine and sneaked aboard. The whole kitchen staff got roaring drunk for the last week of the job and either under-cooked or burned whatever they had in hand. And they ate the peaches.

Breakfast was worse than usual: the scrambled eggs were cooked dry as sawdust; the hash browns were under-cooked and served cold; even the coffee, nasty enough on a normal day, tasted like mud. Jonah, Escargot, and the Idiot Rigger had gathered on the port stern after forcing down a hideous meal.

"I think we should ketch Night Train," the Idiot Rigger said proudly. "I figure he's about de biggest fish I ever see in my life. Everybody'd like dat. No mo worry about when he's comin to visit nex. Only problem is we don have a hook big enough for dat giant."

"What the hell happened to Nelson?" Jonah said, interrupting the Idiot Rigger's speech.

They turned to see Nelson, the galley hand with false teeth, striding quickly their way. His eyes were black and he cupped his right hand over his nose. His upper lip seemed smudged with blood.

"Looks like Nelson be in a fight, him. Looks like he lose," the Idiot Rigger said.

Nelson walked into their midst.

"I needs your help. I broke my nose last night," he said. "Woke up behind the barrels. I was drinkin all night with the cooks, must have hit the deck stone cold an bust my nose. Lucky for me, the Foreman didn't find me out."

"What can we do?" Jonah said.

Nelson lowered his hand from his face. His nose was crooked and swollen. Dried blood and fresh blood clogged his nostrils.

"I tried to set it myself, but it hurt too much. I need one of yous to hold me down and one of yous to set my nose."

"Well lay down here on de deck, podnah. We'll fix it good," the Idiot Rigger said grinning.

Nelson lay down on his back. The Idiot Rigger held his arms down.

"This is going to hurt you more than me," Jonah said.

"No shit."

Jonah pinched Nelson's nose hard, so that he could feel the cartilage, and in one quick motion pulled and reset it.

Nelson screamed; his eyes went wild. He jumped up and paced with short little steps back and forth between them, wiping tears from his eyes and fresh blood from his nose.

Jonah and his friends smiled and watched Nelson strut around, trying to walk off the pain. Nelson wasn't mad at them for thinking it was funny, and even smiled a little himself.

"Thanks," he moaned. "I owes you-all a favor. What do yous boys want, some extra steak for dinner?"

"No podnah, you cooks can't cook," the Idiot Rigger said. "But why don't you git one of your Weldin buddies to make us a shark hook big enough to ketch dat *gran requin-marteau*, Night Train."

The idea appealed to Jonah, but also made him uneasy.

Escargot liked the idea a lot and nodded his head in ready agreement.

"You crazy," Nelson said. "Dat's a real smart fish. En't no regular *gran requin-marteau*. It's plenty dangerous to interfere, to git in *HIS* way. *HE* send dat Night Train fo dem dat run off de egret."

"Mebbe so," the Idiot Rigger said. "But dat en't us. Mebbe *we* cans ketch'm, show him whose boss. What about it?"

Jonah didn't want to do it either, but he could tell by the look of the group that they were going to try and catch Night Train with or without him. "If you hook him," he said, "you'd better be ready. No skimpy fishing line's going to hold him."

"Whut about dat quarter-inch nylon rope you divers have?" the Idiot Rigger asked.

"That would probably work," Jonah said.

The Rigger's eyes flashed with excitement.

Jonah had the strange feeling that he was somehow betraying the hammerhead shark. At the same time, the idea seemed stupid.

"Okay," Nelson said. "If that's what yous boys want, I'll git you-all a *big* shark hook. I'll make it myself."

While Nelson went to get a shark hook, Jonah walked up the control tower stairs to the helipad. As he stepped onto the helipad, he saw Seed power-tanning on a beach towel. The puke had his eyes closed.

Jonah turned and looked out at the ocean. From this height he could see far out over the water and always looked for the sick blue whale. But no luck since the egret left. Maybe the blue whale was dead; he hadn't heard anything about her on the news lately either.

He kept thinking about Olene and what she had said: "I was raped. They left me naked on the roadside." He felt violently angry, and wanted to kill the men that had raped her.

The puke suddenly sat up and looked straight at Jonah.

Ever since Seed had tried to kill the egret, he was treated as a pariah by most of the laborers. It was as if the barge citizens were worried that the Idiot Rigger was right. Nobody wanted to be near Seed when his judgment came. Seed sat on a towel on the far side of the helipad, his shirt off. Lately he had been keeping to himself. Kip had been his main companion, and now Seed had stopped putting on shows because he was less popular and because it wasn't the same with Brockman gone. He also stayed away from the water unless it was his turn to tend. Except for the hardest men and the convicts of the Angola Club, all of his former friends seemed to avoid him. Fuck 'em all—gutless punks.

He saw Jonah and shouted:

"Hey!" Seed's eyes had dark shadows under them. He felt sick. The tiny scars on his torso and arms, cigarette burns from his parents, stood out like a disease. They were nastier than any prison tattoo.

"What?" Jonah said.

"What are you boys doing down there?"

"Fishing for Night Train."

"Really? I'd like to see that . . ." Killing Night Train would be incredible good fun. He pictured the giant shark dead for a moment, and he smiled. Jonah might be his enemy, but he was no punk. Sometimes he hated the man, but there was still something okay about him. Maybe they could make a truce somehow. "Hey, I've been thinking. Even though you backstab me, for some reason I still like you. Remember that day with the octopus . . . and that night you carved those shark jaws? That was fucking wild. Those were good times. Why don't we quit trying to kill each other and just be friends again?"

Jonah let the words sink in. He let out a long, slow breath.

"Really?" he said flatly.

Seed felt himself grow calm. The feeling soothed him and relaxed him like a hot bath. When he felt like this he could see the future. A time was coming when he would tell Jonah who raped Olene and watch him react. Then he and the Angola Club would cut him into pieces—little pieces, while he was still alive.

"Right," Jonah said. "Whatever you say."

As the man left, Seed could see the future very clearly. Jonah would look like red meat in a butcher shop window. But the *chug-chug* of a supply boat broke Seed's thoughts. A supply boat arriving meant there would be stuff to unload.

It brought the last shipments of forty-foot pipe, tar, welding rod, groceries, sand, cement, fuel for the engines, and a small bag of personnel mail.

A letter from Olene came for Jonah while he sat in the galley.

Jonah pushed away his breakfast. He eyed the letter curiously, wondering what was in it. He put it down on the table, then picked it up again. It was in a pale blue business-sized envelope.

He opened it and read:

Dear Jonah,

Sorry I didn't write you sooner, but now you know why. I've been feeling better lately, though I still have bad days and nightmares—but not every night like in the beginning.

I want to make a deal with you. I peeked in the window of your room to look at your shark jaws and I got an idea. I'll trade you a killer home cooked Cajun dinner if you could let me have three or four teeth off your shark jaws. I'd like to make earrings and maybe a necklace out of them. Tell me what you think and I guarantee you it will be the best and spiciest Cajun dinner you ever eat!

And like with her last letter, she had drawn a small heart and signed her name. The letter moved him. He felt an overwhelming desire to take care of her, protect her. He also wanted to find out who had raped her and kill them. Maybe he could take her on vacation to Cancun, any nice place where she could learn to scuba dive and get away from her bad days. Or maybe somewhere where there was a good chance of seeing some whales.

Olene could have as many shark teeth as she wanted.

⚓ ⚓ ⚓

The Idiot Rigger and Nelson, the cook with false teeth, stood by the edge of the barge looking into the waves. The two men were so absorbed by the idea of catching Night Train that they didn't go to bed at all that day. Nelson forged a hook from a twisted piece of scrap steel; the hook was the size of a medium gaff with a sharp barb welded on. The steel was still warm from the burning torch when he tied the hook to the rope. Then the men rigged a long length of rope with a buoy at the end to keep the bait suspended just ten feet under the surface.

With his rod and reel the Idiot Rigger caught a nice-sized barracuda from under the barge. He carefully impaled the thrashing fish on the big hook, doing it in such a way that no organs were damaged. The barracuda wouldn't die right away; he'd be live bait for Night Train.

The Idiot Rigger fed out the line until the buoy floated a hundred yards off the stern. He sent Nelson to tell the rest of the group. He would need help pulling in Night Train, if he hit.

Nothing happened for several hours.

Word spread across the barge city that he was fishing for the black hammerhead and curious laborers wandered aft to see the Idiot Rigger holding the rope.

Once the Idiot Rigger had put the baited hook in the water nothing could get him to leave the area. He had Nelson bring him food and coffee from the galley. He even urinated over the side and defecated into a bucket instead of using the head.

The men waiting for Night Train all worked the night shift and weren't used to the sun and its full heat. They shaded their eyes with their hands when they looked at the buoy and occasionally one of them would bring the Idiot Rigger cups of ice water from the galley.

Mid-afternoon, something tugged on the line.

The Idiot Rigger gave out a yelp and jumped to his feet. All eyes went to the buoy bobbing in the waves rising and dropping across the ocean.

"Somet'ing's bitin," he said breathlessly.

The buoy jerked downwards and the rope pulled out a couple of feet.

"Here comes," the Idiot Rigger said. "Bite on dat hook now Mr. Night Train. Bite on dat hook we got special fo you."

In a flash, the rope grew taut and tore out of the Idiot Rigger's hands.

The line pulled up straight as a rod and flicked water into the air all the way out to the buoy.

Then the buoy vanished into the ocean, taking the line with it.

Coils straightened and the rope slid fast across the deck into the sea.

Everyone leaped up to help. Six strong men.

The tow was monstrous. The incredible power was perfectly steady, out and down, like they'd hooked a cruising submarine. Nobody expected this much force. They knew a fish as large as Night Train would be strong, but not this strong. They had expected erratic changing pressure where they could haul him in when he came toward them and hold him back with their combined arms and backs when he tried to flee. They could barely restrain whatever it was, even with all of them lined up like a tug-of-war team.

"Tie us off! Last man tie us off!" somebody shouted from up front.

The Idiot Rigger was last in the line.

"Okay," he said. "I is de anchor, me."

He picked through the pile of coils on the deck and found the end. He tied it off around his waist, then resumed his pulling stance.

For a long time the men held in a stalemate. There was not the expected quivering or yanking of a fighting fish in desperation. Just the huge steady force.

"It don't feel like no normal fish! It be de *gran requin-marteau*! Night Train!" the Idiot Rigger shouted with infectious glee. "Come on, boys! Let's pull dat rope! Pull dat rope!"

The men leaned fiercely backwards, taking as hard a strain on the line as they could.

As hard as they pulled, no line came in.

It only went out, inches at a time.

Suddenly the line went slack.

"He's comin to us!" somebody shouted.

They began hauling in the wet rope.

Then Seed appeared.

The Idiot Rigger hollered in high spirits, "Hep us pull'im in!"

Seed shook his head sideways.

A huge dark shadow appeared just under the surface of the sea.

"Looky dere, de *gran requin-marteau*! Night Train! Pull dat rope! Pull dat rope boys!" the Idiot Rigger clamored. He screamed and laughed like a happy maniac.

Seed stretched his neck from a safe vantage point to see the shadowy black monster under the waves. The creature's size seemed to amaze him, and he jumped back a little.

A huge black tail broke the surface of the ocean and pounded downwards with a gigantic froth-breaching slap.

Men yelled nervously and shouted at each other, hysterically happy at the sight but at the same time terrified.

It was as if they'd trapped a god.

"Look at him! He en't no leettle feesh. En't no leettle feesh. No sir!" the Idiot Rigger shouted.

The men kept pulling in the line, but Night Train didn't fight them.

His black dorsal fin rose up like a reaper's blade as he came closer.

"Don't you worry, Night Train. We's en't goin to kill you. Jus wan to peek at yo face, us," the Idiot Rigger said.

The animal swam right up to the edge of the *Nez Perce* and put his face upwards. Like a massive double-bit axe, the back of his black head broke the surface. He turned to the side and put a frightening eye directly to Seed, who jumped as if he'd been stung.

"Kill him! Kill that son of a bitch!" Seed shouted.

"No, no," the Idiot Rigger said.

Night Train's head dropped back under. He turned and blasted a sheet of ocean at them with his mighty tail.

"Kill him!" Seed screamed. The psycho sprinted across the deck and grabbed the rope in front.

"Come back here, you son of a bitch!"

The rope went super-taut, speeding out the instant Seed's hands touched the line.

The great shark jerked the men across the deck, like party balloons on a string.

The rope burned through their fingers and palms, cutting into their flesh.

Seed screamed hysterically, "Stop him! Stop him!"

The shark charged away.

The deck edge and the ocean slid up before Seed's boots as the black hammerhead dragged the men toward the deep.

Seed let go of the rope and fell to one side.

In a matter of seconds the shark's effortless power dragged three men into the sea.

As each man fell, the line went out faster and with more raw power.

The Idiot Rigger, the rope tied to his waist, began to panic and shout for somebody to cut the line.

Boots slid and squeaked against the deck as the men tried to drag the rope back in, but it was useless.

All hands touching the rope were now bleeding.

Two more men fell overboard.

Now the Idiot Rigger stood alone, tied to the rope, pulling for his life. His face turned bright red and his eyes bulged with fear.

Seed saw the Idiot Rigger terrified for his life, and watched with a smile.

The Idiot Rigger went overboard with a scream.

He vanished under the ocean. Somehow the other men who had fallen over had scrambled back on board, but not the Idiot Rigger.

Two days later his body was found, adrift on the waves, still tied to the line. At the other end of the rope the big shark hook was no longer a hook. It had become a straightened and shiny piece of steel.

Several massive bites of flesh were missing from the Idiot Rigger's torso.

His heart had been eaten out.

CHAPTER FORTY-SIX

THE PIPELINE FINISHED

The last week of the *Nez Perce's* trek to the end of its job, a huge oil rig rose up on the horizon like a castle standing alone in a glaring blue desert. It was the first oil rig Jonah had seen on the ocean since arriving at the barge.

It grew closer and closer as they were laying the pipeline toward it: the massive rig was their finish line. They could see its lights and flare-off fire glowing at night like a giant alien spaceship hovering over the sea. Soon it loomed close and, during the daylight, Jonah could see men wearing hardhats walking the catwalks and working on the steel decks.

On the final day of the pipe-lay job, crew boats began to arrive at the *Nez Perce* in order to deliver the men back to land. Crew boats shuttled workers back and forth between land and offshore worksites. They motored all over the Gulf of Mexico like honeybees endlessly collecting pollen, then returning to their hives ashore.

However, it wasn't business as usual this time. All ship captains were keeping a sharp eye out for the blue whale while they did their work. The latest news reported that she was probably dead and gave out the coordinates of her last sighting. The Gulf Marine Mammal Institute was offering a $5,000 reward to anybody who could locate the carcass. The whale was very important to the scientists and they wanted to find it for an autopsy before the whale's body sank. If, by chance, she were still alive, the spout would be colored sickly yellow with pus from her respiratory infection. Maybe they could cure her.

⚓ ⚓ ⚓

The last joint of pipe was capped, X-rayed, and rolled down the stinger. The job was finished.

All ninety miles of the new pipeline had been installed on the sea floor, and now that the pipeline no longer lay on Kip's corpse, the body could be safely recovered from the stinger. Finally. It had been ten days in the water being crushed and scraped by the pipeline sliding over it.

Jonah and Escargot pulled his remains to the barge by the umbilical still attached to his harness and to the helmet on Kip's head.

Nothing was left of the yellow Tender but his helmet, and Jonah lifted it from the ocean and set it carefully on the deck.

Seawater drained out of the helmet and he stepped back to avoid the foul puddle.

Jonah's stomach lurched when he saw the raw stump of Kip's neck and the spine protruding out from the decaying flesh like a skeletal snake.

He found a large bucket with a lid and put the helmet with Kip's head in it, face down, and the empty harness on top.

He didn't want to see Kip's dead eyes looking at him when he put the lid on.

Nobody did. Not on the barge anyway, but the men on the oil rig would be curious before long. Word had spread. And there was something wrong with that. Kip deserved better than a bunch of gawkers.

The *Nez Perce* was anchored next to the legs of the gigantic oil rig. The rig towered over the barge like the bare structural supports of a condemned industrial building. A great boom extended out in the sky above them like a horizontal steel arm jutting off the derrick. At the end of the boom, safely over the sea, the flare-off fire burned off impurities and waste gas from the oil flow, casting a hellish orange glow over the barge city. During the night and during the day an oppressive stink filled the air.

Men rushed around in the strange glow and sooty air putting equipment away, as if they were trying to get out of a volcano's crater before it blew.

Beneath the windy rustle and pop of the flame, Jonah brought Kip's head to the dive control shed. The bucket was surprisingly heavy and everyone stared as he carried it.

A crowd of men had gathered on the deck with their duffel bags to board the first of several crew boats mooring alongside. He alone, of all the Tenders, had been asked to come to the dive control shed for a meeting with the Barge Superintendent. He hoped the meeting would be short so he wouldn't miss the last crew boat.

Jonah entered the dive control shed and set Kip on the desk.

The Barge Superintendent lifted the lid on the bucket and grimaced. He put the bucket on the floor and sat heavily on the corner of the desk.

"Tell me about the night you tended Aleck Brockman," he said.

Jonah tried to get all the images into place, but it seemed a hundred years ago.

The middle of the night . . . Brockman dressed in cutom made dive gear . . . ordering Jonah to tend him on a crazy dive to 590 feet . . . no dive bell . . . secret . . . Jonah thought it would kill the old man . . . afterwards Brockman shook and walked like a drunk . . . pressure-related nerve damage . . . face looked white-blue like sculpted marble . . . blood on his lips . . . but Brockman was okay in the end.

It looked as if the Barge Superintendent had been examining Brockman's record-keeping. His eyes were bright and he compressed his lips into a hard straight line.

"I heard a story he took an unauthorized dive and that you tended him," he said in a neutral tone. He made a face that said, *Tell me.*

"That's true," Jonah said. "It was probably one in the morning and the Idiot Rigger told me Brockman wanted to see me in the dive control shed. Brockman told me to tend him, and I did. He dived down to the worksite." He wondered if he was in some kind of trouble.

"The *idiot* who?" the Superintendent asked, annoyed.

"Nickname. A rigger. Lost him overboard."

That didn't seem important now to anyone. But the Superintendent still had questions about Brockman.

"To 590 feet without a dive bell?" he asked.

"Yes," Jonah said. "He knew what he was doing. He mixed his own gas and planned the whole dive and it worked."

"All this happened in the middle of the night?" the Barge Superintendent asked.

"Yes."

"What the hell was he doing?" A look of great seriousness and deep curiosity spread across his face.

"Saving this job. After his dive, the saturation divers suddenly finished the tie-in. Without Brockman, every man on this barge would still be in shit."

"That son of a gun," the Barge Superintendent said with admiration.

The crew boats began pulling out to take the workers back to land.

CHAPTER FORTY-SEVEN

THE LAST CREW BOAT

T he sounds of departing boats bothered and distracted Jonah because he didn't want to be left on the *Nez Perce*. He said goodbye to the Barge Superintendent and the man thanked him for doing a good job under very difficult circumstances.

"All right," the Superintendent said finally. "That's all. We're done."

Jonah bolted across the deck to go below and fetch his duffel bag. He passed by a brightly lit red crew boat about to leave. Too late. Then, further along the barge, he saw a group of angry men cursing and threatening each other. They were waiting to board an old black-hulled crew boat filling up on fuel. The dimly lit vessel looked ugly and menacing like a junkyard dog. One man waved his knife at another, and the air smelled like dope. Blowing the deadline and missing the bonus put a bad taste in everyone's mouth.

By the time Jonah came back on deck there was only one crew boat left—the bad one.

Looking at his home for the last two months, the *Nez Perce* seemed empty and alien; nobody worked at the stations or walked the decks. The cranes were motionless and the horn on the control tower was silent. Only shadows caused by the oil rig's flare-off fire flickered and moved.

The last crew boat started pulling in her lines. She had a large searchlight set up at the bow because the captain was searching for the dead blue whale—the reward money still dangled out there. The boat's hull was battered and black and her decks were empty except for a pile of duffel bags lined up around the cabin door. The boat was either deserted or everyone had gone below. The oil rig's massive flare-off fire reflected and burned in miniature on her windows and portholes. Like she was on fire.

Jonah had a queasy sensation in his guts as he looked at the fiery boat. He didn't want to board her. He also didn't want to be on the same boat as Seed and the Angola Club. But he figured they were already gone, that they had muscled their way onto the first crew boat to get back to the beach as soon as possible.

Suddenly the crew boat's deckhand rounded the gangway. A young amiable-looking man. The deckhand glanced up at him. "Are you coming?" he called.

Jonah hesitated. This was the boat that the men who were shouting and threatening each other with knives had been waiting to board. Then again, he wanted to see Olene tomorrow, not wait three days.

"Hey, bud, we're leaving," the deckhand said. The man waved, and Jonah jumped aboard, wedged his duffel bag in among the others and stayed on deck to see the boat pull away from the *Nez Perce*.

The engine rumbled and the stern deck vibrated under Jonah's feet.

The crew boat parted from the *Nez Perce* and slipped over the waves into the outer dark. Only then did Jonah believe the job was truly over and he was finally going ashore.

It would be a very long ride—something like thirteen hours before they'd touch land. He watched the *Nez Perce* grow smaller and smaller until it vanished. But the oil rig's flare-off fire continued to burn in the sky like a solitary low star.

Oddly, no person other than the captain and deckhand seemed to be aboard. Usually men wandered on the decks to stretch their legs and smoke. Jonah figured that all the passengers were part of the day shift with the habit of sleeping at night.

The crew boat lurched and pitched on the open ocean, and soon the oil rig's flare-off fire vanished in the night.

⚓ ⚓ ⚓

Jonah opened the door to go below, and hyena laughter and smoke met him in the companionway.

A warning came over him, and he squeezed the banister tightly and waited. Another cackle of laughter came up. The men were probably watching a movie. Jonah, moving carefully, went down to see what was on, hoping to find a seat.

The cabin was hot, smoky, and dark. Everyone was smoking either cigarettes or marijuana. Someone had turned all the lights out except for the TV and the light in the galley. The men were all facing the same way, high on liquor and dope. They sat on the floor and in seats with their backs to Jonah, watching the TV screen. They were huddled tightly together so that they could all see it, and some of them had taken off their shirts. A porno tape played on the VCR, the volume up high. A young woman sobbed and screamed through a gang-rape scene. Suddenly the men in the cabin began clapping and screaming the hyena laugh again, voices full of death and lust. A pernicious fog permeated the air and made hazy the figures and faces of the men: veined tattooed arms, hairy broken-knuckled fists clasping cigarettes or joints, severe faces, dark profiles, and ugly smiles.

He looked at the screen to see what prompted them to applaud, and saw with a stab of horror that they were watching somebody's homemade tape. A young woman was really being gang-raped.

The men were applauding because Seed was in the video. He was the one now raping her as she wept and shook her head side to side.

Jonah recognized most of the men watching. They were the craziest and most brutal Riggers and Welders on the *Nez Perce*. Restrained by the regimen of the grind and the need for dollars, these men during the job had been generally isolated from each other. They had worked on different shifts and had been buffered by good men. They were bad men individually, but together under present circumstances, they were capable of anything.

They had chosen this crew boat, the last one, for a party ride in, a party Seed had promised and planned for them the week before. The Angola Club sat front and center in the best chairs.

The shortest one was the boss, the one with huge arms and a giant tattoo of a butterfly spread across his chest. Jonah had heard he worked offshore under a phony name to escape the law. The other two were larger and taller. One had a shaved head and a pitted, pockmarked face; the other was a mulatto with short dreadlocks. The bodies of all three were gruesome with prison tattoos and fight scars which in the cabin's murky light shone out on their torsos like ugly gray lesions.

Seed slouched at the galley counter with a joint in his mouth, holding a half gallon bottle of Crown Royal whisky. He was filling paper cups and passing them out. Now that he was away from the *Nez Perce*, Seed seemed bigger. The swagger was back in his stride. He was the celebrity host running this show. This was his environment, his party.

Suddenly Jonah, in the back of the room, knew his moment with Seed was close at hand.

He looked once more all around the room hoping to find an ally. He glanced from one man to the next and found not a single friendly face. Nobody had noticed him yet, so he stepped back to leave the room, but the young woman being raped in the video began pleading, "Please stop, please stop." The sound on the video was muffled and tinny, but something about the woman's voice was familiar. Jonah looked closely at the screen and saw that the girl being raped was Olene.

He froze.

"Hey, Jonah, my man!" Seed shouted. "Looks like you got on the right boat. Recognize the starlet in this movie? When I found out she was your sweetheart I couldn't resist." Seed burst into crazy laughter. "Come over here and have a shot. We'll drink to Olene!"

Jonah braced himself. Seed was brave when surrounded by his pack. A few turned away from the rape film to look at him.

Seed poured an enormous quantity of whisky into a tall plastic glass right up to the rim.

"Now come here and have your shot. I'm glad you're here. I was just tellin the boys about how we had to find you as soon as we hit the beach. You saved us the trouble." Seed raised the tall glass of whisky toward Jonah. "If I'm going to be drunk when I kill you, you're gonna be drunk when you die. It's only right." Seed smiled crazily, his face deranged, his eyes glossy black, his pupils dilated.

How could he get out of here?

The Riggers and Welders turned back to the rape video; all of them except the Angola Club who now stared at Jonah.

Seed put the glass of whisky down hard and spilled some.

Jonah felt his hip pocket for his knife.

"I'll tell you what, Jonah. This is it. One time. You come over here and take this shot or we'll carve you up right now and throw you overboard in pieces."

The Angola Club still watched him. The one with the shaved head and bad skin started to his feet. His chair swiveled and he drew out a long knife.

Seed shouted, "Speak up, Jonah!"

They were too close. He wouldn't make it up the stairs. His only advantage was that they were drunk and high, and he was not.

The bald convict with the knife stepped toward him.

The hyenas were laughing, and Olene was screaming to the next rapist, "Stop, stop, please stop!"

If he could get into the bathroom they'd have to fight him one at a time.

The bald convict was caught off balance by Jonah's move, but pushed men aside to get at him.

Jonah slammed the door shut, but it closed on the bald Rigger's thick arm and bounced open.

Jonah threw his whole body into it and hit his head against the door. A flash of light burst through his skull.

The Rigger shouldered against the door, trying to force it open by wedging more of his body through the gap.

The convict's bulging shoulder and whole arm were in the bathroom.

Jonah had his knife in his hand and stabbed and dragged the blade deep across the biceps muscle and inner elbow.

He felt the knife jump as it cut through a tendon.

The Rigger screamed and pulled his arm back.

Jonah slammed the door shut and locked it. Heaving for air, he dropped to the floor. The bathroom was small and narrow, but that was an advantage.

He put his back to the wall and straightened his legs against the bottom of the door.

Men started pounding and shouting at him through the door, but it was too small for more than one man to pound against it at the same time.

The wood strained inward with each blow and the lock broke immediately, but the door did not open.

Jonah jammed it shut with his legs locked straight.

He sat with a racing heart and held his bloody knife on his lap ready to cut whatever hand or face came at him. But he could hear noises, noises over Olene, over the men—the commotion had alarmed the crew boat's deckhand. Pounding feet, more shouts.

The deckhand's voice shouting, "Captain! Captain! Get the shotgun!"

It sounded like the deckhand had run out of the room for help.

Jonah could tell by the tinkering sounds at the edge of the door that they were taking off the hinges. Seed was helping, and his voice came through the door in a low, happy tone: "We're going to kill you."

Jonah inched his feet higher up against the door to brace it better, his legs locked hard and straight.

He was sweating like hell, and his shirt and neck were wet.

He looked around the bathroom for anything he could use. There was nothing, not even a plunger. Goddammit!

Suddenly, he heard a new voice outside. "Get the fuck away from that door!" The man was loud and angry; it had to be the Captain, and the sounds of the men unscrewing the hinges stopped.

Then Jonah heard footsteps, followed by a moment so quiet, he could hear the deep rush of the sea under the hull of the vessel.

"Whose blood is this?" the Captain asked. He moved up against the bathroom door and knocked hard. "You in there! You all right?"

"Yeah!" Jonah shouted.

"Come on out. It's safe now. I've got these assholes covered."

Jonah relaxed his legs and started to stand up in the tiny bathroom, but a sudden shout and a gunshot stopped him.

Someone let out an agonizing scream, and men cursed and shouted.

Jonah straightened his legs hard to hold the door, just as a heavy weight crashed against it. It must be the Captain against the door. They had overpowered him and now they were killing him with a knife. He was screaming.

Jonah kept his legs straight and could feel the force of each stab through the door with the bottom of his feet.

Suddenly, the fighting stopped.

The sound of someone dragging the Captain's body off the door, and the men were back unscrewing the hinges again.

Jonah held his knife ready.

He straightened his legs as hard as he could.

Then there was a massive collision.

He hit the wall.

A flash of light.

Everything went black.

Nothing.

Jonah woke up on the floor next to the toilet. He sat up, stunned. How much time had passed? Minutes? Seconds?

The crew boat had hit something big. The impact of the crash had thrown him against the bulwark next to the sink. His shoulder hurt and for a few seconds he could see flickering lights. He also felt a gash on his head. The bathroom door cracked open, barely hanging by one hinge.

He jumped to his feet to shut the door despite a vague feeling that the ship might be sinking. Stunned and groggy, he wiped blood from his forehead. The crew boat's engines had stopped and, except for moans and shouts outside, there was a seeping quiet.

The men were no longer trying to get at him. As he reached for the bathroom door's handle the boat seemed to shift under his feet and he heard a drunk voice yell, "We're sinking! We hit the whale! We're sinking!"

Jonah leaned forward and looked out into the cabin. The Captain's body lay on the floor in an obscene pool of blood.

The ocean poured in from somewhere forward.

The crew boat began tipping nose down.

The floor rose up and men were sliding backwards. Cups, ashtrays, somebody's kit bag, and anything else not nailed down tumbled and clattered toward the sinking bow.

Blood dripped into Jonah's eyes and he wiped it off with his forearm.

He waded through the rising sea and floating debris. The rest of the men were too drunk or too high to react quickly. One man waved his arms for balance, tried to stand but fell into the water in his stupor. Some of the men couldn't swim and began to babble hysterically.

Seed, with his knife drawn, stabbed a man with a life jacket in the face. The man fought back, punching and shouting, but Seed killed him and took his life jacket.

Nobody looked at Jonah as he made for the stairs.

The last thing he saw was Seed putting on the life jacket.

Then the lights exploded behind him and a man screamed, then another.

Jonah scrambled out into the night, just as the nose of the boat tilted and sank all the way under.

The duffel bags on deck rolled and tumbled toward him as the stern jutted vertically up from the sea.

The open cabin door now faced the sky like the lid of a tomb somehow left ajar. The men trapped in the hold, laughing at rape only minutes ago, would drown.

Jonah looked around for a life jacket, but everything was confused.

The boat sank deeper, and without thinking, he jumped out and away so as not to get sucked under.

The ocean felt shockingly cold and his gashed head stung.

He swam a good distance from the sinking vessel and stopped to tread water. When he looked for the crew boat it had already sunk and the ocean fizzed and bubbled where it had gone under. He could see nothing but dark waves. No lifeboats. No whale. Nothing.

CHAPTER FORTY-EIGHT

NOT ALONE

Beneath a bright moon only the whisper of the ocean and wind broke the midnight silence. Within seconds of the boat's sinking, a monstrous splash erupted near him and something floundered in the dark. Jonah turned toward the noise. His imagination invented the worst, a shark. Then he heard coughing and spitting and swam toward the sound.

"Who are you?" he called out.

"It's me." He saw a dark figure, floating.

Seed, wearing a life jacket, had popped up from the deep.

Jonah worked his legs and arms, slowly treading and fanning to stay afloat. Seed floated nearby wearing the life jacket, his head a black silhouette, and he waved a knife and shouted, "Keep away."

Jonah worried more about drowning than Seed's threat. He got rid of his boots and socks, then pulled off his jeans, and the wet jeans pulled off his underwear. He tried to grab his shorts but they were gone. He knotted the ends of his jeans so he could trap air in them and use them to stay buoyant.

The Gulf water was warm enough that hypothermia was not an immediate threat. If he could last the night he had a good chance of being found. Also, he might drift within sight of an oil rig and swim to it. Until then, he needed to keep waving his jeans over his head to refill the legs with air.

He heard Seed hiccupping. It sounded as if he were going to vomit. Seed had to be dehydrated and disoriented from liquor and drugs. He doubted the man could last very long and didn't care, except that if Seed died Jonah wanted his life jacket.

Whenever Jonah would float too far away, Seed scuttled after him, and whenever Jonah moved toward him Seed held up his knife. Its blade glinted in the moonlight.

In the great vault over their heads the stars glittered clearly, like countless pinpricks. It was an astonishingly beautiful night. Easy waves rose and fell around them, with a lulling swish and hiss. Jonah watched the moon's slow crossing of the sky. Odd, but at times he thought it hovered over them like a gold thumbprint.

He tried to bring his mind back to surviving, but he couldn't concentrate. At first he wondered what they had hit, then he imagined that he had floated into the shallows and that bottom was only a few inches deeper than his feet could reach. Jonah told himself again and again that if he could make it to daylight, he would live. He wished he'd not gotten on the crew boat and had instead stayed on the *Nez Perce* for the slow ride in. Something had warned him, but he hadn't paid attention to his feeling.

Seed stopped hiccuping and complained in a hoarse voice that he was thirsty and cold, but Jonah didn't reply.

He was exhausted, and his calves felt close to cramping. He fingered at the spot on his head that bulged like an egg where he'd slammed into the bulwark when the crew boat hit something. Now and then he waved his jeans over his head to refill them with air and watched for lights on the horizon when a wave lifted him, but saw only the dark sea.

Once Seed's face dipped forward as if he were dead, then he broke violently from his sleep, thrashing and slapping the water. He wailed, "I don't want to die. I don't want to die." Now that he was no longer running the show or surrounded by the Angola Club, he seemed small and weak. He began talking, but Jonah tried not to listen to what he said.

Seed turned hysterical and seemed to be mentally breaking. He yelled at unnamed people and wished he'd never been born. For a time Seed wept. He confessed to committing horrifying crimes: raping and mutilating women, torturing and killing men and hiding the bodies. He even claimed to have killed Pike by putting a bag of cottonmouth snakes over his head. At one point he shouted, "*Don't you think I was raped?! Don't you think I was tortured?!*" After each of his outbursts Seed paused as if waiting for a response—if not from Jonah then perhaps from the sky, or the wind, or the ocean itself. Each time, Seed heard only the wind blow and the ocean splash.

After a long pause, Seed hollered, "What about *me?*! What about *me?*! Why don't *I* count?!" He sobbed for a few minutes, then said, "But I made myself better in spite of what they did to me. At least I did one good thing. And I did it for you."

"What," Jonah said, not believing him. "What good did you do?"

"I saved Olene for you. We were going to kill her, but I talked the guys out of it. I did that for you."

Jonah remembered Olene saying her rapists were going to kill her but one of them changed his mind and talked the others out of it. Could that have been Seed?

Jonah started to feel sick. He felt Seed's words demoralizing him, weakening him and trying to kill him with distraction.

If the devil was real, he was wheedling Jonah right now.

"You should thank me, you ungrateful son of a bitch!" Seed shouted. "If you live through this! And if you ever see her again! Every sweet moment! Every kiss! All the love she ever gives you! Should remind you of *me*! That *I* did something good, once!" With this Seed stopped shouting.

"You don't understand," he muttered to himself. "You don't get it."

"Yeah, I do," Jonah said, swimming away from him.

Endlessly the waves rose and fell.

Saltwater kept getting in Jonah's mouth and he spit it out, but the briny taste lingered.

His skin puckered like goose flesh.

In the dark ocean, wide and huge, he was helpless.

He could only keep his hope alive by treading water, staying warm as possible, and doing a dead man's float to save his strength.

Without the life jacket Seed, dehydrated by alcohol and in a semi-stupor, would have drowned immediately.

They floated for hours.

Half dazed by exhaustion, Jonah suddenly saw that the false dawn had started. He had drifted off for a second, and now the sky to the east brightened ever so slightly.

An eerie calm spread over the water. A wispy vapor smoked up from the surface of the sea and curled about his head. He knew it was almost absurd, but a great sense of relief grew within Jonah. He'd made it through the darkest hours. Even a false dawn offered a tiny encouragement and hinted at rescue.

Then something faint brushed against Jonah's naked foot and a vortex fanned into his submerged body.

Something was swimming around him.

He gasped and turned to face the way the thing had passed, and for a moment he was so frightened he couldn't see.

Now the black sea came alive with sharks that seemed to swim between the dangling legs of the two men or graze by them.

The sharks were looking at them, smelling them.

A fin broke the misty surface and sank only four feet away from Jonah as he bent his knees to his chest to protect his legs. He fought his own panic for possession of his mind, and Brockman's words came back to him: "They won't mess with you unless you're dead or in a chum slick."

Jonah pulled his legs up against his chest, but he started to sink as he held that position.

He looked around for anything dead in the water that the predators might be drawn to; he had to know why they were here. He turned in a circle but could only see Seed's head ten feet away.

The sharks glided silently under and about them.

Jonah tried not to imagine the broad wedge-shaped heads, their expressionless button eyes, or their jaws—like the one he had cleaned—and how it would feel if they began forking, gouging, and ripping him apart.

Rough skin brushed his legs.

There it was again, something moving around him, a hard fin, a force of water propelled by a tail, this time strong, the next time casual.

Was a shark testing him?

Jonah convulsed and began to weep.

He closed his eyes, afraid he would die from sheer panic, but the fluttering nervous energy and clenching in his guts wouldn't let up.

Suddenly he heard Seed cursing like a lunatic, and it took him out of his panic.

"I stuck the bastard. I stuck the bastard with my knife!" Seed shouted. His voice was high and gravelly. A shark had brushed past Seed, who pounded the sea with his arms and legs.

Jonah started swimming hard to get away. Maybe they were unknowingly in the middle of some kind of chum slick or above a school of fish. There had to be an explanation for the sudden presence of so many sharks when there were none before.

He stopped for a rest.

A shadow fanned his legs, and a shark nudged him hard.

Every second he expected to feel teeth fasten on him.

His heart felt like a fist punching in the back of his throat.

He gagged and almost retched. Something told him that he was on the verge of self-destructing, of dying from panic.

He had to calm down.

The moon caught his eye, and he stared into its cold glow. He breathed deeply and held it. Then breathed again. He looked up at the moon and it suddenly seemed friendly, and he slowly let the air out of his lungs. The controlled breathing started to work, he felt a little calmer. He told himself that if he was going to die tonight, the sharks would have to kill him. He took another long slow breath. He was coming back to himself.

Then Jonah felt something even better—a calm new energy, a fresh surge of determination like a second wind, except by now it would be a fourth or a fifth wind. Some part of him other than his mind, something outside of himself, seemed to be taking over and working his limbs and starting to move him forward through all that was happening. The hysteria tapered off, and his mind became detached, lucid, and objective. He'd had this sensation before when he took the survival swim test for commercial diver certification; treading water with a weight belt was a battle of heart and durability. Especially because you didn't know how long the test would last. Jonah had learned that if he dug deep down to his bedrock, he could surprise himself, that he could go much farther than anyone would have ever imagined. Anything could happen if you held on tenaciously and absolutely never gave up.

Suddenly just ahead of him the waves dipped, and he glimpsed the long, low outline of something floating.

He heard a splash behind him, and Seed swam up. He was getting over the liquor and drugs.

"I think I see something," Jonah said.

"What? Where?"

"Right there. A raft or a boat."

Again the long, low outline billowed into view, then sank out of sight.

A second later a shark rammed into his chest. It lifted Jonah out of the water up to his waist like a matador thrown by a bull.

He rolled clear of the shark's mouth then plunged headfirst undersea.

In the pitch blackness the shark bit down on his jeans and ripped them out of his hands.

Jonah spun upside down, and his shirt came off.

He imagined sharks circling him, mouths open and lips peeled back to bite. Bubbles escaped his mouth, and he closed his eyes.

There was a flash of light as a tail or hard snout slammed across the back of his head.

He was slowly somersaulting now and his side burned where the shark had scraped off his skin.

This was the end.

The trio of molas, limned in indigo blue radiance, appeared like undersea angels. The vision was so clear, Jonah realized that he was dying. Waving their fins, the molas pressed gently up to him with sad, moonish faces. He still couldn't understand what they were saying.

Brockman said, "You I can trust."

Jonah's grandmother held his hand and smiled at him. He was a little boy and they were at the beach looking at the baby whale.

The molas glided closer.

The egret flew up against the wind, rising high in the sky, glowing in the sun.

He saw Olene.

It was black again.

Then it was black with flickering specks that he was seeing inside his eyelids.

His lungs burned, and he wanted to inhale the ocean and end the nightmare, but he clenched his teeth and held his breath to hold his life in.

Another shark jarred him, and Jonah somehow kicked it away without telling his legs to move. This bit of luck jolted him into action. Once more, he began consciously fighting for his life and was surprised that he could still move his limbs.

His head broke the surface and he gasped.

He sucked in air, felt it cross over his tongue and between his teeth.

He blinked the ocean from his eyelashes, his eyes blurred with the wash of seawater.

The raft was right in front of him.

Jonah swam for the raft with everything he had, pounding the water with his arms and legs in a frantic crawl.

He felt something solid moving under him, a shark, then it squirmed and power-whipped away.

He grabbed the raft, realizing instantly that it was not a raft, but he did not care.

He pulled at it and slipped back, then clawed his way up.

He could barely believe it. He was out of the water by only inches, but that was good enough for now.

CHAPTER FORTY-NINE

THE BLUE WHALE

B reathing hard and shivering, he sat naked on what he now saw was the carcass of the dead blue whale.

The whale's skin felt cold and soft, like a clammy wetsuit.

The waves swished and gurgled against the mostly submerged body.

The moon floated lower in the sky, but it was still night.

Jonah figured it was maybe another half an hour until the real dawn. Now he understood why the sharks were here. They were feeding on the dead whale and anything else in the way.

A scream rose out of the sea, Seed crying that his leg was gone.

Seed shrieked in pain as he swam up to the whale. He was a few feet down from where Jonah climbed up.

The mist cast a bluish light on the sea and Seed's face.

He looked up at Jonah and showed him the knife as a warning.

The water roiled and something splashed next to him.

Then he stabbed his knife into the whale flesh for a handhold and pulled himself, climbing and kicking his legs, up onto the carcass.

Sitting, he turned to face Jonah and point his knife at him. He wheezed and coughed seawater, then suddenly vomited. When Jonah didn't attack him, Seed lay back with a groan and rested the hand with his knife on his stomach.

"Jonah, my leg's gone. I'm bleeding out," Seed gasped.

Even in the darkness, Jonah could see that Seed's left leg had been bitten off above the knee. A dark puddle of arterial blood formed below it and streaked down the side of the whale.

It wouldn't be long now.

After a few minutes, Seed became very still and quiet.

He looked dead.

Jonah crawled toward him, to take the knife and life jacket. As he crept closer, it looked like the blood had stopped flowing from Seed's leg. He had to be dead.

Jonah reached for Seed's knife.

The man stirred, and Jonah moved back.

Seed opened his eyes and looked surprised and confused. He said in a slow, exhausted voice, "I'm glad you're here with me." The words meant nothing. Jonah wanted the knife and the life jacket.

"You're the only . . . *real friend* . . . I ever had."

A minute later, Seed rolled off the whale into the sea. He went in clutching his knife.

He floated, motionless, face up in the waves and bumped up against the side of the carcass.

Jonah scooted further back on the whale, and saw a large shark take Seed by the arm. Then another took him by the torso. The sharks fought over him with casual savagery, ripping and pulling.

Seed went under, then somehow surfaced again.

Now a giant black hammerhead took him by the top of the head. Night Train.

They made little splashes as they ate him.

Jonah climbed to the highest point on his whale island.

His head pounded and Seed's screams echoed in his mind.

He stretched out on his stomach on the center of the enormous mammal.

He was thirsty.

The right side of his abdomen had been chafed bloody by a shark's rough skin and blood started to leak from the wound on his head. He felt sick and cold, and then he sagged unconscious on the back of the whale.

CHAPTER FIFTY

THE FEAST

At dawn he sensed light, but salt had almost crusted his eyelids together.

The sun peered over the rim of the ocean, and the whale's carcass trembled as the gray-bodied sharks tore great mouthfuls of flesh from it. A continual succession of them emerged at his feet just beneath the water—a couple of tiger sharks, Night Train, and the rest oceanic whitetips, the most deadly open-water sharks in the sea; the big ones thirteen feet long, hungry to feed. Hundreds of them.

They glided with savage stealth in and out of sight, only rarely breaking the surface. Stocky and hard-eyed, a legion of ruthless hunters, they approached one at a time, or in twos and threes. Sometimes, just before they knifed their teeth into the whale, they looked up at Jonah sitting so close. Their dorsal and pectoral fins were roundish at the extremities and blotched white. When they rose from the depths to feed, the surface upwelled and rumpled. Shreds and scraps floated and sank through bloody water as the sharks violently jerked their bodies to rip and saw loose hunks of meat.

Gulls and terns gathered overhead and flew close above the water to join in the feast. Several birds boldly paddled in the water. One was plucked from the surface by a shark, yanked under, and vanished for good. Except for the splashes in the water and the cawing of seabirds, a general silence added to the horror.

Jonah shivered, naked and cold. He could see no ships, oil rigs, or aircraft anywhere. All around stretched the wide impassive ocean, tranquil and glassy. A long slick of blood and whale oil smoothed acres of water with a shiny film and drew sharks from miles around. The chum slick glistened in the early light.

The sun was now a fiery ball on the horizon, and the wind blew softly with the coming day.

The sharks circled and recircled their feast.

Light spread horizon to horizon, the inky ocean turned to gray, then to deep blue.

Naked, he sat on his vanishing island and waited for whatever would come.

⚓ ⚓ ⚓

As the morning brightened, the world took on a hazy liquid quality.

A mist was rising, and it was as if the ocean were exhaling after holding its breath all night. In his delirious state, he wouldn't have been surprised to see the sharks cross over the wet, smoky air to feed on him, or Brockman's marble face emerge to gaze sardonically from the water.

By mid-morning the sun was strong, and a warm breeze had risen.

Jonah's lips and tongue were dry and thick. He tried but could barely produce the smallest amount of saliva.

He watched the sea and the sky for help until he couldn't stay alert any longer, couldn't keep his eyes open. Then for a while he hung his head on his chest, craving ice cubes—cool ice cubes for his mouth—and dozed in and out.

Then it was almost noon.

The sun smarted on his naked body, and his wounds had dried.

He rubbed the gash on his head that he got in the crew boat collision the night before. It had become a scabbed, painful lump.

He worked his tongue against the parched roof of his mouth and tried to draw down some wet, but nothing came.

Directly in front of him, a large gray caudal fin burst out of the sea and pounded the water as a shark twisted and tore at the giant open wound in the whale's carcass.

A tern lowered and briefly hovered in the air, before landing on the farthest exposed part of the whale. A second tern landed next to it, and they began to squabble and hector each other.

Again, Jonah tried to moisten the inside of his mouth, but still nothing would come. He felt sickly warm—except for his buttocks and his feet on the cold whale—and his head hurt. He wondered whether he was feeling the effects of a concussion.

He tried to lift his arms but in his weakness could only wrap them around himself.

He put his chin on his knees and tried to think about his island.

How long would it last with so many sharks feeding on it? Would it sink even before they could eat it all?

She was an immense long, blue whale, a full-sized adult, maybe even a hundred feet long.

He was sitting on the highest point—three feet above the water—roughly on the center of the whale's side. A six-foot-wide strip of the body lay exposed to the air. There was a lot more underwater, especially lengthwise. Luckily, the ocean was calm and did not wash over his narrow perch. He could see, maybe twenty feet away, one of the whale's gigantic pectoral flippers. It jutted out at a declining angle under the clear water and looked ghostly gray and luminous over the deep light-shifting blue underneath. Farther down that way he could see under the water the beginning of the whale's gray pleated throat, the deep grooves parallel and long-running, like part of an enormous corduroy trouser leg belonging to a giant.

Brockman had said: "*They won't mess with you unless you're dead or in a chum slick.*" But he was sitting right in the middle of a huge chum slick, all the whale blood and oil. The whale was his life raft, but it was also the reason why the sharks were here.

What if the whale sank? The gasses making it buoyant could dissipate, or the sharks could eat enough blubber to sink it in the next half day. If the whale stayed buoyant all day and then sank during the night with him still on it, he would not be able to see well enough in the dark to get clear of the feeding sharks. Sinking at night was the most dangerous situation he could think of and he wanted to avoid it at all costs. If he could.

In daylight he was sure he could fix his direction by the sun, and if he dived out away from the whale and swam as far from it as possible, maybe he could get clear of the oceanic whitetips—maybe. Many of them, he noticed, were bloated and full from the flesh they'd already eaten off the whale. Maybe they would not attack if he could get away from the carcass quickly.

He looked at the slick of oil and blood glimmering like a silver stain on the ocean. It stretched out of sight; then it came to him that more and more predators had to be on the way—hungry ones that hadn't fed yet. What if he got caught in all that new traffic coming in?

His best chance became clear to him: stay on the whale till the bitter end. And it would be a lot easier for a rescuer to see him sitting on the whale than to see a head bobbing in the waves. But if the weather changed or the ocean got rough . . . *no, don't even think about that.*

If he drifted within sight of an oil rig, even an uninhabited platform, he would have to try and swim for it. He would swim to the platform and hope it had a ladder down to the water. If it did have a ladder, he would climb up and work his way to the highest level on the rig and wait for a passing aircraft or vessel to find him. If it did not have a ladder, he'd have to climb up the cross braces without being sliced to pieces by the barnacles.

If he drifted within sight of an inhabited oil rig, he'd wait as long as he could on the whale for them to notice him. If they didn't notice him by early evening, or if the carcass began to sink, then he'd gamble and swim for it.

He looked down at himself and knew that he was in bad shape. If he was going to swim for an oil rig of any kind and have a real hope of making it, he would have to do it today. He was naked, exhausted, and dehydrated, and becoming weaker as the day slowly passed . . .

⚓ ⚓ ⚓

Twenty feet in all directions the ocean around the whale glittered like a shiny pond, unnaturally smooth and clear because of all the oil coming out of the carcass. Jonah could see the thick torpedo-shaped bodies of countless oceanic whitetip sharks curving and weaving through the cloud of bloody water in front of him. But beyond the glossy, gently eddying water encircling the whale, the sea moved with slow rippling waves.

As Jonah watched his island shrink one mouthful at a time, the heat of the sun became unbearable. His limbs felt rubbery, and he worried that he was becoming helpless. He tried to cool himself by stretching out on his belly, hugging the surface, pressing his face against the whale. The whale was saving him and he loved her. He turned his head and pressed the other side of his face on the cool, damp skin. But then something told him it wasn't the sun making him hot. The heat and aching was coming from inside him, a fever.

He lifted his head and looked to his right. Now the sea sparkled. He stared at the dazzle and thought about ice cubes again. He closed his eyes and felt the whale rocking gently with the sea, almost tenderly. Yes, he loved her.

Finally, he crept on his belly down the side of the whale and crawled to the edge of the carcass to splash his hot head and torso with seawater. If he could wet his hair, it might help his fever. He reached down toward the water and almost had his fingertips in it, and then a small shark, maybe six feet long, glided quickly right up under him, a foot below the surface. So close under his face, he could see its tan-gray hide and the tiny dermal denticles like minute overlapping teeth all pointing toward its tail. The shark turned its head and Jonah saw its cold eye notice him. He sprang back and swore savagely, and retreated from the water without having touched it.

CHAPTER FIFTY-ONE

TEETH IN THE WAVES

The sharks and the sea birds kept coming and coming. He watched them feed and he watched the horizons and the skies and then he watched the sharks and did not dare to go again to the water's edge where they fed.

Some time later the waves picked up a little, and soon the carcass under him began slowly rolling and swaying in the way he had feared.

He had to scramble, pivot, and scoot with demonic intensity every few minutes to stay out of the water. On his hands and knees, or buttocks and feet, or flat on his belly, he clung and gripped and dug at the whale, adjusting to the rocking waves and the pitching motion of the carcass.

Now the ocean splashed him and gave him more cold slaps than he could stand. It also began to slick up the whale's skin that had earlier been dry enough to hold onto.

By late afternoon the paleness of his body—all except his tanned forearms and face—had turned deep red. He stung all over, as if his entire skin had been peeled away, though he knew it was only chapped and flaky with salt. He hadn't been able to huddle or to cover up with his arms since the waves had risen. He didn't know how much longer he could keep up his struggle to avoid the waves. He was getting clumsy and reacting slower and slower to the pitch and tilt of the whale, whose skin had dipped many times into the oily water and was now so slick that he often slipped.

Now and again, he looked to the sky and out to the horizon, but saw only the emptiness around him.

A swell splashed and foamed up the whale longwise.

Jonah scrambled like a fiddler crab to avoid it. He had to squat because he was so weak and because staying on the whale's slick back had become almost impossible.

Even in a crouch his legs slipped out from under him, squeaking faintly on the whale's skin, but he managed to flop on his belly.

Before he could recover, he slid face first down the whale's side into the sea, right where the feeding was heaviest, where the ocean frothed with blood and sharks.

He opened his eyes for an instant and saw blurry pink and dark gliding phantoms.

He spun quickly right-side up underwater and came back to the surface with a gasp; he tried to lunge out of the sea in one frantic desperate motion but failed.

He slid back down the whale's side and his legs dangled in the opening of a giant cavity—a pink crater of gore like the mouth of a bloody cave—while two large sharks tore furiously at the meat next to him.

He clawed and thrashed his legs frantically, and barely got back up.

For a moment he lost his balance and almost fainted, but he lay facedown sobbing and held his place.

All afternoon the sea rose higher and he seemed to see teeth in the waves. Occasionally, if a wave hit just right, it washed over the whale's back. Gradually, and dimly, he felt the buoyancy of the carcass changing.

CHAPTER FIFTY-TWO

A STUPID SEAGULL

He was in a daze when the whale started to shift and twist around. He came alert as the midsection and tail submerged slowly, and her colossal head began to rise. He scuttled and adjusted to the new imbalance. More and more, her head rose to the surface, growing increasingly enormous, like the peak of a new mountain rising. Finally, the whale's massive, royal face broke out of the water. Glistening silver, anointed with her own blood and oil, and the life-giving ocean, the dead whale looked supernatural, like a sea god. Jonah scampered and hopped across her great brow like a stupid seagull and found himself just behind her blowholes. He saw huge open lesions all around them. The whale had been very sick when she died.

Then the great corpse rolled more on her side, her head raised up even further, and one of her dark eyes emerged fizzing from the ocean, fresh rinsed with spume and saltwater. It was shaped like a dark almond and a little larger than a human head. It wasn't the cold eye of a fish and it wasn't as simple as a cow's eye. It stood wide open and seemed to stare back at him with stark, unearthly knowledge. As the carcass rolled in and out of the waves, the ocean rushed and whirled over the eye, and once it seemed to blink in a frightening trick of life.

The weather started to turn bad. A thin blanket of clouds came quickly from the horizon, and the ocean turned gray.

Jonah, now only half-conscious, raised his head and thought he saw new sharks coming in—bigger ones.

A wave rolled lengthwise down the whale, funneled up her side, then rinsed over her head.

He pushed up with his arms and legs, gripping feebly with his toes and fingers.

The sea passed under him and rinsed around his ankles and wrists.

He crawled forward with his naked rear up high in the air, slipping a little as the carcass shifted again under him.

He looked for the next big wave and saw that it was still twenty feet away.

Jonah sat down in exhaustion and looked about with slitted, weary eyes.

Now the whale eye seemed to wink at him, and he looked away.

He felt cold—cold down to his bones, delirious and numb, far past exhaustion. He caught a glimpse of the whale's giant eye, and this time it glimmered with the washing sea—*we'll become extinct together.*

His arms were shaking badly and felt as if they no longer belonged to him. He couldn't scramble any more; it was no use. The sun had broken through the clouds, and he opened his eyes wide to let the light flood and blind him with its immense presence, even as the sea would fill his lungs.

Suddenly, something was different. He sensed it even before he could see it. He closed his eyes for a long moment of darkness, to reclaim his senses.

A blurry white dot just over the horizon began to grow. It kept growing and now he could see there were two of them.

The next wave washed onto the whale, and somehow he had the strength to gull-hop and shuffle out of its way.

He looked back to the sky, steeling his eyes against the brightness that had come—*the dots were bigger.*

Now he could hear the faint machine-gun slapping noise of rotor blades.

Helicopters.

They were coming his way fast.

Whack-whack-whack.

He got his feet under him, stood painfully on the whale's head, raised one arm and tried to wave, but his strength was gone. His arm fell back to his side, useless.

⚓ ⚓ ⚓

The harness tightened and lifted Jonah clear into dry, windy space. It dug into his armpits and he felt it was tearing burnt flesh, but he was safe. He dangled limply, knowing he was red and naked and helpless. The other helicopter hovered near and he caught the glitter of a news camera pointed at him.

As they reeled him in from above, the helicopter's downwash blurred and pummeled the ocean and streams of its surface peeled and broke away.

Jonah swung through the air with sky and ocean whirling around him.

Below him, the gray oval form of the blue whale shrank until she looked like a submerged island, a weather-smoothed tongue of rock. Now only her eye and a small part of her head were still above the surface, surrounded by streaks of foam and the shadows of sharks. She would sink before the predators could eat much more. A ring of brightly shining oil haloed her head, and her open eye, penetrating and dark, looked back at him.

He bumped over a skid, and hands took hold of him. Then someone's arm hooked around his waist. They were pulling him in and onto his side, but all the time he was leaning out and looking down to the sea, into the blue whale's eye.

Finally, they rolled him aboard the helicopter and somebody held a thermos of something sweet and cold to his lips—iced tea.

He drank trembling and greedy, feeling its coldness run down his throat, but they pulled it away before he was done.

The helicopter's powerful turbine engines made an incredibly loud buffeting noise. He heard voices but couldn't make out what they were saying.

Jonah looked at the faces of his rescuers, the concerned eyes, the headphones and little microphones in front of their mouths: a blond bearded man with wire-rimmed glasses that caught the light and a brown, freckled woman wearing a white tee shirt with a humpback whale on it. They looked astonishingly rested, dry, clean, and healthy.

The woman put a gentle hand on his forehead and a life jacket under his head.

He drank more from the thermos, wanting all of it, but the man took it away.

The woman put a set of headgear on Jonah's head so he could hear them talking to him. Suddenly the sound of the rotors and turbine engines became muffled and faint.

He looked down at his naked skin. The cool air felt good, but then someone lay a blanket over him, and he cried out at the burning.

He threw off the blanket and struggled up to lean on his elbows and look out the window down at the sea.

He wanted to see the whale once more, and now her whole body was still visible, barely underwater. Suddenly a black shadow came to the surface and glided toward the carcass. The incredible huge hammerhead passed over the sinking whale, sharp and ink black against her luminous gray, a dark king among the shifting gray-brown shapes of other sharks. With a flick of its tail Night Train dissolved downwards into deep blue and was gone for good.

"Lie down. Take it easy," the woman said, gently pushing him toward the life jacket that was his pillow.

The man who seemed to be in charge said, "My God, how are you doing?" adding that they had been looking for the whale. They were the scientists everyone had heard about on the radio. The man's voice came beautifully clear and loud over the headset.

Jonah tried to say "drink," but the word came out as a moan that sounded like "ink." His tongue was swollen, the saliva in his mouth sticky and thick as paste. When he tried to speak, his lips clung to his teeth.

"You need to wait a few minutes," the man said. "You don't want to shock your system any more than it's already been. We'll take care of you."

Jonah nodded. He was trying to think of what he should say but gave up. It was too hard.

"You've got a bad cut on your head. Did you get that from a shark?" the man asked.

Jonah closed his eyes and shook his head no.

"It looks pretty sore," the woman said as she leaned over him for a look. "But it's clean." He was naked, but he didn't care. He was alive.

"How long were you on the whale?" she asked.

Twelve hours? He shook his head, unsure.

The man leaned over him. "You're lucky we came out searching for that whale. You're lucky as hell. Are you the guy who fell off the cruise ship?"

Jonah lay still without bothering to respond.

"We heard a news report that a guy fell off a cruise ship and was lost at sea," the man said. "Is that you?"

He moved his head slightly, wishing they would stop talking, so he could go to sleep. Didn't anyone know that the crew boat had sunk? That all the men were dead?

"He's in shock," the woman said softly. "Just take it easy."

The man and woman squatted on their heels next to him, and he thought he felt their breath warm on his sunburnt skin. The woman tried to take his pulse at his neck, but couldn't seem to get it, then put her hand on his forehead for a few seconds, and she said again, "Lie back and rest."

Jonah's whole body felt incredibly hot, and he hurt all over. Was he really safe, would he be all right?

He opened his eyes, but the helicopter seemed full of foggy light, and he closed them again.

He could still feel the whale swaying under him and hear the splashing sounds of sharks feeding.

Olene came into his mind, and he began to talk to her about the gold thumbprint of the moon and the three gentle molas who had gathered around to protect him.

Seed's voice spoke in his mind, "*I did something good, once. And I did it for you.*"

The voices of the man and woman irritated him and brought him back. Jonah opened his eyes again, and the woman seemed to realize that he was listening to them.

"Is there anyone we should contact and tell you're alive?" she asked.

It was too much for him now, and he shook his head.

"Well," the woman said, "you're about to be on the news. The whole world will see you being lifted off that whale. The other helicopter is carrying a TV crew. They've been following us and filming our report about the impact of pollution on the oceans. They're going to want to talk to you at the hospital. Everyone is going to want to talk to you."

He raised his head a little to look for the whale and the sharks, but now everything was gone. Only the sea's surface shimmered and rumpled with the pale cloudy color of the sky. An opaque ocean stretched out far below them like one endless undulating fabric, with no hint of where it was deepest or what was hidden in it. Nobody could ever know all the shadows in the sea. Not even Brockman.

The sun came through thinner clouds and the world suddenly brightened. Now the ocean looked bluer and scaled like the flank of some incredible fish too big for the eye to take in all at once. The surface bulged and heaved as if it were alive, breathing in slow motion. At last Jonah lay back and closed his eyes.

He felt the solid, level floor of the helicopter, tilting under him sometimes, and the humming vibration of the turbine engines. He knew he was flying over the Gulf of Mexico toward Louisiana, and in his mind he saw the square-edged shape of oil rigs rise up in the north distance like tiny spires sitting on a smoky mirror, scrolling into view, scattered widely at first, but growing closer together as the helicopter headed north. Some of the platforms were grouped like chains of islands, not soft and green, but ugly and severe, fortresses of steel. About them, like slow honeybees, service vessels shuttled busily and trailed wakes that quickly vanished. Soon, there wasn't a bare stretch of water in any direction under the helicopter. The sea beneath him was dotted with thousands of structures built by the offshore oil and gas industry, their steel I-beams and towers and service vessels glinting like the armaments of an attacking army, an army advancing out to sea.

Back on land Olene waited for him. Her shiny hair was pulled back with a blue headband and she wore a magnificent shark tooth necklace. The teeth glowed sharp white against the soft, tan skin of Olene's throat, and her gray eyes were smiling again and sweet. And like her spirit freed to a nearby bayou, the lovely egret stood in calm water by cypress knees and Spanish moss, fishing peacefully in a cool mist.

Jonah, safe in the helicopter and drifting off to sleep, saw it all with his eyes closed, as if he were a white egret flying above the ocean, soaring on the wind, heading for shore.

⚓ ⚓ ⚓

When he opened his eyes he lay in a hospital bed in Louisiana's Iberia Medical Center. A sterile, air-conditioned room. Clean white sheets, a privacy curtain, an IV drip stuck in his arm, his head wrapped in gauze. He felt relaxed, not a care in the world— like he'd been given morphine. He had no memory of how he got to the hospital. The last thing he could recall was the blue whale's dark eye gazing up at him as he looked down from the helicopter.

Olene stood at his bedside, her hand on his arm.

He tried to talk, but his mouth wouldn't work right. She kissed his bandaged head, said, "Shush, not now. We'll talk later . . ." and pointed to the TV. The nightly news was on and Jonah watched himself being rescued from the sinking whale and feeding sharks.

The voice of the announcer was clean and sterile, just like the hospital room:

"Late this afternoon an unidentified man was spotted stranded on the back of a dead blue whale in open ocean 158 miles from shore. Our news 12 chopper caught it all on camera. Two experts from the Gulf Marine Mammal Institute—trying to locate this particular blue whale—finally found the carcass. The scientists from the marine institute had been combing the sea for weeks, and

it was only blind luck they found the castaway this day. Apparently the rescued man fell overboard off a cruise ship . . ."

Next the news clip showed Jonah being carried on a gurney into the entrance of the hospital. Olene was running alongside. One of the EMTs swatted bees from his face.

The announcer ended the piece, *"Thanks Jay. Incredible story. In other news, the Super-Tex oil company reports that a crew boat from the barge Nez Perce is now twenty-four hours overdue . . ."*

Jonah's eyes closed.

He drifted toward sleep.

TV noise.

Olene holding his hand.

He saw himself on the gurney again.

A bee buzzed slowly around his head.

CHAPTER FIFTY-THREE

THE BEE

By the time Porter finished his story about Jonah, it was dark. We were still sitting on the terrace of the King Fisher Club, facing the Atchafalaya Bay. The hostess lit torches that flickered around the perimeter of the seating area and lit lanterns at each table.

The sky grew darker and the air cooler. Like it might rain. We ignored the incoming weather and stared at the bay and the lights of oil rigs in the distance. Still thinking about Jonah on the whale with sharks tearing into the carcass. Telling the story had unburdened Porter somehow, as if he'd finally gotten something terrible off his chest. The old diver was done talking for the night.

Another honeybee had fallen into the pitcher of iced tea— some time ago, around sunset. Miraculously, the insect was still alive. A faint buzz every now and then.

Porter stood up. "Time to go home."

He turned to leave, but then stopped. His arthritic joints made him move like a man twice his age.

He glanced at the pitcher of iced tea and noticed the bee still alive in the drink, struggling on a piece of ice. Still fighting to live.

Porter's expression softened.

He took the pitcher by the handle and walked to the grass at the edge of the terrace.

He glanced over at me, with a little smile, then gently poured the iced tea on the grass.

He set the empty pitcher on the table.

"God's grace," Porter whispered.

A few minutes later the bee crawled onto the terrace.

It sat still a moment, then the rescued bee flew off into the night.